The McClane Apocalypse
Book Eight

Kate Morris
Ranger Publishing, Copyright 2017

Ranger Publishing
Copyright © 2017 by Ranger Publishing

Note to Readers: This publication contains the opinions and ideas of its author. It is not intended to provide helpful or informative material on the subjects addressed in the publication. The author and publisher specifically disclaim all responsibility for any liability, loss or risk personal or otherwise.

For information about special discounts for bulk purchases, please contact, Ranger Publishing @gmail.com.

Ranger Publishing can bring authors to your live event. For more information or to book an event, contact Ranger Publishing @gmail.com or contact the author directly through KateMorrisauthor.com or authorkatemorris@gmail.com

Cover design by Ebook Launch.com

Author photo provided by J. Morris

Manufactured in the United States of America
Library of Congress Cataloging-in-Publication Data is on file
ISBN 13: 978-1981148448
ISBN 10: 1981148422

Acknowledgments

I would like to thank the fans of the McClane series. Your letters, emails, and shout-outs on social media are encouraging and so uplifting. Thank you for supporting the series and following McClane family.

As always, please support veteran causes and companies like Black Rifle Coffee Company and Article 15. Just don't get yourself an Article 15.

Kate

Chapter One
Paige

A week has gone by since the tornado came through and altered their lives and caused them again to rethink what safety and security truly mean. There were funerals held for the people of Hendersonville who were killed, and two unscheduled clinic days to help with the injured and infirm who were affected by the storm. The clean-up process on the farm has been a slow one as the men have had to go on runs for supplies and to help some of the people in town. There was substantial damage to numerous homes, especially the roofs. Today she is helping at their clinic and is happy to be spending some time with her friend Sam. Paige has missed her greatly since she moved away.

"It was really sad," Sam is telling her about the funerals she attended. "I didn't know most of them, but their families were devastated."

"I'm sure," Paige says with a nod as they scrub down the countertop in an exam room. She adjusts the red bandana on her head to keep her hair back. They have mostly been busy with injuries caused by the storm and then with people getting hurt handling debris during the clean-up efforts. She can't imagine losing Simon to a damn storm after having been through so much just to get to him.

"How's Cory doing?" Sam asks.

"Better, not slowing down, though, like the doctors have advised him to do about a hundred times."

What she doesn't say is that he has become a machine. He hardly sleeps, works his fingers to the bone, and stays up on watch duty every night. He pulled his stitches twice and had to be resewn back together. Herb told him that if he kept it up that the barn wasn't going to be the only thing on the farm that resembled a patchwork quilt.

"That's hardly a surprise," Sam says.

"Simon's doing well, too," Paige offers and watches her little friend's face fall just slightly before she recovers.

"Oh, good. That's good. I'm glad everyone is doing well."

"Are you two ok?" Paige asks. "It just seems…"

"Yes, fine," she interjects. "I've just been so busy at Dave's."

"Yeah, I know," Paige agrees. Since their clinic was destroyed entirely, leveled according to the men who went over to take a look Her uncle decided to temporarily treat patients at Henry's farm again. Henry's kitchen is serving as a patient exam room, but they are still going to hold joint clinic days with the McClanes in Pleasant View every other week. Her uncle had been out of his mind with worry about Sam, too, during the tornado. Paige can only imagine. Dr. Scott just got her back, so she can relate. Paige likes Sam's uncle very much, but there is something truly sad lurking behind his guarded eyes. She doesn't know much about him, but she would guess that he has a dark history hiding behind the brave front and professional doctor facade he puts off.

Paige suggests, "You should come over and stay for a visit."

"Oh, I don't know, Paige," she says and turns her back to her, the swoosh of her black ponytail reminding Paige of Cory's stallion's thick tail.

"Why? It would be nice to have someone to visit with again," Paige says. "Everyone's so busy rebuilding the farm and running here and there trying to gather materials. They haven't let me go on any runs with them, either. Cory says I bring him bad luck."

Sam chuckles. "Well, he does have a point."

Paige joins in and laughs at herself. "Reagan said if I didn't have bad luck, I wouldn't have any at all."

"Probably true. Of course, I think that's most of us now."

"Not you," Paige argues. "You bring good luck to the people around you. And happiness, too, Sam. Everyone loves you."

Sam smirks as if she does not believe this.

"We could gather all the girls and have a girls' night in like we used to."

"That's only because a girls' night out is just us going out to the barn, not a nightclub," Sam teases.

2

Paige laughs. "Huntley's been missing you, too. He mopes around a lot." Her brother does the same, but Paige isn't going to reveal that to Samantha. He mopes, he grouses, he complains a lot, and worst of all, Simon hides from her and everyone else. He's never around when they have a rare, free moment of time in the evenings when it's simply too dark to continue working outside.

"I miss Huntley, too, but with the clinic being destroyed, we're going to have to start all over again. We're in for a long process to get another one reestablished."

Paige shakes her head with disgust, "Any idea yet on where it's going to be located?"

"Not sure," Sam tells her. "Dave and Henry and my uncle have been holding a lot of meetings about it. I don't know where it's going to be- at the farm or in town or just another nearby house. Who knows? Problem is that the house that got demolished was the closest one to Henry's farm. I don't think they want my uncle and me to set up a clinic in town. Hendersonville isn't as well-fortified as here. Plus, Uncle Scott wants to live in the new clinic in case we're needed in the middle of the night or something. Also, I think he wants his own place again."

"Yeah, that must be hard for both of you," Paige says. "I mean living around so many people, strangers."

"Sometimes," Sam confesses. "They've all been so nice, though. But my uncle was staying most nights in the clinic instead of with the other men in the men's barracks. He said he could work and study and do more research there because it was quiet. Everyone's nice, but it's just crowded."

"Not the same as family, your family, the McClane family," she unambiguously hints, earning a laugh from Sam. "You need to come for a stay. Plus, you never even got those herbs you need," Paige reminds her.

"I think my herbs got a little wind-whipped," Sam quips with a smile.

"No doubt," Paige agrees. "Such a shame. Sue's been working so hard to get the greenhouse put back together."

"So much work."

"Yeah, but Simon's been helping her," Paige tells her and then quickly adds so as to not upset her friend, "And Cory's been repairing the building and the roof. The roof took a hard hit."

"Yeah, I saw," Sam nods. "I hope they're able to get more glass to do the repairs so that it all works the same way again. The herbs and the greenhouse are so important. Plus, it's nice to have fresh herbs all winter long for teas and cooking."

"You'll have to come over and get your starts soon," Paige reminds her.

"Maybe. We'll see," Sam says with a smile that doesn't hold promise.

Sam gathers a tray of instruments that will need to be sanitized and leaves the room. Paige recognizes a blow-off when she hears one. Sam doesn't want to visit the farm, which leaves Paige to assume it is because of her brother. He's working at the clinic with them, too, today, but Simon's been in other rooms with Herb. Sam has stuck mostly by her uncle's side, but Paige has floated from room to room helping where she could.

She can't blame her friend for extracting herself from an engagement on the farm with them, one in which she doesn't wish to participate because Paige has been doing the same thing with Cory. She has used the best evasive maneuvers she knows to steer clear of his company lately. The way she felt about him during the tornado, huddled inside the protection of his arms was not something she ever wants to feel again. He wants more from her than she could ever give, ever allow herself to give, either. It has been one of the hardest choices she's made in a long time. Not being around him is difficult, especially when every cell in her body wants his companionship. It wouldn't be fair to Cory because he has made his intention known as far as where he sees their relationship going. Wedding bells are not in her future. They're never going to be. She just tries to focus on helping out on the farm and giving him lame excuses as to why she can't sneak away with him. For the last week, it hasn't been too difficult because everyone's been so busy repairing the buildings and doing farm work. Her own slippery skills in avoidance are the reason she so easily recognized Sam's evasion.

Paige takes the bucket of cleaning supplies and stacks it on a shelf with similar items in the storage room.

"Didn't pass out today, I see," her brother says, startling her.

"Hey!" she scolds. "That was a one-time thing. I don't know what was wrong with me."

He frowns and steps closer. "Probably stress, sis. You always put a lot of pressure on yourself. You don't have to go on runs or even work here if it bothers you. We've got the clinic covered. Dr. Wallace even brought a nurse with him."

"And Sam, of course," Paige corrects him. Her brother still refers to Sam's uncle as Dr. Wallace instead of Dr. Scott or just Scott as the man has corrected many times. "But I think Sam's closer to being a doctor than a nurse by now. She's so smart."

He doesn't answer but nods, hangs his head, and turns away to place a tray of instruments on the counter.

"Don't you think Sam would also make a great doctor?" she pries.

"Sure," he says not turning around. "Of course, she would, but she doesn't have any interest in furthering her studies and becoming a doctor. She told me she's studying with her uncle, but that she'd much rather be doing art. She just likes helping out at the clinic. Her brain doesn't work like that. She has a love of music and art and animals…"

"And kids," Paige adds slyly.

"Yes, she is good with children," Simon admits. "They all love her."

"They aren't the only ones," she tells her stubborn brother.

He levels her with a look, "Sam is a good person. Of course, everyone loves her."

"Even you?"

He scowls and turns his back to her.

Paige, not to be put off so easily, says, "She'll have lots more practice with kids because there are so many that her uncle's going to be giving care to once all those women give birth. Heck, maybe he'll be taking care of Sam's kids someday soon, too."

This gets his attention, and he whips around to regard her keenly. "She's a bit young for that, don't you think?"

"No, not at all," she says as nonchalantly as she can manage. "Lots of women are pregnant right now, many her age. What is she, twenty-one, twenty-two?"

"No, she's just turned twenty."

"Hm, old enough," Paige says. "Mom had me when she was twenty-five. No matter. Maybe you'll get to learn pediatrics with her uncle."

"Why?"

"Reagan told me the other night that they are going to have you do an internship or residency thing with her uncle very soon. I guess they want you to go over and stay on Dave's compound and help them out with getting a new clinic established, too."

"We talked about that before, and I told them that I wouldn't be any help in such matters."

"That's not what Reagan said two days ago to me," she counters.

"I don't have time to go over there and help them," he protests as Reagan walks through the door.

"Doesn't matter," Reagan replies as she places a box on a shelf. "Grandpa and I talked about it. If you could go over there for a few weeks, it would help them a lot. They lost the whole clinic they just about had ready to open. Plus, you could work with Dr. Scott learning peds. He's a great source of pediatrics study for you."

"I can't drop everything and go over there."

Reagan snorts. "We can hold down the fort and afford to lose you for a few weeks. We're suspending clinic day for the two weeks you'll be gone. It's more important to get their clinic ready. Dave and his group have helped us out a lot. We owe them."

"Cory's a lot handier than me when it comes to construction. He should go."

Reagan is quick to say, "We talked about that, too. His going over there is a possibility. He could do construction with Henry and his men on whatever building they find to turn into a clinic, and you could work with Sam and her uncle to get the place ready. And do your internship with him, so to speak."

Paige didn't know Cory was going to need to leave the farm, too. She was glad the family might send her brother over to work with Sam's uncle because she thought maybe she and Simon might be able to work out their problems. Paige knows he'd be safe there, too. However, Cory leaving is another thing altogether. She would miss seeing him every day, but it would help her with the avoiding him plan. Her heart is torn.

"You're right," Simon says reluctantly and with guilt. "We do owe them. Dave's done a lot for our family, and he always sends men over to help keep watch on you guys when we're all gone looking…uh…on a supply run."

She knows her brother means to say looking for the highwaymen. Everyone knows that's what they are doing when they go on runs. The tornado has placed a wrench in their search for those marauders, but she's sure they will continue the hunt soon. Paige has to admit, she's kind of glad they are taking a break from searching for them and are, instead, working on repairs.

"Good, then you'll go over and help them set up a practice? Again?" Reagan adds for good measure and to lighten the mood. She knows he isn't happy about this.

"We'll see," he says, leaving her to guess that he doesn't like the idea.

Her brother and Cory went yesterday with wood signs they made from the tornado-torn barn siding and pieces of plywood lying around the farm and pounded them into the ground beside the freeway. They were painted with a warning for people to stay off the main roads and beware the highwaymen. She hopes people heed these warnings as the messages could save their lives. Dave's men also did the same. They hit the main freeways with six signs from each of the four groups that went out. There was a plenteous supply of scrap metal and wood to make them after the tornado. Dave's town was hit much harder than theirs, so he had even more raw materials to make their own. Paige is now concerned that once the highwaymen spot the signs, they'll know that people are aware of and are communicating about them. They'll want to take retribution against the ones warning people of their dangerous existence. However, they must alert people that dangers await them on the roads. They cannot stand by and allow it to continue happening without doing something about it.

"Just go do it," Reagan states decidedly to her brother as she is leaving the room. "Arguing with you isn't something we have time for, Professor."

Paige chuckles. Her friend is blunt, to say the least, and Simon does not seem to find her amusing.

"It is a good idea," she reminds him. "They need our help. This clinic is a lifesaver for this town. Plus, if her uncle ends up being influential in their town like Doc is here, then they really need it set up soon. Sam said the devastation in Hendersonville was really bad. I feel so sorry for them."

"Yes, we all do," he states simply and swipes a hand through his auburn hair.

"I can help, too," she offers, trying to lift his spirits.

"Maybe," he says. "Not if Cory's going, though. Then you can stay on the farm."

"Simon," she warns. "Stop."

He turns and hits her with an accusing stw33ware that makes Paige feel like a jerk for her recent deceptions where Cory is concerned. She tries not to cringe. She doesn't particularly like all the sneaking around they've done, but she also can't seem to stop having those longings for him.

"Just stay away from him," her brother says. "I don't like the way he's always looking at you and…"

"You have no worries there," she lies again. "I do try to steer clear. He's annoying."

"Yes, he is," Simon agrees as Sam comes into the room with them.

"Did you hear the news, Sam?" Paige asks.

"No, 'bout what?" her little friend asks and secures a stray wisp of black hair behind her ear.

"Simon's going to be coming over to Dave's compound to live and work for a few weeks. Maybe Cory, too."

"What?" Sam asks, a lopsided sneer of discomfort slowly causing her mouth to turn down. "Why?"

"They want me to study peds with your uncle and for Cory and me to help establish and work on a new clinic site."

"We don't need your help," Sam argues, surprising Paige.

"I tried to explain that, but the idea was shut down," he tells her.

"It would be great, though," Paige says, trying to make them both see the light. "Simon needs the study in pediatrics, and you guys need help getting a clinic up and running."

Sam sighs long and with great melancholy, leaving Paige to guess at her unhappiness. She would've thought her brother living over there for a few weeks would make Sam happy. Her assumption was clearly wrong.

"Great," Sam says softly and turns to go.

"Sam, wait," Simon says and follows her from the room.

Paige just shakes her head with confusion. Then she peeks down the hall and retreats into the storage room again. She quickly takes the slim item she needs, conceals it in the pocket of her cargo pants, and places the box back on the shelf. She knows how closely they monitor every single item in the supply boxes at the clinic because they've been robbed before, but she hasn't gone on a run where she could find one without anyone seeing. She just hopes they miscount this one when they do the inventory. She doesn't want the whole family knowing about the missing item or why she needs it.

Chapter Two
Sam

A few days after the bad news at the clinic in town that Simon is going to come over to the compound for a few weeks, Sam doesn't think life could get worse. Then it does.

At four-thirty in the morning, something awakens her. She sits upright in her bed, her covers pooling around her waist. She looks around, rubs her sleepy eyes and waits quietly to see if another noise comes. She's not sure what it was precisely that had awakened her, but it sounded like a door shutting. Everyone in the long room is still sleeping, several snoring. She strains to see if anyone is moving around. The windows above people's bunks are mostly all open, but she does not hear anything troublesome happening outside. It is quiet and peaceful, this still part of the night before dawn. Perhaps someone rose to use the restroom. No other noises come, and nobody is walking around their bunkhouse. Crickets continue their songs outside. Sam swings her legs over the side of the bed and leans toward the window near her. She can see a lantern in the distance near the dairy barn. One of Dave's men. She frowns and sits back down on her bed. She's just jumpy, unused to her new surroundings still. She used to sleep so much better at Grandpa's farm.

She was so sure that a noise had awakened her, but maybe it was a dream about her family again. These seem to be coming with more frequency since she left Grandpa's farm and moved to Henry's. They always leave her feeling melancholy and longing for her mother's loving embrace. She rises and pulls on a clean shirt and the same jeans she wore yesterday. A quick glance around the sleeping barracks again lets her know that nobody else is awake or has come out of the bathroom, so she reaches under her bed and pulls out her

10

small box of art supplies. Then she takes her sketch pad and box of erasers and charcoal pencils and places them in her messenger bag, something Cory found for her years ago so that she could transport her art supplies around the farm.

"Hey, what's going on?" Courtney whispers with a sleepy voice.

"Shh, go back to sleep," Sam tells her. "Just going for a walk."

"Is everything ok?"

"Yeah, fine," she lies. "Just too hot."

Courtney rolls over and is back out again within seconds. She's not sure her friend was even fully awake. Sam sneaks out of the building, closing the door behind her. She walks toward the horse barn, collects a can of crimped oats and makes her way to the end of the barn. She opens a stall door. She enters and takes her usual seat in the corner, which is a bucket, to observe the horse. This particular mare gave birth the other day to a stud colt. She started a drawing of him since it is not every day that there is a newborn baby available. He's in a stall with his mother still, so it works even better that he cannot run off when she wants him to stand still for his first official portrait. The mare nickers through her nose in greeting. She feeds her an apple she took from the cellar yesterday. The colt is skittish and distrustful of her and mostly tries to hide behind his mother.

"Hey there," she says to him. He tosses his head to let her know that she isn't welcome. Sam chuckles. "You'll come to love me soon enough, little one."

With the single wall sconce turned on outside the stall in the aisle, it is difficult to see her drawing, but Sam works for a while on it anyway. It gives her something to do to keep her mind busy for a short reprieve. Something had awakened her, but she's not sure what it was. It wasn't as if Huntley's mother came to her in her sleep like he had experienced the night of the tornado. It was just a noise. Not that it really matters. Sleep here on this compound is usually fleeting for her anyway. Plus, she needs these short breaks away from everyone, even if they don't last nearly long enough. Solitude is not the worst thing ever, she's learned. The mare finishes her grain and comes over to inspect her drawing, her baby stuck to her side like glue.

"No, no, mama," Sam warns softly. "Don't get your slobber on this now."

The mare loses interest in Sam's lack of more food and walks a few feet away, forcing her baby to stand closer to Sam. He does not seem happy about his new position and tosses his head with anxiety.

"Settle down, silly boy," she scolds gently. "I bet you'll make a fine stallion someday, won't you? Or a gelding. Perhaps you'll be a gelding. We'll just have to wait and see. If you end up gelded, you'll probably grow a little taller. Did you know that? No, of course, you don't. Not yet. Most stallions are a tad shorter than geldings. Of course, you'll have fewer girlfriends if you're gelded." She chuckles at her own joke and gets a tiny nicker from the rascally boy.

Although his mother is a gray, he looks like he'll end up being a dappled gray. It's still too early to tell. He does share her long legs and shorter neck. Henry has an Arabian stallion that he's been breeding to quarter horses and thoroughbreds. He says he thinks the smaller stallion breeding with the bigger brood mares makes it easier on the mares to give birth. He's probably right, but he's not going to keep the height of the taller breeds of mares. The stallion is also older, so Sam's not sure what he looked like in his prime. He's mellow, though, which makes him easy to handle. This little guy might be his father's replacement in a few years.

"Knock, knock," Henry says, tapping the stall door so as not to startle her.

"Hi, Henry," she says, trying not to be disappointed that he is there. Henry is very kind, but she just wanted some time alone with her art, her feelings, and the animals.

"That's really good," he praises as he enters the stall.

"Thanks," she replies.

The colt allows Henry to pet his neck, which surprises her. Although he is a veteran of the Marines, Henry has a gentleness about him, which the baby must recognize.

"The medic said you checked the mare last night," he comments.

"Yes, she seems to be doing fine, no fevers or swelling, or anything else that I could see," she answers. "We had an OTTB…"

"A what?"

"Oh, yeah, an off-the-track thoroughbred like her at the barn where I used to take lessons. She had a little colt, too. She wasn't a gray, though. She was a big, dark bay with four white socks."

"Is that where you learned so much about horses?"

"Yeah, pretty much," she answers. "I took lessons from an early age and hung out just about every free day I had at the barn with the coaches and trainers. I never took courses or veterinary classes or anything. I read a lot of books about horses and horse care, though. I was still in high school when, well, when everything went south."

"Maybe you woulda' became a vet," he says.

"No, I didn't really want to go into medicine, not animal or human. In retrospect, that just seems like what someone else wanted for me now."

"He has his ways, huh?" he asks, referring to God.

"Yep," she answers.

He leans against the oak wall of the stall and says, "Well, I for one am glad that you were a little barn rat growin' up. I don't know a whole lot about horses, so havin' you here on the farm is helping all of us. Our poor medic's been trying to study whatever he could get his hands on for the past few years."

Sam chuckles, trying to imagine Sonny studying horse veterinary care. It just doesn't fit.

"I'm a dairy farmer, born and raised, so I can handle the cows' vet care but don't much about horses. Were you going to do something in the horse field?"

"I liked show jumping. That's what I wanted to do."

"You were lucky to know at such a young age what you wanted to do with your life. Seems like that would've been an expensive endeavor."

"Oh, it was," she says, remembering her parents fondly. "My mom and dad would argue about it a lot. It was costly. My coach was expensive, the horses and their upkeep, the travel. It all added up, but my dad was the one who wanted me to stay with it. I don't really think my mom liked me doing it at all. I think it made her nervous. She was scared I'd get hurt badly."

"I can see that," he says.

"Did you always want to be a Marine?"

"Yeah, I guess I did. My uncle was in the Marines and was killed in Afghanistan when I was just a kid. I figured I'd put some time in and then come back here and run the farm so my pops could retire. He was getting up there, and the farm was taking its toll."

"All farms are a lot of work," she says. "We only had my horses, but they were a lot of work and money and time. Dairy farms have to be the worst, though. The milking schedules, never being able to go on vacation because the cows have to get milked twice a day. What a pain!"

"Yes, ma'am," he comments with a crooked grin.

The mare nudges Sam's knee with her nose, causing her to chuckle.

"Ok, hungry mama," she says and rubs her velvety muzzle. "I'll get your hay. I know you're eating for two."

"I'll get it," Henry volunteers.

"No, that's fine," she says, slightly frustrated of never being able to do anything around his farm. The men on Henry's farm are chivalrous and outnumber the women, so she hardly gets to do any barn chores, which she actually enjoys. "I'll get her hay."

"I'll come with you. Kind of dark up there," he says.

Henry follows her to the bank barn next to the one-story horse barn. A fog has settled in on his farm, causing everything to be coated with a blanketing of white mist. The grass is dewy and slippery as she climbs the small hill to the double doors.

"Careful," he warns.

"I got it," Sam returns, hoping he doesn't try to hold her arm.

She leaves the big doors shut and goes in through the small man door to the left of the double doors. Henry is carrying a lantern for them, but she still uses her small flashlight, as well.

"Are you on watch duty?" she asks as she inhales the smell of minty hay. The hay on his farm is more abundant in alfalfa than on Grandpa's. Most dairy farmers usually planted more alfalfa for their dairy herds than on other types of farms so that their milk production was more plentiful, the cows fatter and more heavily nourished to boost their output. She learned a lot about hay hanging around farms during her youth. Horses don't need straight alfalfa. They'll eat just about anything, and unless they are doing work like training or pulling a cart or plow or nursing young, they don't necessarily need heavy calorie dense hay. A balanced mix of Timothy is plenty.

"Yes, ma'am," he answers as Sam walks toward the hayloft.

"Aren't your friends going to wonder where you are?"

He chuckles. "There's six of us on, so I think they can manage."

"Hm," she says noncommittally.

"Let me kick one down from the top," he says before she can object.

He leaves his lantern beside her on the floor of the old barn and begins climbing the massive stack of square hay bales. A barn swallow flies overhead from one colossal beam to another likely catching mosquitoes and flies, causing her to look up. The sights and sounds are so familiar to her and make Sam wish she was back on the McClane farm. A gentle breeze pushes through the hallways below them and up through the slats on the floor and through the open hayloft door that looks down over the first floor. It tufts her hair and cools her. She tries to see the little bird. This is the time of year when the mother swallows should be teaching their newborns how to chase pesky flying insects in the barns. Her flashlight catches a swatch of white in the rafters. She peers closer. There is something up there, up high and moving. A light, gossamer strip of white material flutters in the soft breeze. Sam shines the light directly on the object. Her eyes narrow as she focuses in. Sam's entire body breaks out in gooseflesh before she even realizes what she's staring at. The bumps on her skin are not from the light breeze. Her reaction is borne of sheer horror. Then she drops her flashlight and elicits a scream.

"What is it?" Henry asks, climbs down in a hurry and runs to her.

Sam covers her mouth with both hands and refuses to look up again. She simply points in the general direction. It takes a moment, but he must see the same thing.

"What the…?" he says. "Oh, my God. Oh my…"

Henry pulls her physically from the barn. Her body is shaking uncontrollably in his arms. The tears that can't be helped are running endlessly down her cheeks as the image flashes through her mind repeatedly.

"Don't go back in there, Sam," he says.

She can't even respond, nor does she understand what Henry is saying to her.

"Do you hear me? Don't go in there!" he yells more firmly, squeezing her shoulders with his hands.

Sam nods shakily. She doesn't need to be told. She has no intention of ever going back in his barn.

"Stay here," he orders and sprints away shouting and calling to his friends who are also on night duty.

Within seconds, Dave the Mechanic and four other men are running full speed toward the barn. Sam does not go with them into that place of horror.

"Goddammit!" Dave yells from inside. Then others are cussing and swearing, as well. One man comes outside and runs around the side of the barn to vomit. He is young, probably closer to Sam's age than anyone else.

Dave comes out a second later and says to her, "You ok, kid?"

She nods, unable to form words.

"I'm sorry you had to see that," he says as if it is his fault. "She just wasn't dealing with the death of Bruce. I never thought she'd do that or I would've put someone on her at all times."

Sam just walks away. She can hear the men swearing again and Dave issuing orders. Someone will have to climb up there and cut Reese down from the rafters where she has hung herself. Sam knew that her new friend was having trouble handling Bruce's death, but she had no idea that Reese was going to kill herself over it. He was killed the night he was with Simon in the city. So was Annie. It was a tragic night, one that the whole compound took hard, and Derek was left maimed for life. This is worse. Bruce had helped Reese during her recovery, had sat in the old Victorian house in town across from Grandpa's medical clinic while she was in a coma and had not left her side. Reese was young, only a few years older than Sam. She knows that her friend was severely abused at the sex camp. She was very pretty, probably why she was so popular there and in such high demand. Her life would've been so miserable while she was a captive there. Sam knows this firsthand. Sam and Courtney were starting to hang out more with her, especially since Bruce's death. She'd seemed depressed, but just a few days ago Sam had felt like Reese was getting better. She even laughed and smiled a few times and had taken a shower and cleaned herself up a bit. She must've been hiding it from them. Perhaps she had this planned. Perhaps

16

having fun with them the other day in the chicken coop holding the baby peeps had been a false front she'd put on for them so that they wouldn't hover so much and she'd be able to sneak away to do this. Her body was still slightly swaying at the end of that rope, causing Sam to wonder if she'd only just hung herself moments before they'd discovered her.

Was it Reese she'd heard leaving the bunk that had awakened her? Had she only just exited, the door softly clicking, her light, bare footsteps on the concrete floor padding as she made her escape to seek her own death? The more she dwells on it, the more Sam realizes that it is a very real possibility, although she doesn't want it to be so.

Sam walks on wooden legs back to the bunkhouse, all thoughts of art and feeding the mare gone from her thoughts. She doesn't even stop at the barn to pick up her bag lying outside the mare's stall. Before she enters, Sam changes her mind and keeps on walking. She starts running and ends up at the edge of Henry's farm where the fence ends. She climbs through the wires and hikes into a dense copse of trees where she plunks down at the base of an old elm. She pulls her knees up to her chest and presses her forehead into them, rocking gently and trying to make sense of it all. She'll never get the image of her friend dressed in a long white nightgown swinging from the gallows and a hangman's noose of her own making high up in the rafters of Henry's barn. Sam wishes that she could keep running all the way back to Grandpa's farm.

Chapter Three
Cory

Simon is leaving in the morning to go over to Dave's compound to help with building a new clinic for Sam and her uncle, so they are taking one last run for building supplies to make further repairs to the farm. The cow barn took the hardest hit, and they've worked nearly day and night to rebuild the roof. The chicken coop was mostly leveled, and Cory has been working during his night watch shift with Lucas trying to build a new coop. The chickens have been sleeping in temporary nests in the horse barn in one of the empty stalls while their coop is in process. His stallion had escaped the tornado's wrath unscathed, but other horses were injured, two quite severely. All but one horse was recovered, and they have looked for it for days to no avail. He can only assume it is dead. They also lost three goats and six beef cattle that were grazing in the top pasture. Doc said he thought the cows might have been struck by lightning since they were huddled under a tree. The missing goats and horse are just gone. He's not sure if they were literally carried away by the twister or if they ran off in fear.

Some of the buildings in town were heavily damaged, but Doc's practice survived just fine. They have only gone to town twice for actual clinic days and mostly to offer medical care from being injured by the tornado or people who were cut by metal debris afterward during the clean-up process. For now, the farm has to be their first priority, which pisses Cory off because he wants to track those jackass highwaymen. However, he understands the importance of making the emergency repairs to the barns, especially the roof on the cattle barn so that it doesn't rain in and ruin their hay stored there. The tarps that they've covered the holes with are only a temporary fix, and they all know it. With each passing day, they make further progress on completing the repairs, and that means that the day will soon come when they are back on the prowl. It is a day he much anticipates.

He and Simon are in the truck and driving toward Clarksville where they will try to find more roofing materials, nails, any kind of lumber, and anything else they can use, including items from that hospital he went to with John and Sam a while back. They've already been there a few times scavenging and have had success. Today is the last time he'll be able to forage with Simon before they leave. They need more barn roof materials so that the rest of the men can continue the work while they are gone.

"Did you hear that K-Dog called in this morning about another attack?" Cory asks his friend.

"No, I must've been out in the cabin packing," Simon answers, not taking his eyes off the road where he is looking out his window. "Where was it this time?"

"Farther out, east of Nashville," he explains. "Guess they hit a group of Amish people traveling north from Florida to Pennsylvania to find their families."

"Amish? Are you messing with me?"

Cory laughs once, recognizing how ridiculous it sounds. Then he sobers when he realizes how low people must be sinking to victimize the weak. He knows that Amish don't fight back, don't believe in violence or even defending themselves, that violence of any kind goes against their religion. "No, not messing, bro. They killed everyone but the six who got away."

Simon exhales a hard blow of air and says, "That's insane. What are they going to do with the survivors? Do they know yet?"

"Another group of people who were going north anyway is taking the survivors with them."

"How'd K-Dog find out about it?" Simon asks.

Cory shrugs and says, "I don't know. I think he had a friend in the area or something." They pass one of the signs alongside the road that they built and pounded into the ground on stakes. "Hey, that's a good sign. Literally."

"You need to get some new material," Simon criticizes. "But it is fortunate that nobody has knocked it over, that *they* haven't knocked it over."

"No shit," Cory remarks. "I can't wait to find these fuckwits and obliterate them. They need to go. Soon."

"I agree. We're going to Clarksville," Simon points out what they both already know. "You guys weren't able to check out Fort Campbell when you went with your brother and John and my sister."

"I was a little busy getting shot," Cory reminds him.

Simon snorts and says, "Pussy. Anyway, do you want to run by it really quick? It's not like the others will have the time to do it when we're gone. Heck, we barely have the farm put back together. And we hardly have time for clinic days, let alone looking for jerks."

"Yeah, no kidding. We're far from done with repair work," Cory says, weighing out the suggestion. "Sure. Yeah, let's run up there and take a look. If those assholes are camped there, at least we'll know where to find them."

Simon lifts the radio from the console, "I'll call it in."

Kelly responds and warns them to be careful, use caution, and not engage if they find them. His brother does not sound pleased with their idea, but he doesn't tell them not to, either. Cory knows that Kelly wants the highwaymen dead as much as he does. And John does the most. His brother still can't walk without the use of the walker, crutches, and on bad days even the wheelchair.

"And bring me back a number three from Mickey-Dees," Kelly then teases about fast food.

"Got it," Simon returns without missing a beat.

Cory grabs the radio and says quickly, "Sure you don't want a cappuccino with an extra dollop of gay?"

Simon yanks back the radio with a disapproving frown at their goofing.

"Nah, but Doctor Death said he'll take one," Kelly returns. "Be careful. Out."

"Over and out, big guy," Simon says.

"What an ass," Cory remarks. "Now I'm craving fast food."

"That stuff was disgusting sludge," Simon jokes.

Cory laughs again, "Hey, we weren't all senator's kids. Didn't you ever eat garbage food and hang out with your friends cruising your ride on a Friday night?"

20

"Cruising?" Simon asks as if confused. "You mean for girls?"

This time Cory laughs loudly. "No. Well, that's always an added bonus, but no. I meant cruising in your ride."

"My ride? I didn't have a ride. I was only fifteen, remember? My ride was usually a limo going to some stupid event with our dad or my mom's car taking me to Science Club. My mother never would've permitted me to have a hotrod when I was old enough to drive anyway. She was a nurse. She saw a lot of teen crashes coming through the ER when she worked down there."

"Too bad we weren't friends in high school," Cory says.

"What the heck makes you think you'd have been my friend?" he asks.

"How the hell else would I have passed Chemistry?"

This time Simon laughs. "True."

"Then you could've hung out and worked on my car with me and my old man," Cory suggests.

"Oh, boy," Simon remarks with humor. "I don't think I would've been much help."

"You managed to get you and Derek out of the city. Did you use the hotwiring skills I taught you?"

Simon shakes his head beside him and looks distraught at having to recall that night.

"Too bad we need to get such big stuff, or we could've taken my new bike," Cory says, changing the subject since he knows Simon blames himself for people being killed and Derek getting hurt, although it is ridiculous and not at all Simon's fault.

Simon laughs, "As if I'd ever get on that thing with you."

"Ha! Your sister told me the other day that she wants to learn how to drive it herself."

"Over my dead body," Simon says with certainty. "She's certainly never riding on a motorcycle. Isn't the world dangerous enough now?"

"I told her the same damn thing," Cory adds as he watches closely through the front windshield. They are approaching a cluster of wrecked cars on the road. Simon raises his rifle to his shoulder.

"This wasn't here last week when we came through," Simon tells him.

"No, it wasn't," Cory replies. "It looks like a trap. Be ready."

Cory drives slowly toward the carnage in the road, glad to note that there aren't dead bodies like the other scenes they've come across where an attack had taken place.

"Definitely, feels like a trap or a diversion," Simon quietly utters.

Cory stops going forward and presses his foot on the brake to wait and see if there is going to be trouble. Simon is silent beside him scanning out his window. After a few moments, Simon indicates with two fingers that they should continue. Cory does so with great caution. He even has to drive down into the thick grass alongside the road to get past the vehicles. Nothing happens. Nobody runs out of the forest around them shooting and yelling.

"Phew," Cory says as he speeds away toward Clarksville. "Glad we didn't get ambushed. I hate killing people before breakfast."

Simon lowers his rifle again and says, "No, you don't."

Cory smiles and shakes his head. "Nah, I don't."

"What'd my sister pack? I saw her loading food into a bag for us."

"Great," Cory says with sarcasm, although he feels sentimental about his girlfriend- not that she'd allow him to call her that- packing their bag of food for them. "She probably packed us a bunch of vegan shit. Tofu sandwiches and carrot sticks."

"I like carrot sticks," Simon remarks.

"Ever get called carrot stick in school? You know, with your hair being red and all."

"Sometimes," Simon admits. "And other stuff. Insults. The usual."

"Kids are dicks," Cory adds to which his friend nods.

"How would you know?" Simon asks in a serious tone. "It's not like you would've been teased. Football player, good-looking, muscular, cool car. Yeah, must've been terrible."

"All kids get picked on at one time or another," he tells his friend. "I just had a badass older brother who taught me how to defend myself."

"I had a senator for a dad, so he would've just put a security detail on me."

Cory laughs as Simon reaches for the bag between his feet on the floor. He pulls out a paper sack and rifles through it.

22

"I'm glad the kids on the farm aren't like that," Cory says, thinking fondly of the little ones back home.

"Except for maybe Arianna.

"Hell, yeah. That little stinker's a pain in the ass sometimes. Not mine, of course. She loves me. But she's a pain to her brothers and Huntley. She even harasses Luke sometimes."

"I think it's a girl thing. They have a lot of dominance issues. Must be in their DNA."

He takes the biscuit sandwich from his friend. Two, buttery biscuits with homemade sausage and egg in between. Life could be a lot worse than this. Sometimes he thinks about Paige being out there on her own for so long and the awful things she's told him they ate to survive like edible grasses and herbs, squirrels, rabbits, any canned food they could find. Her group had a much harder time than he did when he was gone on his own for a while. At least he already knew how to hunt and take care of himself. She told him about finding a can of Spam meat product once that they made into a gruel they concocted from mixing a little bit of oatmeal, flour, and water with it. It made him want to hurl. It also made him feel even more protective of her. Thinking about her out there again makes him feel the same way; protective, on guard, uneasy. He's never letting her out of his sight.

"I think you might be right, Professor," Cory agrees with his friend. "Your sister's a bossy pants. So is Hannie. Man, she's got Kelly wrapped so tight it ain't right."

Simon chuckles. "Yes, she sure does."

Cory shakes his head and says, "He doesn't seem to mind, though. Actually, it kinda suits him."

"I can't see you being like that someday when you get hitched," Simon remarks.

"Doubt I'll ever get married," Cory says what he's thinking. He doubts it because he wants Paige, which is so complicated he doesn't know how to work it out without hurting Simon and backing her into a corner. She apparently doesn't want a commitment with him of any kind, just the sex.

"With all the women always chasing after you, I'm not sure you'll have a choice in the matter."

"Neither will the men in Dave's compound," he says, finishing the last of his sandwich and washing it down with a glass jar full of water.

"What do you mean?" Simon asks.

"Doc's going over there soon," Cory explains, figuring that Simon has missed this conversation because he's always gone in the woods picking herbs or in the greenhouse or just about anywhere that he doesn't have to be around the house when Sam is over for a visit, which has been a while, too long in Cory's opinion. "He wants the men who are sleeping with the women from the sex camp to either marry them or knock it off. You know Doc. He ain't gonna be down with any of that premarital sex hook-up stuff."

"That's going to be difficult to enforce," Simon says between bites. He normally eats slower than Cory. "They're all adults. I don't think Herb can force them into marriage."

Cory shoots him a dubious expression. "This is Doc we're talkin' about here."

"True," Simon concurs with a grin. "But maybe some of them don't even want to get married."

Cory tries not flinch, thinking of Paige, "Then I guess in his opinion, they shouldn't be doing it at all."

"Also, probably true."

They roll through Clarksville and north toward Fort Campbell. Once they get within a few miles, Cory stashes the truck on a deserted road that looks to have been an access driveway to a farmer's field. Since the fields have long since been forgotten, gone to seed and overgrown many times over, he feels it is safe to make the judgment call and leave the truck at the end of the road just at the edge of a forest. This is a good place to begin the trek to the base anyway with the cover of dense trees and overgrown forestland.

They exit the truck, grab their packs, lock it up and take the keys. The CNG vehicles on the farm are proving invaluable for their survival. It is better than traveling by horseback. Plus, it saves the horses for their uncertain future travel needs. Others would, no doubt, feel the same way about their truck and take it without hesitation. Cory recently worked with Derek installing kill switches to the positive circuit of the fuel pumps of both vehicles to prevent them from being hotwired. Unless the person wanting to steal it knows about the hidden switch under the passenger seats, then they'll be hotwiring something that isn't going to start. They'd gone back a few days after the tornado and recovered the four-wheeler they'd left behind at the cabin, too. They got lucky it was still there, probably only because the assholes who shot him, likely the highwaymen, either hadn't seen it or were too busy running away from John's deadly shooting rampage. Either way, Cory was relieved to get it back. It helps them a lot, especially on quick runs to their neighbors' houses or even over to the condo unit to meet up with Paul or K-Dog.

They jog through the woods and make it to Fort Campbell unimpeded and unnoticed, other than by the herd of deer they spot in a low-lying meadow. At the same time, they drop to the ground and belly crawl to the crest of a short incline to spy through their binoculars on the old Army base. It was the home of the 101st Airborne, and he's pretty sure Kelly came through here, John, as well.

It is clear that they aren't going to see much from this position since they are so far out, so Cory suggests cutting the chain-link fencing and getting a closer look inside the actual base. Within a few minutes, they've cut through and are creeping toward a tall building that probably housed troops or offices at one time. There are long rows of what appear to be townhouses, apartments or small homes to their west. He wants to get a higher position and check the place out. He gets Simon's attention and signals they should go up, to which his friend agrees. They slink around the corner of the brick building and through a side door that is unlocked. The building appears to be abandoned and not currently inhabited. Cory indicates they should climb, and they find the nearest stairwell and do so. The building is four stories, and he and Simon exit onto a roof that has clearly not been maintained for quite some time. They walk the perimeter instead of the center in case some of the areas that look weak give out and cause them to fall through. They both take a knee near the edge and pull out their binoculars again.

It doesn't take them long to notice movement near another building similar to theirs. Cory watches closely as two children run down the middle of the road. Others come out behind another building and scare them. The children scream and then laugh. They are actually playing. Simon taps his shoulder and points to their south. There are young people working in a garden. Some are also kids.

"Lot of kids," Cory comments quietly.

"Yes, strange," Simon replies as he continues to watch the area. "Actually, I don't see any adults at all. What the heck?"

"There's one," Cory says. "Over there near the door to the building. He's got a gun, too."

"I don't know, Cor," Simon says with doubt. "I think that's a teenager."

Upon closer inspection, he's pretty sure his friend is right. It does not seem to be an adult, after all. They wait for a while watching this camp but don't ever discover adults. Two people on ATV's come through a back gate, dismount and are greeted by some of the children, of which he's counted six so far. They hand them two dead squirrels and what appears to be a string of fish. Cory can tell that the newcomers are also young people, maybe twenty or so.

"Where are all the adults?" Simon asks rhetorically. "This is strange if it's just a bunch of young kids living here."

"Some of them aren't kids," Cory says. "But they aren't exactly very old, either. I doubt if they're the parents of these kids. They don't seem old enough. Think this is it, this is the whole picture? Think they're surviving on their own, a bunch of orphans and teenagers or something?"

"Not sure," Simon allows. "We should report it back to the farm, though. They definitely aren't our highwaymen."

"No, not them. Let's call it in when we leave later. For now, we should get to work," Cory says, getting a nod from Simon.

They exit the same way they entered the base and begin scavenging Clarksville for building supplies. They have a lot of good fortune at a small, family-owned store but not as much at the big places like Home Depot. They aren't the only people looking for materials to repair their homes right now. They do find metal roofing, nails, boxes of screws, down spouting, lumber, and fencing supplies. Cory gathers four, five-gallon buckets of white paint, too.

"That might not be any good anymore," Simon points out.

"I know. I just need it...for a project I'm workin' on."

"Oh, got it," his friend says and doesn't further question. The last place they hit is the hospital where they take everything they can fit in the truck. They work until nearly sundown, tie their loot down

26

with ropes and bungee cords, and head back toward the farm. When they get to the blocked part of the road again, they see that not everyone was so lucky to pass the wrecked cars so safely.

"What the hell?" Cory says, gripping the wheel tightly.

Simon adds, "We just went through here this morning."

"No, shit," Cory remarks. "Whoever did this obviously wasn't here this morning when we passed through. These people got ambushed."

"They just weren't here when we went by," Simon observes. "We missed them."

"They were probably somewhere fucking else killing other people at other ambush sites," Cory says with anger.

He stares out his window at the vehicle on fire with a dead man behind the wheel. There are also three dead men on the road, and another vehicle that has been raided and left behind since he and Simon drove this way. Further up the street, they find two women and a young boy also dead. A few miles down the road away from the carnage, people run out of the woods flagging them down. They are clearly the victims of the highwaymen, who likely just murdered their friends and family members. Cory stops the vehicle to talk with them. They are unarmed and scared out of their minds. Two men are covered in black soot and ash as if they'd tried to rescue their friend in the car but were too late. A woman is crying and holding her baby. Two others are in shock with their vacant, blank eyes and thousand-yard stares. He wonders if one of them was the mother of the dead boy who couldn't have been older than twelve. A rage is building within him as he hustles the people into the back of the truck on top of the loot to take them to their town. They explain to Simon through the slider window that they were headed to Florence, Kentucky, and that they'd heard it was better there. It's not better anywhere. Cory would like to say this, but he figures they just got a huge icy splash of reality in the face enough for one day.

The ticking of the second hand in his mind is growing each day that they haven't caught and killed the highwaymen. He is going to have to go hunting at night on his own like he used to. They can't stand by and allow this to happen again. The predator within him, that malevolent thing he tries to still, will not be confined any longer. It is time to unleash it.

Chapter Four
Simon

He eats a hearty breakfast the next morning with the family and tries not to have anxiety about the trip he's about to make. The journey is not the problem; it's the destination. Simon has no wish to spend the next few weeks living on Henry's farm.

They'd dropped the people from the burnt carnage on the road in town and took time to introduce them to their friends there and, most importantly, the sheriff, who will assess and evaluate them before allowing them to stay on. As the murder rate rises on the roads, the population in their town also increases as they take in new members, victims of the highwaymen.

But this morning, he is in a sour mood. He'd much rather be working on the barn roof, repairing the front porch, building new sections of fence, or pretty much anything that isn't going to plant him in the vicinity of Samantha. There is so much that wasn't dealt with between them from her last visit, the night of the tornado. He'd kissed her in the barn. Like a pathetic, weak fool, he'd been ready to renounce everything he'd worked so hard on regarding Sam, namely his plan to allow her to move on with her life and forget about him and find someone else who can make her happy, someone not like him. In an instant, it had all been erased from his brain, his so carefully orchestrated plan- poof, just gone. All that had mattered was holding her in his arms and making her his. He can't do that, though. Simon knows she isn't his to begin with, never was, and can never be. He could never endeavor to deserve her, not after what happened. And now, as hard as he has tried to move on with his life as best as he knows how and allow Sam to do the same, he's being forced right back into her company. He should've suggested that she come to the McClane farm for a two-week stay. Not exactly subtle, but at least she would've been on the McClane farm while he was at Henry's.

"Try to find a home with at least four rooms on the first floor, Simon, if you find a two-story," Doc is saying. "They'll need that many exam rooms. Plus, her uncle said he might live on the top floor with Miss Samantha when it's done. They'll need two bedrooms in addition to the exam rooms."

"Yes, sir," he mumbles.

"You'll need running water, heat, and a way of sterilizing instruments. Don't forget to build a wheelchair ramp if it needs one," his mentor adds.

"Don't look for a place that's too sandwiched in by a lot of houses all around it," John tells him. "Just in case there's ever trouble and the docs gotta' get out."

This makes his stomach turn. Sam and her uncle running for their lives from people attacking the place? He doesn't understand why they can't run their clinic from the safety of Dave's compound. Probably the same reason Herb and Reagan don't. It would be a security disaster.

"Yes, sir," he answers John.

Reagan butts in to say, "I think Dave's planning on putting armed guards on it twenty-four-seven. I'm assuming they'll be living there with Sam and her uncle, so you might look for a house with at least four bedrooms on the top floor."

This makes him even more nauseous. He just wishes they'd all go into silent mode. Thinking about Sam living in a house in tight quarters with two guards, men he doesn't know at all, causes him to feel a particularly intense anxiety.

"Right," he says anyway.

"A small shed on the property would be great, too," Sue adds. "So that they can get their greenhouse established."

"Yes, ma'am," he says.

They continue to give him advice, even though he just wants it all to stop. Not only does he not want to go over there to help with this project, he doesn't even want to think about Sam living off the compound. It's never going to be safe enough no matter what they do.

Breakfast concludes, and he and Cory make their exit. His friend is going with him for the first week, but then he's coming back without him. Simon will hitch a ride to town with Dave's men in order to get back home, or at least that's the plan.

"I'm gonna miss you," Paige says, hugging him next to the truck so tightly he can scarcely breathe.

"It's just for a few weeks, maybe less," he reminds her and pats her back. Maybe he can come back when Cory does.

"We'd better get on the road," Cory says as he comes around the truck. "Do I get a hug, too, Red?"

Simon passes a glare to his friend and pats her back one more time, ignoring Cory's comment.

"You wish," Paige says to Cory as she pulls back. She leans up and kisses Simon's cheek. "Be careful."

"I will," he says. "Stay close to the house while I'm gone."

She nods, and he turns to go. Cory is speaking with John near the driver's door. They had a meeting last night with the family to tell them of their find at Fort Campbell. He's not sure if those were orphaned kids and young adults taking care of themselves there or if there were adults just out of view that they hadn't seen. Either way, they didn't seem like the highwaymen. They didn't spot vehicles moving around, either, and they know that the highwaymen have cars, motorcycles, vans, and at least one truck that belonged to Henry and was stolen. John said that he might take a run over there and check it out while they are gone. It hadn't gone over well. His wife had been angry about the idea of him going alone. With he and Cory going away, they won't be able to let too many people leave the farm for runs. It just wouldn't be safe leaving the farm unprotected with a shortage of manpower.

It takes a while to make it all the way to Henry's farm, but they are glad to see that Dave's signs are also still erected on the roads. It should help. Anything is better than nothing at this point. Their victims were absolutely defenseless and unaware that the roads were dangerous, deadly even.

They are greeted at the gate by a sentry, who tells them that Dave is expecting them and is in the dairy barn. Simon's not sure which barn that is, so they park near the house and walk toward the cluster of many barns. They greet a few people along the way but get brief, abbreviated greetings in return. The collective mood is off. Nobody seems in a particularly good disposition. He wonders if they are upset by him and Cory being on the farm.

They pass a girl who looks familiar, "Hey! Simon, right?"

Simon regards her, trying to remember her name, "Yes, Courtney?"

"Right," she says with a smile and shakes his hand, then Cory's.

"Cory, ma'am," he says with a smile. "Do you know where Sam is?"

"Oh, I don't know, Cory," she answers. "She's been gone a lot the last few days."

This alarms Simon, but Cory is quicker to question this, "What do you mean by gone? She's been off this farm?"

"No, I don't think so. She's mostly been going off by herself. I think the barns or the woods."

"That doesn't sound very safe," Simon breaks in, trying to control his disappointment at this news.

"Well, it's just that… well, you know it's been hard on Sam," she says.

"The move here?" Cory asks.

"No, she's been great," Courtney offers.

Simon is less than enthusiastic about this information. "Then why is she going off by herself. And what's been so hard on her?"

"Finding Reese," she says as if they understand what she means. They both give her a confused look. "Don't you know? Oh! I guess I just assumed they called over to tell you guys or told you while you were on a run together or something."

"We haven't been doing the combined runs since the tornado," Cory tells her.

"Oh, right," Courtney says with a sad sigh. "Then you don't know."

"Know what?" Simon prompts impatiently.

"Reese killed herself two days ago," she drops on them. "Everyone's been freaked out about it. I guess she was just too sad since Bruce was killed."

She keeps droning on, but Simon is having difficulty processing so much information. Bruce was murdered the night he was with him. It has weighed heavily on his mind and his conscience since. The simultaneous murder of Annie has also plagued him. He can't help but feel he was somehow responsible.

"Sam was the one who discovered her," Courtney says, instantly drawing his attention. "They were friends. She really liked Reese. I feel so bad for her."

"She found her? Where?" Cory asks.

Simon is glad his friend is asking the questions because his brain has stopped working correctly. All he can think is that Sam is in distress and he needs to find her.

"Hanging in the barn," Courtney tells them. "She was so sad."

"Damn," Cory remarks bleakly. "That's too damned bad."

"I just don't think she could take one more thing, and then Bruce was killed. It just…made her snap," Courtney says.

"And Sam found her?" Simon asks again, getting a nod. "And she's been going off on her own since it happened?"

Courtney nods again, then drops her eyes to the ground. Her blonde hair falls over her shoulder.

"Hey, guys!" Dave calls out as he approaches.

"Dave," Cory says in greeting and shakes his hand. Simon does the same.

"Glad you're here," Dave says as a few of his men gather. Henry is with them. "We'll leave soon and show you a few places we've found. See what you guys think."

"Great," Cory says with less enthusiasm. "We're glad to help."

"We had a problem a few days ago," Dave says more quietly.

"Yeah, Courtney just told us," Cory tells him. "Sorry for your loss. I'm sure everyone is taking it hard."

"Yeah, fucking sucks, man," Dave says. "We're holding a service for her this evening. We buried her yesterday morning, but we're giving her a proper memorial service tonight."

"We'll be there," Cory says.

"Yes, sir," Simon agrees.

He scans the property around them, searching for her. At first, he'd been nervous about seeing her and being around her. Now, he's just upset because Sam is in distress.

"Let's load up, and we'll take you to the few houses we've found that might work," Henry says.

Cory shakes his hand and nods.

Henry turns to Dave and says, "I'll catch up at the truck. I just wanna' check on Sam before we go."

He is speaking quietly, but Simon still hears him. It pisses him off. He wants to know where she is and why Henry knows where she is and he does not.

Dave tells him, "See if she wants to go. We could use her advice, too."

"Yes, sir," Henry answers and walks away.

"I'll meet you in a minute. Um, gotta...use the restroom," Simon says quickly to Cory, who nods distractedly as he continues to speak to Dave and his men.

Simon follows after Henry at a distance without him noticing because there are so many people in the barnyard. Henry walks behind the storage barn and past an outdoor pen full of goats. Simon waits near the barn, spying as Henry goes down a short hill to a big tree with a wooden swing hanging down. It is then that he sees her for the first time, and the reaction is always the same. It is as if something has sucked all the oxygen from the air. She is sitting not on the swing but the ground at the base of the tree. It looks like she is doing art. When she sees Henry, Sam rises to greet him. They speak, and she nods. Then she does the unthinkable and very briefly hugs Henry. Simon's eyes nearly bulge out of his skull. A squeaking sound at his side startles him. He looks down to find his fist so tightly clenched around the leather sling of his rifle that it is squealing in protest. He takes a deep breath and retreats as they approach the barn. Simon jogs back to meet Cory at the truck.

Sam immediately rushes into Cory's outstretched arms and hugs him for a much longer time than she had Henry.

"Hey, kiddo," Cory says gently. "We heard about your friend. We're real sorry to hear about that, Sam."

She nods and lowers her head.

Dave walks from the rear of their own truck and says, "Wanna' jump in the bed? We'll ride together."

Cory flips him a thumbs-up sign, and they climb into the bed. He is disappointed that Sam has not acknowledged his presence, and she takes Cory's hand to climb over the closed tailgate. They all find a seat, Henry included, much to his irritation.

"Hello, Samantha," he says, trying at civility, although every fiber of his being is longing to pull her into his arms and stroke her dark hair in a comforting manner.

"Hi, Simon," she greets without affection or emotion.

She won't look at him, which concerns Simon.

"Sorry I have to be here. I'm sure you wish I wasn't," he offers with a morose expression as they pull away. Cory is engaged in conversation with one of Dave's men near the tailgate, and he is sitting against the front. Sam is near him, but also near Henry, who has perched on the wheel well. Simon imagines how easy it would be to push him over the side of the truck. Unfortunately, they aren't traveling at a high enough rate of speed to do much damage. Maybe he'd at least get run over.

Sam doesn't answer but looks briefly at him before turning away.

Simon inches closer and touches her arm lightly, "You ok?"

She nods and looks away again at nothing. She also slowly pulls her arm out from under his hand. He is left feeling impotent. They are in a truck full of people, some strangers. It is a horrible, painful topic to dredge up and definitely not in their current setting. He does not believe she is doing well at all. The wind catches her hair, tossing and blowing it into her face. Sam pushes it back, holding it at the base of her neck to secure it. She is pale and fatigued-looking. He'd bet anything that she hasn't slept since she saw Reese hanging in the barn. Something like this would be traumatic for her, and she's already been through so much. A lot of what she's been through lately has been because of him, and the guilt from the knowledge of it is eating away at Simon.

They drive past a small, brick home about four miles from Henry's farm. He doesn't like the location. It is too far away should her uncle and Sam have a problem. Cory says that he likes the brick construction because it offers more protection from bullets and is more energy efficient. However, he is quick to point out that there are a lot of outbuildings where people could hide. Dave agrees, and they head the other direction. The next place is too heavily damaged from water, causing mold and bacteria to take a firm hold in the basement. Cory jokes that they are trying to treat people, not make them sicker. Dave laughs, and they continue on. This goes on for three more homes until they come to a large two-story about three miles from Henry's farm. Simon really doesn't like the location.

"This is good," Cory says. "No neighbors to worry about. No houses to block the view for security. Not a lot of outbuildings, but that small shed would be a good greenhouse eventually. Pretty close to your compound."

"Not very close," Simon disagrees.

"You think it's too far?" Dave asks him.

Simon nods and says, "Yes, sir. If the doctor is going to live on site, it's awfully far if he were to run into problems."

His eyes dart to Sam, who is standing on the front lawn with them. It mostly resembles an overgrown pasture, not a lawn. She is looking across the street at an empty field. Her gaze is void of emotion, sightless, seeing nothing in particular. He doesn't like this. Simon has seen her like this before, and it is never a good thing.

"He doesn't have to live on site; Scott would just prefer to," Dave explains. "Let us show you the inside."

They go in the abandoned house, which is definitely big enough to use as a medical practice.

"This is a good location between our compound and our town," Henry tells them. "We'll be able to offer medical care to more people in the area."

"And it would keep the compound more private like yours," Dave adds, looking at them.

"That's always a smart thing," Cory nods. "Plumbing still looks viable. I think the front rooms would work as exam rooms. What do you think, Professor?"

"Huh?" he asks, dragging his gaze from Sam. "Yes. The dining room, office, and living room would easily convert. Actually, the living room would be the only room that we'd have to build a divider wall in. And the kitchen is acceptable for a work area, storing meds and sterilizing tools."

"This house has four bedrooms upstairs, too," Henry adds. "It would be perfect for Sam and her uncle."

Dave says, "We could post two men here with them, too. They'll need amped up security."

Simon doesn't agree with any of this, "I don't think it's a good idea at all."

Everyone turns their attention to him.

"It's just that it's far from your compound and going to attract attention. People looking for drugs will hit this place as soon as they hear about them running a medical clinic. There's no perimeter wall or fencing structure around it. Our town has had problems time and again with people stealing from the clinic, probably non-residents of the town but people we've treated that heard about the clinic who traveled there for care."

"We'll be fine," Sam utters stoically, not lifting her eyes from the dusty hardwood floor.

"No, I don't agree," he argues, looking at Sam, who has already lost interest and is back to staring at nothing in a daze. Simon, instead, turns to Dave. "There's no way to secure this house. What are we supposed to do, build a stone wall around it? That's the only thing in our town that's helped."

"You've got a point," Cory says.

"We could establish the clinic but not have the doctors live here," Dave offers thoughtfully.

"You'd have to lug your supplies back and forth from your compound to this house every time you have a clinic day," Cory reminds them. "They'll still break in and steal things, even shit they don't know how to use like medical instruments and supplies. Some of it you could haul back and forth, though."

"That would be alright, I suppose," Dave says.

"Aren't there any houses closer to the farm?" Cory asks.

"No, none that aren't flooded out, molded, or too damaged by the tornado now to bother with," he says.

"There's an old log cabin near my farm," Henry states, "but I don't think it would be very accessible by road."

"How close is it?" Simon asks.

"Less than a mile, but it's just a rustic cabin," he explains further. "It sits back really far from the road. We used it more as a hunting cabin than anything else."

"Could we build small exam rooms in it?" Cory asks.

Henry considers this a moment before answering, "Yes, maybe. It's not big, but we could probably get three exam rooms in there."

"You mean that place back in the woods?" Dave asks.

"Yes, sir," Henry answers. "My family built it a long time ago before I was born. The neighbors let my family build it, and they got to use it for free. They were friends of ours. It's technically on their land, but they're long gone now. They had more woods on their farm than we did, so we hunted over there. My dad and his brothers would sack out there and go hunting and fishing."

"How would we get patients there?" Dave asks.

"We'd have to find a way to clear a path," Henry says. "We used to take ATV's to get there."

Simon quickly puts in, "We could help with building a road."

Cory also says, "What about bedrooms? Could Sam and her uncle live there, too?"

"Um, yeah. There's a loft and two small bedrooms. It's nothing fancy. Pump well in the sink, fireplace for heat. Not much."

"It's better than being out here on this paved road and open to ambush and attack," Simon remarks.

"True. Good point," Cory adds. "Once people figure it out that there's a clinic here, and they will because word gets out quick, you'll already have a security issue. The clinic in town grew so quickly. We weren't even prepared for how many people found out about it and started bringing their families there for care. You'll probably have the same. Doc and Reagan treat people who aren't from our town, too. We let them in and give them care and then turn them back out through the gates."

"Yes, I've seen that. Interesting," Dave considers. "Maybe your old cabin isn't such a bad idea, Gunny."

"What do you think, Sam?" Henry asks, turning to look at her. "You know a lot about the way a clinic should work."

She walks over toward them, having wandered to the front windows to look out.

"Doesn't matter. This place. That place. Anything you guys decide will probably work," she says. "We just need to get a practice set up and do it as soon as possible. There are so many women in town here who are going to have babies. We'll be trying to help with the births when we can, but their babies are going to need a pediatrician. We need a practice unless we're going house to house once a week to check on them."

With this statement released, she walks away again, past them and out the front door. They all stare at one another with confusion. Apparently, he isn't the only who doesn't understand women. Simon follows after her. The men can discuss it further without him. He's given his opinion. It won't change.

"Sam," he calls, not getting her attention. She stops at the truck but doesn't climb into the bed again. She just stands there staring out at the field across the street. "Anything wrong? Did you see something out there?"

He naturally tightens his grip on his rifle sling.

She looks up at Simon and shakes her head. "No, nothing."

He knows she is stressed out. She's exhausted, barely on her feet, but she's still beautiful to him. He's seen her at her worst and was not the only man to find her attractive. That was the problem.

"Wanna' sit?" he asks and opens the tailgate. She doesn't acknowledge him. "Sam? Do you want to sit and rest a minute?"

"What? Sure."

Without thinking, Simon wraps his hands around her waist and hefts her onto the tailgate. She doesn't pull back or argue. She takes his help as if she isn't even aware that he is there. He hops up and sits beside her. Simon doesn't push her. She likely needs some space, but he is concerned. They sit in the silence of the afternoon, the birds chirping and the sun high and bright, although it does seem as if it will rain later. She keeps picking at her thumbnail. Her fingernails are painted, something she must've done while at the farm for her visit. They are chipping, though, and she keeps picking away at the polish.

Her hair is hanging down her back, not pulled into a ponytail or braided as she would typically do in such hot weather. He's just guessing, but it also seems tangled as if she hasn't brushed it yet today. Sam is wearing blue-jean shorts, cutoffs that she's rolled up. They show off her tanned legs. Simon wishes she was wearing long pants, and not just to conceal her sexy legs from the other men. He finds his eyes dropping to them a lot, too, while they wait in silence. Her pale pink, oversized t-shirt has dirt on the hem, leaving him to wonder what she has been doing today. Probably something that has to do with horses, he's assuming. She always looks so pretty in pinks and rose colors; it brings out the flush of her cheeks.

A moment later, the men come out of the house, noisy as ever, unaware of much other than themselves and their discussion. If any of them notices Simon sitting with her or that Sam seems sad, nobody says anything.

They load up and travel back to Henry's farm, but instead of turning down the lane, they drive past it to a field access driveway, which is mostly just an overgrown cow path full of ruts and holes that throw Sam against him a few times. When they come to a fallen tree, they dismount from the truck and walk. It doesn't take long before they find the cabin that Henry told them about. He was right about one thing. It is rustic.

They look around the outside first and discuss whether or not they could build and clear a driveway to the structure. It is quickly decided that they can manage that. Cory and Henry climb onto the roof and declare that it's solid but could use some upkeep. Then they go inside. The house is basically a bigger version of the cabin the McClanes stay in when doing a run to Clarksville. There are signs of spiders everywhere. Normally Sam would cringe at this, but she just walks around the cabin with a glum expression on her tiny doll face. He walks over to the men cloistered in the living room near the fireplace. Cory has his head up the chimney inspecting it.

"Looks clear," his friend says and comes out covered in cobwebs and dirt.

"Can't say the same for you now," Henry jokes.

Cory laughs, and so do the others. Simon does not. He doesn't really like Henry all that well.

They go from room to room, measuring and examining. Simon offers his opinion where he feels he should and listens as others do, too.

"Let's discuss these houses more over dinner tonight," Dave suggests as they prepare to leave. "We got some ideas today, but we need to get back."

Simon looks around to find Sam gone.

"She went upstairs," Cory tells him. "I'll grab her."

Simon offers a nod but still waits in the house for his friend to bring her down. Then they leave together and head back to the compound. She is quiet the entire ride and takes Henry's hand to get down from the bed of the truck when they arrive on his farm. He tries not to be bothered by this.

He and Cory are shown to a small white cabin with chipping paint and a low roofline near the dairy barn where they will be staying while on the farm. It's even smaller than their cabin back on Herb's farm, but it is a little more private than staying in the bunkhouse with a lot of people. He's appreciative, and he is sure Cory is, too. Henry warns them that the shower spits out mostly cold water. Simon's glad he took one before he left this morning.

They join Dave's group for dinner in the mess hall and go over their ideas and plans. Simon glances around several times looking for her but doesn't find Sam in the crowd. There are a lot of people at the various tables, but he doesn't think she is just lost in the crowd. It makes it very difficult to concentrate on the conversation around him. They do make a decision to go with the log cabin for the practice. It's going to take a lot of work, but he's satisfied that at least she and her uncle will be safer there than out on the road in a house not ten feet from it.

After dinner, the entire group goes to a burial site they have chosen for Reese. He can't stand this. Dave further explains to them that so many people were gone on a run yesterday that they held off on her memorial service in order for them to be present. She was well liked. Simon is sick and tired of attending funerals. Dave's compound has a village minister who gives the service. So many people are crying, even some of the men. Reese was a really nice woman. She certainly didn't deserve the life she was given.

Simon looks around the crowd again and still doesn't find Sam. Her uncle is standing next to Courtney, but Sam is not with them, either. He discreetly slips away and heads toward the women's bunkhouse, which is quite a long way from his cottage rental. He doesn't find her. He looks in the barns and still comes up short. A light drizzle has begun, which seems like it will eventually turn into a deluge. He searches a long barn, which must be where they store hay and keep horses because he hears them nickering to one another. Surely, she'll be here. But he doesn't locate her again and is beginning to get worried as he exits out the back of the long building. A two-story equipment shed at the end of the other barns and very removed from the rest of the farm is the only place he hasn't looked. He jogs there since it is the last possible area she'd be. The sun is setting and making it difficult to see in the darkening building. It appears as empty as the rest. Then the soft glow of a lantern coming from the far corner of the pole barn catches his attention as he turns to go. He walks cautiously toward the source. Skirting around an antique truck from what he would estimate to be the 1950s, Simon finally finds her. She is sitting in the bed of the truck on an old mattress drawing by the light of the lantern. She doesn't startle. Sam must've heard him. So much for his stealth skills or his future career as a ninja.

"Hey," he says softly, not wanting to chase her off.

"I figured you'd find me," she doesn't say this with malice or anger, just as if she is stating a fact.

"I was worried," he responds honestly.

"I'm fine," she says and uses her pencil to point to her handgun beside her box of art pencils.

"What are you drawing?"

He steps closer, and Sam immediately flips the sketchpad closed. This worries him. She could be slipping into that dark place again.

"Nothing, horses, stuff like that," she says and looks away.

Her behavior is suspicious, but he won't push, not tonight.

"You're missing the funeral for your friend," he says as he climbs over the side of the truck and sits beside her, propping his gun against the frame of the rear, missing window of the cab.

"No, I'm not missing that at all," she informs him.

Simon frowns. "She was your friend?"

Sam nods.

"I'm really sorry, Samantha," he offers.

She just nods again.

"Don't you want to go to her funeral?"

This time she shakes her head. Simon nods. He can understand. It gets old real fast, and they've certainly watched enough people, friends, and family be buried the last four years.

He replies with a simple, "Yeah."

Simon sits with her for a few minutes in the quiet, listening to the raindrops tinkling down upon the metal roof. Sam packs her art supplies away but doesn't attempt to leave.

"Want to talk about it?" he asks.

Her blue eyes slide to his, and Simon can see her pain, the anguish and something akin to horror that she's been hiding all day by staring at the floor or out at fields or anywhere but at him directly. She barely shakes her head, the motion nearly imperceptible.

"It'll help. You can tell me," Simon offers and touches her arm.

Her breathing speeds up, her chest rising and falling faster and faster. Sam's eyes morph into a haunted stare as she recalls something terrifying.

"Talk to me, Sam," he urges.

"It...it was..."

She shakes her head and looks away. There is nothing to see on that side of the truck but a blank, dark wall.

"You found her?" he asks.

"How'd you know?"

"Courtney."

Sam nods with understanding.

"In the barn she said?" he prompts.

She nods and says on a shaky breath, "Yes. She was...she was hanging there, swaying."

"No, that's terrible," he says, picturing what she must've seen. It is a horrific image to be sure, one that won't dissipate into the far reaches of her memory for a long time to come.

"Henry was getting hay down. We were the only two people awake, and I was drawing in the barn. He followed me to get hay for the mare that just had her baby. Her white dress caught my eye, and I looked up. It was..."

She doesn't finish but looks away again. Simon is also concerned that she was the only person awake and hanging out with Henry all by herself in the barns. He doesn't like it. For now, his concern is for Sam's mental state.

"She was swinging just slightly," Sam explains before he can ask another question. "She looked like a ghost. I guess she already was. Her face, though. Her face..."

"What is it, Sam?" he asks, resting his hand on her shoulder.

She shakes her head, draws her knees up to her chest and hugs them, refusing to talk.

"Was she dead already or had she just dropped?"

"No, she was definitely dead. I'll never be able to get that image out of my mind."

He rubs her back. "You will. Over time it'll fade."

She vigorously shakes her head and looks directly at him. "No, no, I won't, Simon. It was…her eyes, and the purple mottling of her skin. I've never seen anything like that."

He doesn't know what to say. He's never witnessed a suicide. It must've been a ghastly thing to discover.

"I'm sorry," he offers.

Sam nods and rests her chin on her knees. She sniffs hard, leading him to believe that she might be crying. All he wants to do is pull her into his arms and comfort her, but he's not sure if she would allow it. Before she left the farm, she would've turned to him for help dealing with this. She always sought him out for things that greatly bothered her. He just continues to rub her back and shoulders with his left hand. Simon hopes it helps to lessen her pain.

"I couldn't go to her service," she says. "I don't ever want to see her again or even picture her. I just want to pretend it never happened, that I never knew Reese at all."

He doesn't think this is a healthy way to deal with this situation but holds his tongue. Instead, he says, "I'm sure everyone understands. You need to process this, take your time and handle it on your own terms."

"John told me once that one of his friends killed himself when he discharged out of the military and went home. He said it was really hard on him, too. I never thought I'd have to deal with something like that."

"Yes, veteran suicide was a real problem for our soldiers," he tells her. "My father did a lot of work to improve our veteran hospitals and tried to get them the psychiatric care and counseling they needed so that they could find another way, see that there were other options out there."

"Now there's nothing like that, not for anyone. Reese just couldn't deal with her grief, what happened to her, and losing Bruce. It was just all too much. I wish I would've seen it coming."

He sighs and nods. "Yes, I know. Perhaps I should be studying psychology a lot harder so that I can offer help someday with issues like this."

"I think we all should," she says. "Just to take care of our friends."

They sit in the bed of the truck for a while just listening to the rain and not talking. He wants to give her space, but at the same time, Simon would like nothing better than to pull her into his arms and hold her close, tell her that everything will be all right, and that he'll take care of her from now on. This is another fantasy dimension of reality that he has created that he likes to visit sometimes where things are different, and he has the right to live out his life with her.

"Simon," she asks after a long time of silence.

"Yes?"

She looks at him again with bloodshot eyes that have dark circles underneath. To Simon, she has never been lovelier. Sam could be on her deathbed with the plague, and he'd still find her lovely and not wanting.

"Why did you kiss me again?"

This floors him. Simon wasn't expecting this question at all. He swallows hard and pushes his glasses higher on his nose. The night air which had just a moment ago felt cool, a gentle breeze blowing through the open shed, suddenly feels stifling as if the air has grown thin and humid.

"I…I'm…"

His answer is idiotic, and he sounds like a stuttering imbecile. He wants to explain everything to her, tell her how he feels about her, lean in and kiss her again like he had that evening before the tornado struck the farm. He hadn't even been able to see her off or say goodbye. He'd been in the far pasture catching a horse he'd seen wandering into the woods. Nobody else saw it. He knew he had to capture it before it ended up lost to them.

"I don't understand why you did it," she repeats, her dark brow crinkling.

"I…I'm sorry about that, Sam. It was inexcusable behavior," he apologizes, which sounds stupid. She wants an actual explanation, but he can't give her one that makes sense. It doesn't even make sense to him. He finds her irresistible? Of course, he does, but he can't just tell her that.

44

She considers him a moment, looks like she is chewing on the inside of her cheek, and nods. Then she swiftly rises, grabs her bag and flees the barn without another word. Simon is left sitting there feeling like the fool he is.

Chapter Five
Sam

A few days after Simon and Cory arrive on Henry's farm, Sam attempts to sneak away like she does most mornings but is detained by Cory in the barnyard.

"Hey, kiddo," he says in greeting with a big, wide smile.

Some of her bunkmates have already been pestering her about Cory. Sam usually politely smiles and walks away. Poor Cory, to be so devastatingly handsome that women everywhere pine after him. She wonders if he has formed an attachment to someone in town, though, because he does not seem particularly interested in any of the women- of which there are plenty- on Dave's compound.

"Good morning," she says, wishing she could've gotten away unnoticed. She just wants to be alone. She is sleep deprived and exhausted and sad.

"We're going to the new clinic today. Wanna' come and give your input? We'd sure appreciate it."

"Um...I was just gonna go help in the barn," she lies badly.

Cory frowns and looks at her art bag, "With pencils and erasers? Is that the way they muck stalls around here?"

She laughs, something Cory is always able to make her do. She is certainly not immune to his charm and wit.

"Come with us," he implores. "It'll be good to get away from here for a while."

"I'm fine, Cory," she says.

"Do it for me, kid," he teases with a ruffling of her hair on top of her head. "I miss my little buddy."

Sam grins and nods. "Let me get ready. When are you guys leaving?"

"Soon, as soon as the Professor gets out here," he says and adds, "Lazy bastard."

Sam chuckles and shakes her head. Then she heads back to the bunkhouse and pulls on shorts instead of her long pants, which she'd put on in order to sit in the hay and not get scratched by it. She'll wear the same t-shirt she already had on since she's probably going to get dirty and sweaty. They'd decided the same night that the guys had arrived to make the log home in the woods their clinic. Her uncle had also gone out there to check it out and had agreed that it would work just fine. Some of Dave's men have already started clearing a path to make the driveway more accessible. It's a good, safe location hidden away in the woods and one that they'll be able to defend if anyone were to attack.

When she goes back outside to the truck, Cory is there with Henry and three of Dave's men. Simon is also standing there.

"Good morning, Sam," he is the first to say.

She doesn't want to be rude, so she returns the greeting.

"Ready, Sam?" Henry asks and touches her arm lightly.

She turns to him and offers a greeting and a smile, even if she has to fake one.

"Mount up!" Dave's man yells and gets in to drive.

She takes Henry's outstretched hand and climbs into the bed of the truck. Sam doesn't acknowledge Simon, who is also standing there.

"We're short-staffed today," Henry tells his men. "So, keep your guard up, boys."

"Why are we short-staffed?" Sam asks.

Henry turns to her and says, "Because Sergeant Winters took a group for supplies and to work on the damaged buildings and homes in our town. Another group is going…looking for other things."

Sam smiles at him and says, "You can just say that they're looking for the highwaymen. You don't have to protect me."

Cory laughs bawdily. "No, Sam's no wilting flower, Gunny. That's for sure. Plus, she'll cut out your gizzard without you even knowing it. She's pretty handy with a knife. Isn't that right, little sister?"

"Humans don't have gizzards," Simon corrects and gets punched in the arm by Cory.

"She'll still cut *yours* out," Cory says.

Simon scoffs and remarks tightly, "I have no doubt."

Sam chooses to ignore him and not engage in this conversation of mutilation by dagger. It is a morbid topic. Cory brings up security at the compound instead, and the men discuss it while she stares at the surrounding forest. They arrive at the cabin, having made it down the rutted drive. She can tell how much work the men put into the driveway so far. At least there is one now, even if it is overgrown with long grass, pricker weeds, and filled with potholes.

Sam uses a broom to clean the floors and dust cobwebs while the men start laying out exam rooms and hauling in the lumber to build them. Simon insisted that she wear a face mask to protect her sinuses from the dust. She sneered at him but took it just the same. They labor for hours until Dave's wife and a few others bring lunch since most everyone missed breakfast in their haste to begin the workday. Sam grabs a seat on the covered porch, her legs dangling over the side, as she eats her food. They have brought them hardboiled eggs, bread, and roasted beef that is left over from the other day when they'd cooked a large pot of meat for the whole compound. There are also fresh raw vegetables from the garden, sliced into chunks. She is thankful that Cory brought her a few herb starts for their greenhouse. They still need so much more.

Simon stands in the surrounding yard, leaning against a tree while eating. Cory is sitting on a stump beside him. She tries to ignore Simon but finds her eyes sliding toward him more than once. Henry chooses to sit next to her on the porch floor.

"We've got two rooms framed up already," he reports in. "A third is almost done. We're just closing them in with tongue and groove wood. It's the best we can do and will take the shortest amount of time. Most sheetrock is not good anymore, too wet from water damage to the building supply stores. This should work, though."

"I think it'll be fine," she offers considerately. "People will just be glad to receive medical attention again."

They converse as they eat while some of the others return to work more quickly. Cory's laughter at something Simon has said to

48

him draws her attention. Simon is not wearing his glasses today, but his signature ball cap is on and pulled low over his forehead. She can still see his blue eyes, though. He seems sullen and angry and is not at all laughing along with his best friend. When she is finished, Henry helps her to her feet, and they return to the job. She just wants to be back on the compound, engrossed in her art, and not interacting with people. Everything is forced and false, every smile, every comment. The despair she feels over the loss of her friend and what she saw in the barn has haunted her this last week. She'd much rather be alone.

"Sam," Simon says behind her, startling Sam.

She is in the second-floor bedroom that houses two sets of bunk beds. If she and her uncle are going to live here full-time, then she'd much rather sleep on clean bedding and with less dust, mildew, and spiders. Especially the spiders.

"Yes?"

"I was just checking to make sure you're ok," he says, looking around the small bedroom.

"Uh…yes, other than my new spider friends, I'm fine."

He nods and says, "Good. That's good."

For some reason, Simon seems on edge, even nervous. "What is it, Simon?"

He grimaces and replies, "Can we…can we talk later?"

"About what?" she asks immediately. Being around Simon is painful enough without seeking out his company for conversation.

He pulls a piece of folded up paper from the back pocket of his jeans and extends it to her. Sam opens it and finds the drawing she'd been working on the other day, the ghostly apparition of what she'd seen in the barn, her good friend.

"How did you get this?" she asks with flat-out accusation.

"I was worried about you," he says.

No wonder he was nervous.

"You got into my stuff? When? Did you go in the bunkhouse and rummage my things?"

Sam is angry and feels as if her privacy has been invaded. This isn't Grandpa's house.

"No, no. I wouldn't do that. Why? Do you have similar ones there?"

"What? No. Maybe. It's not any of your business."

"It is. You know it is."

"Where'd you get this then?"

He snatches it away from her, quickly folds it and places the drawing back into his pants pocket. "You left it in the truck the other night. In that equipment shed where we were talking, remember?"

"Yes, but I don't remember leaving this there."

He shrugs. "You did. That's where I got it. I didn't break into your bunkhouse and rummage your items. But after looking at this, maybe I should."

Sam glares at him. "Mind your own business, Simon."

He boldly steps toward her and takes her upper arms into his hands, holding there firmly. "It is my business. You know you can't do this. It's not good for you."

"Yes, I can. It's therapeutic. I've been told that it's perfectly fine for me to do."

"Whoever told you that doesn't know you as well as I do," he points out with superiority. Sam turns her head to look at the wall instead of him. "This is not healthy. You can't do this again."

"Don't even start, Simon."

Footsteps in the hall alert them both, and Simon steps away from her.

"Sam," Henry says and stops when he sees Simon. "Oh, sorry. Didn't know you two were talking. We just had a question for you, Sam."

"About what?" she asks, her feathers thoroughly ruffled, her cheeks likely a dark pink from anger.

"They want to know how you'd lay out the sick bay room. Do you want bunks in there or cots side by side?"

"I'm coming," she says, dismissing Henry, who pauses and looks for a moment at Simon before leaving. Once he does, Sam turns her attention back to Simon. "As for you…"

She starts but is cut off by the sound of a loud explosion. Sam instinctively ducks, although the noise seemed likely far off in the distance.

"Are we under attack?" she asks.

He doesn't answer. Simon immediately takes her hand and pulls her after him through the door. They run down the stairs and meet the other men in the living room.

"What the hell was that?" one of Dave's men questions.

Another asks, "Was it outside? One of us?"

Cory rejects this idea with, "No, way. That wasn't us."

"Let's go," Henry demands.

"That actually sounded like some sort of heavy round," Cory says as he jumps over the side of the truck into the bed.

This time, Sam takes Simon's help climbing in. She sits next to Cory, who is perched on the wheel well.

"Possibly heavy artillery, mortar," Henry remarks as they speed away.

They drive back to the compound only to find nothing afoot there. Everyone is safe, and the guards are still standing at their posts at the front gate. Cory insists that Simon stay with her while he takes off with Henry and more men. She paces back and forth near the horse barn.

"I don't need you to hang out with me, Simon," she tells him. He says, "I don't mind."

"How can you be so calm?" she asks as he just sits there on a bucket near the door to the barn. His long rifle is casually perched between his feet on the ground and resting against his shoulder.

"They're fine. I'd be more worried about who they might run into who could've fired off whatever that thing was."

"I'm still worried for them."

"For Henry?"

She shoots him a sneer. "Of course. And for his friends and most of all for Cory."

He chuffs, "Cory's the one you should worry about the least."

There is a park bench near the other door, and Sam forces herself to sit and try to relax. Simon joins her a moment later.

"Sam, can I get your opinion on something?"

"I suppose so," she says, although if it is about her macabre artwork, she'd rather he didn't.

"Do you think Cory and Paige could be…a thing?"

Sam thinks for a moment. "Maybe. I don't know. They aren't fighting all the time anymore. That's a relief."

"That's not really a relief to me."

"She's your sister, how can you not tell?"

Simon sends her a comical look and says, "You have to ask that? I don't understand any of the women on the farm. My sister coming to live there has not improved my insight into the female mind any, and I certainly don't understand her, either."

Sam smiles patiently, "Do you get the impression that she likes him?"

"Sometimes. Then other times she acts like he just gets on her nerves."

"That's something all men do to women," she teases.

He smiles and nods. "Yes, I'm sure we do."

"Some more than others," she hints. "If you're worried about it, Simon, just ask her."

"I have. She's always evasive or outraged that I've even asked."

"Then, there's your answer."

He laughs, "Oh, right. Because women are so forthcoming?"

"And you are?" she reminds him and gets a quick frown. "Besides, they're both adults. They can be together if they want to be."

"Not with Cory she can't," he says. "You don't know Cory as well as I do. He's not the kind of man to commit to a woman. It would purely be…physical on his part."

"I'm also an adult, Simon," she says with irritation. "You don't need to tell me that Cory is a rakish fiend when it comes to women. In his defense, it's not all his fault. Women do tend to throw themselves at him."

"I know. It took all of ten seconds since we hit the ground here before the women started checking him out."

"He could charge a stud fee," she jokes, getting a short laugh out of him. "I saw a few looking at you, too. You're just too naïve to notice."

"Uh-huh, sure."

It's true. A couple of the younger women in her bunkhouse noticed Simon because she heard them talking about him, how cute he was, his jawline and hair color, how they'd like to have him examine them, play doctor. The conversation deteriorated from there, and Sam had tuned them out. She knows they were just teasing around, but it had still bothered her. Plus, she understood that they were actually sexually attracted to him. That bothered her more.

"As far as Cory goes, reformed rakes make the best husbands," she says jokingly.

52

"Where'd you hear that bunch of nonsense?"

"Not sure. Somewhere. It's probably true."

"Rakes are just rakes. They don't reform. People don't change."

"People can change if they want to change. That's where you get confused, Simon."

He shakes his head as if he doesn't agree with her. He looks down at his hands instead. They are dirty from work, and she knows it is probably bothering him. Simon is a neat freak.

"That would be funny if they got married someday," she remarks.

"No, no part of that would be funny at all," he snaps.

She laughs at his distress. "Oh, Simon. If they're happy, then let it be. It's hard enough to be happy and find happiness. We should know. Life's too short to be so serious all the time. Lighten up a little."

"Is that why you're drawing like you used to?"

This cuts hard. It is a low blow and extremely unusual for Simon. Sam's eyes narrow, and her mouth turns down, too.

"Sorry," he immediately states. "I didn't mean that. Forgive me. I…"

He takes her hand in his, but Sam pulls away. Shouting near the house alerts them that the men are back, and they jog there to find out what happened.

The first thing she notices is that Cory is not with them.

"Where's Cory!" she asks Henry frantically.

"Scouting," he replies.

"What happened?" Simon asks next.

"Attack. Couple miles from here," he tells them. "They set a trap, killed some people. Car was on fire when we got there. I'm assuming that was the explosion we heard."

"The highwaymen," Sam says, getting a nod from Henry, although she doesn't need one to figure this out.

"And Cory is going after them?" she repeats.

"Don't worry," Simon reassures her, placing his hand on her shoulder. "He'll be fine."

"Your friend wanted to see if he could get a track on them. He's not going to attack them if he finds them," Henry explains.

"They're getting closer," she remarks and watches the faces of Henry and his men fall. Simon simply nods.

"Spread out," Henry tells his men. "Take up a position or get with our guards on a patrol until Sergeant Winters returns later. Sam, you take Simon to the medical building and continue to work on organizing the supplies for the new clinic. We'll keep the place locked down and secure."

"Sure, Henry," she agrees. She doesn't want to naysay her host, so she goes along with his request. Also, he rarely asks her to do anything, so he must feel this task is important. However, she doesn't miss the look that passes between him and Simon. "Ready, Simon? I'll show you where we'll be working."

They walk away from the crowd as Henry and a few of his men continue to shout orders and scramble.

"I feel like I should be out there with Cor," Simon complains as they walk to a long building.

"I'm glad you're not," she confesses. "I wish Cory wasn't, either," Sam adds for good measure, although, truth be told, Cory will be fine.

"It would help if I were with him. He should've come back to get me."

"I understand how you feel," she says. "That's exactly how I feel, or how I used to feel, every single time you guys left the farm."

"The farm is the safest place for you, or was," he says as they enter the dark barn.

Sam flicks on the lights and leads him to a storage room where she and her uncle have been working on organizing the meds, supplies, and equipment for their new clinic.

"Sam," he says quietly, gaining her attention, "you should move back to the farm."

"Don't start with that."

"No, I mean because of the highwaymen. Do you realize how close this attack was today? There's even a possibility that they drove past here and saw the place. They could come back."

"This place is called a compound for a reason, Simon."

He sighs with frustration and continues, "But no place is completely impenetrable. Come back to the farm, even just for a while. Then you could move back here again. Just let us catch these men and deal with that situation first."

54

"No, I'm safe here, too."

"Damn it, Samantha," he swears and drags a hand through his auburn hair, quickly replacing the ball cap after. "Why do you have to be so stubborn?"

"I could ask you the same question."

His blue gaze drops to his feet for a second before looking at her again. "I'll move into town. I'll stay at the practice. You won't even have to see me."

"Sure," she scoffs and turns to retrieve a box that has yet to be rummaged. "I thought I had that all worked out before, and every time I turn around, there you are again."

"I'm sorry," he apologizes. "I don't mean to hurt you with my presence. It wasn't my idea to come here, and I didn't have a choice."

"It doesn't matter," she says. "We're both adults. Let's just work on this project and try to avoid each other for the next few weeks."

He doesn't respond, so Sam turns to look at him. Simon's expression is one of acute sadness mixed with disappointment. She goes back to her work, and he soon joins in and helps. They pull box after box from the shelving units, and he retrieves others from the main room. Just being near Simon in the same tight quarters causes her pain. Why had the family suggested this?

"Dinner's ready," Courtney says as she enters the room, startling Sam. "Oh, and your cute friend's back."

"We'll be right there, Court. Thanks," Sam returns with a patient smile.

"Good," Simon tells her as soon as Courtney leaves. He places a heavy box on a bottom shelf and stands erect again. "I can't wait to see what he found out."

"You'll have to drag the girls off him first," she jokes.

"Lord, help us," he teases in return, turns off the lights and closes the door.

The night air has turned chilly and cool she notices as they walk toward the mess hall.

"I think you should consider coming back to the farm, ok?" he presses again. "Especially in light of what's gone on here in the last week. First, your friend, now the highwaymen being so close. It might be good to come home for a while."

"This is my home now," she reminds him and picks up the pace, hoping to leave Simon behind. It doesn't work. He sticks with her, and she can hear him grinding his teeth.

Chapter Six
Reagan

"Nothing?" Reagan asks her husband as she stroke's Cory's mutt on the head. It wasn't really a choice. She's a pest. "He didn't get anything? Not even a tire print in the mud?"

"No," John answers. "Cory said he couldn't track them more than a mile from the attack site. These people either know what they're doing or know short-cuts and back roads or something."

"Is he safe? Is Simon safe?" Paige asks with nervous gray eyes.

"Yeah, they're cool, Paige," Kelly assures her.

They are all sitting on the picnic table in the yard, enjoying the morning sunshine. Cory talked to John last night from Dave's compound. Her father recently sent a runner with information from Fort Knox and a ham radio by which to communicate better with him. Reagan would rather he hadn't. Dave's compound already had a similar setup, so now they can use the same form of communication in a more efficient manner with their strongest ally in the area. Derek knows how to use one, so he's been in charge of showing everyone, herself included, how to operate it. She just doesn't like owing her father anything.

"These people know what they're doing, or they're getting really damn lucky," Kelly remarks, expanding on John's thought.

"Language," Hannah warns, although her sister is holding her husband's hand and hardly seems angry with him. The children are playing out by the barn, so Reagan knows they can't hear them.

"I've started an algorithm," Lucas states, surprising her because her new brother is usually so quiet.

"For what?" Derek asks.

"I've tracked the first known attack and the location and every one after. They seem to be moving west to east and then back again on the same roads."

"Interesting," John says.

"Yes, I thought so, as well," Luke says. He pulls a wrinkled piece of paper from his pants pocket and spreads it out on the table.

"What do you have, Lucas?" Grandpa asks, leaning toward the notes.

"See here? The first attack that we knew of was northwest of here. Then the next one after that was even farther west. Then they move east. I have the dates beside the locations."

"Nerd," Reagan comments.

"You'd know," G comes back at her.

This makes Reagan smile broadly at her half-sister. She likes her spunk. The kid is a survivor, that's for sure. And the more Reagan gets to know both of them, the more she understands how close they are and that Luke looks after Gretchen with an intensity that can only be described as fierce.

"Touché," Sue agrees with G, adding a smile aimed at Reagan, who returns it.

Luke doesn't offer a comeback but continues explaining his scientific study. Perhaps they are more alike than she'd first thought when he'd arrived on the farm as an unknown stranger to them all.

"It seems sequential. They're moving in this east-west corridor. Mostly they hit the same freeways over and over. They may have to change the routes now that we've put up signs. I'm quite sure they've seen them."

"I'd be very surprised if they haven't," Grandpa says and rubs the beard stubble on his chin. "They could be raiding areas even farther out than what we know. We just have no way of verifying it other than searching."

John agrees with her grandfather. "These people must have a camp in the tri-county area somewhere, possibly further out but not too far."

"Maybe," Derek adds. "Or maybe they have an unlimited amount of gas that they can come in from far."

"No, they can't," Kelly argues. "They've siphoned gas from every attack. They don't have unlimited fuel."

58

"Right," Derek changes his mind. "What about the compound at the golf course? We should go back there again and check it out."

"I agree," John says. "And soon. We have to know who they are. Cory and Simon checked on it again when they went the other day and said those people were still there. He said they still seemed harmless, but who knows? We need more intel on them."

Kelly says, "And if they aren't our highwaymen, then we should warn them about those ass…jerks."

Reagan grins. He is smart to correct his swear.

"And those young people at Fort Campbell," Grandpa adds. "We really need to know more about them. Perhaps they need our help."

Reagan smiles gently. Of course, he wants to help them. His good will toward his fellow man, especially children is one of his most endearing qualities and why she loves him so dearly.

"They definitely need a warning, as well," Sue agrees with worry.

"Right," John agrees. "We should run over there as soon as Cory gets back. Unless you think I could go with maybe Chet."

Derek shakes his head. "I don't think it's a good idea to leave the farm right now. If Luke's right, then they'll be making their next attack heading this way."

"Yes, I think they will," Luke says, pushing his dark hair off of his forehead.

"Seems like he's right," Kelly says with a nod, examining Luke's paperwork.

Lucas breaks in to say, "I was thinking if we set out more signs on these roads here," he points with a pen on the map, "that we could start changing their routes. Then we could narrow them down, bottleneck them until we've got them moving on the roads that we want them to use."

"Smart," Kelly comments.

John says, "Then we set a trap."

"Exactly what I was thinking," Lucas says.

"You sure you weren't going into the Army?" Derek jokes, earning a crooked grin from her shy brother.

"A salt lick operation," John says.

Derek bumps fists with her husband.

Hannah frowns and asks, "What does that mean?"

"Bait," John explains.

"Oh, no," Hannah frets. "This sounds dangerous."

Kelly chuckles and rubs her back, "This is what we do, baby. Don't worry."

"But one of you would have to be bait?" Hannie asks.

"This is our area of expertise, if you will," Derek adds.

Reagan knows they have experience with this sort of thing. It doesn't make her want them to go on the offensive, though.

"Long-range reconnaissance, anti-terrorism activities, that's the stuff we used to do, Hannie," John explains. "Don't worry. We've got this."

Kelly says, "Remember that time in Djibouti?"

"Yeah, the Djibouti-call in Africa?" John jokes, earning laughter that mostly nobody but Derek and Kelly understands.

"You know it, brother," Kelly answers.

"What do you mean?" Reagan asks.

John turns to look at her, his blue eyes lit with humor, "Dumpy country, Muslims who hated Americans. We got sent in to retrieve a person of interest, when low and behold, it turned into a city of people who all wanted to play the kill-John-and-Kelly-and-their-friends game."

"That sounds awful," Sue says.

"And highly classified," Derek says with a grimace of disapproval.

"I just declassified it," John says with a grin of ornery intent. "It was important. I was making a point and needed a reference." Derek just shakes his head, and John laughs. Kelly smirks, too. "What we're getting at, Hannie, is that we're used to it. Kelly and I were outnumbered about a thousand to one, and we made it out just fine."

"Evac pickup was late, too," Kelly complains.

"Yep, had to stop for a Starbucks or something that time if I remember correctly," John jokes.

"We don't always make the evac spot, either," Kelly reminds him.

"Yeah, for a different kind of booty call," John says, to which Reagan punches his arm. "Kidding, babe.

60

"Hannah," Kelly says, turning to his wife, "we're always outnumbered. Always. The American military is and always has been outnumbered. We're expected to take and hold a position, follow our orders, complete the mission without faltering, without failing. I don't ever remember fighting one on one. It's always some large group of idiots against just a few of us. We're unconventional warriors, and that's what we're good at."

"What about Simon and Cory?" Paige asks. "What about them? They don't have the experience you guys do."

Derek chuckles softly and says, "Oh, yes, they do. You just weren't here for the years of training they went through. They are more than capable of handling themselves in a bad situation. Look at that camp in Nashville we took care of. They were an integral part of that raid."

Reagan doesn't like to remember that night when they went to the sex camp. She was so worried about the men. This is going to be worse. She has a terrible feeling about these highwaymen.

"Look, guys," John says to them, "this is what we've been trained to do. We can handle this."

"I'd rather you didn't, though," Reagan argues softly, holding her hand over her stomach.

Derek says, "We're fighting them. It's either gonna be here on this farm at their time of choosing or out there where the terrain and the element of surprise are on our terms."

John wraps an arm around her waist.

"Hannah," Kelly says, "you make the best biscuits on earth, baby. That's your specialty. If I tried to make a biscuit, it'd taste like sawdust and charcoal. My job is this. I protect you and Mary. I take care of the bad people. I'm better at this job than any other on earth."

"And if you're grossly outnumbered?" Sue asks.

"We'll handle it," John simply states.

"I don't like this," Sue reiterates.

"We've got scores to settle," John adds. "This isn't just about persecuting a bunch of jerks who are harming innocent people on the road. This has affected us, too. I know it was the highwaymen who hit Derek and killed two of Dave's best soldiers. They shot Cory. This isn't going to stand."

"I spoke with my father…our father last night," Lucas states, pausing their arguing. Everyone turns to look at him.

"About what?" Reagan asks.

"I discussed the highwaymen," he explains. "He's concerned. He doesn't want them showing up in his area, either. He's already worried enough about the President doing that."

"And?" Sue prompts when he pauses for too long.

Luke sighs, "Well, he's going to send some men on patrols to look for any signs of these people, as well. If they find them, he'll contact us immediately."

"Good," Grandpa says. "That's good news. We could use all the help we can get."

Reagan tries not to be negative, but she's quite sure her frown is not very well hidden. If Robert helps them, she's positive he'll want something in return. He's nothing like Grandpa. She wonders if Grams got him mixed up at the hospital with another baby.

"We'll wait until Cory returns from Dave's," Derek says. "Then you can go and take one of the neighbors or even Cory could go to check on the golf course compound in Clarksville."

"And make contact with the young people," Grandpa adds.

"Right," John agrees. "We'll make sure to, Herb."

Grandpa nods and smiles.

"Ready to work on the barn roof?" Kelly asks Luke.

"Yes, sir," her brother answers.

John helps Derek to the house, but the younger people head to the barns for chores. The kids have taken off somewhere, probably to play in the barns. Ari is no doubt leading the mission.

Reagan goes inside to use the bathroom, but she overhears her husband speaking with his brother in Grandpa's old bedroom where Sue and he now sleep. She stops in the hall to listen. It sounds heated, which concerns her.

"No way," John says impatiently. "Not gonna happen, brother."

"Just go, man," Derek states. "This is bullshit. I'm not getting any better. Just leave me alone."

"Nope," her husband says in his usual tone when he's being stubborn. "You and I have got a workout waiting for us. So, you either come with me, or I'm getting the Hulk and we're draggin' you outta' here."

"Don't be an asshole, John," Derek says with open hostility. "I'm worthless now. Fucking worthless."

Reagan frowns hard, swallows harder, and her gaze drops to her shoes. This is painful to hear.

"Hey, so you've got a paperweight for a leg instead of a leg that works the way you want it to. So what?" John says. "Crap happens, bro. You know this. It's war. This is what happens in war."

"It's not war, goddammit," Derek yells. "I got hit by a damn truck. That's not the same."

"This is a war," John argues. "It's just a different kind than we're used to. Instead of religious freaks trying to kill us, it's morons trying to rule what's left of this country. And it doesn't mean you're worthless. We still need you, especially for leadership. You think me or the Hulk could run this operation? Get real, man. You make the tough calls. You have the most operational leadership experience. We're just triggers. You've got the brains in this outfit."

"Whatever, John," Derek says with despair.

"Let's go," her husband says firmly. "I don't care if you do have a paperweight, you're still working out with me. Besides, Sue's gonna dump your hobbled butt for some young, hot guy in town if you don't keep up your workouts."

Reagan frowns. That's not true at all, but she knows better than to get involved in the arguments of the men or try to understand them or their strange and sometimes unforgiving way of communicating with one another.

"Hey, sis," Hannah says behind her, startling the hell out her.

"Damn, Hannie," she exclaims.

"Whatcha' doing?" her sly sister inquires, probably knowing full-well that Reagan is eavesdropping.

"Nothing, going to the bathroom as usual," she lies.

A moment later, John comes down the hall with his brother on his heels using his crutches and scowling at John's back.

"Help me in the kitchen?" her sister requests.

"Sure, let me use the bathroom first. Alien kid is pressing on my bladder," Reagan informs her, although Hannah has already been here, done this, got the t-shirt in the baby growing department.

As she's washing her hands, Reagan ponders Derek's predicament, something she and Grandpa do on a daily basis. It's so frustrating knowing they can't perform the surgeries he needs to correct the broken, mangled bones and ligaments in his leg. Her brother-in-law is becoming more and more withdrawn from the family as each day passes. She hopes John tells him soon before she has to. Not understanding the extent of his injuries is unfair to Derek.

Reagan comes out of the bathroom and nearly runs down Paige.

"Sorry," she apologizes.

"No prob," Paige says. "I'm off. Going over to visit my God-son, Elijah. He's so dang cute."

"He is," Reagan agrees, having met Talia's baby in the form of a check-up just a few days ago. He is rather adorable. "Be careful."

"You got it," Paige says and leaves.

Reagan makes bread with Hannah as Sue prepares baked chicken for tonight's dinner. They are cooking three of the injured birds from the tornado that were not going to make it much longer. They had John kill them, and Huntley and Ari pluck them. The kids have to learn this stuff in case they are ever completely alone. It sounds horrible, them being alone or on their own someday, and Reagan doesn't like to think about it happening, but it could. Paige was alone for a while with just the company of two friends and a toddler. Cory struck out on his own. Something could happen that could tear them all apart. The highwaymen could attack the farm next. Perhaps they will have enough men to finally best the McClanes. Or maybe Robert will adopt all of them and then ditch them, too. It could happen.

"Right, Reagan?" Sue asks, breaking her gloomy train of thought about the kids.

"What?" Reagan asks.

"We need to get Sam to come over for a visit soon," Sue repeats. "I miss her. She's our little ray of sunshine. Now we're stuck with you. I miss having her around all the time. So do the kids."

"Don't think that's gonna happen, maybe not ever again," Reagan informs them, ignoring her sister's jab. She knows Sue doesn't mean anything by teasing her.

"Why not?" Hannie asks with a crease in her ordinarily smooth forehead. It seems out of place, that little worry line.

64

"She's not coming back, and I don't think she wants to come for visits anymore. She pretty much told me that the other day at the clinic."

"Oh, no," Sue frets. "We need to get Simon off alone and find out what this is all about."

"She said that basically, she has feelings for him but that they weren't reciprocated," Reagan tells them. "Once when she came for a visit, she was being very elusive when Paige and I talked to her. And then she said some bullshit about wanting to live with Dave's group because of her uncle."

"Reagan," Hannah warns about the swearing.

She grins and continues, pressing her luck, "He's royally screwed this up, whatever this was. Simon's gonna have to fix it, not us. I don't even know why he doesn't want her. He hung on her every word. He followed her around the farm like a love-sick puppy for the last four, friggin' years. And he's more protective of her than anyone else. This relationship shit is confusing."

"Hey!" Hannah says with more earnest this time. Then she continues on in a sweet voice, her Disney princess Hannie voice, "I think we should speak with him. And by we, I mean *you*."

"Me?" Sue asks. "Simon and I aren't that close. I mean, I love him and all..."

"No, not you, Sue," Hannah stops her.

It takes Reagan a second to realize her sister means her. She stops kneading and stares with unconcealed surprise. "What? Me? Why the hell would you want me to talk to Simon? Duh. I just said I'm bad at relationship crap. I'd have no idea where even to start."

"Start at the beginning," Hannah recommends cheerily. "It's always the best place!"

Reagan doesn't reply with the sarcastic comment that's floating around in her head. Hannah is too innocent for such a thing.

"I don't think we should get involved," Reagan says instead.

"Someone should," Sue counters as she places the chicken in a roasting pan and covers it with a large lid. She'll let it marinate for a few hours in a mixture of oils and spices from her herb garden, which is starting to look like an herb garden again and not like a tornado just kicked the shit out of it. Then she'll have the guys put it on the barbecue pit out back.

"Sure as hell not me!"

Hannah slaps the back of her head.

"Hey, I'm pregnant!"

"Exactly why you shouldn't use that sort of gutter language!" Hannah explains primly.

"What?" Reagan asks with incomprehension.

"The baby can hear you," Hannah elucidates. "Do you want him to learn that kind of language from his mother?"

"Good Lord," Reagan says, preparing to duck.

"One more time," Hannah threatens a full attack and points her finger in Reagan's general direction.

"Babies in the womb do not learn swear words or any words for that matter," Reagan corrects her.

"Oh contraire," Hannah argues. "Babies hear a lot more than you think. They like music, too. Mary used to kick like crazy when I'd play the piano."

"You were probably making her ears hurt," Reagan teases. "And that was her only way of communicating for you to stop."

Hannah gives an exaggerated frown, an unusual expression for her dear, darling sister. Sue just laughs at their banter.

"Back to Simon," Sue reminds them. "I do think it'd be a good idea if you spoke with him, Reagan. He trusts you, looks up to you. It's either you or Grandpa, and you know Simon's not going to tell him anything that he thinks might upset him. That would kill Simon. So, if anything bad happened between him and Sam, you'll have to dig it out. Grandpa's not gonna be any help with this one."

"And I would?" Reagan asks, getting a nod. "Oh, geez. Talk about pressure. I'm not good with that sort of shit."

Slap! Another crack to her head.

"Ouch!" she complains.

"I warned you fair and square," Hannah says in a chipper tone as she takes her bowl of bread to the pantry to rise.

"So irritating," Reagan complains about Hannie to Sue, who just grins.

"See what you can do, sis," Sue pleads and touches her hand. "They're both in a lot of pain. Simon tries to hide it, but I can see how much this has hurt him- her leaving."

"Yeah," Reagan says. "It sucks that you're putting this on me, though. I've got better things to do than fix people's relationships."

"Like what? Study gross pictures of diseases or put up your swollen ankles or throw up for the twentieth time in a single day? You don't have a lot of choices right now."

"True. That sucks, too."

Sue nods and smiles gently before tucking a strand of Reagan's hair behind her ear. "Yes, pregnancy is no treat, but it does have a pretty good payoff at the end."

"So I keep hearing," Reagan jokes and takes her bread bowl to rest beside Hannah's. Her sister's looks so much more perfect than her own. Oh well, they shouldn't ask her to step outside her comfort zone and enter the kitchen. Like John's forte is killing people- which they'd sugar-coated but meant anyway- her specialty is positively not cooking.

She sits at the island and munches on a celery stalk, earning a snooty look from Sue who is busy chopping them.

"It's so sad," Sue says out of the blue, her brown eyes downcast. "I always thought I'd throw a baby shower or bridal showers for you guys someday. Now, look at us."

"Neither of those is something I'd need to be done for me if this all hadn't happened," Reagan informs her sister.

"Sure you would have," Hannah corrects with her usual optimism.

"No, I had no intention of marrying or having kids," she reminds her. "You two should know that better than anyone."

"I don't know about that," Sue counters. "If you would've met John at our house sometime, I don't think he would've let you stay single for long."

Reagan snorts but secretly wonders what would've happened had she met him under different circumstances. It was bound to happen. His only brother was married to her sister. They would have run into one another, and likely many times. The only reason they never had was because John was always deployed when she went to visit Sue and Derek, and she was busy in medical school. She knew of him, but that was all. Reagan doesn't even think she ever saw a picture of John at their house. Now she can't imagine her life without him.

"Doubt it," Reagan says. "John wasn't ever going to leave the military, not like Kelly would've. He was bound to be a lifer."

"So?" Sue says. "Doesn't mean you wouldn't have met. Then we would've had to wait and see what happened. I bet John would've given it up for you."

"Most definitely," Hannie concurs with a nod.

She's not so sure. John was a career military man, a natural born killer, something he doesn't necessarily like being but something at which he excels. He is in his element in this world the way it is now. He never would've fit into a suburban husband role where he mowed the lawn on the weekend, grilled food for friends and family, and went on the occasional hunt in the fall. It would've stifled him.

"No matter," Sue says. "He's got you now. And he made it stick, too."

Her sister points to Reagan's stomach with her paring knife and smiles. Then she goes back to work, now chopping potatoes. Reagan just grimaces.

"You seem like you're feeling better this last week," Hannah speculates.

"Yes, not so bad," Reagan reassures her. "Only took me to almost eight months to get there!"

"You always did do things at your own pace," Sue says with a laugh.

"Usually at high speed," Hannah teases with a sly grin.

Reagan rolls her eyes and groans at their criticisms.

"Why don't you go and lie down, sweetie?" Sue suggests.

"I'm fine," Reagan says.

"Then go rest and put your feet up," Hannah says. "And study your books. We've got this, and they certainly don't need your help outside."

"I think I'm being evicted," Reagan remarks with a grin.

"Yep!" Sue says brightly. "Go rest. That's an order."

Reagan sends her a salute and climbs the stairs to her bedroom on the third floor and silently wishes it was on the first floor. The muscles in her groin ache by the time she gets to her room, not before she pit stops in the bathroom again.

She takes up a perch with a book on infectious diseases of the blood on the balcony in a soft chair John put out there for her. Male laughter draws her attention to the equipment shed. She can see Kelly jabbing his fists toward John, who is deflecting. They spar like this a lot. John explained that it keeps them fresh. She worried they'd hurt each other, but so far, no broken anything or stitches. Luke is doing pushups on the ground beside Derek, who is also pumping them out. John goes over to her new brother and pushes his booted foot down on Luke's back. Luke jumps to his feet and begins punching at John with as much skill as Kelly just had. John deflects this time, ducks and comes up swinging. Luke blocks and connects with his right against John's cheek, causing more laughter. They are all loud and boisterous, obnoxious and raucous. Even Derek laughs. It makes her heart lift just slightly, even if he only laughs once.

Chapter Seven
Sam

She's been forced into his company for the last five days and would very much like to avoid Simon for the next week, although that is not likely to happen. Sam is sad tonight because Cory is leaving in the morning. They worked all day again at the cabin and made a tremendous amount of progress. She's had time in the evenings to hang out with Cory and was thankful that Simon did not join them. They played cards a few times with Henry and another woman named Dylan who sleeps in the same bunkhouse as Sam. She's pretty sure Dylan wanted to do more with Cory than just play cards, but Sam doesn't think he's interested in her. At least it hadn't seemed that way to Sam. Dylan, on the other hand, had drilled her with a hundred questions about Cory, of which she'd tried to deflect.

The day is over, the sun set, and she's hanging out in the horse barn watching the baby foal frolic in the sectioned off part of the long barn away from the other horses. His spindly legs crack her up. He trots with a sharp attitude around the small pen as if he is king of the world. Wait until he gets out to the big pasture with the other horses. He's in for a surprise. He'll learn his place in the proverbial pecking order soon enough. A few of his auntie mares will set him straight.

"Sam," Henry says behind her.

"Hi," she greets cordially.

"Boy is he cute," he remarks with his southern accent hanging onto the word 'cute.'

"Yes, all legs and no sense yet," she says with a smile.

"I've seen you working with him," he admits. "I'm not as familiar with horse training as you. I'm glad you're here."

She offers the slightest of smiles.

"Can I speak with you?"

She turns to him and nods. "Of course."

He frowns and sighs first. "I should've said this sooner, but I wanted confirmation of what I assumed."

"What are you talking about?"

"I like spending time with you."

Sam frowns, not sure where he's going with this. "Ok, I like spending time with you, too. Playing cards at night in your house has really helped me feel like I fit in around here."

Henry shakes his head. "That's not what I mean."

"Oh, sorry."

"No," he says, touching her arm. "I'm not saying this right. Sorry, I get a little tongue-tied sometimes. What I mean is that I've seen you around him, around the Professor, I mean, Simon."

Sam feels the air leave her lungs and the room become narrower like a hallway at the sound of his name.

"Am I right in assuming that you two are or were together?"

Sam just frowns and doesn't answer. There is no answer for this question.

"I apologize. That's none of my business..."

"No, we're not together, Henry. Simon's...well, Simon's just...he's a friend."

He doesn't look like he believes her, so he just nods. "I don't want to be presumptive, but I assume you aren't together now or you wouldn't have moved over here."

"We're not a couple," she repeats for clarity.

"Right," he says. "I wanted to make sure."

"Ok, well, now you know," she says, beginning to feel angry about this conversation. She's not necessarily angry at Henry, but Sam doesn't like it that other people speculate what they must see between herself and Simon. He doesn't want her. He's made that clear. She doesn't want to look like a fool when people find out that they aren't together. Her feelings, the ones for Simon, are so difficult to conceal. She's going to have to work a lot harder doing so.

"Good," he says with a smile.

Henry has a kind smile, friendly, open, less guarded than other men she knows. He's quiet, but when he's around his friends less so. He laughs a lot with them, and Sam knows how loyal he is to them, as well. She believes he feels a lot of responsibility for the people on his farm, even the ones who weren't fellow soldiers or friends before the fall. He feels responsible for people like her, the women from the sex camp, and anyone else that comes to reside on the compound.

"Do you like it here then?" he asks.

"Yes, I like it just fine. Thanks for asking."

Sam wonders if he worries with equal fervor about the individual comfort of all the people living on his farm. If so, he's going to get an ulcer. He and Dave have taken in a lot of people.

"I want you to be happy here," Henry says.

"Ok," Sam returns and looks back at the foal, who is nursing on his mother. She isn't happy on this farm, but she isn't about to tell him the reasons for her unhappiness. Finding her friend hanging from the rafters had devastated her. Reese's suicide was like the pinnacle of Sam's already growing depression. She'd been forced back to the farm for a visit, which had turned into a disaster of epic proportions. First, she'd quarreled with Simon. Then he'd kissed her, which had left her confused. She doesn't understand why he does things like that when he clearly does not want to be with her. Is he just lonely? Then the tornado had destroyed parts of the farm. She just felt melancholy when she'd left Grandpa's farm. Then her friend killed herself because she hadn't felt she could go on.

"If there's anything at all that you need, just ask," Henry says, interrupting her thoughts about Reese.

"Thanks, Henry," she says. "I've got everything I need."

It's true. She has her uncle, a roof over her head, food, and security. Today, that's a lot. So many are not as fortunate as she.

"I really like you, Samantha."

"I like you too," she says without looking at him. The mare is annoyed with the foal and walks a few feet from him. Sam smiles. Poor mother. He's a pestering little guy. She knows if he bugs her too much, then she'll push him away with her body language. She studied horse behavior extensively when she was younger, read every book and concentrated her studies eventually on the late and great Monty Roberts. The stud in a herd is not the boss. It is always an older mare, and she has the ability to banish other horses if they displease her.

"Sam," he says, pulling her attention away again.

"Yeah?" Sam asks and looks up at him.

He reminds her, "You've been living here for quite a while now."

"Yes, like four months or something."

"Almost six," he states.

"It's been really nice, Henry. Thanks for letting me stay here."

"Do you really want to live with your uncle in that cabin?"

Sam frowns. She hadn't considered not doing so. Living there with Uncle Scott was assumed. She doesn't want him to live out in the woods all by himself, even if one or two of Dave's men decide to live there, too.

"I guess so. I wouldn't want him to live there without me. He may have emergencies that he needs me for. Besides, we're family. We need to stick together. I lost him before. I don't want that to happen again."

"You could stay here."

She looks up at him and furrows her brow. His brown eyes are soft. "Hm, I don't think that's a good idea."

"You could live in my house instead of in the bunkhouse with the other women."

"Oh, I couldn't do that. I've made friends there. I wouldn't want anyone to get mad at me and think I'm getting special privileges. Plus, there aren't any other available bedrooms. Someone would have to move out."

"Dave is going to finish up the house behind the horse barn soon. He wants the space for himself and his family."

"Oh, yes, I've seen the structure. That would be great for him…and his wife and kids, too."

"It's just taking a little longer to erect because of everything that's been going on."

She smiles and says, "I'm sure you'll be glad to have fewer people living in your house. That must be crowded."

"It's not so bad, but there is plenty of room up at the house for you."

"I don't know. I don't want to have tension between the other girls and me."

"I think they'd understand," he argues softly.

Sam smiles patiently and says, "I'm perfectly comfortable where I am."

He sighs hard and says, "I wasn't just thinking of your comfort. I was also considering mine."

"Why? Are you not comfortable there? I don't understand."

His frustration is evidently growing with her as his mouth turns down, and he sighs again.

"I don't mean that. I'm saying there is plenty of room for you in the house. With me. In my room."

"I don't think that'd be appropriate," she murmurs awkwardly and instantly feels less comfortable around Henry. What is he thinking?

"I'm in love with you," he blurts with a lot less patience.

"What?" she whispers.

"That's what I've been trying to tell you," he says with a wide smile. "Apparently not very successfully. You aren't making this any easier, Samantha."

"What?" she repeats with the same level of confusion.

Henry surprises her by taking her face gently between his hands that are rough and calloused from hard work. He quickly presses his mouth to hers. Sam is too shocked to move. She's not frightened. She's just taken aback. She can tell that he has kissed many girls in his past. He seems to know what he's doing. His lips are warm against hers. His eyes are closed, but hers are wide open as he has startled her thoroughly. His thumb strokes her cheekbone. His kiss is gentle, and he seems very sure of himself. It feels wrong. She has no idea how this happened. Sam jerks away and takes two steps back from him. She'd go farther, but the fence panels are pressing against her back.

Henry looks down at her with an expression of disappointment.

"What was that?" she asks.

He grins and says, "It's called a kiss, the last time I checked."

Sam can't help but smile, too. "No, I meant why did you do that?"

"I told you that I like you," he says, leveling her with logic.

"I thought you meant as a friend."

He frowns and then smiles again. "No, not exactly. Maybe just a little more than a friend."

"Oh," she whispers, embarrassed. "I'm sorry. I didn't know."

"I'm not great with communicating my feelings," he says. "It's my fault. I do like you, though. Actually…"

"That four-legged little stud ready to find a girl yet?" Cory yells loudly and obnoxiously as he enters the enclosed paddock, causing them to both turn with surprise.

Sam blushes, hoping her friend didn't just witness Henry kissing her. Cory looks at Henry with suspicion, and her new suitor excuses himself and leaves them. She also hopes that Henry isn't mad at her. Cory doesn't say anything for a few minutes but watches the baby horse with her.

Just as Sam is about to bring up something mundane like the weather, Cory breaks his silence, "Do you like that guy?"

"Sure, he's nice."

"Do you like Gunny kissing you like that, is a little more what I was getting at."

"Oh, geez," Sam laments, completely humiliated. "I was hoping you didn't see that. I should've known."

Cory chuckles. "I see all."

"I guess you do."

"Are you his girlfriend over here?" Cory asks. "I see you two hanging out a lot. He likes you. I thought as much but didn't want to bring it up and cause a problem."

"Oh," Sam says again. "No, I'm not his girlfriend. I just now found out how he feels about me. He's never done that before. Apparently, I'm the last one to the party."

Cory chuckles softly and pats the top of her head. "It's ok, kiddo. Nobody expects you to be a love expert."

"No, I don't love him, Cory!" she vehemently whispers and shakes her head. "I didn't mean it like that."

"It's cool if you like him. I'm ok with it. He seems like a good guy from what I've gotten to know about him."

"Yes, he is. Henry is a good man. He's very generous."

"Generous, huh?" Cory remarks. "Hardly sounds like the sparks are flying."

Sam laughs. Cory is such a goofball. "No, I don't love him. He's just a nice guy. There are no sparks."

Or are there? She's never thought about him in that way.

"Could you love him?" Cory asks in a more serious tone.

Sam shrugs.

"Could you love him more than Simon?"

Her cheeks burn. "I don't love Simon."

Her lie burns her throat even more than the embarrassment of his assumption has flushed her cheeks.

"That's fine if you don't love Henry. I'm not here to judge, little sister. Just be careful. You don't want to lead Henry on. If you don't like him in that way, just be honest. You also don't owe him anything, either. Don't feel obligated to be with him just because he's letting you live here. That had as much to do with Dave as it did with Henry. They run this place together. I'm sure that the decision to allow you to live here with your uncle was put to a vote between them."

"Probably."

"Do you think you have any romantic feelings for him?"

Sam looks at her dirty riding boots and says, "I don't know. I never really thought about it."

"Looks like you'd better start. There are going to be men here on this compound that want to be with you. There are also going to be men who come to your clinic when it's ready who will want to make a play for you, too. I mean, pretty much you'll have your pick of the litter. You're super sweet and also hot if I'm being honest, which is gross since you're like my baby sister."

"Thanks, Cory." She also thinks of Cory as a brother, and he's helped to fill the void in her heart where the love of her older brother used to live. "But I'm not hot. I'm just…not that kind of girl."

Cory grins at her and says, "So you think. Take your time. Choose someone or choose no one. It's up to you."

"I think you're giving me too much credit, silly," she jokes.

"No, I'm not. Trust me. I'm not. You're a real catch, kid. Any of these men would be lucky to have you. I think they all see it, too."

"Yeah, right. I'm a mess. Men should run and hide. That would be a much better choice…for them!"

Cory covers her hand resting on the railing with his own. He smiles patiently and pauses before saying, "You aren't a mess. What happened to you, doesn't define who you are. You are a special person, Samantha Patterson. Nobody can take that away from you.

Any guy would be blessed to have you. Besides, if people are still alive today, then chances are they've been through some rough shit, too. You aren't the only one who's had it bad out there. Everyone has lost someone. Everyone has had pain, either physical or emotional, inflicted on them. We just have to survive. That's all any of us can do anymore. And we have to hold on to the people we do have, even if they aren't our blood relatives. You're important to me, Sam. I want you to be happy. If Simon wasn't making you happy, then I'm glad you left. He's miserable and being an asshole most of the time now because you're gone, but I'm glad you're happy here. I want the best for you, little sister."

"Thanks, Cory," she says and hugs him around his waist. He returns it with a strong embrace of his own and kisses the top of her head. "I want you to be happy, too. You deserve it. Em would want it, too."

The tiny laugh lines around his eyes crease for just a second as he remembers his sister, her good and dear friend.

"Yeah, I know, kid," he says. "I miss her, but I know Em would want me to move on and be happy."

"You need someone to love, Cory."

"I'm workin' on it."

He winks, leaving Sam to wonder what he's been up to. Cory has always been private about his dalliances, of which she's sure he's had plenty. But he seems different lately, more settled, stiller, calmer as if something or someone has helped to quiet his demons.

"If any of these men attempt to mistreat you in any way, you get your uncle to bring you to the farm immediately. I'll handle it from there."

"I don't think any of them are like that. I've never gotten that impression from any of them. They all seem very decent and respectable.

"Good. Now, let's go find the Professor and torment him for fun, shall we?" he suggests.

"Cory!" Sam exclaims and giggles.

Sam follows him from the barn but leaves Cory to his devious plan of seeking out Simon and instead heads for the women's bunkhouse after she has checked on a gelding with an eye infection.

Later, Sam lies awake in her bunk thinking about Henry's kiss and what it means to her or what it could mean to her. She is genuinely confused and not sure what to think of him at all. A few times she'd thought he might be flirting with her, but she's never sure of these things. He is a really nice man, but she just doesn't think her heart is ready for a relationship. Maybe it never will be.

Courtney comes to the women's hall next and slips into her bunk beside her. Most of the other women are asleep already. A few are snoring, which means Sam won't find sleep for a while.

"Sam," her friend whispers in the dark.

"Yeah?"

"Guess what?"

Sam rolls to her side and raises to her elbow. "What?"

"Thad proposed," she says, her smile so evident, even in the dark building.

"Oh, Courtney!" Sam exclaims. "That's so great. I'm so happy for you and Lieutenant Stevens."

"Thanks," her friend says.

The next thing she knows, Courtney is kneeling beside her bed and hugging her. Sam returns it with great affection. She has come to like her so well. She's glad for her friend. Sam knows how much she loves Thad, the handsome Army lieutenant, who can't take his eyes off Courtney. She knows they'll have a happy life together. She can't help but feel just a hint of jealousy. It is gone in the briefest of seconds later, and she is left feeling nothing but pure joy for Courtney.

She wonders if Cory will tell Simon what he saw but hopes he doesn't. Sam would rather Simon not know what's going on between her and Henry. Technically, nothing is going on, so there would be no point in making him think that there is. Her feelings for Henry are non-existent other than friendship, although he now wants something more. She's not sure if she is able to feel more than friendship for him.

Sam lies awake, tossing and turning and debating the pros and cons of having a relationship with Henry. She still has feelings for Simon, but he does not want her. He's made that clear, or somewhat clear. Henry is kind and giving and generous and maybe someone who could someday make her happy.

Chapter Eight
Cory

He leaves the next morning before dawn, making Simon promise to tell Sam goodbye for him. Cory doesn't want to be on the road at the usual daylight hours of travel. He has a plan.

He drives west toward Pleasant View and the farm, out into the countryside on an old, bumpy, and not often traveled road. It is difficult in places to see where the pavement ends and the grass beside it starts. He took this road before with John a few years back when they were going on runs from house to abandoned house looking for any supplies that would be useful on the farm. He's learned so much from his friend over the years, things like clearing a house, perimeter checks, hotwiring vehicles, setting up tripwires.

In the dark, quiet hours before the sun rises, Cory parks the truck on a high ridge and leaves it. The spot he has chosen is about eight miles or maybe less from Pleasant View. The main road below him runs virtually parallel to the freeway where they've left warning signs for travelers to beware the highwaymen. If the creeps avoid that road and take the less traveled one in hopes of catching more prey, then those murderous thieves could possibly run right below him. He's been thinking about this all week while working on the new clinic for Sam and her uncle, who seems like a nice guy. So, he decided to leave early and perch himself on this ridge in the hopes of catching them in the act. Cory knows it's a long shot, but it's worth a try.

A screech owl in the distance cries out in the night as he descends the steep incline beside the road and into the forest.

Prickers latch onto his jeans, mosquitoes fly toward his face, and he gets smacked in the back of the head with a branch, but the payoff at the bottom will be well worth it. The hike takes him a few minutes to get to the lower ridge where he finds a well-concealed position and takes up residence to watch over the road even further below him. Cory props his rifle against a tree base and removes the sack of food from his pack that Dave's wife packed for him. He can understand why Samantha wants to start an herb garden over there. The smoked trout, dry, crumbly biscuit, something green in a jar, and dried berries and apple slices do not rise to the same level as Hannah and Sue's cooking. He chokes it all down with a canteen of water anyway, knowing that he needs the sustenance to get through the day.

This quiet, still time allows him to reflect on Sam and catching her with that guy Henry. Cory has nothing against him. He always seems like a good person whenever he's been around him. Plus, he knows that Dave would never be friends with an asshole. That helps to ease his mind about the man throwing his hat in the ring for Sam. It's just that he'd hoped she and Simon would come together. He's not sure what keeps them apart, but Cory estimates that it has more to do with Simon than Sam. His friend has a tortured soul when it comes to Samantha. He doesn't know how to fix their problems, or if they are even repairable, but he'd like to help. So far, he's stayed out of it, steered clear of the issue, but he hates seeing her looking so miserable. Cory knows that some of her misery lately is because of the girl that hung herself in Henry's barn but not all of it.

He can't imagine thinking that was the only option left in life. He feels bad for that young woman. He's been through enough to know that pain eventually does fade, though, even the kind so intense and agonizing that it seems as if it will never go away, that it will most surely kill you slowly first. Losing his little sister was the absolute worst thing he's been through. Em was his whole world. Now he feels the same way about Paige, even though she does not seem to return a similar depth of feeling about him.

He consults his watch and begins packing leftover breakfast items away. It is nearly eight a.m., the sun having risen a few hours ago. The last thing to go inside the bag is the canning jar of green stuff, which he hadn't felt brave or desperate enough to try. It looks like swamp water mixed with something the animated character Shrek would consume. The low murmur of a vehicle approaching on the road below him alerts Cory, and he tosses his bag down and snatches up his binoculars.

A dark truck goes slowly by, followed by a full-size white van, two motorcycles and three ATV's. It has to be them. Cory runs up the hill to his truck and fires it up. He slams it into gear and floors the gas, throwing gravel and grass out behind it. He angles the vehicle expertly but quickly down the road and comes out west of where he'd spotted them. They should be ahead of him. He takes a breath to relax and keep his cool.

Cory spots them stopped in the road about a few hundred yards away. They are easy to see, parked in the middle of the road like they are, all out of their vehicles and having a pow wow. He spies through his binoculars but quickly places them back on the seat beside him. They are turning around and going to head toward him again. He has to get off this road and hide. This time, he actually peels out in his haste to accelerate. He veers onto the first road to his right and flies down it, turns in an abandoned access road to a farmer's field and slowly circles back to the main road. He waits, though. If they travel down this road, they'll immediately see him. If they don't, he can get in behind them again.

They must've gone as far east as they wanted and not had any luck robbing people. Now they are circling back in the opposite direction going west. He waits a long time, longer than it should take. They don't go flying past on the road again. He was sure they were turning around. Cory rolls slowly toward the road and puts it in park. He gets out and jogs into the weeds and spies down the street with his binoculars. They're gone. They hadn't come this way. He sprints back to the truck and gets in. Had they changed their minds again and kept going? They were all turning around.

He pulls out onto the road again, turning left to pursue them in the eastward direction. He drives a few miles and doesn't find them. His frustration is growing. They are gone, vanished into thin air. Cory turns around and heads back west. Then he turns left onto the road where he'd spied on them from the ridge. He realizes that they've taken this road. The grasses growing up through the concrete, thick in some places, are completely smashed down by multiple vehicles and four-wheelers. He comes to the spot where he'd parked and slows down. There is no one in sight. He looks behind him to make sure he isn't being followed. He can see for at least a mile. Nobody's there.

Cory drives forward another thirty yards and spots the place where he'd gone down the hill to spy on them. The grass was stomped from him. Only now it is trampled down from many people having gone through it. There is a sign, a white, wooden sign staked into the ground. It reads: you are dead asshole.

An unbidden chill races up his spine. They knew he was here, or discovered it when they took this road to look for helpless victims. Cory gets back in the truck and turns around. He heads back down to the main road and continues west, still hoping to catch them. He doesn't think there are so many that he can't gain the upper hand and kill them. He just doesn't like that they knew enough about tracking to realize he'd been at that spot watching them. They obviously know that someone is onto them because of the warning signs that they've no doubt seen in their travels. The ante has just been upped. He can't speak for them, but Cory is ready to call.

He doesn't catch sight of them, which pisses Corry off to no end. He wants blood. He wants them dead. They've killed so many innocent people, taken family members from their loved ones, and raped at least two women. Both women had been strangled to death, as well. They have a serial rapist, strangler in their group and are accepting of him. This makes them his enemy. Any man that would stand by and do nothing while another violated and strangled a woman to death is his mortal enemy. They remind him of the creep who killed his little sister. He'd like to find them all tucked in their beds asleep and shut them in their building and burn them alive like he had her murderers. They deserve no less in his opinion, but the trail runs cold.

Cory drives around Pleasant View and home to the farm, which is always a sight for sore eyes. It becomes an even bigger one when he sees Paige come out of the greenhouse with Sue. She is biting her lower lip and trying to conceal a smile. At least she's happy to see him. Everyone comes out to greet him as a rumble of thunder echoes in the distance. They take their meeting into the big house where Hannah is setting out platters of cold meat, cheeses, and breads. It feels good to be home and surrounded by its comforting smells and sounds. The sounds are mostly coming from the kids who are playing the board game Risk in the music room on the floor. Arianna immediately spots him and comes running.

"Cory!" she squeals and hugs his waist, which is all the higher she can reach.

"Hey, monster," he greets and rubs the top of her dark head affectionately. "Keep the boys in check while I was gone?"

"You know I did!"

"I have no doubts, Ari. No doubts."

She smiles up at him, her eyes full of mischief. He's well aware of her crush and finds her amusing. She's a rotten little monster and a real tormenter of the boys on the farm. Huntley snorts with irritation from the floor.

"You did nothing of the sort. Don't be so ridiculous," Hunt offers sarcastically, gaining a roll of Ari's eyes.

"I'll play you a round of chess later, 'kay?" he says to her. "Right now, I need to talk to the guys and your dad."

"All right," she agrees with a coy grin.

He gathers everyone into the dining room, and Doc closes the pocket doors. Then he relays what he saw this morning, the location, and the threat that was left for him. John is angry, but his brother seems more concerned. Kelly just acts nonchalant, as if the outcome is already sealed.

"They are threatening the wrong people," John says.

Derek says, "The fact that they were able to tell that Cory was on that ridge watching them is what worries me."

"And they got away from him. They gave Cor the slip," Kelly adds.

"It's a big area," Cory explains. "There are a lot of back roads out there, lots of possible routes to take. The next time, we'll pick a spot that's a lot more congested with vehicles and debris so that they don't have so many options."

"That's what we were talking about when you were gone," Luke says.

"Soon," John says. "Soon we'll take them out. First, we need to assess the situation at the golf course in Clarksville, make sure they aren't our highwaymen."

"I don't think they are," Cory says.

John continues, "I agree. I don't think so, either. But we have to find out who they are. Then we need to check out Fort Campbell, find out if those kids need help or what the heck they're doing there by themselves. At least warn them."

"My guess is orphans," Reagan says. "I don't know why they're there, but we should definitely vet them."

Doc jumps in quickly to add, "If those young people need our help, then it is our obligation and responsibility to do so. They may require medical attention, food, housing. We won't know until we are able to make contact with them."

"Hopefully, they don't put a bullet between our eyes," Kelly says.

"We'll go at this carefully," Derek says.

They discuss strategy, a plan, a date and time before the meeting convenes and everyone goes their own ways. They want Simon back on the farm with them when it goes down. He's a valuable asset to the team. However, Cory is going on the trip to surveille and hopefully talk to the people at the golf course depending on their willingness to be friendly. He'll also probably be with John when they try the same approach with the kids living at Fort Campbell.

Cory catches Paige in the hallway before she can leave.

"Hey, Red," he says, touching her arm. "Miss me?"

Her gray eyes dart around nervously. He knows she is looking to see if anyone heard him. Everyone else split immediately following the meeting to do evening chores. The only person in the house is Hannie, and he can hear her in the kitchen working. Whatever she's doing, it's sure to be some magic food spell that makes everything she cooks taste so fantastic.

"Cory, I'm going out to feed the goats for Reagan. She's tired tonight."

"Then I'll help," Cory says. She looks hesitant. "I don't want them to attack you or anything."

This time, he gets a smile. "I'm not afraid of the goats. Well, maybe that one billy goat. I don't like him. I think it's mutual."

"I'd be scared of you, too," he teases. "I am."

"Yeah, right," Paige remarks with sarcasm. "I doubt if you're afraid of anything."

He doesn't tell her that she's wrong. Mostly he doesn't tell her because Cory doesn't want to admit that the thing which scares him most is losing her. Instead, he walks with her to the barn where they've done massive repairs the last few weeks since the tornado. It looks like John finished the barn siding that was missing while he was gone. They'd been in the middle of it when he had to leave for Henry's farm. He decides to broach the subject of Henry with Paige.

"What do you think of that Henry guy?"

She looks up at him, "Henry? He's nice. He seems like a good person. He sure lets a lot of people live on his farm. That has to mean he's pretty charitable."

"Yeah, guess so."

"Why? Did you not find him that way when you were there?"

"No, no. It's not that."

Paige frowns and says. "Then what do you mean?"

"I saw him last night kissing Samantha."

She stops in her tracks and turns to him. "What?"

Cory shrugs because he doesn't know what to say. He just offers a nod.

"Are they sleeping together? Is that it? Does Sam have feelings for him?"

Paige fires off a lot of questions, most of which he doesn't have an answer to because he doesn't know if Sam was being honest that she has no feelings for him. And also the fact that he doesn't really understand women all that well.

"What about Simon?" she asks.

"I don't know," he says. "I asked her if she's in love with this dude, but she said no. I don't know. I don't think she's over your brother, but she sure avoided him as much as possible while I was there."

"She's just angry. Hell, I'm angry with him, too."

Cory nods again and says, "Yeah, guess everyone's feelin' a little like that about the Professor. We just want Sam to come back. Now that this Henry is making a move, she may not."

"I don't understand Simon," she says and resumes their walk. "I know he has feelings for her. I've seen it. I can see it in his eyes, Cory. I know him better than anyone else here on this farm. He's my brother. I just don't get it. And he won't even talk to me. I don't know what to do."

"I don't think there's anything that we can do," he says and would like to hold her hand in his as they walk but refrains. "I've got the same problem as Sam if you think about it."

"What? Did you kiss Henry, too?"

Cory laughs aloud at her quip, knowing full well that she is being evasive with humor.

"Not exactly," he says. "Although, I would say he is rather dreamy."

She punches his shoulder playfully and laughs. He missed her.

"You've been doing a lot of avoiding lately, too, Red. Me! It doesn't make any sense. I'm a total catch. I'm a stud, obviously. I'm handsome, funny…"

"Don't forget humble."

He chuckles and says, "When are you gonna just let go of all this denial stuff and just marry me?"

"Marry you? Was that your idea of a proposal, Neanderthal?"

He chuckles as Damn Dog joins their path. "Sure. Or did you want flowers and a ring and a wedding planner?"

Paige chuffs. "None of the above. I'm never getting married. I don't want a commitment."

"You seem fine with the sex," he points out. He knows this worries her because Paige quickly peers around.

"Shh, don't be crazy. You think I want everyone on the farm knowing that?"

He doesn't tell her about John's conversation with him that night on watch duty. That's one person who knows. Maybe others do, too. Even though they've been discreet, the farm is only so big. There are many sets of eyes on it, too, which makes discretion even more difficult. He knows that John won't tell anyone, but he can't guarantee her that others don't know. Probably Hannah.

"So, you like the…perks, you just don't like the commitment that should come with them."

"Pretty much," she says.

He shoots her a frown of his own. "Maybe I'll cut you off."

She snorts. "Yeah, right."

"Yeah, probably not. I'm pretty easy," he teases with a grin, getting one in return. "But sooner or later, you're gonna have to marry me. Doc's not gonna allow this to continue if we're caught."

"Then we should stop," she says, surprising him.

Cory sighs, "Not as easy as it sounds, Red. You've cast a spell on me that I can't seem to shake."

"Ask Simon. I'm sure there's some herb you can rub on it to make it go away," she jokes bawdily.

"Ha!" he says with a loud guffaw. "I don't think an herb'll fix it. This is an itch that can only be scratched by my red-haired witch."

She gives him a snarky expression and goes into the barn. Cory is content to follow her since the view isn't so bad from this angle, either.

"Hey, Cory!" Huntley calls out, jogging across the barnyard toward him. "I haven't been able to talk to you since you got back."

"What's on your mind, little brother?" he tells him.

"Not much. How's Sam?" he asks of his friend.

"Good. She's doing good, Hunt. Don't worry about her."

Huntley looks at his shoes for a minute before saying, "Kind of hard to do. I miss her. I worry about my little shadi."

"I know, man," Cory says with a nod. "But, hey, if you can keep a secret, I'll tell you something."

"Sure, Cory. I'd never tell."

Cory smiles, knowing the kid is loyal nearly to a fault. "I'm going out tonight to look for the highwaymen pricks. You wanna' come with?"

"Really?"

"Yeah," he says. "I'm going tonight because I don't have guard duty. Luke's taking my shift so I can rest. I'm not resting. I don't need extra sleep."

"Heck, yes, I'll go."

"Good, be ready at oh-one-hundred hours, and I'll meet you at the equipment shed. Keep it on the down low, little brother."

Huntley bumps his fist against Cory's and smiles widely. Cory knows how much this means to him being included, and they are not in any danger tonight or he wouldn't be taking him.

"And leave the bow. Bring a rifle instead. This ain't the 1700s, bro'," he teases and gets a laugh before Huntley jogs away.

He has no doubt that Huntley will be up, ready and probably early for their mission. The kid is always asking to tag along on pretty much any trip they make either for supplies, a run for building materials, or a more serious mission like the freeing of the women at the sex camp. He wants to contribute more. Huntley is an excellent shot, a great tracker, and a good soldier so far. He needs more practice, though, and a hell of a lot more practical experience.

Cory meets up near the goat pen with Paige again and helps her feed them.

"You never did answer my question," he reminds her.

"You mean whether or not I think you're the most annoying person on this farm? The answer is yes."

He smiles at her and slips an arm around the back of her waist.

"Hey, don't," she warns as her gray eyes dart around nervously.

Cory kisses her quickly and releases her. Paige flits away to the other side of the small goat enclosure. "I missed you enough for the both of us, Red."

He continues on with his work but notices that she has gone silent. Cory looks over at her to find Paige just standing there as if she is surprised.

"We need to stop this," she says as if she has come to some difficult summation of a problem. She even nods.

"No, we need to take this to the next level and stop all this foolin' about."

Paige shakes her head in disagreement. "No, I mean it."

Her tone is serious, solemn even, and she is wearing a frown.

"What's going on? Did something happen while I was gone?" he asks and walks toward her.

"Don't, Cory," she says, holding out her hand. "Stop. I mean it. I think this is over."

He really doesn't want to hear this from her. He'd missed her. He'd wanted to skip the asshole surveillance and rush home to her instead. The way she is so resolute in her behavior leads him to believe that something is amiss, something she is concealing.

"You didn't up and ditch me for another dude, did ya', Red?"

"No," she answers simply.

Cory isn't so convinced. She's been separated from him for a full week. Maybe that dick Jason from town has made another move for her. He wouldn't be surprised. That guy also dumped Jackie from the armory. He's a real playboy. Cory will probably deck him when he goes to town next. It's been a long time coming anyway. Likely no one will even be surprised or care.

"What is it then?" he presses.

"Nothing…I don't want to talk about it. This is just stupid and a lot of people, including you, are going to get hurt. There's no good, happy ending to this, not for us or Simon or the McClanes, nobody."

"Sweetheart," he says softly and steps into her space, "just talk to me. Tell me what's going on. If I'm pushing too hard too fast, I'll back off. Don't shut me out. Talk to me, Red."

"Cory…" she says, her eyes tearing up.

"What is it?" he asks with more concern and rubs his hands up and down her bare arms.

"Nothing," she blurts, pulls free and rushes from the barn, leaving him standing there in a perpetual state of confusion. Usually, she's a lot easier to read. Not tonight. He's thoroughly screwed on this one. He missed her and wanted to come home to see her, maybe even spend some alone time with her while Simon is still gone at Dave's compound, but she is clearly not in the same mindset.

He's been so worried about her since she passed out on their run to Clarksville. That had been a terrifying experience, one he doesn't wish to repeat. Seeing her hit the deck not to resurface into his line of sight had been scary. He cares so much about her now. He'd even taken a minute to discuss it with Simon while they were bunked together at Dave's place this week. Her brother is equally concerned about her. He'd gone through a lot of complex medical diagnoses of what could have caused it to happen, but none of them sounded like a good outcome in the end. He'd gone to Simon to find some sort of reassurance about her health but had come away with more questions and concerns afterward.

Cory heads to his cabin, cleans up, and prepares for the long night ahead of him with Huntley. He'll take his motorcycle and let Huntley ride behind him. He's worked tirelessly on the machine to get it quieted down. In the past, bikers wanted their motorcycles as loud as they could get them, but Cory needs it to be as silent as he can tweak it to be. Moving in stealth mode is optimal for tracking and creeping on assholes who kill innocent people.

He kills the lights in the cabin with the intention of sleeping a few hours before he rises to go on his mission, but Cory finds himself thinking about Paige's newest relationship edict of it being over. He simply won't accept it.

Chapter Nine
Simon

Cory left three days ago, and he's been in misery since his friend's departure. He has, however, been learning a lot from Sam's uncle, who is working with him on pediatric studies. He enjoys the work, the long hours at their new clinic, and the hands-on experience he's getting with her uncle. Simon's just not too keen on the time at night when Dave's men try to include him in on their activities because he doesn't want to be around Sam. He has no answer for her legitimate question of why he kissed her again. Again. He'd slipped again like an idiot and let his feelings and emotions take over for his logic and level-headedness. His own weakness makes him sick.

That night before the tornado hit and changed everything, Simon had been so angry with her for calling him a coward. He's not a coward. He's trying to do the right thing by her. She deserves better but making her see that has not been an easy thing to do. He's not sure if she sees it still. Sam mostly seems like she's been avoiding him this week, too. She stays up until the wee hours of the morning playing cards and games with her new friends in Henry's house.

And Henry is another subject altogether. Simon doesn't trust him. He may be a nice guy, but Simon is sure that the man is interested in Sam. He's seen it in his eyes. Sam doesn't seem to notice, though, or else she is mutually interested in Henry. He hopes not. Simon wants her to be happy and to find someone good who can take care of her, just not Henry. The reason he knows she stays up late with her friends every night is because he can't sleep, either, and has seen her and Courtney coming out of Henry's house smiling and laughing gaily as if they've had a grand old time. Simon is usually wide awake, wandering the compound aimlessly, or sitting at his desk in his temporary housing looking out the window which happens to face Henry's side door.

He's also spent the last week and a half avoiding a few of the women from Sam's bunkhouse who have let their interest in him be known. They seem like perfectly lovely girls, but he does not return their affections. He believes one was rescued from the sex camp and the other was an orphan who came to live on Dave's compound a few years ago. They are both close to his age. He hasn't committed much about them to memory other than that the blonde is named Ashley, and she is very pretty and a bit shy. He just has no consideration of her because he must stick to his studies and stay focused on becoming a doctor now and has no time for romance. Or at least that's what he tells himself.

"This is great," he tells her uncle. "I have a lot to study from this."

They have been working on pediatric growth charts and childhood nutrition. He had no clue that children were so much different than adults. Her uncle taught yesterday about the similarities and also the differences between standard birth weight babies versus preemies. Then he spent most of the night studying the notes he has taken for the last week and a half while working with him.

"Good," Scott says. "I'm glad I can help. We need all the doctors we can find or teach. This isn't getting any easier. Babies are being born every day. They need care; so do the mothers. Out there...out there, these children aren't going to get any help or medical care. I've seen so much malnutrition and disease..."

His words fade away as his eyes take on a haunted look.

"Where were you the last four years?" Simon asks because he and everyone else on the McClane farm has been curious about her uncle. He's very quiet, not open to talking about himself or really much of anything with them.

"Where? Close by. Not far."

"At a camp like this one?"

Scott shakes his head, "No, not like this. If I had been, I wouldn't be here tonight with you. The places I was at were a lot less fortified, not secure at all. It's not...safe out there. I've learned that many times over."

"Sam once told me that you were working and living in Nashville when it happened and that you had a girlfriend or fiancée or something."

"Yes, girlfriend. It was serious," he says. "I was going to propose on her birthday the next month, April."

"What happened?" Simon asks, his interest growing.

"She was killed," he answers. "I was at the hospital. I thought I could still hold everything together, go to work, help people."

"My mother did the same," Simon says, remembering his mother's devotion to her patients. He wishes so often that he could go back in time and forbid her from going to work that day. It was already becoming unstable in their country. Then it collapsed in the blink of an eye.

"I'm sorry," he says. "I know about her. Samantha told me. I was doing the same thing she was. We were dedicated to helping people. It's why we all went into medicine in the first place. I had so many little patients who needed me."

Simon nods with understanding. Her uncle has a big heart, or did. He's not so sure if Scott is the same as he used to be as far as generosity goes. He is great with the kids at Doc's clinic, but he is very reserved around everyone else.

"It got bad at the hospital. Police were called in to protect it, guard it against being raided by people looking for drugs. I could literally hear the city collapsing outside the windows of the hospital. I saw fires, looting, all of it. We got as many of the children out and with their families as we could. Some of the staff stayed on. I went home to make sure Steph was all right. I promised to return for a night shift since so many of the staff had already abandoned their jobs. When I got to our apartment, she was already dead. The building was looted. People were dead everywhere. She'd been…"

He doesn't finish, but Simon knows the horrible fate his girlfriend and future wife suffered at the hands of the same kind of men with whom he'd traveled from Arizona. The same ones who'd abused Sam.

"I'm sorry."

Scott nods and continues, "I wanted to bury her, but the looters were still in the building. Or maybe it was a fresh hoard. I don't know. So, I packed what I could and left. I went back to the hospital. It was no better than my home. The police and guards were either gone, abandoned their jobs, or were killed. The druggies were already there taking everything that wasn't nailed down or locked up and some that was. I took a few of my patients and got out of there."

"You took other people's kids?"

He shakes his head. "You don't understand what it's like to work on the peds floor, Simon. Some of these kids don't have families. They get dumped in the hospital, especially babies, and the mother checks out after giving birth, and they never come back for them. It's a sad and depressing place to work sometimes."

"Wow," Simon says softly. "That's horrible."

"People are horrible. The kids were innocent victims of bad parents. I couldn't leave them. I knew how to care for them, so I took two, which is all I could manage and fled. I made it down to the parking garage and to my car with a case of baby formula and a diaper bag full of stuff I'd need. Then I got to an Army post. Do you know what I mean?"

"Yes, sir," he says. "My sister was able to do the same."

"Good for her," Scott says. "They were great. They even took one of the babies for me and sent men back into the city to rescue more kids from the hospital. I lived there for about a month. That's all the longer that anyone lived there. It was attacked and overrun. The military men did a good job of getting us out of there, though. Most of us survived, and none of the children were harmed. We retreated to another position. It happened again, but the second time we weren't so lucky. Many people were killed. Some children, too. I fled on foot that time. I was only able to keep the one baby with me, but I also took a little boy, Terrance. He was a sweet kid, five years old, orphaned. I found other survivors and lived with them for about a year. Then I knew I had to find my sister and her family."

"Sam."

He nods and continues, "Yes. You have to understand. In the beginning, it was so chaotic. I never would've made it to them. Once I got set up with the military, I was doing medical work immediately with their medics and nurses and any doctors who were available. Kind of like a mobile clinic. Then again with the next military group, I did the same. And again, with the people who took us in. I was always needed. When I could make my break for it, I did. I came back to find the house empty and ransacked and them gone. I didn't know where to look."

Simon's eyes fall to the floor. He's glad that her uncle didn't look behind the barn. He would've seen the gravesites of Sam's family.

"I kept searching and searching. Then I met up with a nice group of people and decided to stay with them for the winter. I looked for my family every chance I got. Then we were overrun last year, and I ended up with Dave's group."

"That's a stroke of luck," Simon comments.

"Yes, I know. I also know what's out there waiting for me and Samantha if we were to leave. I have no intention of ever putting her in harm's way."

Simon tries not to think of Sam being in her uncle's care. It's hard to rationalize that he is not in charge of her well-being anymore.

"I know how close the two of you are, so I'm telling you this so that you don't have to worry about her."

He tries to offer a smile but fails. "Thanks."

"I've been worried about her myself lately. Ever since her friend hung herself in the barn, Samantha's been very depressed. She tries to hide it, but I've seen it. I've tried talking to her about it, but she clams up on me."

"Yes, she can do that," he agrees, although Sam actually did talk to him about it a little. If she doesn't want to talk, she won't. That's just Sam. At least she does confide in him on most things, especially anything that bothers or frightens her.

"Simon," her uncle says. "I know you two traveled together for a short time. And maybe you know what happened to my sister and her family. All I know is that they're dead. Samantha won't talk about it, but I worry about her. I know something's wrong."

He feels his cheeks begin to burn, but not from embarrassment. This is also not a source of comfort, this topic of conversation, for Simon, either.

"Would it be imposing on you to ask what happened, if you know, that is? I want to be able to help her."

Simon swallows and runs a hand through his hair. Her uncle is still speaking, but Simon cannot follow his words or make sense of them. He doesn't want to think about that time. He blocks it as hard as he can from his memory. It is a daily struggle, this trick he plays on his mind. The room feels too small all of a sudden.

"I don't think that's a good idea," Simon blurts suddenly, surprising her uncle. "Excuse me, sir."

He rushes from the room in her uncle's small cottage and out into the stifling night air. Their study session is officially over. He never would've probed her uncle about his past if he thought the man would bring up his and Sam's. He can't talk about that with anyone, especially him.

Simon turns the corner and nearly runs down Sam, who squeals with surprise.

"Simon!" she exclaims.

"Sorry," he issues.

She's wearing an oversized, white t-shirt that is two sizes too big and knee-length blue-jean shorts. Her dark hair is pulled into a ponytail, and she has leather boots on her feet. She's never looked prettier.

"Aren't you studying with my uncle?"

"Oh, yes, we just…finished," he lies to cover himself.

She frowns and says, "I thought you two would be going for at least another hour or so."

"Nope, got done early," he says. "Big day tomorrow. Gotta get some rest."

"Hm," she remarks as if she is considering whether or not he is lying.

"Are you headed to your boyfriend's house for another night of fun and merriment?" he goads, trying to dissuade her questioning stare and also to find out if she really is going to Henry's.

"As if that's your business. But, no, we're not playing tonight. The guys are having a meeting."

"About what?"

"The highwaymen," she says. "I guess Cory saw them the other day when he went home to the farm, and now they're planning an ambush or something. I'm sure I won't be allowed to go."

"Of course you won't be permitted," he agrees and gets an immature facial expression from her in return. "It sounds like I should be in on this meeting, though."

"You're welcome to join them, I'm sure."

Her eyes are mischievous tonight. Simon often wonders what is going through her brain.

"What's the catch?" he asks.

"They're all still out at the cabin. You'll have to run through the woods all the way to join their meeting if you want in on it."

"Funny," he mocks. "I think I'll pass and hit the shower instead."

"A nice cool one, no doubt," she says.

Simon frowns, "Yes, they don't have the hottest water going around here, do they? Another reason you should move back."

"Why? Am I going to die from a slightly off temperature shower?"

"You're full of pithy comments this evening," he remarks, staring her down.

"And you expecting flattery and high praise?"

Simon chooses to ignore this and moves on to a topic that is pulling at his curiosity.

"Sam, why...why have you not told your uncle what happened to us, to you?" he asks with great caution.

"What?" she croaks out. "Why are you are asking me that?"

"Because he asked me. I didn't tell him. You know I'd never do that. I don't feel it's my place."

She nods and looks down. Then she looks up at Simon again, hitting him with those mysterious blue orbs.

"I will. Someday. Maybe. I don't know."

"It's ok. I don't think he expects you to. He was just worried. Maybe it would help..."

They are interrupted from further comment when a loud boom followed by the cracking of gunfire sounds off in the night.

"What the heck was that?" he asks.

"I have no idea," she stammers with equal confusion.

Then more gunfire as one of Dave's men runs past them.

"What's going on, Thad?" Sam calls after him.

"Get to safety!" he yells at them. "We're taking fire."

Simon doesn't waste a single second and grabs her hand and runs for his cabin. He needs his rifle, which he'd left on the small table in the main room. Within a minute, he has his rifle slung over his shoulder and is strapping his pistol on his hip, as well. He takes her hand again and leads her back out. Then he hooks a right and jogs to her uncle's small cottage.

"What's going on out there?" Scott asks with worry as he ushers them inside.

"Not sure. I'm going to find out."

"Me, too," Sam says.

"Sam, stay here," he says and turns to go.

"I want to help," she argues and is pushing past him to go out the door.

"No!" he barks loudly as more shots in the distance ring out. "Stay here. I don't want you shot in a crossfire. I don't know what this is. I'll come back as soon as I can to let you know when or if it's safe. I mean it. Don't come out there. Sir, keep her here. Stay here and get out through the back of the farm if it's overrun. Get to Doc's farm if it comes to that."

"Fine," she says, her eyes worried and wide. "Don't forget me here."

"I'll keep her safe, Simon," her uncle says, hitting him with a strange look as if he is surprised to see this side of Simon. He notices the man has a handgun drawn.

"I won't forget about you guys. I promise," he says and slides past her. "Lock this!" he yells through the door.

Then Simon sprints for the front of the compound where he meets up with some of Dave's men.

"What the hell's going on?" he asks in a rush.

"Someone just launched a grenade at us, at the gates," the man answers.

"Where's Sergeant Winters?" Simon inquires after Dave.

"Not back yet," the other man says, his eyes jumping to the barrier fence separating them from their enemy.

The man Sam called Thad says, "They're still out there. Come on. Let's get you in a good position."

He follows Thad into Henry's home and sprints up to the attic.

"How bad are we outnumbered?" Simon asks.

"Not sure. Dave should hear the shots and be here soon. No worries. Let's just do what we can to prevent them from breaching."

"Got it," Simon says firmly.

"Over there," Thad says, pointing to the small window. "See what you can do. I'm going back out."

Simon sets up his rifle in the window and spies through his scope. He watches a man outside the compound's gate run in front of a small truck, backlit by the headlights. The man blasts off a few rounds toward the fence and gate. Simon takes a steadying breath and squeezes, disabling the man with a shot to his leg. Two cars fly in from the south and pull up behind the truck. At least a half dozen men immediately jump out and begin shooting through the fence at Dave's men. Simon shoots and kills one of them with one shot. He attempts to do so on another but misses. He slows his breathing further and expels a heavy breath of air.

Dave's men are laying down a barrage of suppressive fire. He sees through his scope some of Dave's soldiers take an offensive position on the other side of the road in a gully, having flanked the men parked there. He's not sure how they managed it, but he's glad they did. They push forward catching the men in a crossfire situation. Some swing toward Dave's men and others try to keep shooting at the fence and gated area and through the sections where there is chain link. He hears a woman scream out in terror or pain. Simon hopes it isn't one of the women on the compound being shot but just one that is frightened.

Simon aims at another man near the front of the first car and fires. It's a direct hit to the chest, and the man falls backward, splayed on the hood of the car, the spray of his blood staining the windshield.

They are shouting orders at one another. Some of it sounds frantic. A man between the two rear vehicles lobs a grenade over the high fence protecting Henry's farm. It makes a loud boom when it lands. Simon keeps his cool and squeezes. The shot disables the human grenade launcher, and he falls to the pavement with a scream of pain. Dave's men continue to rain down fire from the opposite side of the road, but he no longer sees them. Every once in a while, Simon catches sight of a red flash from a tracer round from deep in the brush where Dave's men must be concealing themselves. It's a solid tactic and one that seems to be working. Two more men fall to their deaths on the road.

The squealing of tires to the west draws Simon's attention. Another vehicle approaches at a high rate of speed and comes to a screeching halt at the scene. It's a full-size black van. At least eight men jump out and join the fight. They are stealthier and immediately take cover behind their vehicle and the others in the street. Simon zeroes in and takes out the driver before he can even get out of the van or move it if that was his intention. It's a clean kill.

Shots ring out at a constant pace as they trade fire with the enemy. Simon reloads and takes aim again. He wants to hit one of the newcomers. A squatting man who has not concealed himself well enough has his back to Simon and his left shoulder leaning against the side of the van. They obviously don't realize he is in a high, sniping position. Simon squeezes, and the man goes down in a slumping posture with his forehead resting on the pavement. He does not move again. His friends scatter and try to take cover. Simon is able to lead one and wing him in the calf. His friends pull him to cover. This is life or death, this fight. His only concern is keeping these men from breaking in. Samantha is in here.

His teammates' voices grow very loud in the yard below him, and Simon watches as Dave strolls calmly into the melee without a care in the world. He is shouting orders to his men. Simon isn't sure how they got into the compound, likely from a side entrance, but he's glad they are here.

He takes a shot at another man from the black van who has become unwisely brave and is standing slightly exposed but only manages to clip his boot. He screams in pain, too. It was the only thing sticking out of the side of the van that he could aim at. They are smarter than their comrades from the cars and the truck. Instead of wasting time with another miss, he concentrates on a different area. A man runs toward the gate and manages to toss something over. It immediately explodes, but Simon doesn't think it was a grenade this time. He is swiftly taken out by Dave's men.

A second later, another item is tossed near the entry gate, which also explodes but with a much louder boom. The gate is now hanging askew. Simon wonders if they will be able to breach it. He sweeps right and looks through his scope in time to watch yet another man mimic the other two, tossing his own device over their fence. This one lands closer to the house where he is hiding in the attic and sniping. Simon zeroes in on the man who threw it. He sites in and…pop. The man goes down in a cry of agony. Someone from

Dave's group takes the kill shot. It doesn't matter to Simon who does the killing, as long as it gets done efficiently.

The battle seems to rage on for hours but is, in reality, likely only about twenty minutes. The men in the black van retreat first, but not before everyone takes a shot at their vehicle. They are able to speed away even though their headlights are off, leading Simon to believe they were wearing night-vision gear. A few of the remaining fighters jump into the truck and also take off. Simon shoots one in the bed of the small truck, killing him instantly with a headshot.

He rushes from the attic and out the back door to the yard where he jogs over to Dave in the crowd. Men continue to pound at the remaining creeps in the road.

"Eliminate whatever survivors are out there. Keep anyone who's injured alive for questioning," he orders his men. "Rusty and Tank, take a team and go after those fuckers!"

"Anyone hurt?" Simon yells over the shooting.

Dave points and says, "Over there. They'll need your help, Professor. Someone fetch Dr. Wallace. Get a room ready!"

Two of his men quickly return with, "Yes, sir!"

Simon runs to the men near the side of a building who have been dragged there by their comrades in arms. A woman is, indeed, there and has very obviously been shot. Before he can even press a bandage to her abdomen, she dies. She has bled out, which is very evident by the amount of blood on the ground. It bothers Simon, but he has to push aside his shock and assist the living.

Sam and her uncle show up a moment later with his bag of emergency supplies. They work on stabilizing their three patients before having the men move them to the men's barracks where they've established an emergency clinic. He works with Sam and her uncle for the next two hours sewing the poor soldiers back together, either from gunshot wounds or shrapnel spray. He's thankful they have such a surplus of medical equipment and supplies. It is nearly midnight when they get their patients bedded down and resting for the remainder of the night. He and her uncle scrub up at the sink, and Sam goes to the women's bunkhouse to shower. She received a sizable splash of arterial spray when her uncle had placed heavy pressure on a man's thigh wound. Scott volunteers to stay up and keep an eye on their patients as Simon seeks out Dave and his men.

He finds them in the top of the cattle barn interrogating two men. It looks as if it is not going well since both men are badly beaten and bruised.

"Oh, you'll talk, motherfucker," Dave is saying as Simon enters the space. He sends a grin toward Simon and then goes back to lecturing. "You assholes think this is my first questioning?"

One of the men spits on the ground in front of Dave. His saliva is heavily mixed with blood.

"Nah, me and my boys used to do this for fun in our downtime. You'll talk. Your buddies abandoned you, but I got you, bitch. You're mine now. I got you for as long as it takes. You'll talk."

"Are you the ones robbing people on the roads?" Henry questions, his stance one as formidable as granite.

No answer. Another soldier punches the side of the man's face, the one to whom Henry was speaking. This goes on for another hour until Dave finally kills the one in front of the other. Simon has to look away. Everything about being a doctor goes against this sort of treatment of human beings. However, he wants answers, too. People were hurt, killed tonight. Sam could've been killed. They need this last remaining man to give over secrets so that the people he cares about don't get their blood spilled by the enemy.

The man finally breaks a half hour later and talks.

"Yes, we're the ones. It's us," he says weakly as blood drips from his face in several places and from many open wounds.

"Where's your location? Where are you holed up?" Dave asks.

He laughs, maniacally and without a care for the consequence of doing it.

"Answer or we'll take care of you the same way we did your friend here," Dave warns.

More laughter.

"I'm not so sure I'd be laughing if I were you, boy," Dave taunts the man, who is clearly not a boy.

The man laughs again. Henry punches him.

"Not so funny now, is it?" Dave asks.

He chuckles. "You'll see. You'll see who you're fuckin' with soon enough, assholes. You're so fucking screwed."

"Unless the Spartan king Leonidas is in charge, I'm feelin' pretty sure of my abilities to defeat your fearless leader just like we whooped your asses tonight," Dave says.

"You're so outnumbered, you have no fuckin' idea," the man says with a chortle.

"Enlighten me to these great numbers you have," he jeers and squats in front of the man, who is tied to a chair.

"Over six hundred, asshole. Like I said? You're fucked."

And for the first time, maybe since joining the McClane family, Simon feels like they may just be defeated.

Chapter Ten
Paige

She feels terrible for the way she broke things off with Cory the other day, even if he seems to have completely ignored or blocked everything she said and is acting like they are still in a secret relationship. He drives her crazy. But she'd needed to do it. It isn't right to lead him on, especially since she is so steadfast on the direction she wants her future to move. Being involved with Cory put more than a wrinkle in her plan. He's the worst possible scenario. Paige's feelings for him were growing, and she wanted to put an end to it. The only possible outcome is Cory is killed on a mission, and that isn't something she can go through. Her only concern needs to be keeping herself and her brother alive another day. The highwaymen alone may end up raiding their farm and killing most of them. As intimately as she knows Cory now, Paige is positive he'd throw himself in harm's way to protect the family, which means he is killed. Every conclusion is always the same. Cory is killed. She's not going through that.

She plods through any result that means he isn't killed in the end and comes up short every time. It's a good way to pass the time as she sits on her bed reading a book- one that Cory looted in a bookstore in Nashville about ancient Greek architecture. Her postulations also reaffirm in her mind that there is a zero percent chance that she and Cory marry, have the children he wants, and they live happily ever after. He's going to die from some bizarre disease, plague or pox, or he will be killed, murdered by cruel, insensitive people who only have their own greedy interests at heart. No thanks to any of those possibilities.

The pregnancy test that she took the night before she ended it with Cory came back negative, something for which she'd readily thanked her maker. When Reagan had suggested that she passed out due to being pregnant, it had made Paige consider that she was so. Stealing the test from the clinic had made her feel guilty. Sneaking around behind her brother's back also gives her a dirty conscience. Simon is the most important thing in the world to her. She doesn't want to hurt him unnecessarily by being secretive and immoral. She was just relieved when the stick showed a negative symbol. Seeing the positive one pop up might've made her pass out again. She wrapped it in paper and hid it at the bottom of the wastebasket in her bedroom. She certainly doesn't need anyone to find it. That would be slightly difficult to explain, another reason that she has to stop sleeping with Cory. She doesn't want the lies, nor an unexpected pregnancy.

Paige has no doubts that she'll never have children. That just isn't going to be a part of her future. As safe as the farm is, there is always a danger, a predator lurking out there now. Her children could someday end up like she did, out on her own in the wilds of new America dealing with evil people. She desperately wants to believe in happy endings and marriage and babies and family, but that isn't going to help her and her brother survive. Those are the fantasies of a naïve schoolgirl, someone she used to be.

"Hey!" Reagan says, barging into her room. "Something's going down over at Dave's. You'd better come downstairs."

Reagan leaves a second later, and it takes a moment for Paige to catch on to what she means. She slams the book shut and rushes down to join the family in Doc's office where Derek is using the new radio to communicate with Dave's camp.

"What's going on?" Paige whispers to Cory who is standing farther away from the family members who have assembled around Doc's desk.

He is biting the inside of his cheek as he rubs at the stubble on his jaw. "Not sure yet. Sounds like they're under attack."

This frightens her. Simon is over there. She listens intently as Derek turns the knob on the radio and speaks into the mic. Dave's voice comes back at them as Paige remembers that Sam is also over there.

"I'm going," Cory announces and turns to go.

John stops him with a firm, "No. We'll wait and see. Don't run out just yet."

It is hard, but he stays. Paige can read the frustration in his stance, the tenseness in his shoulders, the hard stare of his dark eyes. He wants in this, whatever it is.

"Wait," Derek says to them. "I've got a better link. Hold on."

He adjusts the radio again and gets a clearer connection with Dave. The attack is over. People are injured or dead. They believe it was the highwaymen. They are calling an emergency meeting. At first light, they are heading this way. Paige thanks God. She hopes Simon returns home and does not go back there ever.

"Is Simon coming?" she blurts her feelings without a care for what people might think.

"Maybe," Derek says.

"Make him come home, Derek," she openly pleads. Derek nods and issues the request to Dave. The radio goes dead, so she's not sure if her brother is coming or not. Paige will never sleep tonight.

"Don't worry. He's fine," Cory assures her.

She frowns, not sure if she should believe him. She won't rest until Simon is back on the farm with her, and she can see for herself that he is unharmed.

"How do you know?"

Cory touches her shoulder, his hand warm and comforting, "If he was dead or injured, Dave would tell us. Same goes for Sam. They wouldn't make us wait till morning to find out."

The family discusses the situation, what little they know of it, for a long time before John notices his wife asleep on the sofa behind them. Paige consults the antique clock on the mantel and notes that it is after two a.m.

"Everyone, go to bed and get some rest," Doc says. "We may be needed tomorrow. Who knows in what capacity, but we should be prepared for this meeting and whatever might be coming this way."

"I'll take watch," Kelly says.

Lucas hops to his feet as if it is early afternoon and he is full of energy. "I'll help."

Derek nods and says, "John, I'll pull you on at dawn with Huntley."

106

"I can keep watch then," Cory says.

"I figured you'd want some sleep," Derek says with a grin as he tosses his pen onto Doc's desk. He'd been taking notes on their assessments of the situation. Cory shoots him a quizzical look. "What with all the nights you've been gone and such."

Cory's gaze narrows, and he leaves the room but not before Derek calls out for him to go to bed and stay there. Cory snorts loudly from the hall.

Paige catches him in the hallway and grabs his forearm to stop him, "What was that all about?"

"Nothing," he lies.

She sends him a look that lets him know she doesn't believe this.

"Just been going on some scouting runs," he tells her.

"By yourself at night?"

He smiles, "Yes, Red. At night. All by my lonesome. I'm a big boy. Remember I lived alone for almost a year? I think I can handle a few nights of tracking by myself. Well, one night I let Huntley tag along. He needs to learn. Kid's a good tracker, but I was able to teach him a few new tricks."

"Cory, that's not safe. You shouldn't be going anywhere all alone."

"Well," he pauses and grins, "you won't let me come up and visit you upstairs, so I gotta do something to pass the time."

She glares and slaps his shoulder. "Stop. That's not funny. Someone could…"

She pauses as Sue pushes her husband past them in the wheelchair. They both look exhausted.

"You're ridiculous," she says when they are gone.

"Just spittin' the truth."

Paige rolls her eyes, then narrows them at him. "Be careful what you say. There are too many people in this house to go around joking like that. You're going to raise suspicion. More suspicion."

"I wasn't joking. That's the part you don't get."

He yanks her to him, kisses her on the mouth and retreats before she even has the chance to react. Paige groans and goes to bed. So much for breaking up with him. She doesn't sleep much because her mind either focuses on Cory and her feelings for him, or it travels to Dave's camp and worries about her brother and his welfare.

The bark of Cory's dog alerts her in the morning that they have company. She fell asleep for a few hours despite her distress. Paige quickly dresses and pulls her hair into a ponytail. She races down the stairs and out the back door in her bare feet. Expelling a sigh of relief at the sight of Simon, Paige is also relieved to see Sam get out of Dave's new truck, as well. Sam steps down from the extended cab door, and Simon jumps to the ground over the side of the bed. She embraces her brother for a long time, longer than he wants. She doesn't care and clings tightly anyway. He smells like a campfire, gun oil, and sweat.

"I was so scared. Are you all right?"

"Fine, sis," he says with a low level of patience. "I'm just fine. No holes, see?"

He stands back so that she can look at him.

"That's not funny, you jerk!" she hisses. Then she takes his hand in hers and asks, "What the heck happened, Simon?"

"We're about to go over it," he tells her.

"I'm glad Sam's here, too," she says, looking over at her little friend hugging John around his waist.

"Yes, she was shaken up. I don't think she's even been to bed yet. Dave said it might be a good time to take a break from the farm for a few hours and get her out of there..."

She interrupts and asks, "Was she hurt?"

"No, no. She's just upset. She didn't want to leave, though, but Dave ordered it. She's been through a lot the last few weeks."

"I heard. Cory told us about her friend," Paige says, referring to Sam's friend who committed suicide. "That's so horrible."

"Dave said the change of scenery might be good for her for a few days. She wasn't too happy about it, but his word is the final one."

"What about you? Did you get any rest yet?"

"Not a wink," he says with a grin. "We were on edge afterward, nobody slept. I stayed up in the top of the barn on sniper watch with Dave's sniper. Some of the others went looking for the people who attacked us."

"What about the wounded?"

He frowns, "Yes, that was difficult. I helped Sam's uncle and their nurse and Sam with them. We lost a woman, and one of Dave's men is still in critical condition. It doesn't look too good, though. Her uncle's keeping a close eye on him."

"That's terrible."

"It could've been a lot worse. Dave's place is definitely a compound, though. It's hard to penetrate it. They gave it a good effort, but they didn't get in. If they ever come back, they might breach. If they come with the numbers they say they have."

"I'm just glad you and Sam are safe."

"Yes, she's fine. I left her with her uncle when it happened, forced her to stay put. She'll probably stay here a few days and want to go back, though."

Her brother scoffs at this. He certainly doesn't seem to think Sam should return to the compound. Neither does Paige. Samantha belongs on the McClane farm. Heck, she's more of a McClane than Paige. She's lived here longer and has a deeper connection with the family.

"Unless, of course, Dave says no. He runs the place, and nobody naysays him. His word is final."

"Yeah, I guess it is because she's here and not there. I'm glad, though. I miss her a lot. Did everything… work out with you two?"

"Yes, fine," he answers noncommittally. Then her brother pulls his bag from the back of the truck.

"Brought home my dirty laundry for you to wash," he teases with a wink.

Paige scowls at him as Dave's men, including Henry, join the McClane clan gathering near the picnic table in the side yard.

"We've set up a roadblock on either end of our road now," Dave tells them after explaining the attack.

"Good idea," Kelly says.

"Also got an LPOP going full-time."

Reagan asks, "What's that mean?"

Dave looks directly at her and says, "Listening Post, Observation Post. It's essential to keep an eye out for them to return."

Henry adds, "They got away too quickly last night, and we weren't able to find them. That won't happen again."

John punches his fist to Henry's and nods. There is an intensity in John's eyes that frightens her. He is out for blood in this. Paige would rather they avoid them instead.

"Did you get the impression that they knew who you were? That they had intel on us?" Kelly asks.

"No, I think it was random. They were just looking for stuff to steal, people to rob. It was definitely them. Same modus operandi," Dave answers.

Cory says, "This sounds like a job for high explosives."

"Absolutely," Dave says. "As soon as we locate their hovel, we'll use the application of all the little tricks we know."

He grins, and the men laugh. Paige does not. She is too stressed out about the idea of her brother and Cory going into this battle. It's enough he was in it last night.

By the time the meeting wraps, Paige is more worried than she was last night. One woman from his compound was killed and a few of his soldiers badly injured. Dave's men are as trained as the McClane men. If it could happen to them, the family is in danger, as well. This is bad, really, really bad. These people are figuring out where the farms are in the area, the compounds like Dave's. They could find them next. They'd tracked Cory and left a threatening message. Her brother was in a battle last night. All the old fears she used to have while on the road come back in a swoosh of panic through her system. Her palms sweat, her heart races, and she feels lightheaded.

They agree to keep a tighter security schedule. This is the one thing that both camps agree on. Dave says that he'll start night runs to look for the highwaymen. John and Derek agree to do the same. Little does Dave know, Cory's apparently already been doing this.

"We'll set an ambush, like we talked about before, Derek," Dave says.

John nods, "As soon as we know if their claim of having six hundred men proves true or false. I want intel first."

"Agreed," Dave says with a firm nod. "Then we go on the offensive. Take them out."

"If they have that many men," Herb speculates, "how could we ever defeat them? We'd be grossly outnumbered."

"Not necessarily," Kelly insists.

Reagan says, "I don't understand. How the hell would we not be outnumbered?"

"Let's just get the information on their numbers first. We verify that, then we go after them."

Reagan doesn't question him further but lets it go. Paige is also curious why the men don't consider being so heavily outnumbered is a disadvantageous situation.

Dave and his men leave a short time later. She's sure they are in a hurry to get back to their farm. They have many people to keep safe and their compound to defend. Those men could come back tonight if they choose. She watches Henry hug Sam at the side of their truck, and there is something in the way that he touches her cheek that seems intimate to Paige. Her brother glares openly and hops down from the floor of the porch where he'd been sitting with her waiting for them to leave. Paige quickly follows and grabs his arm. She shakes her head.

"What are you doing?" she demands.

"Did you see that? The way he just touched her? Asshole," he hisses under his breath.

"You don't like him? I thought you wanted her to find someone and be happy."

Something Henry says causes Sam to laugh. It's a good thing. Her little friend does seem depressed. Simon's jaw flexes.

"Don't go over there and start something, Simon. You look like you want to."

"I want to do more than that," her brother confides through gritted teeth.

"You can't, Simon," she tells him. "You have to let Sam decide for herself. She's an adult. We can't tell her she isn't allowed to be with Henry. Besides, he seems nice."

"Nice," he says with a snort.

Dave's men mount up and leave. At least Sam stays, which gives her some relief. Herb insists that her brother and Samantha both go and get some rest. Simon heads for the cabin. More accurately, he stomps away to the cabin in a huff of rage. Sam doesn't seem to notice and goes upstairs to her shared bedroom with Paige. The rest of the family proceeds to have a planning meeting about the highwaymen. Cory is ready to leave and find them by himself, but his brother manages to get him calmed down. Reagan is barely able to manage her own feelings, as well. John does less to calm his wife. He looks fit to be tied, too. Everyone is on edge, thirsty for revenge of their fallen friends and the many innocent people they've found murdered on the road. Paige is the only one who is ready and willing to flee to another area, somewhere maybe a few hundred miles away and start over there. This is the only way she knows to survive because it's what worked for her and her friends.

"Six hundred," John says with a heavy sigh. "That's a lot more than we'd figured."

"Too many," Reagan is quick to say.

Paige couldn't agree more. These people are well organized and have the numbers to wipe them all out.

"Dave's right," Derek says. "We need to find them first, find their permanent camp or house or farm or town, whatever they've got. We can't just go by some idiot they questioned. The guy could've been lying his ass off just to intimidate us."

"I agree," Kelly puts in. "We need more intel. We can't assume the numbers are right. We have to find them, scout it out first. Let's not plan an ambush just yet, not if they've got those kinds of numbers."

"We've fought worse odds," John says quietly.

Paige believes him to be ready to take off after them just like Cory. Those two barely keep their tempers in check most of the time anyway. John may be a loving father and devoted husband, but he's also a trained soldier and killer. Paige has seen his darker side. The ferocity with which he fights is only matched by the intensity of his feelings for protecting his family and the love he has for his wife.

"True," his brother agrees. "But this might bear further looking into."

"I still don't understand how we'd ever sack six hundred people, John," Reagan persists.

Her husband looks at Derek and then back at her without answering.

"What?" she asks.

"There are ways. Depending on what their compound looks like and how many of them there really are, we could do it."

Kelly adds, "Don't forget, Little Doc, there are people in town, Paul and K-Dog, allies of ours who will want to be involved, too. It's not just us few men with Dave's."

"True," she says but frowns heavily.

Paige isn't so sure if fifty of them, if that's a better number, could defeat six hundred.

"Simon told me that the two men they held for questioning were wearing Kevlar and night-vision and had good weapons," Derek says. "I think that's something we need also to consider."

"They're more organized than most we've come up against, too," Cory adds.

"Right," John says. "They're organized, outfitted for the job, and have mobility. It won't be easy."

"What are our other options, other than fighting them?" Sue asks.

"We allow them to continue to kill people, and when they accidentally discover the farm, kill us, too," John snarls.

He is losing his patience with them. Paige can see it in him that he wants this fight badly. He wants to eliminate the threat from their community.

Sue nods and refrains from commenting further.

Derek pats her hand on the picnic table and says, "We don't go in blind. We never do. Let's see if we can't set up an intel mission tonight. John, maybe you and Cory could go. I'll take watch duty with Kelly and Luke."

"I can help, too," Huntley says, standing near Cory.

"Good," Derek says, surprising Paige that he would do so. Huntley's only fourteen and a half. Having him on watch duty is a big responsibility.

"I could go tonight, too," Paige offers, wanting to help.

"Maybe tomorrow night if we don't find them," John allows.

The men go back to planning their mission for the night while Paige follows Reagan and her sisters to the garden where they weed and hoe it. The discussion while they work focuses on the highwaymen and concentrates on their concerns about their men battling it out with them. Hannah is even with them wearing dark sunglasses and a wide brim hat to shield her delicate eyes. She is worried about her husband and brothers-in-law. Reagan is concerned that John and Cory will engage these highwaymen tonight if they find them. Paige also has concerns about this. She's glad Simon was asleep during the meeting or else he might've wanted to tag along. Sue is unusually quiet, which leads Paige to assume she is too distressed to discuss the matter with them. She knows the feeling well. Just thinking about her brother being in harm's way last night when he was so far away makes her feel a panic attack coming on.

An hour later when they finish up, Paige is ready to start packing her bags and fetching her brother to leave with her. It's the first time since coming to the farm that her desire to run is this strong.

Chapter Eleven
Sam

Everything went along nicely that day. She rode with Huntley before dinner, helped the girls prepare the meal, played with the little ones, and successfully avoided seeing Simon until dinner was served. All in all, it was a good day on the farm. However, the next day went a lot worse. Actually, it could best be described in Sam's opinion as all hell breaking loose.

The men did not locate the highwaymen's lair last night, so they will go again tonight. Sam would like to tag along with them. She's also curious about these people who would attack the compound on Henry's farm and people on the road. She doesn't at all understand why they are doing it. There is enough pain and anguish in the world without adding more to it. So many questions surround these people. Where are their families? Is it just men living on their compound, wherever it is? Why are they attacking people?

"Grandpa's going to Fort Knox next week," Huntley says from the back of his paint mare.

They are riding through the woods about six miles from the farm. Cory is guiding them, and they are scouting for anything they can find that would give them a clue where the highwaymen are traveling and if they are close to their farm. The woods are dense and sometimes difficult to maneuver in, which Cory says could be a good place for people to hide. It scares her that they could be living this close to them and that they never knew it.

"Really?" Sam asks, surprised. "Why?"

G answers for him, which causes Huntley to roll his eyes. "He's going to see my dad. He wants to check on his health and his camp and see if they know anything about the attacks."

"Oh," Sam says. This will worry her. Grandpa shouldn't leave the farm on such a long trip. It's dangerous. The highwaymen are still out there, and he could be harmed or put in danger.

"I know, right?" G says, reading Sam's reaction so expertly. "Totally not worth the trip."

Gretchen is riding alongside her brother, who is quiet, probably thinking about the same thing Sam is questioning. She and Lucas have both become proficient riders and seem to enjoy it.

Cory calls to them from a hundred yards away in an open field. Sam takes the opportunity to bump her favorite mare into a gentle canter. The rest naturally follow suit since horses do not like to be left behind when traveling together. They trail after Cory into the woods again.

Her big brother hops down from his stallion and squats. Cory points to the ground in front of him. "Look here, Hunt. Tracks. This might be what we've been looking for."

Sam also dismounts to get a better look and hooks her reins to the low branch of a maple tree. Huntley is touching the ground in front of him.

"See here?" Cory instructs, pointing with a stick. "They're not that fresh, but you can see them anyway. I'd say four-wheelers, maybe three or four. There's also human footprints, many different sets."

"And broken twigs on some of the trees," Lucas says as he touches one near them. "Yeah, not fresh. Probably a few months old if I were to guess."

"How do you know that?" his sister asks.

"Look, G, the branch is no longer green inside, but brown and dead looking."

"Hm," Gretchen says in response.

Huntley tells Cory, "No small prints. No children or women."

Cory nods, "Good. I was hoping you'd notice that, too."

Sam asks, "Think it's them?"

"Could be. Let's follow it," Cory says.

They all mount up again, and this time Sam rides next to Cory.

"Where does this go?" she asks of their new path.

"Not sure," he says. "I think it will eventually run into Pleasant View, but it looks like they took a turn west up ahead."

Sam spots the area he means where it opens back up into a short patch of what was probably a hay field at one time. They ride through the field and end up going slightly north into another section of forest. There are clouds on the horizon which look like they may become displeased with the world and dispense rain later today, but she hopes it holds off until they get back home.

"Keep your heads up," he warns. "Watch for signs of danger."

Sam nods firmly, sits deeper into her saddle, and tightens her reins. The mare responds immediately by slowing her pace and stepping gingerly around a fallen tree branch. Horses intuit a human's anxiety and react in accordance with their rider.

They follow the broken branches, footprints and smashed down flora for probably two miles until it comes to a road, or what's left of a road.

"Wait here with G and watch our backs, Sam," he orders and motions for Luke and Huntley to follow him.

Sam knows he is being cautious of them all going out into the open. She watches as they ride down the road that is merely the suggestion of blacktop now, nature having taken root and sprung many offspring. Her mare prances twice beneath her, but Sam is able to bring her under thumb easily enough. She pats her neck for her good behavior.

"This is freaking crazy," G whispers to her with wide, hazel eyes.

"Why?"

"What the hell are we gonna do if we run into them?"

Sam doesn't answer but looks away. She knows what they'll do. If they are spotted, it will end in a fight. If they aren't seen, then they will return to the farm unharmed. That is precisely how scouting missions go. They never know what the outcome will be, but they are all heavily armed.

Huntley canters back to them and lets them know that it's safe and that Cory wishes to continue. She and G join the group, and they keep going.

"The path shoots up through here," Cory says as he pushes his stallion up a steep hill.

"Lean way down on him, G," she instructs her since she is newer to riding. "That's it. Just like that. He'll follow along. Don't pull back on his reins. Give him his head. He knows what to do. He'll follow me. Hang onto the saddle horn with your hands and with your thighs on his sides. Lay down on his neck if you have to. He's not gonna run off or spook. He doesn't want to be left behind."

Sam guides her horse up the treacherous bank around trees and dense brush and avoiding bothersome rocks. It must be close to a half mile climb. By the time she reaches the top, Sam is practically laying on her own horse's neck the hill is so vertical. Luke brings up the rear, and he and his sister both look surprised that they are still alive when they reach the top of the long incline. Luke wanted to go with them this morning when they set off after Cory caught a few hours of sleep. He'd spent most of his night on the road with John. When Gretchen found out her brother was going, she'd started begging to go, too. Sam already knew that she was going because she discussed it last night with Cory when she awoke right before dinner. The aromas of Hannah and Sue's cooking had brought her out of a deep slumber. Not such a bad way to wake up in her opinion. Simon hadn't looked like he slept as well as she did because his hair stood on end and his clothing was rumpled. That is definitely not how Simon prefers to present himself. However, after dinner, he'd gone into Doc's office with him to discuss the fatal shooting of the woman from Dave's camp. He was distressed and wanted to know what they could've done better. Sam doesn't think there was anything they could have done to prevent that outcome from happening. She'd been shot twice, once in the shoulder, the other in her abdomen. She bled out before Uncle Scott and Simon could even work on her, cardiac arrest setting in. Nothing was going to fix her. He can't let things go, though. He never does. This is one thing she hates about Simon. It is also what keeps them apart if she were to speculate on it.

Sam really hadn't thought they'd find any trails since the guys have been going out from different locations; the condo village, both towns, their neighbors also hunting, and most importantly Dave's men and the men on the McClane farm and not spotted them yet. This could be another dead end, but it does seem like quite a few people were traveling this trail.

They ride for another half hour before Cory's fist shoots up, ordering them to stop. He spins his stallion and charges everyone to turn around. They do so, and he leads them a half mile back the way they came.

He vehemently whispers, "Dismount!"

Everyone gets off their horses.

"What's going on?" Sam asks, since she was behind Cory, Huntley, and also G. She and Luke were bringing up the rear this time.

"I saw a camp down below. A house and three, small log homes. We need to check it out better."

"G and Huntley, you guys wait here and watch our backs," Cory commands quietly, getting nods. G looks very concerned about this. "You'll be fine. Hunt, use your bird call, the hawk, if there's danger coming."

"Yes, sir," Huntley says.

He can copy many animal sounds, Sam has learned. His mimicry skills are bar none.

She follows Cory with her rifle slung over her shoulder like his. Luke has his own out front in the ready with two hands. She doesn't know a lot about him, but he seems like a man who can take care of himself and especially his little sister.

They come to a slight incline and Cory has them belly crawl to the top. She slides in beside him and pulls her binoculars from her backpack. Luke and Cory do the same, and they all spy on the small village below them.

"Four-wheelers," Luke whispers. "Three of them."

"Motorcycle over there on the side of that shed," Cory says.

"A van and a car," she points out.

Cory says, "This isn't six hundred people. This can't be them."

"Unless that guy was lying and this is all there is to the group," Luke says.

Sam considers both options. "There are kids over there playing. And I see a woman hanging clothes out to dry on a line."

"I see them, too," Cory remarks. "No men, though."

"How the heck were they taking ATV's and vehicles on that path we just went?" Luke asks.

"The tracks stopped down near the road," Cory explains. "I came this way on a hunch. There has to be a driveway in somewhere on the other side of their camp."

"Oh, I see horses," Sam remarks as soon as she spots three horses in a small corral.

"I never saw their tracks," Luke says.

"Me, neither," Cory adds. "They have another way in. We just stumbled on their camp by accident."

"We should head back and tell the others what we've seen."

"Yes," Luke agrees, and they shimmy down the hill and jog to the horses.

They ride back at a more vigorous pace, which the horses love because they know they are going back to their farm. Cory skirts around the steep hill and takes them another way, circumventing the need to ride vertical going head first. Luke and G seem relieved. When they arrive, John is in the barnyard using the portable mill cutting slabs of barn siding for repairs, which still aren't finished from the tornado damage. The family also hasn't completed the chicken coop yet, either. With the highwaymen issue, there is just never enough time to get it all done.

Cory relays what they've seen near the back porch where they have gathered the family to listen. Everyone seems as puzzled as they were at the discovery.

"It was very well hidden," Cory says.

"Yeah, it was," Luke adds. "That was not a location anyone would ever look for someone. They had to be miles from the nearest road."

"We also didn't run into anyone doing perimeter checks, standing guard or perimeter fencing," Cory says.

"We'll run over there tonight and try to find their access point," John says. "We need more information on this group."

"Right," Cory says with a nod. "They didn't look familiar. I've never seen them in town. Have you, Sam?"

"No, never," she concurs. "I didn't recognize any of them. And their men weren't there. That was weird, too. Unless they were out hunting."

"Could be a possibility," Kelly says. "Let's get back to work. We'll discuss this further after dinner later and set a schedule for another run tonight to check it out."

"Got it," Cory says, "I'll help you finish that wood, John."

"Thanks," he returns.

"Hey, Simon," Reagan says, gaining his attention. "Can you run up to my room and get that book on osteopathic manipulative treatment."

"Yes, ma'am," he utters and turns to go immediately.

"Oh, and bring down the second-floor trashcans, please. I don't think I can do those stairs one more time today," she jokes and rubs her ever-growing stomach.

"Yes, ma'am. And you probably shouldn't."

"Oh, I don't know, Simon," Sue says in a teasing voice. "I'm getting anxious to see the little guy. We might think about making her jog up and down the stairs a few times each hour."

"That is highly illogical. You should be careful and not run up and down the stairs at all," Simon lectures. "Walking would be more prudent…"

"Don't be a dork, Simon," Reagan criticizes.

Simon leaves on a scowl, realizing he is never going to get anywhere with this. Sam smirks and is glad he left. She doesn't want to spend a lot of time around him right now. Her feelings are torn. She really likes Henry, but she doesn't know if it will ever be more than just a friendship and Sam knows he wants more. He's made that very clear.

"Doesn't matter," Reagan says, still thinking about running the stairs. "I'd probably fall on my fat ass."

"Hey!" John scolds his wife. "I like your ass just the way it is."

This causes everyone, including Grandpa, to laugh out loud. John never swears. The curse sounds funny on him. For good measure, he pulls her close and kisses her. Then he does the unthinkable and pats her bottom in front of everyone.

"More to love," he says with an ornery smirk and a quick double raising of his eyebrows at the crowd observing them.

"Gross," Huntley says and walks away.

"John!" Reagan corrects with feisty anger. "I'm a fat cow. You're just being nice. And don't worry about my ass. Fat or not, I'm never letting you get near me again after this kid gets out."

"Yeah, sure," he says cockily. "I can't keep you off of me. It's so ridiculous. I always say, 'no, babe, not tonight' but you never take no for an answer."

"This is gettin' deep," Kelly jokes.

"And rather personal," Grandpa remarks with a chuckle.

Everyone laughs again. Reagan is outraged and backhands her husband's stomach. He just flinches and holds onto her small hand. Then he jerks it to his mouth and presses a kiss there.

The screen door to the kitchen slams against the wall of the house, startling everyone. Sam even turns to look in time to see Simon flying out of the house. His face is full of anger and rage. His eyes are wild.

"You son-of-a-bitch!" he roars and comes off the back porch, missing all the stairs and instead vaulting the railing like he's running hurdles in a track meet.

He barrels toward Cory and shoves him.

"What the…?" Cory manages to get out before Simon punches his best friend in the face.

Cory goes down. He goes down hard and does not get back up.

"What the fuck, Simon?" Kelly yells and shoves him back from his brother.

"He's out cold," John remarks as the rest of the family circles around Cory on the ground.

He is coming to, shaking his head, and sitting up.

"What…?" he mumbles, then startles. "Damn."

Simon lunges forward, but John shoots out an arm to hold him back. Of all the people on the farm, Simon would be the last one that any of them would peg to knock Cory out cold. He's not as big or strong or usually as lethal and prone to sudden spurts of violence. He just proved everyone wrong, very wrong.

"Get up!" Simon shouts angrily.

"What's going on, Simon?" John asks as things escalate.

Cory is getting back on his feet with Kelly's help. Simon is trying to break free of John to get to Cory again. It seems everyone is yelling and going crazy.

"Let me go!" Simon blurts fiercely and tries to get around John. "Come on, you bastard. Get up and fight me."

"Dangit, Simon! Stop! What's going on?" John yells loudly.

"Get out of my way, John!" Simon yells right back in a tone Sam has never heard from him before. It actually frightens her.

"Stop! Stop it!" John says. "Just calm down."

"No! Move!" Simon yells.

Cory is also trying to get around his brother, but he does not seem angry. He is definitely confused. All of them are now.

"He knows. He knows what he's done, and he's gonna pay for it. Now move!"

"No, calm the hell down, Simon," Kelly bellows.

"Yes, calm down, Simon," Derek joins in the melee in a more rational manner. He is hobbling with his crutches.

"I will not! Move it!" Simon continues to yell. "Get out of our way. We'll handle this like men."

John finally backs off, throwing his hands in the air with bewilderment, obviously seeing no point in trying to calm him down. Simon is acting completely irrational. Strange that he's always accusing her of this, although Sam has never outright physically attacked someone. Unless she were to count the night she slapped Simon in the face in the barn. That was pretty bad behavior, very irrational, indeed, but she did and still does believe he deserved it.

Kelly also stands aside, and Simon squares up on Cory ready to fight him. By the look of pure rage in his blue eyes, probably to the death.

"Bro, what the hell? Why the hell'd you punch me like that?" Cory asks.

"Put your hands up and fight," Simon orders.

Grandpa stands next to Sam and rests his hand on her lower back. She thinks he would like to lead her away, but Sam isn't going anywhere.

"No!" Cory shouts. "What the hell, man? Why'd you do that?"

"You know why, asshole," Simon swears, also uncharacteristic of him, especially in front of women.

"What?" Cory asks and rubs his sore jaw. "What the hell are you talking about?"

"You said you were my friend. You told me nothing was going on. You've been lying the whole time."

"What do you mean?" Cory asks and shoves back when Simon rushes him. "Stop it, Simon. Dude, I don't want to fight you. Tell me what's wrong."

Simon jabs and catches Cory in the side of his face before he can react in time. This is starting to piss Cory off, Sam can tell. He clenches his jaw tightly together and his eyes narrow.

"Cut it the fuck out, man. You'd better stop. Now!"

"No, fight me, asshole. You're gonna get your ass kicked, and you deserve it."

"Why? What the hell did I ever do to you?"

"You know what you did! Paige! My sister? Remember? Or do you screw around so much that you can't remember her?"

Everyone swings in one fluid motion to look at Paige, who is blushing and staring with her mouth wide open.

"Simon, stop this," she finally says uncomfortably.

"No, he brought this on himself, and I'm gonna kick his ass. Right now and in front of everyone. It's what you deserve."

"What are you talking about, man?"

"I told you to stay away from her, damn it! You lied. You said you weren't interested in her. You're a damn liar. I thought you were my friend."

"Simon," Paige says, but he interrupts.

"No! Don't defend him. He did this, and he'll take his ass whipping and not whine about it. Then I'm moving to town, and you're going with me. I told you to stay away from him."

"What do you mean?" she asks cautiously.

Simon jabs at Cory again. This time, Cory deflects it, which seems to piss Simon off more. Within seconds, they are in a locked embrace, but not one of affection. Simon is punching Cory in the side and the stomach. Cory is trying to block his friend but is mostly failing. Then they're on the ground in the dust and dirt, causing it to plume up around them. It goes on for a few minutes, too, this grappling. Simon finally gets on top of Cory and manages to punch him in the face again. Then again before Kelly pulls him away. In Cory's defense, Simon is in a rage, and Cory isn't fighting back much.

"You stay away from her, or I'll kill you the next time."

"For goodness sake, Simon! Just explain to all of us what's going on," Sue demands, her patience at an end.

"He's sleeping with my sister!" Simon shouts, spittle hitting his chin, which he wipes, leaving a smear of dirt there. Sam notices that his knuckles look bloody.

Cory is to his feet finally and dusting himself off. He looks mad but not as insane as Simon. There is blood dripping from his lower lip.

"What? I don't think so, honey," Sue says gently.

"No, he is. Ask him," he prods.

Sue asks, "Is that true, Cory?"

Cory doesn't answer right away but looks instead toward Paige. She, in turn, looks at everyone with flame red cheeks.

"I found a pregnancy test in her trashcan upstairs just now. I thought I'd be nice and empty hers, too. The test was used. There's only one reason she'd have that. And who the hell else would she be sleeping with?"

Grandpa steps forward and asks, "Is this true, son?"

Cory looks at Grandpa and must realize that the truth is not something he can escape and nods.

"Cory!" Kelly says with a loud exhale of disapproval. "What the hell, Cor? That's not cool, brother."

"I know," he admits and hangs his head. "I didn't mean for it to happen."

"Neither of us did. It just sort of happened."

"Seriously? It doesn't just sort of happen. It's a conscious choice one makes," Simon reminds everyone, the pitch in his voice going higher and higher with irrationality.

"We didn't mean for anyone to find out yet," Cory says.

"Or ever. It's over. It's never going to be something," Paige is quick to correct, leaving Sam and probably everyone else even more confused.

"No, that's not true," Cory says.

Simon tries to rush him again but is stopped by John.

"What do you mean?" Kelly asks. "Do you have feelings for her?"

"Yes, absolutely. I wouldn't have...I'm not..."

Simon laughs again, this time loudly and rudely, "Yeah, right! You are exactly like that. You use women for sex. You sleep around with women in town and neighbors and whoever you can. She doesn't mean any more to you than they did."

Cory looks angrier now than he had after Simon punched him, "Hey! Bullshit. That's not true. I do care for her. I wouldn't have done that if I didn't. I wouldn't have done that to her or you. I want…"

"No! Nope. No way," Paige interrupts, waving her hands, and steps toward Simon. "Don't say it. Look, everyone, it's over between us. We ended it. We didn't want everyone to know or anyone to get hurt by it. It was just a one-time thing, and it's over, and we're both really sorry to all of you for this…misunderstanding."

Cory looks surprised to hear this, leaving Sam to believe that Paige isn't quite telling the truth.

"Then why did you feel the need for the pregnancy test?" Simon demands.

"Was it positive?" Cory asks, his voice painfully and transparently hopeful.

"No!" Paige says with a nervous chuckle. "I wouldn't even have taken it had Reagan not made me think I could be because I passed out. It's not positive. So you see? That makes it even easier to end this once and for all."

"No, it doesn't," Cory argues.

Now Sam feels as if she is in the middle of a very private couple's fight. This just keeps getting more and more awkward.

"Oh, yes, it does!" Paige counters.

"That's not what I want, and you know it," Cory says with pleading brown eyes.

"Too bad!" Simon yells and steps into Cory's space again. John moves him back.

"Simon, you don't understand," Cory explains.

"I don't need to. I know everything there is to know about you. You aren't going to be with my sister. You're the wrong man for her. She deserves better."

"Back 'er down, little brother," Kelly says with anger, warning Simon that he is going too far.

"Easy, bro," John says, staying his friend.

"He's never going to have Paige. He's never going to have my blessing, and as long as I'm in charge of her- and I *am*- then it's not happening. He can find some other woman in town," Simon informs them.

"I want your sister..."

"Never happening..."

"Wait!" Paige shouts above them but is still ignored. "Don't I get a say in this?"

"No! She's moving with me to town first thing tomorrow," Simon tells Cory.

"Simon, man, don't be like this," Cory says. "I'm trying to explain..."

"I don't want to hear any more of your bullshit lies," Simon swears again. "I repeatedly asked you if you were interested in her and you denied it."

Hannah is going to go and get her rolling pin if they all keep up with the cussing.

"I'm not lying..."

"Bull!" Simon blurts. "You don't care about anything but getting laid."

"No, that's not true. It's also not fair," Cory argues.

John says, "That's true, Simon. You aren't even giving him a chance. He's your best friend."

"Was. He's no longer my best friend. He's not even a good friend. Not after this."

"Simon, damn it!" Cory says, his frustration showing as he rakes his hand through his messy, long hair. "I'm in love with her, bro!"

Everyone gasps. This is quite the declaration, one done in front of the whole family. Paige even looks stunned.

"Yeah, got that?" he says to everyone. "I'm in love with her. Paige, I love you. I want to marry you. I've told you that a dozen times that I want to marry you."

"No fucking way," Reagan expresses her shock.

"Reagan," Hannah corrects softly. The f-word must've sent her over the edge. Sam actually smiles. She's happy for Cory. He needed something or someone to love. He needed more than just his dog to heal his poor, broken heart from Em's death.

"No way is right," Simon states firmly. "That's never happening. Not while I'm still in charge of her."

"Uh...what?" Paige asks with great exaggeration. "You aren't in charge of me. Nobody is. I'm in..."

"Wrong," Simon says. "I am in charge of you. It's the 1700s again. You're my sister, my only living blood relative, and I'm the only male relative you have. I am absolutely in charge of you, especially your safety. Even if that means keeping you safe from making bad decisions. You aren't marrying him."

"Uh, no, but we can talk about this later since you're acting like some sort of medieval tyrant. I know I'm not getting married, but not because you say I can't. I don't want to. I don't want to marry anyone."

"I know you're scared," Cory says. "But it's ok, Red. I'm not going anywhere. You won't lose me. I should've told you how I feel. I shouldn't have waited. But we can fix this. We can be married. Right here on the farm would be great."

Simon lunges again, but John is there to stop it.

"You know what, Simon?" Cory taunts angrily. "Why don't we talk about your love life, huh? How 'bout we all have a round circle meeting in front of the whole family about you?"

"Stay out of my business, Cory!" Simon roars. "You've already done enough. You're a liar and a fraud and a shitty friend. Don't even think we're changing the subject now."

"No, we can, and we are!" Cory laughs. "Why don't we get into this right now in front of everyone? Why don't we discuss why Samantha left?"

"Shut your mouth!" Simon yells, pointing angrily.

"Why don't we talk about why she lives on Henry's farm now and not here? Also, why don't we get it out in the open that she was kissing him the other day, and you are throwing your whole life away while she makes a new one for herself? Let's get into that, right? Let's talk this thing out in front of the whole damn family. You want to expose Paige and me. Let's talk about your love life."

There is another sharp gasp that ripples through the crowd again, and Paige looks at Sam. Everyone does. Her cheeks are burning. Simon is also staring at Sam. Then he turns back to Cory.

"Shut up. I'm warning you," Simon says with a sneer and points his finger at Cory for good measure.

"No, we're just getting started. You want to humiliate Paige and me in front of everyone. Let's talk about you for a second."

"You say one more thing…"

"Tell everyone why Samantha left, Simon," Cory taunts.

"That's it…" Simon growls and shoves past John.

Then they are in the dirt again.

Chapter Twelve
Paige

Her belongings have been moved to the cabin, care of her brother. Cory will temporarily sleep in the basement with the children, and she will reside in the cabin with Simon. The family hadn't put in opinions on the matter, but had, instead, let them work it out themselves. Basically, Simon decided it, and Paige hadn't argued because he was already running on a short, clipped fuse. Earlier today was a mess, a nightmare of epic proportions. She can't believe she was so stupid and careless as to have left that damn pregnancy test in her wastebasket. She should've taken it out in the woods and buried it like the albatross it had become. Now everyone knows about them.

"Simon, we need to talk," she says with caution as she approaches him carefully in the med shed.

After the fight, the men had finally got him calmed down enough that he was just barely more rational. His lower lip was cut, but she's not sure if Cory ever actually punched him. She doesn't think he did. There was a lot of wrestling on the ground, though. She definitely got to see a different side of her brother. She never knew that the men put them through such extensive hand to hand fighting training until she saw it for herself. She also had no idea that Simon was so strong. It was quite the scene to behold. It was also violent and horrible. She'd just wanted it to stop and was glad when it did.

"There is nothing left to talk about, Paige," Simon retorts angrily and returns to his work at the counter.

130

It bothers her that his knuckles are bruised and scraped. It also troubles Paige that they got that way from hitting Cory, who has a bruise on his cheek, a cut lip, and a black eye. She hasn't even had a chance to talk with him yet. Right after the melee, Simon ordered her to pack her belongings so he could carry them to the cabin. When she paused for a mere nanosecond, he'd sprinted upstairs and started without her. Paige didn't want to fight with him or further hurt him and figured the family wouldn't like the fact that she slept with Cory, so she complied. She is completely humiliated. Paige knows how Doc feels about this subject. He is old-fashioned, and this is his farm.

"I want to talk about how you reacted," she beseeches her brother.

"I reacted exactly like any brother would when he's been betrayed by his sister and his best friend."

This stings hard. Paige actually flinches. "Sorry. I'm really sorry. I didn't mean for it to happen at all. It just did. And I knew it was wrong, and I didn't want you to get hurt. I knew it would be hard to hear. I told Cory it was over. I didn't want this to happen. It's exactly why I ended it."

"But you shouldn't have lied to me. You broke my trust, Paige," he retorts angrily.

"I know, Simon," she says, her voice cracking. "And I feel like shit about it, too. It wasn't like I wanted to tell you about me and Cory."

He turns to her, setting down his jar of whatever salve he was working on. A tear slips down her cheek as she looks at his split lip. This is all her fault. Everyone is in pain, physically and emotionally tonight, and she is definitely to blame.

"I didn't mean to hurt you," she says, tears flowing unfettered now. "I love you, Simon. I'm so sorry."

Her brother rushes to her and pulls Paige into his arms. He rubs his hand up and down her back. His embrace is comforting, although she knows it is only a temporary respite from the pain they are both feeling.

"I'm sorry, Simon," she repeats with true regret.

Simon pulls back and places a hand on either side of her face, cradling her gently. "I will forgive you, Paige. But not him."

"Simon, it's not his fault," she says, trying to explain.

Her brother shakes his head and walks back to the counter where he was working.

"Don't. Don't defend him. He's not worth your defense."

"But..."

"No, we're done talking about him. You should go to bed and get some rest. We have a lot to do tomorrow."

"No, please, Simon," she pleads. "I don't want to move to town. This is our home. We're safe here. We need this place."

"No, we don't," he retorts.

"I'm not going. I won't move to town."

He swings around on his stool and looks at her with disbelief. "We are moving. That's final."

"No, I get an opinion on this. You know I'm never going to leave you, but I don't want to move from the farm. I've thought a lot lately about running away with you, you know, because of the highwaymen and the danger they pose, but I like it here. I feel safe for the first time in years. Well, mostly safe, and I don't want to leave the family. If it comes to a fight here on the McClane farm, I want to be here for that. I could never leave them to fight without us. Plus, it's safer here than out there or in town. It's more hidden away. I feel a heck of a lot safer than I have since it all happened."

"I'll keep you safe."

"I know that. I'm not saying that you wouldn't or that you can't, but there's more to this than just being safe. You know that. I love the McClanes. I want to be here with them. They're our family now, Simon."

He snorts. "Some of them are."

"No, he is, too," she argues softly, not wanting to upset her brother further. He's been through a lot today.

"Don't say that."

"He is. Cory loves you. What happened was just stupid. We were just being stupid. You know how it is now. You get really lonely. That's probably why it happened. He lost his little sister. I was lonely. He was lonely. It just happened."

He actually looks like he's trying to wrap his brain around her theory. His eyes drop to the floor.

"And you do, too. You must. It's not normal to go through our whole lives without the companionship of someone. Someday, you'll find someone, too. Unless you already have."

132

Simon's blue eyes jump to hers. "You know I haven't."

She treads lightly but has to know, "Simon, what did Cory mean about Sam? He was acting like you drove her away or something bad happened between you."

"Nothing bad happened. I told you this before."

"But what did he mean, Simon?"

"I don't want to get into this right now," Simon quickly says.

Paige decides to let it drop. She goes back to the move. "I want you to think about moving to town and reconsider. I don't want to move. Cory and I are done. I promise. I won't ever be with him again. I don't want your permission, but I also don't want to upset you."

"Do you love him, too?" he asks, flooring her.

Paige clears her voice. "Um, no. No, Simon. I didn't want a relationship with him. He knew that. It was just a mutual, temporary companionship."

"Are you sure? You seem hesitant to answer. Is it because you don't want to tell me?"

She swallows hard and says, "No. I have come to like Cory as a friend. I don't hate him anymore."

"Obviously."

Paige frowns and says, "Right. But I don't want to get married to him. I'm glad the family isn't forcing the issue."

"I wouldn't get ahead of yourself. I don't know what they're saying."

"Oh," she whispers.

"Go get some rest," he says and turns back around. "I'll be out later."

"I'm going to talk to Sam first. She wanted me to visit with her before I go to bed."

There is a long pause, so long that Paige turns to leave because she doesn't think he will say anything. Then he does, "Fine."

"Ok, great. See you in a little bit."

This time he doesn't answer, so she leaves the shed. Paige heads to the house and upstairs to Sam's room. She is thankful that the girls are not in the kitchen. She did, however, spy light coming from under Doc's office door, though, and heard voices in there.

She knocks softly and enters, "Hi, Sam."

Her little friend rises from the desk near the window and rushes to her, hugging Paige for a long time.

"Are you alright, Paige?" she asks with deep concern.

"Um… yeah. I guess. Don't have much of a choice."

"I know. Oh, this is so terrible!" Sam frets, her blue eyes threatening to spill the tears balancing there.

She sighs deeply and finally pulls back from her friend. They sit on her bed, or what was only a few hours ago her bed. Now it will be someone's bed because she will be sleeping in the cabin with Simon.

"Where's Cory? Do you know?" Paige asks.

"I haven't seen him since this afternoon. I know his things are in the basement. I went down to talk to him, see how he was doing, but he wasn't there."

"Did he leave the farm, go somewhere?"

"I think so. I'm not sure."

"Simon really hurt him."

Sam nods vigorously. "I know. I never would've guessed that Simon was strong enough to beat Cory."

"No, I didn't mean like that. I mean that Cory is hurting emotionally. I know he feels bad about this whole mess."

Sam rests her hand on Paige's and says, "You could've told me. I would've kept it a secret. That had to be terrible walking around with such a burden."

"Especially when he didn't want to keep it a secret."

"I'm so glad Cory loves you, Paige. I'm so happy for you two."

"Wait, that's not… I mean, Sam, we're not getting married or anything."

"Maybe you will. You never know," her delightfully optimistic friend says.

"I do know. I don't want to get married."

"Why not?" Sam asks. "He loves you. I can see it now. It all makes a lot more sense."

"What do you mean?"

Sam sighs softly and explains, "I've seen Cory looking at you. Like, a lot. Whenever he'd see me watching, he'd chuckle or roll his eyes like he thought you were a dork. But I saw through it. I kind of thought he liked you, but it didn't seem like it was mutual."

134

"It's not."

Sam tips her head to the side and gives Paige a look that lets her know that she doesn't believe her.

"Well, it's not mutual in the love department. I admit I'm attracted to him, but marriage is out of the question."

"Why? I don't get it."

Paige shrugs. "I don't ever want to get that close to someone. Not anymore. I've lost too many people, Sam. Besides, it's not like Cory is a cautious and careful person. He runs into battles like he's been waiting impatiently for one to strike up. You know how he is. Don't get me wrong. I like him. I actually like him a lot more than I thought I ever could, especially when I first met him. But he's going to get himself killed, and I'm not going to play the grieving widow. I've already played the grieving sister when I thought I'd never find Simon. I was the grieving daughter when I lost my parents. The grieving friend when I lost people on the road that I came to care about. No thanks. This world is hard now. I'm tired of feeling grief all the time."

"But he could live to be eighty. You're passing up on him because you're just afraid."

"Yes, I know. I am afraid. I admit it. But that doesn't mean I'm going to change my mind, either."

"Don't you love him back?"

Paige shrugs again. "I don't know. I don't let myself get that close. He's..."

She thinks in her head about all the adjectives that describe Cory: loyal, sexy, funny, ornery, fierce, bluntly honest, challenging. But she doesn't voice them. She doesn't want to give Sam a false sense of hope about their relationship. Or herself.

"Are you really moving into town across from the practice?" Sam asks, realizing that she's not getting further information on Paige's feelings.

"I hope not. I don't want to. I feel safer here than when we go to town."

Sam nods with understanding. "I heard Reagan and John talking about it. John is very much against you moving."

"I don't think he's pleased with my brother lately anyway."

"Why? What happened?"

"He drove you away?" Paige questions.

"Oh," Sam says after a heavy pause. "No, he didn't. It's not Simon's fault I left. It was mine."

"How do you mean?"

"If you knew Cory before the fall, would you have wanted to marry him then?" Sam asks, entirely avoiding Paige's line of questioning.

"What? I don't know. I doubt very much we would've ever met. We only did because of what happened. Same as you and my brother or any of the rest of the family."

"Say Cory was going to the same college as you on some sort of sports scholarship. Would you have dated him?"

"I don't think we would've run in the same circles."

Sam smiles and says, "Maybe you had to tutor him in something…"

"Etiquette?" Paige jokes.

Sam laughs quietly. "Yes, something like that."

"Cory's not a dumb jock. He's actually really smart."

"I know that, silly. I'm just saying for instance. What if you met him at a college party then. Would you have gone out with him?"

Paige thinks about this for a minute. She was dating someone back then. He was definitely nothing like Cory. He was perfect on paper. He turned out to be a real scumbag who slept with her roommate and friend.

"I doubt it," she finally answers. "He's not my type."

"Doesn't sound like it after what we found out about you two today."

Paige shakes her head and rolls her eyes. "Yeah."

"I bet you would've. I bet he would've asked you out enough times that you would've relented. He's like that…"

"So annoying!" Paige complains.

"Then you would've gone on a date, probably something strange since we're talking about Cory."

"A ribs eating competition," Paige teases.

"No," Sam exclaims with a laugh. "He's not that bad. He probably would've taken you hiking or fishing or something. He told me once that he always liked doing stuff like that. He went with his dad a lot and sometimes took Em."

136

Paige lets her gaze fall to her hands in her lap. His tough, exterior shell keeps the pain of his own losses concealed so well that she forgets how many loved ones he's also buried.

"He said that Kelly would come home on leave and go hunting with them. They even took trips up north to hunt big game."

"I can see that," Paige acknowledges.

"Then he would've charmed the pants off you, Paige Murphy," Sam says. "Oh, geesh! Sorry, I didn't mean it like that!"

This time they both laugh. After such a horrible and humiliating day, laughing for a moment feels good.

"That was brutal," Paige admits with a smile.

"I don't think you should discount Cory's good intentions. He may know you better than you think he does. And he does love you. Of that much, I'm sure. Cory isn't the kind of man to throw words like that around."

"Yes, I'd say so since today was the first time I've heard of it."

"I thought he said he's been asking you to marry him quite frequently."

Paige nods and explains, "Yes, he has, but he's never outright said that he loves me. He implied it a few times, but never said it."

"Well, he said it today all right!" Sam boasts. "I think you should consider his proposal. He's a good man, Paige. And he wants to commit to you. I mean, come on! That's kinda' hard to find, even at the end of the world!"

She and Paige share a laugh again, ending up on their backs on the bed.

"Men are so much trouble," she complains.

Sam rolls to her side and says. "Some more than others."

"Sorry about whatever is going on with you and my brother."

Sam nods and says, "I know. I don't hold anything against you, Paige. You'll always be my sister."

This revelation brings tears to Paige's eyes. She's never had a sister. Now she has a house full of them. Hearing Sam say this is almost as poignant and meaningful as Cory's declaration of love.

"You can tell me. I can also keep a secret," Paige offers and strokes Sam's hair back from her forehead, tucking it behind her ear.

"There really isn't much to tell, not any more than you already know."

"What about Henry? Do you love him? I guess that's out in the open now, too. I didn't know you were interested in him."

Sam frowns and says, "I don't know if I am. I'm very confused right now."

"That's ok. You're allowed to be. You've been through so much. You deserve to be confused. And you deserve to be happy. If you can't find happiness here on the farm, then you should seek it elsewhere. It's only fair, Sam."

She nods, tears forming in her eyes again. Paige rests her hand against Sam's soft cheek.

"Thanks, Paige, for understanding."

"What are sisters for?"

Her friend smiles and nods. They talk a while longer before Paige leaves her room. When she goes back downstairs, there is still a meeting taking place in Doc's study. She tiptoes. Paige doesn't want to discuss her relationship with Cory with anyone else in the family, and she's sure there are a lot of people who are curious about it.

She is almost out the back door when Hannah's voice stops her. She comes from the mudroom holding an armload of linens. Paige had been hoping that most everyone had gone to bed already.

"Hey, Paige," she says, knowing full well that it is she who is trying to make a hasty escape out the back door.

"Oh, hi, Hannie," she mumbles awkwardly.

"I was just getting you some fresh linens for your bed out in the cabin," she says, handing the stack of clean bed sheets to her.

For some reason, Hannah's kind gesture of thinking about Paige's comfort almost breaks her numb state.

"Thanks, Hannah. That was nice."

"No problem," she answers and walks around Paige to the kitchen.

"Need help?" she offers, not wanting to be rude after Hannah just thought of her needing clean sheets.

"No, not really," she answers. "Have a seat a moment. I just made tea."

Paige pauses a moment. Then she says, "Sure," although she'd like to turn Hannah down and flee to the privacy of the cabin. Facing the family is not something she's ready to do.

138

She takes a seat at the long island as Hannah places a mug of steaming hot tea in front of her.

"A good hot beverage makes everything feel better," Hannah informs her.

Paige would like to tell her that tea, coffee, or even a glass of bourbon isn't going to fix her woes. She sips the tea anyway.

"Thanks, Hannah," she says.

"Rough day?" she inquires.

Paige laughs, chokes on her tea and says, "Just a little."

Hannah takes a seat across from her and stirs her own tea. "I figured you two wouldn't be able to carry on much longer without someone finding out."

"What? You knew?" Paige asks with surprise.

"I had my suspicions. Cory's like my little brother. I knew he was in love with someone. He's been acting differently for a while now. I figured it was you. I'm just sorry it all came out the way it did. It had to be difficult to have all of your problems and personal issues bared to the whole family."

Paige nods, remembers that she must respond with words and says, "Yes, it was pretty rough. I feel like a complete idiot."

"No, don't feel that way."

"I'm sure everyone is angry and...disgusted with my behavior. And your grandfather? Oh, good grief! I don't think I could possibly face him."

Hannah chuckles and says, "You think this is the first time Grandpa's ever been surprised by things around here? He figured it out about me and Kelly before everyone else knew. At his age, I think he's kind of seen it all."

Paige smiles and says, "Yes, but I don't want to disappoint him. And I certainly don't want everyone to think badly of me, especially him."

"I think you're safe," Hannah says and reaches for her hand. Her hands are small but warm and comforting. "Don't worry, Paige. Nobody is going to have a negative opinion of you, dear. I think Cory might be in a hotter seat than you."

Her turn of phrase makes Paige smile, but then it fades as she realizes what Hannah is saying.

"Wait, that's not fair. I don't want Cory getting into a lot of trouble over this. It wasn't his fault."

"I know. Trust me, I know this well. Cory is a reputable man of good character. But he does really love you."

"If it would help, I'll move to town with Simon like he wants to."

"Do you want to move?"

"No!" Paige whispers vehemently. "I really don't want to, but if the family is going to punish Cory for what we've done, then I'll move to town. I don't want to leave here, but I would. I just feel safe here."

"We don't want you to move, either, Paige," Hannah reassures her. "Nobody does. It's just that Grandpa is set in his ways. If Cory wants to marry you, then he'll likely want the two of you to get married. Or else stop…well, you know, stop doing that."

Paige blushes and is glad that Hannah is blind, although she is quite sure that her friend knows of her embarrassment. It seems that Hannah knows everything about everyone. Paige feels like she did that time back in high school and she got caught sneaking out one night to meet her friends. She'd gone to a bonfire, even drank a beer, and kissed a boy. The exit wasn't the problem. The re-entry is what got her busted by her mother, who'd just come home from a night shift at the hospital. She'd not been too happy. Paige had been grounded for a month. She'd spent the time feeling more and more foolish as the punishment had gone on. It was a life-changing month. She'd never wanted to displease her mother again. Not because she got caught, but because she didn't like the look of disappointment in her mother's eyes that night. She never wanted to see that again. Now she feels the same way about the McClane family. They probably think she's some sort of harlot that came to the farm to seduce the first single man she found. It's all completely irrational, but it doesn't stop the idea from entering her mind and weighing down her conscience.

"Of course. It was already over before today. I had no intention of carrying on anymore with Cory."

"Do you have feelings for him?"

"Yes, he's a good person. I like him just fine. I just don't want marriage and kids and all that."

140

Hannah doesn't say anything to this but is silent. She sips her tea and nods. Paige wishes she could read her mind.

"I know he's your brother-in-law, but I just don't want to be married."

"Ok, that's your choice. We won't judge you for it."

"Thanks," Paige acknowledges.

She talks for a while longer with Hannah, all the while hoping not to see the look of disappointment in her sightless eyes. It never comes, but Paige wonders if Hannah isn't just a little disenchanted with her that she has no desire to marry Cory. She doesn't want to hurt him.

"Have you seen him?" Paige asks of Cory.

Hannah replies, "Yes, he's gone. Went to check out that camp they found. John went with him."

"Oh," she says softly. Paige wishes she could've talked with him before he left. She feels dreadful about this whole situation, especially if he is taking the brunt of the blame for this.

"He'll be back in the morning," Hannah supplies.

"Right."

She leaves Hannah to her tea and heads to the cabin for the night. Paige goes to her bed in their little cabin, the place she used to sleep and until this afternoon, Cory slept before her. It smells like him, even with the clean sheets care of Hannie. His manly scent lingers in the pillow and mattress as if he has permanently left his mark there. She tosses and turns for what seems like hours, the day's events playing over and over again in her mind. What a disaster. She is so humiliated by the revealing of such a personal circumstance. Cory hadn't seemed embarrassed at all. In fact, other than the fight with Simon and the pain of lying to her brother, Cory had acted like he was relieved. This bothers her. He needs to let it all go.

She finally falls asleep with a good dose of regret and guilt riding along the edges of her consciousness.

Chapter Thirteen
Cory

"Are you going to talk to him?" John asks beside him as they lie on the ground.

"I'll try. I don't know if he'll listen," Cory answers. They've been spying on the camp for the last sixteen hours. They have lain on the forest floor all night, morning, and now into the afternoon. Movement at the camp has been almost constant. Men returned last night around midnight. There were about thirty of them that came in on motorcycles, a couple of trucks, and ATV's. He and John circumvented their camp and found their entry point. Then they'd come back to their original post and waited for something to happen. So far, that hasn't been much. However, the men had unloaded boxes and crates of materials from the backs of the trucks. They looked to have contained random items from clothing and canned goods to car supplies and building materials. They undoubtedly could've been looted from people on the road somewhere, but they also could've been lifted from stores or abandoned homes. All totaled there are about sixty people living in the camp that they've accounted for.

"You have to try," John tells him. "He's your best friend."

Cory sighs and says, "I know, man. I didn't think this would happen. I wanted to talk to him about his sister, but I couldn't get her on the same page with me."

"Yeah, and he was already in a mood," John says.

"Really? I hadn't talked to him much since he got home."

John pauses as he looks intently through his binoculars. Then he finally says, "He's been in a funk since Sam moved. He was complaining to Reagan that Sam shouldn't be allowed to go back to

Dave's to live because the compound was attacked. He wants us to stop her from returning. He doesn't think it's safe over there."

"Sounds like they handled those assholes just fine," he returns. "Dave said that nobody made it through their gates or fences. Seems safe enough. Seemed even safer than our place when I was over there visiting last week."

"I agree. He's just being overprotective."

"Gee, wonder why," Cory mocks with derision.

"Yeah," John agrees quietly.

Cory points, "Over there."

It looks like the men are awake again and joining the women. If they leave, he and John plan on following them.

"Got it," John says as he follows Cory's viewpoint.

They continue to watch the men moving around. It seems like they are preparing for the day ahead.

"Do you know something that the rest of us don't about why Sam left?" John asks.

"No, not really. It's just my hypothesis."

John just says, "Hm."

The men are throwing gear into their truck and on the backs of two ATV's and one motorcycle. A woman walks forward and hands over a satchel to one man, who promptly backhands her across the cheek.

"Asshole," Cory says.

"Agreed."

Other women come forward to comfort and shield her. Another man shouts, and the women disperse. A few of them gather the children who were playing in the yard and take them inside the smaller house.

"Interesting," Cory remarks.

"Uh-huh," John agrees. "Let's go. They're getting ready to move."

He runs alongside John, keeping pace easily and covering a lot of ground in a short amount of time. They make it to their truck, well-concealed in a thicket of brush and long grass. John fires it up and carefully backs out. Then they are speeding along a back road to circle the broad expanse of woods and make it to the entry point of the hidden forest camp. They pull off about a half mile from the camp's concealed entrance and into a driveway which leads to an abandoned farm on the opposite side of the road. John drives slowly back the long, gravel driveway and pulls around behind a barn. They will be able to see the hidden entrance to the forest dwellers. Cory isn't sure why those people aren't living on this clearly empty farm instead of in the middle of the woods. They could've developed the farm into what the McClanes have, a place that would flourish with a little hard labor and some livestock. John puts it in park but doesn't cut the engine. They will wait to hear or see if those men pull out onto the road.

"Did you really see her kissing Henry?" John asks, still hung up on the issue of Sam and Simon.

"Uh, yeah," Cory answers uncomfortably. "I don't know how thrilled she was about it or if she likes him all that much, but he did kiss her. She didn't slug him, so maybe she might like him a little. Hell, what the shit do I know? I'm in love with a woman that can barely stand me."

"I'd say she can stand you," John teases.

"Enough to get in my pants all the time, but not enough to marry me."

His friend laughs. "She's just using you for sex, and you're complaining about it?"

Cory laughs, too. "Yeah, I guess I am."

"Sometimes they just need a nudge."

"Wow, what a couple of pussies we are," Cory jokes, getting more laughter out of John.

"I'm ok with that," his friend says. "As long as I got Reagan in the end, I was willing to do just about anything, even humble myself."

"I could get down on my knees in the back yard and beg her, and Paige would still deny me. She's got issues, bro."

"We all do," John retorts quietly.

"True," Cory says, knowing that John is likely thinking about his wife and what she's been through and what has made her the way she is.

They watch a few minutes more, and finally, the vehicles come pouring out the lane like rats coming up out of a sewer drain during a hard rain storm. John gives them a minute to get ahead and finally follows at a far distance. They are heading south.

144

"Keep an eye out," John warns him. "We don't know where they're going or if they're moving in a random pattern looking for people to rob."

"Or if this is even them," Cory says.

"Right," John agrees.

They drive for about ten miles until the vehicles ahead of them turn off to their left. Again, it is a hidden drive on a road that is not well-traveled or by the looks of it often used. John goes past the turn off point very slowly and then drives about a mile away where they stow the truck in an attached garage of a home with the garage door open. Then they sprint on foot back through the woods and fields and a small suburban neighborhood until they come to the hidden drive again. They stay in the woods so that they don't blow their cover. It doesn't take long before they locate the place the men have gone. There is a small log home nestled in the woods. There are quite a few compact, tiny shacks around it in the woods. They don't appear to be very old but, instead, recently built. The ground around them looks freshly cleared out. He and John hunker down to spy on them.

The men have gone into the primary log home structure, but occasionally one or two come outside to retrieve things from the back of the truck.

"Women," John says, indicating behind one of the shacks.

Cory watches through his binoculars and as two women cook on an open fire. Three little kids run around the shack to join the women. They seem happy but are dirty and unkempt. Of course, most of the kids at the farm look like this until their parents force them into the shower. These children seem different from the kids on the farm, though. They look hungry and dirty like little street urchins or like the pictures of children he saw in textbooks during the Great Depression.

"Here we go again," John says as the men exit the house and get into the vehicles again.

This time a few of the men from inside the cabin go with the men from the other settlement. Some from the last camp stay. They are exchanging people for some reason, and a few of them are carrying papers, perhaps maps with them to their vehicles.

"Looks again like about a hundred people," Cory says.

"Right," John agrees. "Let's go."

They run to the truck, but this time don't see the other vehicles exit the path. They've lost them.

"Maybe they went out another way," Cory suggests.

"Could be," John says. "I didn't see another way out, but maybe they have it hidden and covered over except for when they use it."

Cory thinks about it for a minute. John could be right, but where were they going next? Were they headed out to rob people and kill innocents? Are these even the right people?

"Let's head back," John says. "It's getting late. I want to let everyone know what we found."

"Sounds good," Cory agrees. "If we time it just right, we might miss evening chores."

"You know it," John jokes and nods.

They drive for another ten minutes when Cory spots someone up ahead turning left.

"Hey!" he alerts John. "Look. Was that them?"

John accelerates and follows closely enough without the vehicle in front being able to spot them. They make the same right turn and fall back even more. The truck in front of them turns left through what looks like a field of hay that has not been harvested in years. John approaches slowly and cautiously. They drive past the field.

"I don't even see a driveway this time," John remarks as they accelerate away from the site.

"No, I think they just drove through the field."

A mile down the road, John turns around and drives back toward the field at a measured crawl. The vehicle is gone. The other companion ATV's, motorcycles and the additional truck from the last place that joined the caravan are gone. There are dense woods at the end of the open pasture. They had to have gone into it to disappear so quickly.

"Let's head home," John says.

Cory would like to pursue them into those woods, but John seems reluctant. He'll defer to his friend's experience on this one.

Suddenly, a squeal of tires behind them alerts Cory, and he spins in his seat.

"Oh, shit! They're on us!" Cory shouts as John hits the gas.

"Take care of them. Try to leave a survivor," John orders.

"Yes, sir," Cory answers and opens the slider window to the bed of the truck. He climbs through in one fluid motion, grabs his rifle off the front seat and pulls it through, too. Then he kneels on the bed of the truck as the first round is fired off from the truck behind them, whizzing past John's door. It is the same red truck they followed here. They have either been flanked by these assholes, or else it is merely a coincidence that they pulled out and saw them when he and John were driving by. Either way, if they want a fight, they're about to get one. If these men are the highwaymen, then they may have been hoping to rob him and John. They only thing they'll be stealing today is a bullet.

Cory fires back, hitting their windshield. John swerves to miss debris in the road, and Cory is knocked slightly off-kilter. A bullet whirs past the truck like a whistling roman candle. He ducks. John floors it, sending them speeding at around fifty miles per hour. With his arm extended up in the air, Cory lies on his side and flips the selector switch to fully automatic. He fires off about ten rounds at the other vehicle while staying down and protected by the metal tailgate. Along with the driver and two men crammed in the cab, there are six or seven in the bed of the truck. So, he rises to one knee and takes more precise aim since the other vehicle is veering all over the road to avoid his first spray of suppressive fire. He squeezes three times, connecting with the windshield, the hood, and the grille and finally manages to hit the front, left steer tire, causing the already swerving vehicle to slide at an odd angle before the tires catch and cause it to roll. The men in the bed are sent flying. The truck rolls three times until it comes to its final resting position on its roof. The commotion is loud, deafening in the typical apocalyptic silence of the afternoon. There is no other vehicle noise on this freeway, no moving cars commuting to work, no delivery trucks trying to make their daily routes on time. It's always like this, quiet, sometimes silent other than the sounds of birds.

John slams on the brakes, causing Cory to slide backward slightly. They both jump out at the same time and stalk toward the carnage. John signals that he'll flank their position and sprints up into the woods beside the freeway. Cory moves cautiously forward, then squats behind an abandoned, turned over semi cab in the road when one of the survivors shoots at him. The trailer is jackknifed into oncoming traffic and also on its side. He will be able to use the entire big rig for cover.

He peeks around the tire where he's hiding to scan the scene of the accident. The pick-up has smoke coming out of the crushed hood. Cory wishes Simon were here to snipe them from a high spot. Instead, he half bear crawls half shuffles to the other end of the truck's trailer. If they are moving toward him, they'll first head to the cab where he ran for cover. Cory finds a spot where the box trailer is hanging off the side of the road, a good fighting position for a few rounds, at least. He climbs down into the ditch, uses the trailer for cover and takes aim at the survivors.

Three men, who must've been thrown from the truck, are clamoring for cover. He fires a round, hitting one in the calf. The man goes to his knees with a cry of pain. Cory hits him again with a shot to his side. This will likely be a fatal wound, so he moves on to another. He fires quickly but misses, the round pinging off the bumper of an abandoned sedan with a metallic hiss. It pisses Cory off. He detests missing. The man dives for cover and immediately blasts Cory's area with a fully auto burst. His firing pattern isn't suppressive or precise at all but wasteful and angry. Good. If they're angry, that means they've grown cocky and careless. They will be easy to defeat because they aren't thinking clearly.

A shot rings out from his east, and Cory knows John is taking care of business. The men have scrambled and are hiding from them now. He has to push forward and trust that John has his back for cover fire. Cory rises from his place in the ditch and sprints toward the group. Shots ring out, but so do some from John's position. He skids to a stop and slams his back against a bread delivery short cargo truck and waits a moment. He reaches around the corner of the back bumper and fires a blast toward them again. Then he gives up the cover of the truck and dashes toward their enemy. A man is crawling on his stomach out from under the wreckage, barely able to move. Cory puts him out of his misery with one shot. Then he fires a few more toward the hiders. He doesn't hit anyone, but it keeps them down for a moment while he sprints closer. John is also laying down more rounds on them, this time from a new position further past the wreckage but still in the woods under heavy concealment.

Cory sprints in a hunched over position until he is at the empty cab of their truck. The other man or men who were riding inside are gone. He is left to assume that he is now going to be fighting them, too. Cautiously, he peers around the corner of the overturned truck and is nearly struck by a bullet. The smoke is providing additional cover, so he volleys a few rounds back at them and takes off for a silver SUV. They are too busy shooting into the woods to try and take out John. Cory would like to offer them some advice. Nothing they do will take him down. John is an animal when it comes to war.

He squats low and pauses before swinging around to take aim again. Spotting a man moving between the other empty cars, Cory plugs him, hitting him between the shoulder blades. He screams out and falls forward. He doesn't get up or move or make another sound, leaving Cory to believe he is dead or paralyzed. He sees another run for his friend, so he takes a shot at him and misses. John is there for the pickup and takes him out, a clean headshot from behind.

Cory creeps silently toward another parked car and hunkers down before he ends up in the same predicament as John's last victim. His adrenaline is pumping, but he feels no fear. If this is where his life will come to a halt, then so be it. But he's determined to eliminate as many of their enemy as possible. The roar of an engine in the distance alerts him, and Cory snatches his binoculars. Two trucks, led by a motorcycle are fast approaching in the distance. He and John must get out of here before they are overtaken.

Cory fires off on fully auto again a good spray and sprints back toward their truck. As he's running, he radios John to let him know to fall back. John is already on his way. They meet up at the truck and get in as quickly as possible. Cory rides in the bed again and hits their enemy with a barrage of gunfire as they speed away. They are not pursued as far as Cory can see in the distance. It is not for at least ten miles that they finally manage to pull off into a neighborhood and drive around back to a rear-facing garage where they can hide and wait it out.

"What the fuck?" Cory asks rhetorically when he meets John at the side of the truck.

"Think they radioed for help?" John questions.

"Maybe," Cory says. "They have tactical gear, so they probably have radios. We had them pinned down. I was two seconds from rushing them. I knew you had them pinned on the other side of the road."

"Yep," John agrees. "I think they had to have called in for backup. Reload. Get ready. We'll move out soon."

"Got it."

Twenty minutes later, after John decides it's been enough time, they head out again. He pulls out of the driveway and then out of the neighborhood slowly and with great caution. They wait a few minutes at the stop sign before pulling onto the main road again. The only thing Cory sees is a deer in the field across from them casually grazing on the long grasses. John looks both ways a few times, not for oncoming traffic but for creeps driving vehicles while shooting like they are angry at rush hour traffic and committing felonious road rage.

"Let's roll," John says and accelerates away.

A few miles down the road, they spy two of the ATV's that were traveling with the group that was after them. They are parked alongside the road. Nobody is in sight.

"Disable 'em," John orders.

John pulls up slowly, and Cory hops out. He stabs his dagger into the front and back left tires of each. Then he jumps into the truck, and they take off again. Whoever was coming back to these is going to be disappointed when they get there. Cory knows they are most likely searching the woods right now for them.

"Wish we could stay and pick them off," Cory laments.

"Not a good idea. They could radio for backup again. Now is the time for E and E. Not the time to be heroes who get shot before the war has a chance to kick off."

He nods but still wishes the situation were different. They travel at a high rate of speed until they reach their town. John checks in with the guards to ascertain that nobody has attacked the town, and they are both relieved that it's been quiet all day. He warns them to be on the lookout and to call it in if they see them or need help. Then they head for home.

Cory calls on the radio to the farm, and everyone is gathered in the barnyard when they arrive to hear of the incident.

"Do you both think it was them?" Derek asks after they explain the situation.

John shrugs, "Seems likely. They're a threat. That much I'm sure of. They took no pause in shooting at us."

"That's for sure," Cory chimes in.

"We need to go back out," John says.

"Wait," Reagan says quickly and with fear in her voice. "I don't think that's a good idea."

"Me neither," Paige agrees.

She looks at Cory but for just a brief second since her brother is standing next to her.

"If Simon had been with us, he could've taken out the rest of them. Easily," Cory tells them. His best friend sends him a glare of contempt. "It's true."

"We should sneak in at night," Kelly says. "Take just the one camp, the smallest. Snatch and grab. We'll snag a dude and interrogate him."

"I doubt if that will be an easy operation," Derek says.

Doc puffs on his pipe and says, "Sneaking in and out of their camps will be very difficult. I don't want you in that kind of danger."

John says, "The men left both camps. I don't think many stayed behind. They were all making plans or something."

"We should let the stress from today's skirmish settle before we try this," Derek says. "They'll likely stay close to their camps for a while to protect them. Then they'll let their guards down. That's the time to make our move, after they leave their camps again."

John adds, "Right, that's a good idea. They probably leave their camps often, so once they get back into the swing of things, that's when we snatch and grab."

Kelly amends his idea and says, "We should get a woman instead if we can. Take and interrogate her."

"Kelly!" Hannah exclaims with shock.

"She'll talk before the men will," Kelly tells her. "We wouldn't hurt her, baby. We'd only talk to her."

"He has a point," Reagan says in agreement. "They could return her once they're done. Take her back a few days after and release her near the camp."

Cory jumps in to suggest, "We could go in when the men leave one of the camps and grab a woman and talk to her. Maybe they aren't there of their own free will and would want to talk."

Sue says to him, "You said they slapped one of the women in the face. There's a good chance they don't want to be there in the first place. They may need our help."

"Something to consider," Doc says.

They discuss the situation a while longer until the sun falls on the McClane farm, and everyone goes about performing their evening chores. He rushes through feeding the cattle in the paddock. Then he moves on to watering the horses. They are strange animals sometimes. He's noticed that most of them seem to drink more in the winter than in the stifling heat of summer.

Finishing quickly, Cory jogs away to look for Simon. He finds him milking cows. John is also there, but he discreetly leaves and offers to let Cory finish for him.

"Hey, man," he says. "Can we talk?"

He can't see Simon since he's on the other side of the Jersey, the milk cow that provides them with butter and cream. Cory is milking a Holstein, which will give them drinking milk, especially for the little kids.

"I have nothing to say to you," his friend returns.

"We should talk, Simon. You're my best friend."

"Was. I was your best friend. Friends don't do what you did. You betrayed my trust."

"I know," he says as Simon stands and places his bucket in the sink behind him. Cory notices his bruised knuckles, and it makes him depressed that his friend had to do what he did.

He quickly finishes before Simon comes back from releasing his cow. He places his own bucket in the sink, too. Cory unties the heifer and releases her, as well. He shortcuts it and sends her out through the barn gate instead of walking her out to the paddock.

"Hey, wait," he calls to Simon, who is walking down the aisle with his bucket. "Wait up, man. Let me explain, Simon."

His friend swings around swiftly, making Cory wonder if he's about to get punched again. It's fine if he wants to. Cory won't stop him. He didn't yesterday. Simon is right. If the situation were reversed, Cory would beat the shit out of the dude, too. He doesn't blame his friend or his reaction to hearing about himself and Paige.

"There's nothing to explain, Cory," Simon says with fervor.

"I want to. Just let me," Cory says and continues before Simon can stop him. "I didn't mean for that to happen. Your sister is…well, she's not just a conquest. I have feelings for her. I really do love her. I didn't think after Em…" the words get stuck in his throat and he has to clear it because speaking his little sister's name out loud is difficult for his heart to bear. He collects himself and keeps going, "Well, after Emma died I didn't think I'd ever… that I'd ever let myself feel vulnerable like that again, but Paige changed that. She made me want to try. I love your sister. I didn't mean to disrespect you with what we did, and I know I did. That shit sucks. You're my friend, my best friend, Simon, and I wouldn't hurt you on purpose. I wanted to tell you. I did."

Simon glares at him. "It shouldn't have happened in the first place. There shouldn't have been anything to explain. I never would've done this to you. I never would've slept with Em, even if she was closer to my age or I liked her or whatever."

"I know, brother. You're the better man. Clearly. You always have been. I couldn't stop myself. I literally couldn't. I liked her almost immediately. Damn, I mean, I think I fell in love with her the first time I met her in the woods. She's just so…different."

This isn't helping because Simon is still fuming. He decides to change his tactic.

"I just wanted to say that I'm sorry and that I should've come to you before. I want to do the right thing, though. I want to marry her."

"No way. Not happening. I'd never let her marry someone like you," Simon says through his teeth and stalks away.

Cory is left feeling even more frustrated. It's going to take a long time to regain his friend's trust and respect, if he ever does. He has to find Paige and speak with her, too. That's going to be even more difficult. He just hopes he gets to talk to her before Simon tries to move her away from him. That thought both angers and frightens Cory more than being shot at earlier.

Chapter Fourteen
Simon

Instead of going after a hostage to interrogate, Derek and Doc devise a plan to find out more about the people at the country club in Clarksville and to introduce the McClane group to the kids who are staying on the Army base near there. The two camps they found will have to wait a few days, which John agreed would give them time to let their guards down anyway. It all pisses Simon off, though. He has a lot of pent-up rage he'd like to let loose on some jerks right now. So, instead of hunting down the men who took shots at John and Cory, he is driving to Clarksville with Kelly, John, and Sam. And to make matters worse, he is riding in the bed of the truck with her to keep watch for the road terrorists.

Sam doesn't speak to him the entire ride to the city, which is thankfully uneventful. They get dropped off at the country club while John and Kelly go to spy on the Army base full of youngsters. They will do a little recon for a while and reconvene in a few hours.

"Let's set up shop over here," Simon instructs after Kelly has driven away with John. Sam just nods and follows him into a small section of woods. "This will give us good cover. Watch for trip wires and the like."

"Got it," she says as she picks her way carefully along behind him.

Simon wishes that someone else would've come with them. Not Cory, of course. He has no desire to be around him right now. It's best that he is at the farm on patrol while they are on this mission. They'd dropped Paige off with Talia on their way out of the farm, which had relieved Simon that she'd be spending her day over there and not near Cory.

He'd had a lengthy discussion last night with his sister in the cabin where she'd begged him not to move them to town. He couldn't resist her pleading and had relented in staying on the farm as long as she kept her distance from Cory. If he even gets one whiff of them carrying on again, then he's moving them the same day. He'd told her as much, to which she'd given him a snotty look. He doesn't care. She can give all the looks she wants. It won't change his mind about how he feels. They'd sneaked around behind his back, made a mockery of his trust, and betrayed him with lies. Cory he'll never forgive. Paige is his sister. He told her already that he forgives her, but she has a lot to prove to gain his trust again. He still can't believe it had happened in the first place. She'd assured him that it won't carry on, that it's completely over, and that she's moved on. He'll believe it when he sees it. He knows it isn't over for Cory since he said he's in love with her. Simon will just have to work harder to keep them separated until Cory finds someone else. Judging by past exploits, it won't take him long.

"Over here," he instructs and takes a knee behind a hickory tree with a wide, thick trunk. Simon smashes down the prickly brush beside him so that Sam can kneel without getting poked.

They rest their rifles on the ground beside them and take out their binoculars.

"I still think I should've paired up with Huntley," he says.

"Gee, thanks, Simon," she returns with sass. "And he's not ready yet. You know that."

"I know, and I didn't mean it to be offensive. I just like it better when you're back on the farm where it's safer."

"I'm going back to Dave's soon anyway, so what's it matter?"

This is news to him. News he doesn't like. "What do you mean? When?"

"I don't know. Soon. That's my home now. I can't stay on the McClane farm forever. I need to get back to help my uncle."

"He's not even ready for you yet. He's still doing clinic days in town with us. They're at least a few weeks away from having the cabin ready to see patients."

"I can help. I'd be more help over there than I would be at Grandpa's."

"Probably not. They have it covered. Besides, they've got that nurse now, too. It would be more helpful if you stayed on Doc's farm and worked at our clinic. We don't have as much extra help now that you're gone. Soon, Reagan's going to have her baby, and we'll be short staffed."

"Yeah, that's true. I hadn't considered her not being able to come to work for a while. Of course, this is Reagan we're talking about. I can't exactly see her taking the standard, prescribed six weeks of maternity leave, either."

"I don't think she'll get a choice. I'm sure John will see to it that she takes some time off and slows down."

Sam chuckles. "I'm sure he'll try. Don't know if he'll succeed or not."

"Right," he agrees with a grin.

They observe the country club for a while but don't see anyone moving around. There aren't any vehicles coming and going like last time, either.

"This is strangely quiet," he says.

"I agree. Should we move in closer? See if they've relocated their housing to another end of the building? Maybe we're just on the wrong side."

"Could be. Come on," he says and helps her stand. Sam immediately releases his hand and snatches her rifle from the ground.

She follows him through the woods until they come to a clearing.

"Go first," he indicates to the short, open field they must cross to get to the next, thinner cluster of trees on the other side. "I'll cover you."

"On it," Sam says and squats low and sprints through the tall grasses.

Simon diligently scans the area through his rifle scope, fully prepared to blast anyone who would take a shot at her. She makes it, gives the thumbs-up sign and squats just inside the tree line behind an old oak. Simon does the same, knowing she'll cover him in a similar way. He is quite a bit taller than her, so Simon is nervous he'll be spotted. However, he joins her a few seconds later, and they travel in a wide arc until they are on the other side of the country club's buildings.

"You should give Cory a break, ya' know," she instructs, her dark hair blowing in the wind that has tufted the silky strands.

Simon doesn't answer but gives her a hard frown in lieu of words which he cannot offer because they would be rude and probably angry and crude and inappropriate to say in front of a woman. His frustration is off the charts. He found out during the argument with Cory that Sam has been making out with Henry, although he'd stayed on that man's farm for nearly two weeks and had not seen it happening right under his nose apparently. He's always been suspicious of that dirtbag.

"Really, Simon," she urges with less patience than she used to have. "You can't judge him for sleeping with your sister. Paige is beautiful and funny and smart. She's going to attract men. If I were you, I'd be glad that it was Cory and not someone else."

He snorts and resumes looking out at the horizon to watch for would-be accosters.

"At least she wouldn't have to move off the farm if they were married. He'd always take care of Paige. Of course, he would. I mean, he's Cory. I'd be scared to cross her if Cory was her protector."

"I'm her protector," he corrects quickly.

"You can't be forever," she says. "She's going to want to have someone in her life."

A twig snaps somewhere behind them, causing Simon to swing his rifle in that direction. Sam hunkers lower and brings up her own gun, an M4 that Cory modified for her with a shorter stock so she could keep it closer to her body. A good sixty feet away, a mother elk and her calf are grazing with carefree abandon. She even lifts her head to observe Simon and Sam for a moment before going back to plucking small berries from a bush.

Sam chuckles and says, "Don't mind us."

"They don't know to fear humans anymore."

"They should. People are the most dangerous things on this planet. Look at what we did to it," Sam laments with sadness. "I wonder if elk were in Tennessee before."

"I don't think so. They've probably migrated since there aren't people around anymore. Cory said he saw a zebra in Pennsylvania."

"Escapee of a zoo, no doubt. Anyway, back to your sister and Cory. She's eventually going to want someone in her life."

"Not him. And, besides, she doesn't want to get married. She told me so. She doesn't want to marry Cory or anyone else."

"She'll change her mind. We're hardwired to seek mates. If we weren't, then the population of people would've died out a long time ago, and animals would've run the planet."

"She can have a family someday, just not with Cory. You don't know him like I do, Samantha."

She chuffs through her pert little nose and says, "I know more about Cory and his rakish ways than you think, Simon Murphy. He wasn't always as discreet as he thought he was. Plus, I've seen the women swoon over him. Good grief, I had a lot of them asking about him when he came to stay last week at Dave's camp."

"See what I mean? It's not a good match. He's not like her. He's always going to have women chasing after him."

"So? Doesn't mean he'll act on it. As a matter of fact, I'd bet anything you want to bet that he never would. Kelly isn't a cheater. Their dad never did, either. Cory told me what a good man his father was, that he never abused or cheated on his family. Cory will be just like him. All boys grow up to be like their fathers. And, besides, some of the girls were asking about you, too. That doesn't mean that you guys are gonna run over there to sew your oats."

"What? I doubt anyone inquired about me. And what do you know about oat sewing? You don't need to be thinking about stuff like that."

"Oh, yes, my feminine sensibilities have been offended. Get real. Hanging out on a farm for the last four years with a bunch of soldiers hasn't exactly kept my ears innocent."

"That's something I'd rather not think about. The guys should be more cautious when you and the other young girls are hanging out with them."

"Seriously? Simon, I'm not a little kid. Remember?"

He mumbles, "Of course, I remember."

He'd like to forget this about Sam. Instead, he thinks about how much she isn't a little girl but an adult woman with all of the finer, softer attributes of one.

Sam ignores him and continues on, "I think she's just scared since she's lost so many people she cares about. She'll get over her fear. She loves him. I'm sure of it. I've seen it. She cares a lot about Cory, and that's a good thing, Simon. She's perfect for him. Paige will never take a lot of crap from Cory, and he'll always cherish her. She's given him a replacement for Em in his life. He needed that. Cory really needed that. He's an adult. He needs companionship, and Paige is great. She's tender and sweet. Well, sometimes she's a little feisty, but she's mostly a big sweetheart. Cory needs a bit of softness in his life. Everyone needs someone."

"Oh? Is that so? Just like you need Henry?"

Sam looks swiftly away with a scowl on her tender face. "That's none of your business."

Simon snorts again. "I see how you are. When it comes to talking about everyone else's love life you're fine with it, but not when the tables get turned."

"Ok, then. How about your own love life? Care to discuss that?"

He sends a glare her way. She is being obtrusive and bull-headed again.

"You didn't answer my question," he says.

"Neither did you."

"Don't be so difficult," Simon censors.

"If you don't want to discuss your own relationship issues, then you can't get involved in everyone else's, Simon. And you shouldn't be trying to keep Cory away from your sister. It's not right. They're both adults. They'll work this out. Think about it, if you were just considering Cory's character and your friendship, then you'd think he was a good man, the best. He's loyal and kind. He's a good friend. He's great with the little kids on the farm. Gosh, they all look up to him or want to be him. He is your best friend. There's nobody else better than him in your eyes. Now there's just nobody better for her, and it doesn't matter that she's your sister. Take that out of the equation. He'd never cheat on her. He's protective. Good grief, Simon. Remember when she got shot? That was horrible. And Cory never left her side, only when you were on watch duty with her did he even allow himself to leave long enough to eat and shower. We should've known something was going on back then with the way he was with her during all that."

He doesn't like thinking about that time when Paige took a bullet for Kelly. As much as he admires Kelly and looks up to him, he doesn't want his sister doing things like that or taking such a huge risk with her own life. He wishes he could go back and take the bullet instead. There are so many 'would,' 'could,' and should's' in his life that he can't ever find an end to them. When it comes to Samantha, that list of woulda', coulda,' shoulda's is bottomless. Regret is an integral staple of his daily diet.

Instead of discussing the matter of Paige and Cory, which he'll not change his mind about, Simon asks her, "So, are you and Henry together then?"

She groans softly. "Seriously, Simon? Were you even listening? I'm trying to help you."

"You're trying to sway me. I'll not be swayed, even if you think you are trying a case in front of the Supreme Court. I was listening. I always listen when you talk. It's not like you'd allow otherwise."

She backhands his shoulder.

"And you're still evading my question," he points out.

"Simon," she says in a more serious tone, "I still don't see movement. What do you think's going on?"

He turns away from staring at her, something he lets himself do way too often. Pulling his binoculars up again, he searches the grounds and the buildings more thoroughly.

"I don't know. I was thinking the same thing," he agrees.

"Should we go in and check it out?"

"I'll go. You…"

"No, I'm going, too. I'm not staying out here by myself."

This time Simon groans. It's more of a moan through gritted teeth that he's grinding, another lousy habit care of his never-ending frustrations with Samantha. There isn't a person on earth who can vex him more than her. Maybe this week, his sister.

"Fine," he says and stands, which she does, as well. "Stay close. Be alert."

"Duh," she returns with an attitude.

160

Simon sneers at the top of her head and turns to go, knowing that arguing with her is pointless. They walk carefully through the woods, looking for traps, trip wires or any other devices that would alert the camp. They come to another section that opens up to a once-manicured part of the grounds and sprint through the overgrown yards to hide behind a rather long gazebo. They squat again and surveille their surroundings.

"Nothing," she whispers.

"I've got nothing, too," he confirms and rises.

Sam jogs in a hunched over fashion alongside him toward the main clubhouse where they both press their backs against the wall. Simon slides along the wall until he comes to the corner. Then he takes a quick peek.

"Anyone?" she whispers at his shoulder.

"Not one," he returns and turns to glance over his shoulder down at her. "Let's keep going. Stay close."

She nods, and they move out quickly. Simon leads her to another section of the building where some rhododendron bushes have grown to the height of the first-floor roof behind it. He slips in behind them and keeps going to the next corner where he squats with Sam.

"Something's wrong here," she whispers nervously, her hand tightening on the hand grip of her rifle.

Simon places his hand on her shoulder. "Easy, Sam. We're ok. Let's just keep pushing forward and check it out."

She nods but seems afraid.

"Stay frosty," Simon orders softly and rises to a squatted run. They make it to another section of the building that opens up into an outdoor seating area complete with dining tables and chairs and wide umbrellas that have seen better days.

"Oh!" Sam cries with surprise.

Simon swiftly spins to find her standing with her rifle lowered and her hand over her mouth.

"Oh, man," he mumbles.

Simon stares at the same scene Sam spotted a second before him. There are dozens of dead people lying on the ground in the overgrown grass below the dining patio.

"Stay here. Cover me," he says to her and goes to inspect the mass murder scene a little closer.

Simon skirts a table with an umbrella that is bent over sideways and rusty from being left out in the weather. The club's pool and tennis courts are not far from view, although they're both in terrible shape- the pool having turned to a swamp of black water, and the courts with cracked and uneven pavement and grass growing up through. He goes down the steep hill toward the people, sliding part of the way, his work-boots catching and gripping near the bottom. Seeing them up close is even worse. He gingerly steps around, over and between them. They have been assassinated. These people who were trying to build a new community for themselves have been slaughtered. Some of their hands are tied behind their backs. He has no doubts they were killed by the highwaymen. There were simply too many people living on this compound to be overrun and killed by just a few people. They fought back. That much he can tell. There are a few guns near the bodies of the victims. There were likely many more but were taken by their murderers.

"Sam," he calls to her, confident they are alone, "call it in. We need an evac."

She gives him a thumbs-up.

Simon goes back to reviewing the scene of the crime. It is ghastly, not more than a few days old at his best guess. There are children, too. This makes him sick. He wonders if any of this group was able to escape. Surely, they did.

He moves to their enclosed, fenced off area where they must've kept livestock. A little shelter had been erected, not much more than a three-sided, wooden structure only big enough to hold maybe goats. There is also a chicken coop. Their farm animals are gone, the pens empty, the gates left in the open positions. He wanders cautiously toward a smaller, fenced-in space, an obvious garden with tidy, hoed rows of vegetation. The gardens have been picked clean, nothing left. He scans the area and goes back to Sam, not wanting to leave her alone for very long. She is standing under the overhang of the building, probably trying to avoid having to look down at the carnage.

"They're on the way," she tells him.

Simon nods. "Good. There's nothing to see here; nobody left to talk to about this."

162

"Yeah," she agrees in a melancholy tone. "What do you think happened?"

"Could've been the highwaymen, probably was. Looks like their assassination method. They probably didn't stand a chance, got overrun quickly. The animals and food are all gone."

"Should we check out the buildings?"

"Yes, let's do it quickly before the guys get here."

They enter through one French door of the many sets connecting the brick patio and are greeted by another dining area, this time much grander in size and décor, except that it's dusty and filled with cobwebs. The club must've held wedding receptions, banquets, and events in the large room. This obviously wasn't where those people were making their sleeping and living quarters. They go through the double doors which lead them to the main lobby and reception area. Again, not a soul is in sight. Sam taps his arm and points to their right down a long, dark hallway. He nods and walks ahead of her in case there is danger awaiting them in the shadows.

By the time they make it to the end of the building, they've passed many rooms which were apparently where the murdered people were housing themselves. They look like former offices of the hotel employees, and in the next wing, they find hotel style suites. Every room appears to have been lived in by the looks of the beds and some personal belongings like backpacks and plastic bins of belongings on the floors. Most of the rooms have been ransacked, as well. He figures whoever killed the people and took their livestock also raided their compound for anything they could take with them to use.

They cross to another section of the country club where he and Cory saw vehicles parked before only to find that their vehicles are missing. The raiders must've confiscated them, as well. The only modes of transportation now are a few once-white but now filthy golf carts. He's surprised the thieves didn't steal these, too. Simon nods to Sam, and they enter through a single door to another, smaller building of the compound. It might've been an employees-only facility because there are lockers and offices. A shuffling and clicking sound at the other end of the small building alerts Simon. Sam must hear it, too, because she stops abruptly and freezes.

He holds his fist up to stop her. Then he signals that she should hold her position and provide cover fire if he needs it. Then Simon walks swiftly to the other end of the hallway and swings left with great caution into an open door. He startles two small children and a woman, all three cowering in a corner. However, the woman, who is clearly frightened by him, is pointing a revolver at him.

"Hey!" he says firmly. "Don't shoot me, ma'am."

She hesitates and flinches. In her defense, Simon is pointing his own rifle at her. It's an intimidating piece with the high-power scope and long barrel.

"Don't shoot us!" she cries after a long, assessing pause.

"I won't," he reassures her.

"Simon," Sam's small voice comes from his side.

"Sam, stay back!" he calls to her so that she doesn't approach any closer in case the woman with the gun develops a sudden tick in that finger on the trigger.

"What's going on?" Sam asks.

Simon doesn't take his eyes off of the woman long enough to glance towards Sam. She could make a move, lunge at him, shoot him.

"Please, lower your gun, ma'am," he says.

"We're here to help!" Sam calls into the room.

"Sam, get back," he says, wishing he could swear at her. He doesn't want to frighten the woman any more than she clearly already is. "Ma'am, please. My friend's right. We're here to help. Can you tell me what happened out there?"

"Who are you?" she asks with fear.

"We came here today to make an alliance. Our people spotted your group a while back, and we've been watching your compound."

"You're with them, aren't you?" she asks and raises the gun higher.

"What? The men who did…that?" he inquires, referring to the mass murder in such a way so that the children don't understand. They look scared out of their minds, hungry, tired, and mentally drained. She nods with trepidation. "No, no way, ma'am. We're not like that. We came to offer our alliance, our friendship. I think whoever did this is the same group we've been hunting for a while now. We know they're attacking people on the roads. We were coming to warn your group about this and also to offer our help if you need it. I see we're too late."

Her eyes fall to the floor, and tears slip from them. The gun in her hand begins to shake, and she finally lowers it.

"I'm sorry we didn't make it here in time," he apologizes as Sam brushes past him into the room with the woman and children.

"I'm Sam," she says and squats to the eye level of the children. The little girl offers a nervous smile.

"What happened?" Simon asks.

"We…we were working out in the gardens. Some of the men were gone."

"When? Was it daytime or at night?"

"Middle of the day. It happened the day before yesterday."

Static on his radio interrupts their discussion, and Simon answers John. He tells them of their location and to meet them at the entry door to the building. Within minutes, John is there with Kelly, and Simon is telling them about the woman, who they introduce them to. They learn her name is Bianca, and the little girl is her own and the boy an orphan that she managed to save from the carnage.

"They came without warning and just started shooting people," she explains. "I grabbed my daughter and Oliver here and ran. My husband was one of the men who was gone."

"Gone where?" Kelly asks.

Her brown eyes jump to Kelly and show a certain tentativeness. Everyone is always afraid of him, even though Simon only knows Kelly to be kind and gentle. He is as lethal a killer as John or Derek and definitely Cory, but Simon also knows he doesn't enjoy it.

"They went to hunt deer. We have to go to the woods, the countryside to find deer or to catch fish," she tells them. "It's usually the only meat we have. We had a few dairy cows and goats, but they took them, too. They took everything."

"I saw," Simon remarks.

"Did you know these people?" John asks, earning a more relaxed expression from the woman. If she only knew how deadly John could be.

"No, sir," the woman answers. "I've never seen them before in my life. They were…"

She shivers and lowers her gaze to her hands which are folded in her lap. Sam has taken the children to a nearby table and is sharing their packed lunches that Sue and Hannah made of sandwiches, apples, berry scones, containers of water, and chopped vegetables.

"What?" Simon presses. "What were they?"

"Monsters," she says stoically, awful memories assailing her senses.

Nobody says anything for a moment as the heavy mood settles in on the room and her tears reside enough to allow her to speak again. This woman is highly traumatized.

"How many others made it out?" Kelly asks.

"Just me and the two children. I looked for survivors," she says.

"What about your husband and the other men?" John asks.

"He didn't make it, either," she explains. They wait for her to continue. "They ran into the men on the way back in. They just picked the wrong time to come back home from their hunt."

"Did your men come and go at the same times every day when they left the camp?" John asks.

"Yes, sir. They usually left in the morning and tried to be back before dinner each afternoon. They were good about being home to make sure we closed the club before dark. We felt it kept us safer. We were wrong."

Kelly breaks in to say, "No, you were right. That was smart. These people were probably watching your camp. They saw the pattern. They knew when to ambush the ones left behind and when they'd be able to take out the men returning to it."

"Agreed," John says with a nod and a frown. "They canvassed your place and knew when the best time to attack was going to be."

"Probably," she agrees with a nod. "I don't know what I'm going to do."

"Why were you staying here…after what happened?" John asks.

"I didn't know where else to go," she answers honestly.

Simon asks her, "No family? Friends nearby?"

She shakes her head, and Simon looks to the guys. They will definitely be taking three extra people with them when they leave the city today. They would never even consider leaving her behind to fend for herself and two small children, especially since her food is likely mostly or all gone.

"We have another place to go today," Kelly informs her. "Maybe you might even be able to help."

This gets her attention.

"We have also been watching another place nearby," Kelly continues. "There seem to be a lot of kids, young people living together at an old Army base near here. We'd like to approach them and see if they've heard or seen anything about these men who attacked your group. You could help us, explain, talk to them, let them know we aren't going to hurt them."

"I can't leave here. I need to stay and take care of the children."

"We might have another option for you," John offers. "That is, if you're interested. We wouldn't force it on you."

Her eyes skirt to his and rest there with unconcealed hope.

John continues, "You could live in our town. It's safe. Safer than here, even before what happened. There's a wall to keep people out. You could live in one of the houses, even live with people who would take you and the kids in until we can get a house opened up. It's not far from here."

"Hell, I feel bad we didn't approach you sooner," Kelly says. "We weren't sure if your group was the ones we've labeled the highwaymen."

"It's not your fault, sir," the lady says. "You couldn't have known this would happen."

Kelly looks as if he doesn't believe this as if this will weigh down his already troubled conscience that they let this happen, that it's the Rangers' faults.

"Where are you from?" John redirects. "Around here?"

"No, my husband and I are from Texas. After the first nukes went off overseas, he brought us north for fear of what could happen. His parents lived near Knoxville, a house on a big lake. We lived there for a few years until the lake community was overrun."

"By people like the ones who did this?" John asks.

She shakes her head. "No, dissension from within. It was so sad. We had a great system. Everyone was bartering with one another. The community was gated, small, manageable. But then the fighting started. We didn't have a good crop season last summer, too much rain. People started stealing from one another. Then murdering. After his father was killed, my husband got us out of there, us and a small group of like-minded families."

"We've heard that most of Texas was hit with flooding and tsunami waves," Simon puts in. "Were you still down there when it all happened?"

"Yes, a lot of it was flooded and destroyed, but we were north of Dallas, so we made it. Then we went to Knoxville. It worked for a while, but people being what they are now, it didn't last. Nothing does."

Her eyes turn toward the children and grow even sadder. This woman has seen her fair share of death and tragedy. Simon understands her woes all too well. It seems that everyone they meet has dealt with the same things, loss of loved ones, murder, rape, robbery, and deceit. It makes him think of Paige. He wonders if Sam is right about his sister's feelings toward Cory. Does he make her happy? And if so, is it right to keep her from seeking that happiness with him? Life is so short and mostly bleak. His dictate of keeping them apart could be a selfish act and one he may come to regret like so many other bad decisions he's made. He only wants his sister to be safe, even her tender heart.

"Ready?" John asks him, standing directly in front of Simon.

"Yes, sir," he answers, not sure if he missed something.

John hits him with a look that lets him know that he did. "We're taking her with us, and we're going to talk to the kids at Campbell. Stay alert and help her gather whatever she wants to take. We'll move in ten."

"Yes, sir," Simon repeats with a nod.

Sam continues to keep watch on the two surviving children because they trust her as all children do, while Simon helps the woman pack, and Kelly and John surveille the area. Half of the pick-up's bed is jammed full of articles and boxes of items that she wanted to take with her. They don't argue. It's all she has left, and most of it looks like things for the kids.

John decides to forgo the need for a covert breach at Fort Campbell and instead drives up to their makeshift gate. Immediately they are met by a young man who can't be more than sixteen. After

168

some gentle coaxing and a lot of convincing by Sam and the woman that they are not here to harm them, they are permitted entrance into the old Army fort, which has seen better days.

They are met in an open courtyard by more young people and are introduced to their leaders. Simon is guessing that maybe they might be in their early twenties.

"We need to warn you about some people…" John says but is interrupted.

"We know who you mean," the young woman says. "We've managed to avoid them so far, but we've seen the messes they've been leaving on the roads."

It is interesting to Simon that she would refer to the mass murdering of people as a mess. Perhaps she is shielding the children nearby who are aptly listening to their conversation or else she is just that hardened by this world now that she thinks such disgusting acts of violence against fellow human beings is nothing to concern herself about. Her name is Melora, and she has long, dark blonde hair that is pulled back into a single braid. Her eyes are a light hazel green, and they seem as cold as her demeanor.

"We want to offer your group help," Kelly tells her.

Her eyes become much more guarded at the sight of Kelly, which is nothing new.

"How?" she asks, looking at the young man beside her who is around Simon's age. His name is Hardy, and he seems much more open to conversing with them, although she does most of the talking.

"We have a small town that is completely secured and fortified with trained soldiers and a wall that surrounds it," John explains.

"And there are other children there and a school- well, a library that we use as a school," Sam adds.

Hardy says, "That sounds pretty good."

His further comment is shut down by a look that Melora sends him in haste.

"We don't need help. We're doing fine on our own," she tells them.

"You won't be when those jerks find this place," Kelly says. "And, trust me, they will."

Their new friend from the country club says, "Yes, they will. They found us. It was much more well-hidden than this place, too. Our men were armed. The women were trained. It shouldn't have happened to us, but it did. It'll happen here, too."

Kelly jumps in to say, "Once they run out of people to terrorize on the road, you better be damn sure they're gonna start hitting places like this."

Simon adds, "And we've heard from a source that there could be as many as six hundred of them in their group."

"Six…?" Hardy says and trails off. "Melora, we can't go up against that many. They'd clobber us."

Her eyes dart to his again and then to Simon and the rest of his group.

"We're not trying to pull one over on you, ma'am," John says gently. "We saw your place a while back. We've watched it a few times. If we can do that, so can they. And they will. We believe they researched the country club before they attacked. They knew when the men would be gone. These aren't just unskilled idiots running around robbing people. We think they have experience, tactical equipment, and the numbers to make it happen."

Sam says, "And we have allies. I live on a different compound, and the man that runs it is an ally to John and Kelly. They'll tackle this together. It's what they do. They're all ex-military and have the experience to take out this group."

"When it's over, you all could come back here if that's what you'd want," Simon tells her. "We wouldn't stop you. We don't force anyone to stay in our town that doesn't want to."

"Right, we'd never take away your free will," Kelly says.

John points to the cluster of children who have gathered near the wide door opening of a building. "I don't want to see anything happen to these kids. If you've seen the stuff on the freeways, then you know that these scumbags will not give quarter to children. They are ruthless."

Melora nods and says, "Yeah, we know. We've seen it, too."

"I don't feel comfortable leaving those little ones unguarded," Kelly says. "If you don't come with us, I think I'm gonna have to stay."

Kelly looks at John, who nods with understanding.

"Can we have a few minutes?" Hardy requests, getting another nod from John.

They walk away, leaving Simon and his group to await their decision. It doesn't take long before Melora and Hardy return with an answer.

"We'll go, but only if we can keep our weapons. You aren't disarming us," she says with a stubborn raise of her chin.

"We'd never do that," John says. "More guns and trained fighters, the better. But we will put you through the ringer and make sure you are trained the way we specify, and if you can hack it and want some responsibility in town, then you could even sign up for guard duty."

"Awesome," Hardy says without pause. Melora elbows him.

"And we don't want anyone interfering with the kids. We're in charge of them. Not you guys."

"No, ma'am," Kelly says. "We've all got enough kids of our own that we don't need to raise yours, too."

Hardy chuckles and says, "I don't know about that. I could use the extra help."

A few of the other older teens laugh, as well.

"Well, they'll be welcome to join the school, and there are always chores in town that the kids get to help out with," John says. "It helps them have a sense of belonging and purpose."

"It's run in a way that people help out and barter what they can," Kelly explains. "If you have a skill that would help someone, then maybe they have food or firewood that they'll share. You're expected to take care of yourselves, but since you're leaving this place, then they'll help you out until you get on your feet."

"We'll need time to pack and gather everything," Hardy says. "Our garden is in full bloom right now. I'd like to take as many plants as we can."

"You can give us directions to the place, and we'll just head there in a few days," Melora suggests.

"Ma'am, I don't think I'd be able to live with myself if we came back and found the same scene as we just did at the country club," Kelly says. "We'll help you pack. We'll work together and get your group outta' here."

"Cool," Hardy says before she can object to the offer.

They split up and work in teams helping their group, and Simon sticks by Sam since he doesn't know any of these people. Some of them are their ages, but most are just little kids. He finds out from Hardy that Melora is his cousin, and that they are orphans. All of the children are orphans, as well, and rescued and taken in by Hardy and Melora when they found them wandering alone in cities. They have moved around a lot, too, going from one location to the next hoping for improved safety. Fort Campbell was their fifth move in the last year. They are responsible for the underage children in their care and take the job very seriously. Simon believes them to both have a lot of honor, and he respects them for what they've done.

It is nearly nightfall when they get on the road for home, which feels good to be doing so. They help them pile into vehicles and the back of the pick-up with him, Sam, and the woman and two children from the country club. They only had one, running vehicle, a mini-van, which is filled to the brim with children and belongings. Hardy and Melora have ATV's, which they are also transporting two kids each on the backs of. A few of the teens have dirt bikes and are carrying kids on them. Now their only goal is to get them to Pleasant View safely in such a sizable, conspicuous caravan without being attacked by the highwaymen.

Chapter Fifteen
Reagan

Nearly two weeks have gone by since the guys brought back the people from Clarksville. Sam left the next day, which made everyone sad and Simon grouchy. John took Cory and has spied on the camps in the woods multiple times, but the people who had lived there are gone, disappeared like apparitions in the mist. They aren't sure if the people moved because they realized that they were found or if they were killed by the highwaymen and actually weren't a part of that group to begin with, which they'd assumed they were. Their possessions are also gone, leading them to believe that they have uprooted and left their homesteads behind because they realized they were being watched. John and Cory tracked through the woods and could not find their trail. They likely left using the main roads, but even Cory has not figured out which way they've gone. So, for now, they must wait and keep searching for the highwaymen. Reagan knows that soon the men are planning an ambush, but first Grandpa had insisted that he travel to Fort Knox to visit with her worthless father, even though she'd tried to persuade him not to go.

Derek, Cory, and Paige have taken her grandfather to Fort Knox, which had also pissed off Simon that she was permitted to go. However, Derek had the final say on the matter and felt that Paige would be a valuable asset to the team. Plus, she wanted to go because she was curious about the base and their daily operations. Reagan agreed that it was a good idea for her to tag along, which only further irritated Simon. He'd even volunteered to take Cory's place, but with Grandpa leaving, Reagan needed his help with the clinic day that her grandfather would be missing. Sam and her uncle are also joining them for a combined clinic day and are bringing pregnant women again.

Lucas went with them, too, which had pissed off Gretchen, so she is in an especially bad mood. Grandpa had offered her to go with them, but her new sister had refused, which makes Reagan wonder why she didn't at least want to see her mother. The girl definitely dislikes their father, but Reagan thought G would've wanted to see Lucy. Perhaps she is angry that her mother left the farm with their father.

She and Simon are working on starting files on all of the children from the Fort Campbell group, as well. Some of them were sick with a flu of some sort, and others were malnourished, underweight, and even anemic. Hardy and Melora were doing the best they could to keep their little group thriving and alive, but the children still need medical care and a more well-rounded diet. Melora told Reagan earlier today when she'd brought another sick boy in to the clinic that their diets mostly consisted of wild game, whatever vegetables they could grow, and any berries they could find. The children remind her of Paige when she'd first arrived on the farm. The McClane family has already donated crates of supplies and food, especially grains to the large home they've opened up for them near the clinic. Others in town have also given them things, as well as Paul and K-Dog, who brought over their own offering yesterday once their group had heard of the Campbell Kids, as everyone is now calling them.

In the hallway scribbling notes on a chart, Simon walks up to her and says, "Third kid I've seen this morning that had that cough."

"Yeah, I've had two. It's from whatever flu they've got. Hopefully, our antibiotic solution will kill it."

"Well, getting some hot tea and nutrition into them should help, too," Simon remarks as he makes his own notes.

"Right," she agrees. "Did you dose a fever reducer, too?"

"Yes, ma'am," he answers.

"Make sure Sam gets weights and heights on these kids. We don't want to forget because we won't be able to tell six months down the road whether or not they are growing at the correct rate."

"She is, although I don't get the impression from Melora that they are going to stay here in town permanently."

"We'll see," Reagan says with skepticism. "We lure them in with the idea of a hot plate of food and a warm place to lie their heads, then we hook 'em for high taxes and condo association fees."

Simon chuckles, knowing she is making a joke.

"I think they were lured in by the fact that they don't have to worry about being murdered by the highwaymen."

"Yeah, well that, too," she agrees with a grin. "Back to the grindstone."

"Yes, ma'am," he says and turns to see another patient that Sam has shown into his exam room.

Reagan and Sam's uncle are working alone, and she has paired Sam with Simon since they are both still learning. When they are finished treating the children, they work as a team and manage to get through the long line of pregnant women.

One of the women from Dave's town of Hendersonville is due any day now, and Reagan worries that she'll not have medical care when it happens. Sam's uncle and probably Sam will likely be the only ones close by to offer assistance. Reagan makes a note on her chart which she'll convey to Dr. Scott before he leaves.

She's also pretty sure that one woman from their town has preeclampsia, which is very dangerous. Her blood pressure is high, she's only thirty-one weeks, and she's complaining about pain in her back. It could all be pointing to kidney problems, high blood pressure and the typical symptoms of preeclampsia. Reagan is going to run a protein test on her in a week and see if her urine comes up positive. They may need to induce her labor soon and hope for the best. If they don't take action, she could have seizures or even die. They will need to do a risk assessment and decide if labor induction is the right step. They'd rather lose the baby than the mother, and they don't have the same medical science at their hands that they had access to before the fall. Saving this woman's life will take priority over her child.

She is making her final notation for the day when a sudden cramp strikes in her lower stomach, which is as large as a beach ball. Likely it is just more false labor, but she'll have to monitor it just to be sure. She's only thirty-five weeks, so this is too soon for full-blown labor. Her body has become its own science experiment. Lately, she's been craving Twinkies. It's not even a food she ate before the fall, let alone after. Reagan doesn't even remember the taste of one, but her body wants it. Her system seems to vacillate between the sweet, creamy goo of a Twinkie filled with artificial ingredients and preservatives enough to last through the next three apocalypses and the salty brine of pickles and whole, raw carrots from the garden, unwashed, unpeeled and sprinkled with salt. Bizarre, inexplicable cravings are a rather annoying side effect of this alien invasion.

The cramping subsides quickly, and she finishes her work before joining the other doctors in the reception room of the clinic.

"I have a few files to give you to study," Reagan tells Scott.

He seems overwhelmed with the caseload he's already handling at their new clinic. Sam told her that it is operational, albeit a little rustic and unfinished. She goes over two of the high-risk patient files with him, and he leaves to pack their gear into the back of a truck.

"Sue said you might come back to the farm tonight?" Reagan asks, wanting it to be true.

"We talked about it," Sam tells her.

Reagan doesn't miss her blue eyes shift suddenly to Simon, who looks away quickly as if he hadn't been eavesdropping with keen interest on the topic. Reagan would like to club him over the head with her clipboard.

"To get the herbs?" Reagan inquires slyly.

"Yes, I still haven't collected much."

Simon interjects to add, "Well, the tornado destroyed so much. It's a lot better now. The plants are all producing modestly. I think it would be a worthwhile trip to take some back with you."

"Cory said he'd give you a ride home in a couple days since he has to come that way with Kelly on a scouting trip," Reagan says.

"Oh, good. I guess just a few days wouldn't be so bad," Sam agrees with an unsure nod.

She leaves to speak with her uncle who is standing next to the truck talking with Dave's men who brought them.

"Real hot, Simon," Reagan chides.

"Excuse me?" he asks with a perplexed expression on his gentle face.

"Plants producing modestly, a worthwhile trip? Good grief, that's hardly gonna get her in the sack," she teases.

176

"Reagan, really," he admonishes. "That's disgusting."

"May be disgusting, but someone out there's thinking about all the ways he can get Sam to fall for him. As a matter of fact, I think we both even know of one for sure."

His strong jaw tightens and flexes, the muscles of his neck straining from the effort. She knows he dislikes Henry, although John assured her that the man is decent and good-hearted and that Simon's loathing of him is purely one of jealousy and frustration.

"And I'm not trying to seduce Samantha," he continues. "She's my friend, and I just care about her. And I care about her getting a good supply of herbs."

"There you go with the sexy talk again," she jokes and clenches her own teeth when another cramp seizes her stomach, causing the muscles to tighten.

Simon is at her side in an instant, "Are you alright? What's going on? How far apart are they?"

"Not far apart. Not contractions. Just the usual."

He looks at her with skepticism and narrows his blue eyes. "Are you sure?"

"I think I'd know," she informs him as the tightening subsides.

"This is your first…"

"And last!" she corrects. "Don't get that screwed up. First and last. Period."

"Perhaps. But what I meant was that maybe you don't know. I mean, you certainly know when it comes to your patients, but you don't have practical application to apply to your own symptoms."

"If you think I'm letting you do a pelvic exam, you are out of your freaking mind."

He chuckles and pushes his glasses higher on his nose. "No, thanks, Dr. McClane Harrison. I'll pass, but perhaps your grandfather can do a cervix check tomorrow when he returns."

"If they return. This is my father we're talking about here," Reagan alludes. "He's the master manipulator of the situation. He'll probably convince Grandpa to stay a few weeks."

"Not with Derek in charge of their trip," Simon says pointedly.

"True. He's not going to be in the best of moods having to take Grandpa up there in the first place."

"I know how he feels," Simon agrees with an angry nod and a firm set to his full mouth.

"He'll keep his distance, Simon," Reagan tells him, trying to thwart his worries about his sister. "Don't worry about Cory. He's not a total asshole, at least not most of the time."

"Says you," he remarks sullenly.

"You'll have to forgive him sooner or later. We all live on the same farm and have to get along."

"Which is exactly why I wanted to move into town with Paige," he points out.

"Right, but she doesn't want to, and it's not fair to make her. She's family now. You both are. We don't want anyone to leave. It's bad enough that Sam did. If you guys both move, too, we'll be crying the blues."

"You wouldn't."

She laughs and closes the front door, locking it. "No, I wouldn't, but other people might. Or maybe they wouldn't. What do I know? You are an annoying little shit. They might start cheering."

"Gee, thanks. You're a real self-esteem booster. As a matter of fact, you should write books about it."

"I just might," she teases as they approach Sam and her uncle.

"I'll tell Henry you'll be home in a few days," Scott is saying to her as he hugs Sam.

Reagan immediately looks at Simon, who seems like a teapot ready to blow steam.

She jumps in to help the situation. She's not John, but at least Reagan can try. "So, you're staying?"

Sam steps back from her uncle and nods. "Yes, he said I should go to the farm to get the herbs. We need to get them transplanted into the greenhouse. It's ready. The men have added a new section just for the herbs."

"Oh, great!" Reagan says with way too much enthusiasm as she tries to lighten the situation and, more importantly, calm Simon's simmering temper. "Simon, why don't you take the truck and deliver the supplies we brought for the Campbell Kids? Maybe Sam could help since she's staying."

"All done, little Doc?" Kelly asks as he strolls over to them.

"Yep, you?"

They've been helping when they can with tornado repairs to buildings and homes, library repairs from the fire, and finishing the remaining sections of the town wall. It is difficult for them to find the time since summer is the busiest season on a farm, but they help where and when they can, even if it is only on clinic days. Kelly and John also conducted a meeting this afternoon in the town hall with the sheriff and his deputies. Condo Paul and K-Dog even came over for it. They are devising a plan, scheming and hatching a good one to ambush the highwaymen, beat them at their own, sick game. She hopes the situation is resolved soon. Reagan is tired of hearing about the violent murdering of people every time her family or husband returns from a trip. She just hopes the intel they've received on these peoples' numbers is incorrect. There would be no way to defeat that many, especially if they are heavily equipped and armed.

"Yes, ma'am," Kelly answers.

"Plotting and planning?" she jokes.

He nods. "Sewing and patching?"

"Pretty much," she returns. He ruffles the curls on the top of her head before walking away. "Where the heck is John?"

"Oh, he's coming," Kelly says over his shoulder before rounding the corner of the clinic. She knows he'll double check the locks again. "Saw him talking outside the courthouse with some of the people from town."

Reagan decides to walk down to the meeting and see what's going on. She is assailed once more with a mild contraction but is still able to walk through it. Definitely not labor. Usually, if a woman can talk through a contraction, they aren't severe yet. She's still walking, so it can't be a real one. Just more Braxton Hicks getting on her nerves.

She spots her husband easily in the crowd of people gathered near the steps of the community building, and he's answering questions about the highwaymen. She also notices a dark-haired woman in a long, flowing gypsy skirt standing so close that Reagan wonders if her arm is around the back of John. She is gazing up into his eyes with a bold and brazen longing. Her spaghetti-strap camisole top is low cut and revealing her assets. Reagan recognizes her as someone they let into their town from the former Sheriff Jay's side of the village, a woman they'd taken pity on because she was a single mom of two small boys. The way she is looking at her husband, Reagan wonders if they shouldn't have forced her to leave with Jay and the rest of his people, after all.

John sees Reagan and extricates himself from the group, leaving them behind and greeting her with a warm grin, a typical expression on her handsome husband's charming face.

"Hey there, beautiful," he says and wraps her in a strong hug. Then John kisses her cheek. Then her neck.

She doesn't say anything but pulls back instead.

"Everything ok? What's wrong?"

Reagan shrugs and says, "Nothing."

"What is it? The baby?" he asks, his concern growing.

Reagan just begins walking toward the clinic again, anxious to be home on the farm. "Just wondering if we should've allowed Jay's people to stay, some of them."

"We only let a few stay on. Most of them left."

"I don't know if that was smart."

John takes her hand in his and walks with her. "I haven't heard anything negative about them. Have you?"

"Hm," she answers noncommittally.

"They seem to be getting on all right around here. People have told me that they're helpful."

"I bet," Reagan says, remembering the way the brunette was sizing up her husband. And why wouldn't she? John is so good-looking, his dark blonde hair lighter from the sun's natural highlighting, his blue eyes flashing with good humor at all times, his biceps huge and bulging under his dirty, white t-shirt from long hours of hard labor. He still makes her heart skip when she sees him. That woman had looked at John like he was a deer and she the wolf.

"Some have worked on the wall, too. That's good. Any help we get on that is good. Less time we have to put in on it."

"Super," she says with sarcasm.

"Hey, babe, what is it? Do you not like them here? If you don't, we'll get rid of them. Tell me. If it's some sort of women's intuition thing, just say the word."

"Ha!" Reagan scoffs. "I don't need women's intuition to see through some of them."

His eyes darken and narrow. "What's going on? Is one of them a threat?"

"To our town? No." Reagan pauses and bites her lower lip. "To our marriage? I'm not so sure."

"What?" John nearly shouts with surprise. "What the heck? What are you talking about, babe? Who is he?"

"Not a he! That woman. The one, you know. Jesus, John, she was all but humping you in the town square in front of everyone."

"What?" he asks with confusion and turns to look at the crowd, which has mostly dispersed. "Who? What do you mean?"

"The one with the eyes, the flirty, come hither eyes. She was all but hanging on you. And you didn't seem to mind, either."

"Seriously? Are you crazy? Is this a hormone thing?" he asks tentatively.

"No!"

"I don't even know who you mean, babe," he says, his frustration growing as he rakes a hand through his hair.

Reagan gives a solid harrumph and crosses her arms. Then she gets even more pissed because her arms can only rest on the top of her disgustingly huge stomach.

"Are you serious right now? You're picking a fight, acting jealous of some woman I don't even know who you're talking about? Reagan, honey, don't do this. We're in the middle of a worldwide apocalypse, and you're mad because some woman was hitting on me, or so you say. I still don't even know which one you mean."

"Yeah, sure," she says with childish anger. So her behavior is irrational, she doesn't care. It seemed at the time that she saw something, perhaps a flicker of interest in John's eyes.

"After what we've been through, you think I want someone else? Really? Babe, come on."

She pokes her nose into the air another inch higher.

"You're so cute. This jealous thing is kind of adorable actually," he comments, making Reagan madder.

"I'm not adorable or cute or even attractive. I'm a fucking elephant right now!" she hisses angrily.

"You're my elephant, and I wouldn't trade you for ten flirty eyed women, whoever they might be. I like you just the way you are, big ol' pregnant belly and all. And the bigger boobs are kinda' nice, too."

"You aren't even allowed to touch them. They hurt all the damn time."

"Sometimes you let me," he reminds her, getting a grin from Reagan. "Not often. Not often enough, but sometimes."

She rolls her eyes as John pulls her close again. He whispers something indecent in her ear, causing Reagan to chuckle at his wicked implication.

"Now, no more of this silly talk about other women. You're my boss. That's all the bosses I need."

"Don't forget it, either," she warns, pointing her finger at him. John grabs it and bites gently. "Ouch. Idiot."

"And I'm your idiot. The only one you need."

"As if I needed you," she says with a frown as John presses a plucky kiss to her mouth before she can continue.

"You know you did. Face it, woman, you're stuck with me for the long haul."

"Great," she remarks with sarcasm. Then a grin splits her features when he nuzzles her neck, his five o'clock shadow abrading her tender skin there.

"Now, let's get your big butt home so I can act out some of those things I just whispered," he says, getting jabbed in the ribs from her for the comment about her derriere.

"Don't be a jerk," she warns.

"I like your new curves. All of 'em." He winks for good measure.

"Not me. I can't wait to have my own body back, minus the alien invader."

"Have you given any more thought to names? It's getting closer, boss," he reminds her as if she needs him to.

Reagan just groans. Then a cramp seizes her, causing her to groan in earnest. "Damn."

"Babe?" John asks, his demeanor instantly changing to focused and concerned.

"It's nothing. Braxton Hicks," she says as the contraction ends a few seconds later.

"Are they supposed to be that hard?"

"Are you circling back to the conversation you whispered?" she teases with a grin. John will have none of it, even though it was a funny reference. That's what she gets for trying to joke with the best jokester on the farm. He's always funnier.

"Babe, could this be...?"

"No," she insists, cutting him off. "Nothing to worry about. We're weeks away. You've got plenty of time to pack the bag, finish picking out a name, and gas up the car."

John doesn't smile. His beautiful face is still worried.

"Hey! That was funny this time!"

Finally, he cracks a smile and chuffs. "It was just mildly amusing."

Reagan glares but can't help the smile she tries to suppress from coming through.

"Shut it," she warns.

John takes her hand and continues their walk. "You could've said something like checking our HMO, calling the midwife, and sharpening the knife."

"Mine was way funnier," she challenges with a smile, tucking her head into him as he wraps his arm around her.

"Yes, it was. It was a good one, boss," he allows and squeezes her shoulders to bring her closer in an embrace.

She doesn't let him know that during the ride home, another tightening of her abdominal muscles occurs. There's no sense in worrying John. He has enough on his mind.

Chapter Sixteen
Paige

"Whoa, this looks a lot different than it did the last time we were here," Cory remarks from behind the wheel. Luke is riding in the back seat with her and Derek. Doc is in the front passenger seat next to Cory. She has a blue bandana around her head holding back her hair, even though Cory teases her about wearing them.

"Really?" Paige asks him, thankful they hadn't run into problems on the ride to the fort.

"Yeah," Kelly agrees. "This place looks like some work progress has been moving right along."

"With my father in charge now," Luke states, "it won't take long to make this place into the bunker. He's an excellent delegator and planner."

"I guess so," Derek concurs.

"Look at the fence. Repairs have been made. And the gardens? Geeze, they make us look like chumps," Cory says.

"That's a good thing, though, right?" Paige asks them.

"It means they're making progress and thriving as a community," Doc says. "That must be a good thing I would think."

She offers a smile but reserves judgment on the matter. She knows how much most of the family dislikes Robert and his plans.

They are greeted by men who are in charge, a man named Parker, in particular, and are offered a tour of the grounds. They ride in the back of their truck with the others as Parker's man drives them. Robert joins them halfway through their tour, and Lucas helps him up. In Paige's opinion, he doesn't look so hot. His color is pale and waxy, and he coughs a lot. The man, Parker, greeted Lucas with a handshake of familiarity, but Luke's eyes fell to the ground between them as if he doesn't find him likeable or desire further conversation. They obviously know each other, but if Paige were to guess, she'd think Luke dislikes him. His father greets Luke in the same manner and with just as little affection. She tries not to judge Robert so harshly, but he certainly doesn't make it easy. He could've offered his son a hug, but instead, gave him a firm handshake. However, the look of hopefulness in Luke's eyes reveals a lot about him. He wants his father's attention and approval, even though he's an adult. Paige doubts that he's ever been able to live up to Robert's standards and expectations.

She was surprised even to be allowed to go on this trip since Cory was also assigned to it. She has avoided him at all costs, barely speaks even in the company of the family at dinner time, and never goes anywhere alone with him. It's been very hard, staying away from him, but it's the right thing to do. She doesn't want to further hurt her brother. What they did was wrong, and Paige feels horrible about it. She also feels bad because she knows how Herb feels about that particular subject. Pre-marital sex on his farm is like a slap in her host's face, and she hadn't wished for him or anyone else to find out about her relationship with Cory. Now it's too late. Everyone knows, and she's very embarrassed over the matter.

Robert shows them the rainwater barrels they have set up, the sewer system that had to be modified to manage so many people, the massive gardens that probably total three acres, the kitchens where food prep and storage is occurring, and the children's school.

"This is a rather impressive amount of progress, Robert," Herb says to his son.

"Yes, well, I know you'll want to see the new medical center and research building."

"Oh, yes. That would be wonderful."

They drive there and get out of the truck again. They follow along, Derek on his crutches, which he's using slightly less on the farm. Sometimes he uses just a cane, but she has heard the doctors and her brother discussing his case. This may be as well as he gets. She certainly hopes that's not correct, but Paige doesn't understand enough about medicine to know.

"We're using the medical clinic they already had here and have shut down areas of it that we won't need to conserve energy," Parker tells them.

Paige is not crazy about this Parker guy. She knows from Simon and Cory that he seemed like a jerk when they met him, but she has her own reasons. Every time he looks at her, it's as if he is undressing her with his eyes. She'd like to suggest a cold shower but doesn't want to draw attention to it. Instead, she sticks by Cory's side as they take their tour.

Robert shows them around a few more places like the housing and animal shelters.

"How many are living here now?" Derek asks.

"Nearly twelve hundred," Parker answers.

"Whoa," Cory remarks. "How'd the numbers jump so fast?"

Parker levels a stare directly at Cory as if he finds him displeasing in some way. Knowing Cory as she does, they probably had words the last time he was here. Nonetheless, the other man says, "I told you. We can build a community quickly. We've been sending out messages, scanning towns nearby looking for anyone who wants a fresh start in a safe place. We even had a small community from Cincinnati show up the other day. They brought over fifty people with them."

"It's very fast," Herb notes. "Can you handle the growth that this will bring?"

"Yes," his son answers. "That and more. With the community working as a team, we can handle ten thousand if it comes to that. We have the housing, as you've seen. We have a medical facility, a school..."

"But how do you feed this many people?" Derek questions. "You said before that you will run this place in a similar fashion as the bunker with people working as a group to survive instead of each family looking out for themselves like we do in our town."

"Yes, but we find that it helps doing it our way," Parker answers for his boss. "More hands towing the line, so to speak."

"And the food?" Derek repeats.

Parker takes the lead again, "We've formed a hunting party, a fishing crew, butchers and food prep. We've got this down to a science."

186

"And when people want to make their own way? What about then?" Cory asks.

Parker hits him with a sardonic smile that has little to no genuine feeling behind it, "They won't. Why would they? This will become a utopia to many."

Paige glances at Luke for clarification, who avoids eye contact and stares at something in the distance.

"That sounds a lot like communism. You're controlling the food, the rations, the supplies?" Derek prompts.

"It works best this way. It's less complicated," Parker says with less patience.

"But people will eventually want their own land, to own a piece of land," Herb says. "It's what man has always done. Community living is going to be fine for the time being, but what will happen when men want work for pay and want to live outside the gates and tend their own farms?"

Parker is about to retort a response and not a very pleasant one by the reddening of his face when Herb's son butts in.

"We'll take the trucks to the clinic," Robert tells them as they come to the end of the street. "We can discuss the city later after dinner. Let's not take up time debating this in the street and waste daylight."

Paige believes he is being evasive, but she'll reserve judgment until she knows more. They drive through the growing community, which is thriving and flourishing well. The people don't seem oppressed, and that must be a good sign.

Two young men jog up to them and call out Luke's name. The truck stops, and he jumps over the side of the bed. He must know them from the bunker because he greets them with smiles and even hugs one. Then he excuses himself to go with his friends. Paige is happy for him that there are some people here that he knows and apparently likes. She can't, so far, say the same, especially about Robert's right-hand man. She hears one of Luke's friends ask about Gretchen as they drive away from him and his friends.

At the end of the street, she can see the clinic coming into view, which used to be called something-ELAND ARMY COMMU__TY HOSP_TAL. She isn't sure of the exact name since some of the letters have fallen to their final resting place, likely in the overgrown shrubbery that used to be landscaping. The building looks like it housed three to four floors before the fall, but some of the windows on the top floor are broken, and it appears that a fire scourged the place at one time because black soot crawls down from the roof to about the second floor.

The men are discussing the medical facility, but all Paige is thinking about is the viability of the big building.

Reading her expression of doubt, Parker remarks, "Don't worry, miss. The building is sound. We inspected it. The sprinkler system must've put out whatever fire hit the place years ago."

"Hm, ok. Good," she tells her new stalker. The guy gives her the creeps. He's sitting right next to her in the bed of the pick-up truck, which isn't helping improve his newly appointed stalker status.

Her eyes flit to Cory's, but he seems preoccupied with something the soldier beside him is explaining. Of all the ridiculous times for him to not be allowed by her brother to be around her, this is it.

"Just stick close by," Parker continues. "I'll keep you safe."

"I've got my own security detail," she informs him by displaying the .38 on her hip.

"Smart. I like an independent woman who is capable with a weapon."

Her eyes widen, and she turns away to stare off into the distance. Yuck. She's got to shake him somehow, or it's going to be a miserable day. They are supposed to head straight back to the farm tomorrow, though. Thank God. Unless, of course, Herb decides they need to stay for some reason. She wonders if two hours into their visit to his son's camp is too soon to suggest vacating it. Damn. Probably so.

When the truck comes to a stop near the entrance, Paige hops over the side of the bed for fear that Parker will attempt to help her down from the tailgate. That would mean touching his hand. No thanks.

"Careful, Red," Cory says as he passes by her.

He goes right back to his conversation with the other soldier as they enter the medical building. As usual, she'd like to pick up one of the fallen letters from the sign and throw it at the back of his head.

"To our right is triage," Robert points. "Beyond those doors are our patient rooms. We have quite a few more than at your practice in town, Dad."

"Good, with this many people living here now, you'll need the rooms," Herb answers.

"And to the left is our new research facility. Our doctors from the bunker who came and another who recently joined our group are working tirelessly day and night in there setting up and preparing the unit for their research. Two of the doctors are from the CDC."

"What will they be studying?" Paige asks.

"Diseases mostly," Robert says. "We've lost too many people to various diseases, some simple that could've been cured before this all happened. We want that capability back."

"That's the first good idea I've heard since we got here," Cory comments, earning a downright hateful glare from Parker.

"You'll find we have many good ideas, Cory," Robert counters. "Our medical team is doing very advanced work with extremely archaic supplies and the limited tools they have at their disposal. You may not like all of our ideas, but we need those doctors working on cures for more than just our community. Infections can spread quickly, viruses can wipe out entire towns now, and diseases need to be battled more effectively than what we've managed so far since our country collapsed."

"True," Doc says, rubbing the silver stubble on his chin thoughtfully. "I wouldn't mind going in there and having a look around. If you all would like to meet up later closer to dinner time, I'll be along shortly."

"I'll stay with you, Herb," Derek volunteers.

"Fine with me," Doc says. "Cory, why don't you and Paige go and take a look at their other facilities. Maybe you'll be able to borrow some ideas."

"I'll show you around," Parker volunteers.

"No, no!" Paige is quick to say. Then she has to cover her random outburst. "I just want some fresh air. I think I'll look around the grounds a little. You're probably really busy."

"True, Parker," Robert says. "Why don't you take a detail and check on the fence repairs along the northern border." He turns to

Herb to explain. "Nothing to worry about, but we do need to get the place one hundred percent secured soon."

"No place is fully secure. Not anymore," Cory says and nods to Derek before turning to go.

Paige isn't waiting around for an invite. She follows right on his heels as he crosses the street. They walk for a while in silence, which feels as heavy as the dense fogs that blanket the farm sometimes.

Suddenly, Cory grabs her hand and nearly drags her through a grassy area and then between two buildings.

"Where are we going?" she asks with uncertainty.

"Somewhere more private," he tells her.

He takes her into the alley and comes to an abrupt stop. As the sun begins its descent, there are darkening shadows slinking further down the narrow roadway that cause her the usual uneasiness.

"What's going on?"

"I needed to talk to you, Red," he says and turns to face her. He doesn't release her hand, though. "Damn. I'm sorry I haven't been able to talk to you since it happened."

She knows Cory means the confrontation with Simon.

"I know. Sorry. I've just been trying to keep my distance. I don't want to upset Simon."

"Again," he adds.

"Exactly."

Cory touches her cheek, letting his knuckles brush against her skin. She suppresses the urge to lean into his hand.

"I'm the one who's sorry. We should've gone to Simon together and told him. It was wrong to dupe your brother, and I feel like shit about it."

"Me, too," Paige admits, looking down the alley to make sure they are still alone.

"No, this is on me. It was my job to deal with this, and I didn't," he says.

"Don't blame yourself. You wanted to tell him. I wouldn't let you."

"Doesn't matter. I have to make this right with him," Cory says, clearly having been in turmoil these past weeks. "I can't stand this, and I can't stand being away from you, either."

Paige doesn't say anything. She feels the same way but doesn't want Cory to push the issue. He takes her hands into his own and pulls her forward.

"I'm also really sorry that you had to deal with the whole situation in front of the family. I didn't want that to be the way you heard about my real feelings for you, Red."

"You were just saying that because you knew Herb would be pissed if he found out we were just being casual. I understand. I get it."

"No, that's not what I did at all."

"It's ok, Cory. It's fine. Don't worry about it," she says, trying to come off as nonchalant.

He leans down to kiss her, but Paige turns her head.

"What's wrong?"

She tries to slide her hands-free, but Cory only tightens his grip.

"I think we should just keep this the way it's been the last few weeks. We can't do this anymore."

"End it? Is that what you're saying?"

"Yes, Cory. I thought we did, right before Simon found out," she says, each word feeling like sandpaper gliding across her tongue.

"We're not ending this," he says vehemently and tugs her close again until Paige is pressed up against him. "I'm not giving you up."

"Cory…"

"I love you, Paige," he says quietly. "I wasn't just saying it to appease the family. You should know me better than that by now. I'm not going to lie just to save my ass from getting bitched out."

"Don't," she says, trying to stop him.

"I love you. My answer's not going to change. Not ever."

This is more staggering hearing it from his lips without the rest of the family around and him yelling the words over the melee of the squabble with her brother. It hits like a ton of bricks, piercing her heart.

"I didn't exactly want this to happen," he continues. "I wasn't looking for anything like this when I met you. I still wasn't over the loss of Emma. I sure as shit didn't want a relationship with anyone."

"And I don't want one now," she counters.

"Damn it, Paige," he says, using her name again, which he never does.

"Don't be angry. I don't want you to hate me. I just think it's best if we end this now before anyone else gets hurt."

"You? Before you get hurt?"

She grimaces and looks at her feet. Paige has no desire to get into this with him. Revealing her fears is a horrible idea.

"Sweetie…" he starts.

Paige can't take anymore. She leans up and kisses him, surprising Cory. He recovers quickly and wraps his arms around her back, holding her tight. His mouth moves on hers with expert skill. He knows every intimate detail about her body but still decides to explore it with his hands.

"Damn!" she hisses and jerks away.

"Our break-up didn't last long," he says with cocky confidence and a smug grin.

"Cory!" she admonishes and takes two steps back from him.

"See what I mean? We belong together," he says.

"No," Paige retorts.

"You can't resist me, Red," he taunts.

Paige grits her teeth and retorts, "Yes, I can. I've done it for the last few weeks. You were just getting all mushy and hardcore feelings with me to manipulate my emotions. Go back to calling me Beanpole."

He laughs loudly and leans back against the wall, folding his arms over his chest, which only draws her attention to his thick forearms.

"I don't know why you try to deny it all the time," Cory says. Then he sighs and continues, "We have chemistry. I know you care about me, too, but you don't want to admit it. That's ok. We'll get to that eventually." Cory shoves away from the wall and places his hands on her shoulders. "I know it's not easy. But we both deserve this, Paige. You deserve to be happy. I punished myself for a year over Em's death and left the family. But you know what I learned? That she wouldn't want me to live like that. Am I still angry? Yes. Do I still blame myself? Of course. It was my fault, completely and totally my fault and mine alone. But my little sister wouldn't want me to spend the rest of my life alone just to punish myself because she's gone. If I could go back and trade places with her, I would. You would for the family that you've lost, too. But we don't get that choice. Those are made for us. For whatever reason, we're still here, and we should live each day doing the best we can. You're definitely the best I can, everything about you is the best. I just don't want to throw away what we have because of our fears. Then we'll only be left with regrets someday."

Paige bites her lower lip and studies the red bricks of the building behind him instead of looking directly at Cory.

"I gave you some space the last few weeks, and I'm going to continue to do so until I've got things squared away with Simon. And, hell, I know I need to talk to Doc, too. Kelly already warned me that'll be coming. But I'm not giving up on us. I don't want you to, either. Once I've atoned for what I've done with Simon, then we'll have an opportunity to be together, and I don't want you to throw us away."

"It was just sex, Cory," she says lamely.

There is a flicker of pain in his brown eyes before he says, "Not for me. And it wasn't for you, either, Red. You can fool yourself into thinking that if you want to, but you can't fool me. That wasn't just sex, not even once, not even the first time. Remember it?"

She allows her mind to drift to that night in the Belmont Mansion in Nashville. The cold weather outside, the fireplace crackling, his hands on her body. She tries to hide her shiver. When she looks up at him, Cory is smiling broadly. His confidence irritates her, and Paige locks her jaw to regain her composure.

"Simon's never going to give us his blessing, and I'll never concede to it if he doesn't."

"You let me work on your brother," he says with way too much self-assurance.

"If he works on *you* anymore, you're going to need plastic surgery," she teases.

"That's ok," Cory says with a smug grin. "It'll help keep the ladies at bay."

Paige rolls her eyes at his arrogance. "You weren't exactly fighting back. You kind of just let him beat on you."

"It's what I deserved," he casually offers up. "I would've done the same if the roles were reversed. Simon just did what he should've. That's how I would've handled it, too. Hell, I probably would've handled it a lot worse than he did. Probably not if it was Simon who was interested in my sister. I trust him. He's got good judgment and honor. But men handle our differences like that."

"He went berserk. I wouldn't have thought he had it in him."

Cory laughs at this and replies, "Oh, I did. I knew he'd lose his shit if he found out that way. I gotta hand it to him, though. Those extra workouts we've been putting in have really added to his upper body strength."

"He knocked you out cold," she reminds him.

He laughs more heartily this time and rubs his jaw as if remembering the moment, "Yeah, no kidding."

"You got knocked out. I passed out. We're a real pair."

"We should probably concentrate on staying on this side of consciousness," he jokes, making her smile.

"Good advice," she says.

"Come on, Red," he orders and reaches for her hand. "Let's head back. Don't want anyone getting suspicious."

"Do you really think it matters now?"

She slides her hand from his grip as soon as they reach the end of the alley.

"True," he remarks. "I should just throw you down right here in the middle of the street and kiss every square inch of you."

"I think I'll pass," she says and clears her throat to erase those thoughts as they walk side by side toward the mess hall for dinner.

"Wonder if Parker is saving you a seat next to him," Cory remarks.

"Oh, gross," Paige says. "I sure as hell hope not."

"No? No love interest there?"

"Cory," she warns quietly. "That guy creeps me out. And if you come here with Sam, keep her away from him, too."

"I don't know. I think he might have a thing for gingers," he says, referring to her red hair and even takes a cluster of it in between two fingers.

She moans with disgust. "I don't know, Cory. He seems odd. Not just because he seems like a creeper and won't leave me alone, but he seems like...I can't describe it."

"Yeah," he says, ushering her through a gate in front of him. "I know what you mean. We talked about it when we left here the last time. Just don't go anywhere alone with him."

"I don't think he'd be that bold."

He shrugs and holds the door to the mess hall open for her. "I don't know. Just don't take any chances. He's a power-hungry freak and thinks he can wield it around since the general's his bestie."

Paige laughs at his phrasing as they join the others for dinner. Herb is absent, and they find out that he's still with the CDC doctors who came to this camp. Robert does not join them, but Paige wonders if it is because of his health. Unfortunately, Parker does eat with them. Lucky for her, he mostly engages the men in conversation about the camp and fortifications.

They finally meet with Herb and Robert after dinner when she forces Herb to eat something. He seems highly distracted and suspects this is exactly the way he used to be when he was a younger doctor in a country that wasn't in the state this one's in. For a man of his age, he is suddenly energetic and jazzed up on science.

They are gathered in the general's private quarters. It's not a five-star hotel, but it is comfortable and well-appointed with working electricity, running water, and a fireplace for heat. Lucas is nowhere in sight, which leaves her to believe that he is still hanging out with his friends.

"Robert, we have a problem with these highwaymen that I told you about," he says to his son.

"They are definitely dangerous," his son agrees.

"If the reports are accurate, they have big numbers, possibly near a thousand," Herb tells him.

"That's a lot more than you originally thought when we last spoke," Robert says.

"They are destroying families and killing entire groups of people, just wiping them out," Derek explains.

"The men I was telling you about," Robert says to his man Parker.

"Ah, yes, I see," Parker says.

"We believe that they have some tactical experience, as well, which is making it difficult to track them down," Cory adds.

"Former military?" Robert inquires.

Derek shakes his head, "I sure as hell hope not. But we can't be too sure, and as of yet, most of the people we've run into who have actually survived an attack have reported that they seem like ordinary people."

"What else do you know about them?" Robert asks.

Again, Derek answers, "Some of them wear masks to conceal their faces. We recently found this out from a group we helped. They don't leave survivors unless, like the people we've found, they've escaped unknowingly. There doesn't seem to be females with them when they are attacking, but we did see some in what we believe were their hidden camps in the woods in our area."

"Odd. We never came up against any group this big at the bunker. We had problems with groups like these people you are describing, but they had their women fighting, too."

Doc says, "One of our people saw a woman being struck, physically abused by one of the men in their forest compound. They may not allow the women to fight alongside them because there is the possibility that they aren't with them by choice and are being held against their will. We've run into this before, as well. Perhaps they feel that the women will flee if allowed to leave the camp. We're not sure on any of this yet."

"How did you handle situations like this out there?" Derek questions. "You said you had similar problems."

"Yes, of course," Robert says. "There are problems like this everywhere. Not necessarily with such a large group, but people like this are out there. We simply sent our top security men out to deal with it. Sometimes it went well, smoothly, no casualties, and other times, not so well."

"Then you had casualties, you mean?" Derek prompts.

"Yes," Parker answers. "Our missions were always successful to one degree or another, but sometimes things happen, as I'm sure you're all well aware of, that can't be helped. Our men were trained, some ex-military like the general, but not every factor can be accounted for before a mission. They fought with dignity for the greater good."

And there is the collectivism that she has come to loathe from Robert and his men. Why does he always express their bunker facility in such a way? It makes her uneasy. She also wonders what the general will want or require in return for his help with the highwaymen. Moving away and hightailing it far away from the farm is sounding better and better every day. She knows her brother will never go for this idea, though. And worse yet, Cory will absolutely refuse, too. Her own love of the family would also be a bit of a problem. She's stuck.

"Keeping your unity is the most important thing," Derek says. "I agree. But we have people all over the area, the condo community, our town, our friends, neighbors, and allies. It's going to be more difficult than simply fighting for the greater good of one community. If we don't get this situation under control soon, we may lose a lot of our friends and allies, maybe Pleasant View."

"*If* it's attacked," Robert says. "However, it may not be. It may never be."

"From what we've been seeing lately they are moving on from merely attacking people on the roads. We think that they might be pushing inward onto farms, towns, and the like. That is probably what prompted them to attack our allies."

"Unless they knew it was them and what you all have been doing in the area to push them out," Parker says.

"Possibly," Derek agrees with a nod. "But if they didn't know who Dave the Mechanic was and how he's been working with us and that we're all responsible for the signs to warn people on the roads, then they are getting ready to start waging war on communities now."

"If the people stop using the main roads to travel because of the signs, then the highwaymen assholes are going to need to source their supplies elsewhere," Cory tells him.

Robert says, "And their numbers are great, and the people not expecting them will fall victim like the poor people on the freeways."

"Exactly," Derek says.

"We may need help defeating them," Doc hits him with directly.

There is a long pause before his son answers, "I see."

Derek inserts, "We have numbers, too, but not like them. Plus, if our last intel mission proves right, then we've got a more difficult situation to deal with because they have small camps all over the place. They're very well-hidden. And they have weapons and supplies."

"Interesting," Robert says.

"Plus, we're pretty sure they attacked one of our closest allies, Dave's compound. People were hurt," Derek continues.

"That's unfortunate."

Parker, who insists on constantly shadowing the general, says, "And you want our help taking on these people?"

"Possibly," Derek answers. "We'll be gathering more information on them soon."

"We'll do whatever is asked," Robert says quickly. "Of course, we will."

This surprises Paige. She hadn't expected him to be so agreeable. It instantly makes her suspicious.

Then he continues, "We need to keep the area secure down there. You all are also our allies. We mustn't allow people like that to ruin what we've all worked for."

Derek says, "If we don't deal with them soon, they could come this way."

"And they are leaving a path of destruction everywhere they go," Doc says. "They are murdering innocent people."

"I understand completely, and I agree," Robert says as his wife enters the room. "Let us speak more of it in the morning."

Paige and the rest of the family are shown to a small home where they dump their gear and hit the hay. She is exhausted, but she knows that Cory and Derek are still awake on the first floor because she can hear them talking. They are probably just as nervous about this alliance with Robert against the highwaymen as she is. From what little she has come to know about Robert McClane, he will not be helping them out of the goodness of his heart. He's going to want something in return.

Chapter Seventeen
Simon

"This just feels weird," Sue says at the dinner table that evening.

"Yes, I agree," Sam remarks beside him.

"What do you mean?" Simon asks.

"Without Grandpa at the table," she says and looks at him as if he is an idiot, which he usually is where Sam is concerned.

"Oh, yes. I suppose it is strange," Simon agrees and turns back to his meal.

"And Derek's gone. That's also a bummer," Sue adds.

John says to lighten the mood, "That's kind of a relief actually. He gets on my nerves."

Everyone laughs at his joking about his own brother. It's especially funny since they all know it's not true.

"Too bad you aren't gone, too," Kelly tells him.

"No, too bad you aren't gone," John quips. "There'd be more food."

This makes everyone laugh again. Leave it to John. Simon isn't witty like him. He wishes he was, but he's never had the cool factor like that. There is certainly enough food; there always is. Tonight, they are having stewed chicken with peppers and onions, mashed potatoes, and sweet corn on the cob. It's a heavenly feast, as most meals the girls make usually are. He's glad for summer, too. The fresh produce is always even better than the canned or frozen. Sue also made Gram's famous baked beans, which are sweet and a little bit tangy, as well. They are so much better tasting than the kind his mom used to make that came from a can. He also knows how much work goes into making any dish with beans since they have to soak overnight before being cooked, something he's learned since coming to the farm. It's worth all the work they require when everyone heads to the garden during harvest times to pick the produce.

"Well, we're thankful Sam is here," Hannah says, changing the subject. "She's an addition to our dinner table that is more than welcome, even if our loved ones are absent."

"Thanks, Hannie," Sam tells her. "I'm glad I'm here, too."

"If you're so glad, then why don't you move back?" Simon asks, his voice a touch angry-sounding. Everyone grows quiet.

"Good one, bro," John chides. "Way to ruin the moment."

Simon looks at his plate, embarrassed as usual for saying something stupid.

"Sorry," he apologizes.

Hannah says, "Oh, it's fine, John. He just misses her. We all do. Isn't that right, Simon?"

He freezes. Is Hannah putting him on the spot on purpose? No, she wouldn't do that. She's Hannah. Sweet, unassuming, kind and caring. Simon's eyes flit to her, and he watches as she demurely takes a bite of her potatoes. She's too innocent to have done something so nefarious and calculated. Or is she?

"Um… sure. Yes, of course. We all miss Samantha," he answers, his words lame even to his own ears.

"Wow, praise, indeed," John scolds.

Simon looks at his friend, who seems terribly critical lately and, if he's being honest with himself, kind of mean sometimes, too.

"He's just being shy," Hannah says. "We all know that Simon has missed her just as much as the rest of us."

"Probably more," Sue adds.

He feels as if they are ganging up on him, and he can't shake the feeling that Hannah is involved, too. He squirms.

"Not as much as *me*," Huntley says rather firmly from the other side of Sam.

Samantha chuckles and replies, "Ditto, bud."

Simon sees Huntley smile at her, then when she turns her attention to her meal, he sends Simon a dirty glare. What gives? Everyone is acting like he is a piece of dirt on their shoes. Of course, he misses Sam, but he's not about to spout off love poetry to her at the damn dinner table in front of everyone. He's kept a tight lid on

200

his feelings for her, even to her. It's nobody's business how he feels about Samantha.

"Mmm," Reagan murmurs beside John.

"Babe? What is it?" John asks quickly.

"Nothing, just a little…twinge," she replies and rubs her hand over her stomach.

Simon noticed earlier that she wasn't eating much. Actually, it doesn't look as if she's even touched her food. They are eating a bit later than usual since it took longer to perform chores without Cory, Luke, and Paige home. Derek doesn't help as much as he used to, but he's starting to pitch in where he can. However, Simon still sees a lot of signs of depression in his friend. He does not know how to treat it, though, and has taken to having conversations with Reagan and Doc regarding the topic of Derek's physical, as well as, mental condition. They both agree to give it time, and Simon is not one to argue with them, especially when he is out of his league. He suspects that John let his brother go to Fort Knox to take his mind off of his afflictions and give him something productive and useful to work on for a while.

Simon regards her with concern. "Anything of regularity?"

She hits him with a hard look, one that clearly states that there is regularity and that she is, in fact, irritated about it.

"How close?" Simon asks.

"About twelve minutes."

John literally jumps out of his chair, knocking it over to the floor. "Are you serious? Are you in labor? You didn't say anything! What's going on?"

"I'm fine," she retorts nastily. "This kid isn't coming out yet."

This perplexes Simon as he watches Reagan try to calmly reach for her water glass. She doesn't drink any and places it back down again. Her behavior seems erratic and strange, even more bizarre than most women's on a good day.

"How do you know?" John asks. "You said you're having contractions that are twelve minutes apart for God's sake!"

"John!" Hannah scolds. "Don't take the Lord's name that way."

"Sorry, Hannie," he apologizes. "But what in the heck's going on here? Did you guys know?"

Both sisters shake their heads, and Sue says, "If we'd known, you would've known before us. She hasn't said anything to us since she got home. She went upstairs to "rest.""

"Stop with the air quotes and talking like I'm not right freaking here!" Reagan complains.

"But twelve minutes. That's close, right?" John asks.

"They aren't contractions. I never said they were contractions," she corrects them. "They're just…twinges."

"Twinges that hit every twelve minutes," Sue says with sarcasm.

"Remember when I had Mary?" Hannah asks. "She was awfully fast once it got going. If you're twelve minutes apart, you might go in the next few hours."

"Going to be a night owl like you if you have the baby in the middle of the night," Sue says.

Simon looks at her and frowns. He's never heard of this or read about this theory in his textbooks. He'll have to confirm it with Herb when he comes home. There is a possibility with so much medical cramming that he just missed it. Sometimes the women on the farm say odd things like this, though, and Simon is never sure if they are serious, passing around old wives' tales, or have factual information that could help his studies. Again, they are so confusing.

"Whoa!" G bellows in her typical, unladylike fashion. "You aren't gonna have it right here, are you? Gross!"

"I'm not having this baby tonight!" Reagan practically yells. "Everyone, shut the hell up and leave me be."

She rises, brushes past John- belly and all- and leaves the dining room in a waddling shuffle. This is the same way every woman he knows who has given birth has walked at the end. They get a kind of duck waddle. He understands that it is because of the shifting of bones and musculature in their hips and joints. He does not envy the miracle of childbirth that women must endure, nor does Simon wish he could do it himself. Women, as he understands and has been instructed by Herb, are much tougher and more resilient than men. This is a fact, a written law of nature, not something he needed to study in a book because he's seen it in real life. Herb sometimes says if men were in charge of repopulating the earth, there would've only been Cain. Simon would have to agree.

"I'll speak with her," he says and rises quickly. He folds his linen napkin and places it on the table before leaving, though. He doesn't like it when people have to pick up after him.

"Thanks, Simon," Sue says as he leaves.

He looks in the kitchen but doesn't find Reagan. The music room is next, but again she is not there, either.

"I think she went outside," Sam says, surprising him.

The kids have begun clearing the table, and the clanking of dishes in the kitchen sink and the energetic noise of the house has risen to its typical, nerve-rattling roar.

"Thanks," he says to her. Sam looks so pretty tonight in her pale blue tank top and white, cotton shorts. Her hair is pulled back into a ponytail. Her cheeks are pink from sun exposure today. He has missed her. The girls were right about that, but he isn't going to go shouting it from the rooftops. She's better off away from him since he can't seem to keep his hands off of her. "Want to come with me? Might help to have you with me."

"Sure," Sam says with a nod.

She follows him out the back door, and he asks, "Do you have any idea where she went?"

"Med shed?"

"Yes, that sounds likely," he concurs as they walk toward it. There is a faint, yellow glow coming from under the door. "Looks like you were right."

"When am I ever wrong?" she taunts, jutting out her small chin.

Simon chuckles and shakes his head. "Probably never, Samantha. Most women usually aren't."

"You *are* getting smarter," Sam says with delight and a bit of smugness.

"Thank you. I try," he replies with a smirk.

This makes her laugh gaily as they enter the shed. Reagan is sitting at the side counter reading a medical book.

"Watcha' reading?" Sam asks lightly as if they aren't there to ascertain the status of her labor.

"*What To Expect When You're Expecting*," she retorts with unconcealed sarcasm.

"I think you should've started that one about nine months ago," Simon remarks, earning a sneer from his mentor. "Your grandfather says that it's mostly drivel and that I should in no way ever refer to it for anything."

She flips the book over and shows him the title, which is not what she'd said. It is a book on functional histology, and Simon knows that she has read it many times. So has he. This is clearly a distraction technique.

"Can I at least take some vitals, Little Doc?" he asks.

"No!" she hisses and turns away from them.

Sam looks at him with confusion before saying, "What's going on, Reagan? Do you really think you're in labor or is this just false labor or Braxton Hicks?"

"Neither," Reagan states. Then she inhales sharply and says nothing.

"Another one?" Simon asks.

She doesn't answer but nods. Simon steps forward and boldly places his hands on her stomach. It's a noticeable contraction. He can feel the muscles of her abdomen tightening under his hand. Before she can shove him away because she is very distracted, Simon presses two fingers against her neck to get a pulse, timing it to his watch. Her pulse is elevated, which is an indicator that she is in pain and duress. He nods over his shoulder to Sam who rushes to a cupboard and pulls out a blood-pressure cuff. By the time she gets back, Reagan has pushed his hand away.

"I'm fine. Stop," she asserts.

"Just a quick check," he says.

"No!" Reagan counters. "I'm not in labor, damn it!"

"Au contraire, my liege," he teases and slips the cuff on her arm before she can argue further. Simon speedily pumps air pressure into the cuff and allows the air to release slowly. "It's up a little."

"What is it?" Reagan asks, ever the doctor.

"Note it," he says to Sam. "138 over 83."

"That's a little high."

Sam writes on the paper she started for Reagan's case and says, "Not for a woman in labor. It's perfectly normal since your body is under stress."

"I'm not in labor," she argues again.

"Less than ten minutes apart, I'd say," Sam states. "You haven't been out here long."

"Shit," Reagan murmurs.

Simon touches her slim shoulder and says as gently as he possibly can, "Reagan, I do believe this is labor. Your contractions are regular, timed, and intensifying."

"Shut up, Simon," she blurts and swipes a few curls away from her forehead. "I'm the doctor, and I say it's not labor. Everyone's just overreacting."

"I could perform a cervix…" he starts.

"Hell no! Are you crazy? That's not happening. Christ, why isn't Grandpa here?"

Sam steps forward and says, "Reagan, I understand that you want him here, but he's not. All you've got is Simon and I. Let us just give you a quick once-over; it really is for your own safety. If this is labor- even though you are pretty sure it's not- Simon would be doing the right thing. We don't want you in danger."

This stops her from saying something mean. Then she rolls her neck as if it is sore and rubs the back of it.

"Grandpa was supposed to be here," she whimpers finally.

Simon gets it now. She's afraid. Her grandfather, the most renowned doctor in the state of Tennessee, the man who wrote papers published in medical journals, the same person who used to be one of the best OBGYN's in Boston, is absent. This has upset her birth plan. All women have one, he's learned. Changing their plan is not something they like. He should've known that Reagan being Reagan she'd have this all planned down to the last push.

"We're going to be all right," he says softly and takes her hand in his. When she looks up at him from her seat, there are tears of genuine fear in her bright green eyes. He doesn't feel that same fear. He's only worried about his mentor and friend. "I'll help you through it. Sam will assist. If you want John and your sisters…."

"No! No, none of them. Fuck!" she swears with renewed anger, the fear momentarily displaced. "Fine. Just you and Samantha. If you run into problems, I'll have to help you."

"There won't be any problems. Don't worry," he insists.

"Simon, I'm early. This baby is almost four weeks early," she informs him.

"I know," he admits. He and Herb have been very carefully monitoring her progress and tracking her numbers on her chart. "But you're healthy. You've kept up with your exercise and eating healthy. The baby will be just fine, too. He'll be big enough. You could have your dates a little off, ya' know?" he points out to alleviate her fears just slightly. "It happens all the time. And you were irregular with your menstrual cycles anyway. You could be full-term. We don't know for sure."

He's pretty sure she's early. Herb showed him her tummy band measurement the other day. She's not where she'd be if she were full-term. He only wants her to be safe.

"Why don't you shower and try to relax. The hot water will help. Do some slow walking. Let John help you. Sam and I will go to Herb's old bedroom and get the room set up."

He nods to Sam, who disappears, having read his mind that she should fetch John.

"No, I want to do it in here," she counters. "I don't want to have the baby in the house."

This, he finds strange but won't argue. He'd lose anyway.

"Ok, great. The med shed will be perfect. Our equipment's in here. You're used to it, and it's sterile already. We'll get it set up."

"Ok," she finally murmurs and slides off of her stool.

John storms into the room a second later with Sam on his heels.

"Well?" he asks.

"I think she'll go tonight sometime," Simon tells him, watching John's face turn from worried to truly terrified. "She'll be fine. We've got this all under control. I just need her to get a shower, do a little light walking, relax if she can while Samantha and I set up the shed."

"The shed?"

"Yes, Reagan would like to deliver in here," he says.

John doesn't argue, either, because he is obviously a wise husband and a smart man.

"Are you all right, boss?" John asks her directly.

"I'm about to squeeze a watermelon out of my vagina. So, no!" she barks at him.

"I'm right here. I'll be here…"

"No, just Simon and Sam. I don't want the distraction of you and my sisters in the room."

"But…"

"No," she says with finality and presses her palm against her lower back.

"But you can help her until the big moment arrives, John," Simon offers. "Just do the shower and walking. Help her breathe through her contractions. When they get too tough to talk through, bring her back. She'll be close then."

"Got it," John says and takes her hand. Then he wraps an arm around her lower back and leads her from the shed.

"Wow, this is gonna be a stressful night," Sam frets when they are gone.

"No, we'll be fine."

Sam looks at him with skepticism, "You're awfully confident."

"Just take a deep breath. I'm nervous, too, but we can't let that show, not to Reagan. She'll pick up on it the second she senses our doubt and will panic. We want her calm and under control for this. We're definitely in for a long night."

"That's the understatement of the year," Sam tells him.

Gretchen comes into the shed a second later and says, "Is there anything I can do? I just heard it's going to be tonight."

"Yes, actually," Simon orders. "Take this bag of equipment to the house. Have Sue boil it all. Then make sure the sisters are preparing clean towels and linens. Reagan will have her baby out here in the shed, not the house, so we'll need things brought to us."

"What else?" G asks, taking the cotton bag of delivery and surgical instruments and readjusts her gun belt hanging on her slim hips.

"Keep her calm. Tell everyone else. Spread the word. Doc's not here, so she's nervous as all get out. We need her calm."

"And caffeine for us," Sam adds, making Simon chuckle.

"Yes," he agrees. "That would be great, huh?"

"No, doubt," Sam jokes as she pushes the EKG machine closer to the delivery table.

They both know short of an herbal tea that coffee is out of the question. She found some K-cups of it in a hospital for Doc, but nobody else has touched it. The find was so special, so meaningful to him that nobody had the heart to ask for a cup. He only allows himself one cup every third day so as to ration it, too. Simon wishes he had so much self-control.

"Tell Kelly to do a test on the generator to make sure it's in perfect working order in case we need it," Simon adds.

G leaves a moment later, and he is left with Sam in the quiet of the late evening, the sun having set while they were dealing with Reagan.

"Do you think the baby will be all right? He is coming early," Sam asks with hesitation.

"I think so. It's not that early. Remember, the mother's life must come first above all. Reagan is our priority tonight. We must take care of her before worrying about the baby. If it should come to a life-threatening situation, she is the one we save."

"I know. I hope we don't have to make a decision like that," Sam says sadly. "I wish Grandpa was here."

"Yes, me, too. But, he's not, and we have to handle this just like any other deliveries we've done in the past without him."

"Right."

He regards her for a moment, watching her flit about the room in a flurry of graceful movements before saying, "I don't think the family would forgive me if something happens to either of them. Everyone's already angry with me for driving you away."

She stops moving and pauses. Her eyes meet his momentarily before dropping to the metal cart in front of her. "You didn't drive me away. I'm an adult. It was my choice to leave, and I left."

"I think we both know that's not true, Sam," he says.

She looks at him and says, "Doesn't matter why I left. I can still come back for brief visits like this. And, besides, I'm happy over there, too. Just like I was here."

"I don't believe that, either."

"Believe what you will. I am."

Simon can't help what he says next, "Because you're with that Henry guy?"

Sam doesn't answer, which makes him edgy. Does it mean that her relationship with Henry has progressed since he last spoke with her about him? Or does she not want to talk about him because they have broken it off? He lays out more instruments and grabs a stack of towels from the overhead cupboard.

"I'm technically here with you right now," she mocks.

Simon chuffs and says, "If you are going to be with him, then you'd better start practicing some precautionary tactics, or you'll end up in this same birthing suite."

"Don't be a jerk," she derides.

"I'm not. I'm just being realistic. You could end up pregnant."

"No, you're fishing for intel. I'm not stupid Simon. I know what you're doing, and you're not very smooth at it."

"I'm not prying," he argues. "I'm just trying to offer solid advice. As your friend."

"I've already told you that we aren't friends anymore," she reminds him. "What I choose to do with Henry is my business. The only things I have to tell you are what I choose to tell you, which is nothing. Especially not about my love life."

This hurts. They were friends first, before and above all else. Throughout their harrowing ordeal with his aunt's group and before he started lusting after her, they were good friends.

"I really wish you wouldn't say that," he says, hating the sound of his own weakness. When he's around Sam, all he ever comes off as is weak. It's pathetic really.

"Here," she says, walking over to him and handing Simon a pair of sterile scissors.

"Thanks," he replies and snatches her wrist before she can walk away again.

Sam doesn't look up at him but continues to stare at his hand.

"I don't want us to fight all the time, Samantha," he admits quietly. Still, she will not look at him. There is so much he wants to say and so little time before the room will be bombarded with people. "I hate that our relationship has turned into this. I miss you." This gets her attention because her blue eyes rise to meet his. "I don't like this. I don't want to fight with you. I don't want to hurt you, either. I just want to be your friend again."

"That's not true, Simon," she says. "You want to control me even if we aren't friends anymore. I don't even live here now and yet, you want to tell me who I can and can't date."

"I just don't like him," Simon remarks and drops her hand.

"You don't like him, and you probably wouldn't like anyone that I decide to be with because you're overly protective of me and think you're my father figure. There is nothing wrong with Henry. I've spoken to people about him and have found out for myself that he is a good and caring man. Nobody has ever said a single, negative thing about him. As a matter of fact, you are the only person I know who doesn't like him. I wish you could just come to terms with the fact that you aren't in charge of me anymore."

"Fine. I will. You can make all the bad decisions your little heart desires. Then can we go back to being friends?"

"No, and that was condescending. It's never going to go back to being the way it was," she informs him with sadness in her soft voice.

"Why not?" Simon asks, trying to ignore the anger that is edging its way into his tone.

"Because I have…*had* feelings for you, and we just can't pretend that I didn't. Simon," she says, stopping to look at him, "I bared my soul to you, and you completely rejected me, rejected the idea of us being together, and basically ruined it for us. Or maybe I ruined it by chasing after you. Had I known then what I know now I probably wouldn't have confessed my feelings. I should've just kept them bottled up inside. Then we could still be friends. But it just doesn't work that way. I can't take the words back, and we both can't just forget they were ever issued. It changed our relationship. Everything's different now."

"But the night of the tornado, I was the one you came to for comfort, not him. That has to mean something."

It definitely meant something to Simon. He was so afraid that she was going to be killed. Simon didn't particularly care if he was, but the idea of Sam being in harm's way had greatly upset him. He wanted to go out and fight the tornado, look it in the eye and fend it off from hurting her.

"Yes, it means I trust you and took solace in what you were offering. But, if you remember, the next morning, you split. You didn't even stick around to say goodbye when I had to leave."

"Wait," he says, holding up his hand, "I didn't say goodbye because I didn't know you were leaving. I was out in the woods or something with Huntley working on cleaning up the tornado debris and chasing animals. I was mad that I missed you."

Sam shakes her head and walks away to the patient bed where she begins pulling a clean sheet over it. "It doesn't matter, Simon. It's over. It's never going to be anything now. You've made yourself clear many times on the subject. You don't feel the same way about me that I felt about you."

He hates it that she keeps referring to her feelings about him in the past tense as if she has completely moved on and forgotten about him. Simon is pretty sure it's true, and that bugs him even more. She doesn't even want his offered friendship.

"That's not..."

"It's ok," she says. "Don't lie. Don't cop to something just to make me feel better. That wouldn't be you. You're not a liar."

This makes him frown hard. If she only knew what a fraud and a liar he truly was. She'd probably hate him even more, almost as much as he hates himself.

"You're a good person, Simon. You'll find someone. I'm sure you will. And then you'll be happy..."

She drones on about this for another minute while Simon mentally kicks himself. There is so much he'd like to tell her, but doesn't.

"Can I just ask you one thing?" she says, startling him from his thoughts.

"Anything. You know that," he says, glad to have any interaction with her.

"Why did you kiss me? Why had you kissed me in the barn the night of the tornado? Why did you do it at my parents' house and at the clinic? I don't understand. You seemed like...I don't know...like you had feelings for me. It didn't seem fake."

Simon's pulse quickens. He'd like to pull her into his arms and do it again, but Sam is right. It's over. He has no right to even think about kissing her ever again. This is what he wanted, for her to move on and find happiness elsewhere so that he could stop being a lecherous bastard about her. So far, it hasn't worked out according to plan.

"Sam, I… I'm just… I can't help…" he stammers and sighs. "This is a horrible, sick…"

Huntley bursts through the door, always at the most inopportune time, in Simon's opinion. He never gets more than a minute alone with her, not here, or the clinic, and certainly not over at Dave's compound where she seems to always be in high demand. He wants to confess to her how depraved he is where she is concerned. He certainly doesn't want to disgust her, but Simon would like Sam to understand. It isn't an easy subject to broach, and it is humiliating and debasing to admit to, but his lust for her is like a physical sickness. He wishes he could move on, but Sam is always on his mind, in his thoughts, his dreams, his fantasies. Especially his fantasies. And that's the biggest problem of all.

"Hey! I just found out. This is awesome!" Huntley declares with excitement.

"Yeah, Hunt," Sam says. "Kind of scary, though. I wish Grandpa was here."

"Nah," Huntley says with way too much confidence in them. "You'll be fine, shadi. And you've got the Professor with you. You guys'll be great!"

"Thanks, little brother," Sam answers.

She offers Huntley a soft smile, which warms Simon's heart. He wishes that he didn't think about her so much, but then she goes and smiles like that, and it's as if the sun itself has illuminated her from within. Or her dark hair will swish and shine in the moonlight, or she acts in a defiant manner that makes him long to snatch her into his arms and kiss her into submission.

"You'll take care of Little Doc, right, Simon?" Huntley questions.

"Yes, sir," he answers and wipes down the countertop. "She'll be just fine. We have everything we need here. Are Sue and Hannah preparing the other items?"

"Yep, G brought them in earlier," Huntley answers and rolls his eyes. He and Gretchen don't always get along so great. Simon understands completely. G is a sassy girl with a fondness for cussing and smoking, and Huntley wouldn't even dream of breaking a rule or doing anything bad. "I'll go check on them."

He leaves in a flurry of long black hair flowing freely tonight. Simon smiles and shakes his head.

212

"I'll get a bucket and a mop," she volunteers and walks past him toward the back of the shed.

Simon snags her arm and holds on firmly. "Can we talk later, Sam? I feel like I just…I just wish I could explain to you…"

Her blue eyes are beseeching and filled with curiosity and wonder. Or perhaps her eyes are always like this. Her dark pink lips are slightly parted, making Simon wish he could kiss her. But that would just further confuse their situation. She deserves an explanation, not more confusion.

"Got the towels," Sue says as she strides through the door. "Looks like it's gonna rain."

Sam breaks away as inconspicuously as she can, although Simon is sure that Sue saw him holding her close to him. She sniffs out whatever Hannah does not, which isn't much. Together they are a fearsome team in action.

"What? Oh, yes, rain. It might," Simon concurs.

"I'll make sure Kelly checks the generator in case you need it," she says and walks toward the door. "I think I saw him heading that way."

Simon is distracted because he is watching Sam walk away to the back of the shed to obtain more supplies.

"Everything ok, Simon?" Sue asks, garnering his attention.

"Yes, ma'am," he says, turning back to her.

"Are you going to be able to do this?" she asks with real concern.

"Of course, Sue. Don't worry," he says. Simon knows she is fretting because Reagan is her little sister. He doesn't blame her. He would be, too, if it were Paige in this situation. He thanks God that it isn't. He probably would've killed Cory for that. "I've got this under control, ma'am. No worries, all right?"

She nods unsurely and leaves the shed. She's right. Simon needs to get his head in the game and stop troubling himself over his relationship with Sam. She's a distraction, always has been, but tonight, his mentor is in his hands, and she needs him. Simon can't let her down. He shoves aside all thoughts of further conversation with Sam and gets to work, trying hard to remember every tiny thing he's learned from Doc over the past four years on obstetrics and gynecology. This is the single, most important medical procedure he's ever handled. The entire McClane family is counting on him.

Chapter Eighteen
Reagan

After midnight, her contractions increase to the point where she can barely continue walking through them. Her groin muscles, which have been sore and tugging lately, feel as taught as metal cording instead of human muscle tissue.

"I have to use the bathroom," she tells John in their bedroom.

"Let me help you down the stairs, babe," he says.

Reagan sends him an impatient look.

"All right," he answers with apologetic eyes. "But I'm right on your six. Be careful."

She makes it to the second-floor bathroom where she relieves herself. Then she washes her hands and accidentally pees some more on the floor.

"Damn it!" she curses loudly.

John blasts through the door with a startled expression and asks, "What is it? Is everything ok?"

"I just peed on the floor. So, I'd say no. No, John, I'm not ok. That's probably my water finally breaking. Turn around! I have to go again."

Her husband swiftly spins and presents his back to her so that she can finish leaking into the toilet instead of on the floor. It seems to go on forever.

"Done? Can I turn around now?"

If she weren't so miserable and in such pain, Reagan would laugh at the hesitation in his voice. John is not the kind of man who is ever unsure of himself.

"Yes, I think I'm finally done, and yes, you can turn around. Ooooh….."

"Another contraction?" he asks, flushing the toilet for her and taking her by the hand and elbow and leading her toward the sink. He has already wiped the floor dry.

Reagan nods and tries to control her breathing, tries to slow it down because she is on the verge of hyperventilating. John rubs her back as she leans down on her forearms against the countertop. The contraction recedes, leaving her sweaty and breathless.

"Want another shower?" he asks patiently. "You said it helped your back pain."

"No, it's time to walk some more," she says. "Can we do it outside? I need some fresh air. The house feels too stuffy and hot."

"Got it, boss," he says and sweeps her into his arms.

"John! Put me down. You're going to drop me. I'm so fat," she argues.

Her strong husband only chuckles as he carries her down the stairs.

"I'd rather it be my fault that you take a tumble than to watch you trip and fall down these stairs on your own," he tells her, then kisses her cheek. "And you aren't fat, dear. You're pregnant."

"Doesn't mean I'm not fat."

"You've hardly even gained weight. You still feel the same weight as you were before you got pregnant. How much have you gained?"

"Twenty-one pounds. And that was enough. It was hard enough keeping food down, let alone trying to gain the appropriate amount of weight," she tells him as he places her very gently on her feet in the kitchen.

"Hey, guys. Doing ok, sis?" Hannah asks as she rushes over and reaches for Reagan's face. Her sister's soft, cool fingertips feel heavenly against her skin.

"Yeah, this is great. Awesome, actually," she replies with deep sarcasm.

"Oh, my poor darling," Hannah says and kisses her forehead. "Let me get you a cool towel. It really helps, especially the farther along it goes."

"Thanks, Hannie," Reagan tells her as Hannah moves away. "My water finally broke."

"Not long now," Hannah says, returning from the sink with a damp, cold rag.

"I'm going outside to walk," she tells her sister and slides her feet into her grandfather's canvas, slip-on shoes. For some reason, these are the shoes she wants to wear. She wants him here, but he can't be. This is as close as she's going to get to having him with her tonight.

"Remember your breathing. It does help. Or screaming. That works, too," her sister offers.

Reagan manages to chuckle. Then she nods to John, and they leave through the back door. She makes it all the way to the equipment shed before she has to stop again to deal with another annoying contraction.

"Damn," she says with a hiss. Then her stomach does a flip, and she turns instantly nauseous. She bends over and vomits beside the equipment shed, pressing her hand against the wall of the building. John holds back her hair. When her stomach is empty, Reagan stands upright again.

"Is that normal?" John asks in an irritated, anxious rush of words as he strokes her hair and back.

Reagan nods. "Yes. It happens. I should've known I wasn't getting out of this pregnancy without puking one last time."

"Can I get you something?"

"An epidural?" she jokes.

He chuckles nervously and says, "Anything else?"

Reagan shakes her head and motions for them to continue their walk. They circle back around and end up down by the hog barn. Another contraction hits. This time it is sharp and stabbing. She actually moans, scaring John.

"Take me to the shed," she says when it passes.

He bends to pick her up, but Reagan pushes him gently back.

"No, I want to walk. Let me walk, John."

"Ok, babe," he agrees with a nod.

Reagan looks at him as they walk, him with his arm behind her back for support. Her handsome husband's hair is standing on end. His eyes are glazed over with fear and worry. His sculpted jawline is tense, and a vein works in his neck. Reagan rests her hand on his thick forearm.

"Don't worry. I got this," she tells him. "Don't worry about me. As a matter of fact, go to bed and get some rest."

"What?" he says an octave higher than his normal voice. "Are you crazy, boss? I'm not going anywhere. You don't want me in there? That's fine. I'll wait outside the door."

"John, just relax. Ooooh," she says tightly and inhales a sharp breath. This is the worst one yet. It's getting impossible to talk through it. The time is coming. She knows she is likely nearing the moment to start pushing. Has she waited too long? It passes again, but the shed feels so far away in the distance as if they have five miles to walk instead of fifty yards. "John," Reagan says in a pleading tone. "I don't think I can make it."

He doesn't even ask. He simply hefts her into his arms again and nearly sprints while still managing not to jiggle her too roughly against him.

"Simon!" John barks, although Simon is just inside the door. "Oh, good. You're here."

"Nowhere else to be, sir."

Simon is smiling, charming, dimples showing. Reagan would like to strangle him.

"What do I do?" John asks with panic.

"Put her down, sir," Simon tells him. "We've got it from here. Right, Little Doc?"

Reagan barely manages a nod.

"How close?" Simon asks as John places her on her feet again.

"Five minutes. Maybe three. Severe. Can't talk through them anymore. Can barely breathe through them," she reports.

Behind him, Sam is jotting notes quickly on a chart.

"Sam, can you help Reagan get changed into something more comfortable?" Simon asks in a calm tone.

Reagan follows her behind the screen, but she can hear Simon talking to John. When she emerges in a sterile hospital gown, her husband is gone, and the three of them are alone just as she'd requested when this all started about four hours ago, not counting the full day of light contractions.

"He's just outside the door, Reagan," Simon tells her as if to help subside her fears. "Now, why don't you lie down and let me get some vitals, alright?"

218

She nods but hates this. She should be in charge here. Simon is still a student. Reagan reminds herself that he's delivered quite a few babies, though. She has to trust him, even though it's hard to do.

He takes her blood pressure, checks her pulse, dilates her pupils with a tiny flashlight, and checks her ankles for swelling.

"Everything looks great," he replies and places his hand on her knee. "We're going to need to do a cervix check, Reagan. I know you don't want me to, but I have to know how far along you are."

This is humiliating, but she is in so much pain that Reagan is confident that at this point she'd let one of the neighbor's do it. Or a passerby on the road. Or one of the highwaymen.

"Fine. Just get it over with."

They help her get her feet into the stirrups that Simon flips out, and she scoots down to the edge of the bed.

"I heard your water finally broke. I can tell. That's good. Everything is presenting normal. You're in good shape. We're ready with everything else," he says as he checks her. "Don't worry, Reagan. Sam and I are on top of it. Our equipment and tools have been sanitized. The towels are ready and clean. I have a bucket already in place for the afterbirth. We don't want you to worry about a thing. Just concentrate on what you need to do and leave the technical stuff to us."

Simon is done a split second later, and Reagan is pretty sure he didn't even look down there but performed a basic cervix check with his fingers. His manner is professional and calming.

"You're at a seven," he announces and nods to Sam, who writes it down along with the time on her chart.

A contraction hits, and she can barely breathe this time.

"Wow, shit!" Reagan swears. "This is sucking!"

Simon takes her hand in his and encourages her to squeeze. He wipes her brow with a cold rag and tells her to breathe slowly.

"Focus on my face, Reagan," he says. "Easy. Slow. Just like me. Follow along. Slowly in, and…there, out. You've got it."

A few seconds that feel like hours later, it subsides again. Simon nods and takes her pulse.

"Good," he remarks. "You got through that one like a champ."

"This fucking sucks. I'm never doing this again! God, I'm such an idiot! I hate John!"

Sam chuckles and presses another cool rag against her cheek. It helps a lot. She wishes she had a Dr. Pepper in a glass full of ice. She has no idea where that thought just came from, but she can taste the bubbly, sweet soda in her mouth. One final craving that is bizarre and inexplicable.

"Oh, I forgot to tell you. I threw up out by the equipment shed."

"All right, we'll note it, but that's normal," Simon tells her.

"Duh! I know that! I know...fuck!" she swears again as an intense one hits.

Simon helps her breathe through it and even holds her hand again. She doesn't care if she's crushing it. He deserves it. This is his fault, too. She's not sure how that makes sense, but it does to her.

The contractions go on for another hour and a half until Simon rechecks her and declares that she is finally ready to push. Then the real fear sets in. Reagan begins to feel an unnatural panic. Something doesn't seem right. Her breathing goes berserk as a contraction hits. Simon tells her to push, but Reagan can't concentrate. Her body just seems wrong. Something is wrong.

"Nothing is wrong," Simon answers her.

She hadn't even known she'd said it aloud.

"You're doing just fine. I need you to push," he says.

"No, something isn't right, Simon," she argues and moans as an intense pressure in her stomach forces her to bear down. Reagan groans loudly, swears once, and collapses back onto her pillow as the contraction eases.

"Get ready because the next one's coming," Simon warns her. "Rest. Breathe. Prepare yourself."

She can't shake the feeling that something is wrong, so she starts asking Simon questions about the baby's presentation, the placenta- if it is presenting first, to which he says that it is not. He tries to reassure her that everything is fine, but Reagan knows it isn't. Then she's pushing again against her will. Her body is forcing her to do the work she doesn't want to do.

"Good. That's it. You're doing great!" Simon tells her.

Sam is also encouraging her and holding her hand. Reagan pushes Sam's hand away. This tiny hand she is positive she will break.

220

"Damn it!" Reagan swears and lets her head loll back to rest. Feelings of foreboding and dread come over her so strong that she starts hyperventilating. "Something is wrong. I can feel it."

"Easy, Reagan," Simon orders. "Take it easy. Relax and rest between contractions."

"I can't do this!" she cries out. "I can't, Simon. I'm going to die. I know I am. Something's wrong."

"Reagan, look at me," he says. "I am monitoring everything. Your vitals are perfectly normal. Everything looks great. I can almost see the baby's head. You're doing so great. Just keep breathing and try to relax."

She vehemently shakes her head and starts crying. "I'm going to die and so is this kid. John is going to be left alone. He'll have no one."

"Oh, no, Reagan," Sam says, smoothing Reagan's curls away from her head. "No, you're doing so wonderful. John is fine, too."

And then it hits her. John. She needs him. He is what is wrong because he is not with her. She needs her John.

"I'll get him!" Sam answers her unspoken question. Or had she said it out loud? The world no longer makes sense as another fierce contraction takes over her mindless, spent body.

"Bear down, Reagan. Keep going," Simon encourages and begins counting. Reagan would like to tell him to go to hell.

"Babe!" John says as he rushes into the room.

Reagan grits her teeth and pushes. The pain is excruciating and never-ending. When the contraction subsides, and Simon stops counting, Reagan collapses back onto her pillow again.

"I can't do this," she says with exhaustion.

"Of course, you can," John says and kisses her forehead, which is matted with sweaty curls. "You're my Reagan. You are the toughest woman I know. You got this, boss."

He continues to talk to her as another contraction strikes. John has a soothing effect, and she calms down enough to concentrate on pushing. He also holds her into a more squatting position, supporting her back and weight.

"Eight…nine…ten, good," Simon coaches. "The head is out, Reagan. Take a few breaths. Get ready."

Within seconds she is pushing again.

"God, I'm never doing this again!" she yells and pushes again. Then she yells a few expletives, namely at John, who just smiles and keeps encouraging her. She'd like to punch him in the face.

"Almost there," Sam says, standing at Simon's shoulder now instead of by Reagan. "Great! Awesome. You're doing great."

"One more...good," Simon says as the baby is finally expelled.

Reagan breathes a deep sigh of relief that it is over and feels her entire body become suddenly empty again.

"How is he? Is he breathing?" John asks with concern.

Simon doesn't answer because Reagan knows he is likely suctioning the baby's mouth and nose. Sam is right there in the same rushed manner swabbing it with towels.

"Well, *she* is doing great," Simon finally announces as the baby cries out in protest of the cold air hitting its recently incubated body, and the light in the med shed stinging its eyes.

"She?" John asks.

Reagan looks at her husband. There are tears in his eyes.

"And her lungs are very strong. Yes, they are," Simon says more to the baby than them. "You are a screamer, little one."

"Oh, Reagan, she's so beautiful," Sam exclaims.

"Cut the cord?" Simon offers, to which John refuses. "That's all right. There. All done."

"Is it ok? Is it too small?" Reagan begins blurting. She asks the weight and length, which she knows have not been taken yet. "Is it breathing ok? Heart rate?"

"Doing fine, one-thirty-five. Normal rate. She's small but seems just fine to me, Reagan," Simon tells her from the back counter where they have placed blankets and towels as padding to examine the newborn. Simon is working quickly, but Reagan can't see what's going on.

"Is it breathing all right?" she calls to them.

"Yes, fine. I'm listening to everything. Lungs seem clear," he calls back and says to Sam in a quieter tone to dictate on Reagan's chart some notes about the baby. It makes Reagan nervous. She wonders if something is wrong.

"What's going on?"

"It's ok, honey," John says. "Let Simon check her out."

"She's great, Reagan," Sam says over her shoulder as she hands Simon another towel. "She has all her fingers and toes and a good, strong heartbeat. Her lungs are clean and clear. Her eyes are responding to stimulation. Everything seems perfect."

The baby screams at them in protest of being wiped down again by Simon. Its sleep was just interrupted to be brought into this loud, cold, annoying world.

A few moments later, Samantha brings the baby over to Reagan and places her down into her arms.

"Our little alien invader," John says, tears now slipping loose. He quickly whisks them away and smiles proudly at her.

Reagan looks down at the swaddled bundle lying in the crook of her arm. All this time, she never knew. She never understood what her sisters, mother, or Grams went through and what they felt in this moment.

"Don't call her that," Reagan reprimands her husband softly. "She's not that anymore. She's our baby girl."

John kisses her forehead, smiling broadly, but Reagan can't seem to stop the tears from flowing down her cheeks at the wonder and incomprehensible feelings that are washing over her. The baby stares at her in the same manner.

"Hello," she says to the baby, who blinks slowly. The infant stops crying the moment Reagan speaks. It makes Reagan smile. This is what she's been waiting for her whole life. She'd thought it was John. Now she knows that he's just the icing on the cake. This baby girl was what she was meant to do with her life. Bringing this little life into the world was her real destiny, not being a famous doctor or discovering new surgical techniques or curing some disease. This little girl was her destiny.

"Another contraction, Reagan," Simon says to her and nods to Sam, who takes the baby and gives her to John.

"Why don't you help me over here with her, John?" Sam suggests, leading him away.

The afterbirth is even more painful to expel, but then it is over, and Reagan wants the baby back in her arms. Suddenly they feel empty without her resting there.

A few minutes later after Simon has finished cleaning her and placing warm, sterile towels under her and packing similar rags against her, Reagan is covered with a blanket and finally able to rest a moment. The room that was just moments ago stifling and hot now feels freezing cold. Her body is shaking terribly. Sam brings another warm blanket over and covers her. Reagan smiles, which Sam returns and kisses her forehead.

"You did so great," Sam praises as she presses two fingertips to her wrist for a pulse.

"You guys did great. I couldn't have done this without you two."

Sam gets tears in her eyes and walks away. Simon adjusts her bed, folds the stirrups back under and raises the bottom again so that she can place her legs down more comfortably. Sam returns with John, who is carrying the baby. He immediately places her down beside Reagan again.

Simon dictates from her chart, "Born at 3:20 a.m. Five pounds, nine ounces. Seventeen and one-quarter inches. I'm not sure she was all that early, Reagan. Perhaps your week of conception was off a little. She's an awfully good birthweight for being so early, which leads me to believe that she isn't as early as you suspected."

Reagan barely hears him. This is the most important stuff of a baby's birth- the weight, length, lung function, vitals, responses to stimuli. Or at least that's what used to be the most important to her. Now, all she wants to do is cuddle her new daughter. She can't seem to stop kissing her downy forehead. She smells strange, not in a bad way, just different, odd. Perhaps it is purity, the only truly pure thing left on this planet.

Sue and Hannah come in a moment later, and new tears of joy are sprung, this time by her sisters. Hannah touches the baby, feeling every little crevice and detail of her fingers, toes, and face.

"Oh, she has a little hair," Hannah comments. "What color is it?"

"Dark brown," John tells her.

"Weird," Sue says.

John smiles and announces, "My mother had dark hair."

"So did ours," Sue tells him. "That's where I got it."

Hannah kisses Reagan on the cheek and smiles. Reagan touches her hand to her sister's own soft cheek and returns the smile.

"What are you going to name her, guys?" Sue asks with excitement.

John looks at Reagan with anticipation and hope. They've discussed this a lot. Mostly it was John who was enthusiastic about it, and Reagan who didn't want to talk about it. Now she knows exactly what she wants to name her daughter.

"Charlotte Rose," she tells them. "After both of our grandmothers."

"Oh, that's a perfectly lovely and romantic name, isn't it?" Samantha says in her light, whimsical voice.

Reagan grins and kisses Charlotte on the forehead again. At her request, Simon hands her a stethoscope so that Reagan can listen to her heart and lungs. They seem good and strong, fast and excited, even though she remains calm and quiet. Everyone leaves a short time later, and Simon and John help her into one of the more comfortable, lower to the ground beds. Sam adds more towels under her, and Simon changes her padding so that she doesn't bleed everywhere. He takes her vitals again and then Charlotte's. Then they leave.

"I can't believe she's finally here," John says and kisses Reagan softly on the mouth.

"I can't believe we made this," Reagan teases with a gentle smile that her husband returns.

"She's so small."

"Not really. She's a good weight. She'll be fine. I'll check her out thoroughly in the morning."

"I have no doubt this baby will be checked daily."

John kisses her again, and Reagan returns it with as much love as one person can feel. Then they both kiss Charlotte.

He eventually falls asleep in the chair beside her with his head lying on the bed next to her. Simon comes in from time to time to check on her and Charlotte, and she tells him how proud she is of him, which, of course, makes Simon blush. But for the most part, Reagan is left with the baby alone in the peace and quiet of the pre-dawn hours.

She's never seen such a perfect creation of God's doing. Her daughter is intelligent and wise beyond her years as if she is hiding some deep secret of the universe in her cloudy, unfocused blue eyes. Reagan wonders what her life will be, what she'll do with it and what the world will be like as Charlotte grows up.

She doesn't even cry. She just seems content to lie in Reagan's arms and stare up at her. She is at peace with the world and satisfied to have her mother holding her. Reagan sends up a prayer that her daughter's life will know happiness and love and that things will get better so that she will understand the world as Reagan used to know it. She even takes a moment to talk to Grams, knowing her grandmother is smiling down at her, and likely laughing at her for being so stupid that she didn't want this precious gift. Reagan smiles at Charlotte before drifting in and out of consciousness, not wanting to lose sight of her new baby for more than a few seconds. She still can't believe she was given such a perfect, beautiful little life for which she is now responsible. For the first time since becoming pregnant, Reagan doesn't feel afraid.

Chapter Nineteen
Cory

Two days into their stay at Fort Knox, Cory is ready to pack their shit and head home to the farm, but Doc is in the middle of some work in the research lab with the CDC doctors and isn't ready to leave. Cory's going out of his mind with boredom and wants to be back on the farm, or more importantly, back on the road searching for those dickhead highwaymen.

Yesterday, they heard over Robert's radio that Reagan had her baby, to which they'd all celebrated. Doc, however, had been upset that he wasn't there, but Reagan had assured him and the rest of them that she and the baby are doing fine. To Cory, she'd seemed happy, which is not an emotion that Reagan exhibits often.

It makes him think about having kids. He likes to tease Paige about having kids with her, but Cory sure isn't ready for such a responsibility just yet. Just getting her to bend to his will and marry him someday is proving a difficult task.

"Oh, yes, it'll work. You'll see," Parker is saying to her as they walk along a narrow corridor in a dorm-style building.

"I don't see how that'll be possible," Paige argues. "People aren't going to want to live like this forever. If they could develop their own land and farms around the area, you'd have a more productive community."

"Doc was saying last night that some of the people in Pleasant View are considering moving right outside the town and starting their own farm. It would be a possibility for your settlement to barter livestock and produce with them in exchange for whatever it is that you might have to trade in return," Cory says to them. He is walking behind them, and Derek has taken Doc to the research clinic again. Derek has also been shadowing Robert McClane for the last few days learning everything he can about the fort and their way of life here. From what he told him and Doc and Paige last night after he'd tagged along with Robert all day yesterday was that it seems more and more like a socialist model than anything else. They even keep the food and weapons under lock and key and armed guards. People are being fed rations right now, too, since their food is still growing, and they don't have too much in the way of livestock and have had to hunt for meat. Cory doesn't like the changes he's seen on the base. The people of their town don't run Pleasant View like this. The only thing that is community-driven is their security. The sheriff has deputies, and they train new men and women to act as sentries and outriders. It helps to keep the place safe, but they don't have community gardens or a shared reserve of food that is kept locked up. Anything that is shared is either bartered or given away because it is not needed by that family.

Their town has been generous and giving with the newcomers, especially the Campbell Kids, but Cory knows that each child over the age of twelve has been doing chores, gardening, cutting firewood, and helping out in the form of payment for what they are being given. It will help them learn responsibility and discipline, and the kids seem to like having something to do. So far it has worked out just fine, and he really doesn't anticipate them ever leaving again, even if their leader Melora says the opposite.

The two women who are now teaching classes in town are being paid in fresh produce and canned goods to get them through the winter because the town decided that if they were in the library teaching school all year long, then they weren't going to be able to tend a garden, as well. Medical care by Doc, Reagan, and Simon is usually paid for by surrendering any medicines that family has, items they have salvaged on a run for supplies, or repairs that need to be done to their clinic. The people in town also keep the grounds around the clinic maintained and cleaned up in exchange for their medical care. People who keep dairy goats or cows trade their milk with others who grow more bountiful gardens or raise meat chickens. Whatever trade one man might have will come in handy in exchange for a skill that another one lacks. Their system of taking care of one another has worked beautifully; however, forcing people to work as a group for a community store of doled out food is eventually going to implode. It seems to Cory that Robert's plan for the fort is all too similar to what they just left in Colorado, but he'll reserve judgment until he sees more.

"I don't see why we can't continue to grow community gardens and produce livestock here within the walls of the fort," Parker argues.

"Because there is no incentive to continue at some point," Cory explains. "Eventually, people will grow tired of pulling the weight for those who don't want to put in the same amount of time and effort. Models of community living have always proven to fail or dissolve over time. Some will become lazy and complacent to have others do the work for them. The ones doing the work will become frustrated and revolt against the system."

"I don't see that it will become a problem here," Parker continues as if he doesn't believe Cory at all.

"Oh, it will," Cory says, ignoring his rival's sneer.

"Why don't I take you for a ride around the complex, Paige, and show you some of the more progressive areas of our system that we've already implemented."

Cory notices that he is not included in the invitation.

"Oh," Paige says, stammering slightly. "Um, sure. Cory, let's take a look at what they've done, 'kay?"

"Sure. Sounds fantastic," he says brightly, hoping to piss off Parker even more with his agreement to go with them.

Cory just can't shake the feeling that Parker is a worm. It doesn't help that he's been hanging on Paige for the past three days straight. Her feet barely hit the ground in the morning before Parker is pouncing. Although he is supposedly ex-military, Cory finds himself wondering if the guy has ever seen active duty combat before. He sure as hell doesn't seem like it, and Luke doesn't like him, either. He's sure of it, although his new friend has never said as much. Cory can tell by the sidelong glances of barely concealed loathing that he's seen Luke giving Parker, especially when he's boasting about something, either the compound, his achievements as second in command, or his success stories of fame at the bunker. Cory also wants to vomit when he's around but has refrained out of respect for Doc. Not Doc's son, but Herb himself.

He escorts them in a golf cart, and they tour some of the base they haven't seen yet. Parker shows them the meager livestock they do have, which isn't much and certainly won't be enough to sustain the base through the winter. Then he drives along some of the perimeter fences they've been building. The other was way too far out to keep the small area of the occupied base safe and secure, so they are tightening down the acreage with new fencing. It's a good idea. Fort Knox is a massive complex and difficult to secure without the benefit of thousands of soldiers living on it. From what he's read on the yellowing posters in the hallways promoting the base, it is a massive amount of acreage. Great for an actual town someday but not right now with so few people to defend such a significant amount of square footage. Parker explained that they will try to keep a small, centralized area sectioned off until the group expands and continues to grow.

Yesterday, they went through the gold depository, which was certainly empty of any gold. The building was cool, Paige loved the architecture, and the general said that he one day hopes to make it his military command base. When asked where all the gold was moved to, Robert hadn't answered but evaded their question. Cory wonders if it is in the bunker in Colorado, not that it matters much since gold, silver, or paper currency hardly seem to carry any relevance anymore. Perhaps someday it will count again, but for now, mostly just surviving a winter with enough food on the table is all that's on most people's minds. Bullets and guns seem to be a better bartering tool than cash.

"And over that way is the school. A lot of the single women here on the base are offering classes," Parker tells them, pointing into the distance at a brick building. "You could do the same if you decide to come and live here."

"What? Are you thinking about that, Red, moving here?" Cory asks with agitation from the back seat of the golf cart. Paige is conveniently sitting next to the jackass.

"Me? I don't know," she answers as if she has been put on the spot.

"Well, let me tell you, Parker," Cory states, "if Red here teaches a class, it should be survival skills like foraging for food and setting a snare trap. She's no schoolmarm, single woman who wants to teach kids their ABC's. She survived out there with just two friends and a baby for three years on the road."

"Really?" Parker asks. "Fascinating."

Good grief. He'd been trying to dissuade the guy's feelings about Paige being a passive and quaint woman who wants to be the next Laura Ingalls Wilder, and here he's gone and caused Parker to be even more intrigued by her.

"Hm, not really," Paige says in response to Parker.

"You can tell me all about it over dinner later," he says.

"It's kind of loud in the mess hall, and there's not much to tell," Paige says.

Cory can only assume that she is not into this guy by her body language. At least, he hopes she isn't. His estimation of her would take a severe hit if she were interested in him, which would make Cory question his own manhood.

"Oh, I meant dinner at my place, my private quarters," he corrects and drives them to another area of the base.

"Um, I kind of told Derek that I'd help him with some things later," she fibs badly.

"I'm sure whatever it is, we can delegate the task to someone else here on the compound. That's the great thing about being in charge. People are eager to help out when we need it."

There is always something about the way he seems to enjoy wielding his authority over people that doesn't quite sit well in Cory's gut. His instincts are not usually wrong about people. It's also what kept him alive for almost a year on his own.

"Oh, I couldn't do that. It wouldn't be right. Besides, I stick to my word once it's given. I have to help him. It just wouldn't be me if I went and reneged now."

"Raincheck then," Parker pushes.

"Uh...sure."

"What's going on over there?" Cory asks and hops down from the moving golf cart. Parker pulls to the curb and gets out, as well. Paige also joins them. She places herself right next to Cory, though.

In the distance, behind a fenced off area, there are people working on what looks like military maneuvers.

"That's our training facility for future soldiers."

From what he can see, most of them will need a lot of training. Some are women and what appear to be young children.

"Women and kids?" Cory questions.

"Yes, well, they need to be able to protect themselves in the case of an invasion," Parker explains.

Cory begins walking closer; Paige follows, which means that so does Parker, although he looks disappointed to be doing so.

"So, you wouldn't expect them to join your army?" Paige asks.

"Only if they wanted to, and not the kids. We do have women in our army, though. They go on supply runs, work in the munitions room, too."

"I would hope you aren't training them to go on combat missions, though," Cory remarks.

"Again, only if they have the desire," Parker says.

Cory shakes his head with disappointment. That doesn't seem right to him. On the farm, they try to keep the women out of the fight, even if it isn't always a successful venture. He watches as the people in training pair off with partners and spar. He walks around the end of the chain link fencing and stands off to the sidelines observing them with interest. Paige seems curious about it, too. Either that or she doesn't want to continue her private tour with Parker by herself. Cory's fine with the result either way.

Two young boys, probably around the age of ten or twelve are going hand-to-hand but are mostly just flailing about. Older teens, likely seventeen to nineteen are in the next row over, and Cory moves there to watch them. Most of them are doing about as well as the little kids, and the "drill sergeant" is too busy working with adults with the same low skill levels. It's too hard to stand by passively and allow them to continue. He steps forward and shows the young men a few better moves. They are practicing with carved, wooden knives so that nobody gets seriously injured.

"Here," he says and takes the knife from one young man. "When he steps in on you like that, you gotta deflect and then jab. If you just go stabbing and don't put forth any defense, you'll find yourself on the sharp, pokey end of his own dagger."

The teens chuckle and nod. "Yes, sir."

He's not sure if they think he's their instructor or not, but he's surprised by their show of respect. He gives them a few more

232

tips all the while Paige and Parker stand on the sidelines observing. Then Cory moves to the young couple next to him and offers some advice, too. They seem appreciative. He learns that they are husband and wife, likely in their early twenties, and are wanting to learn more about self-defense. They came from the bunker with the latest group of refugees and tell him about their arduous journey before going back to their practice. He goes down the aisle working with people and children until he runs into the actual instructor.

"Sergeant Dale McKenzie," the man introduces himself. "Boy, I could sure use your help around here. Glad to have it, too."

"Oh, I'm only here for a few days, and then we're leaving," Cory tells the man, who looks like he's around thirty-five or so. Cory can tell the guy's seen some shit. It's hidden behind his charcoal brown eyes, but he's seen it in people before, even in his own eyes from time to time when he looks in a mirror.

"I know. You're one of the McClanes," Dale acknowledges. "You guys are well-known around here. General McClane talks about his family's group a lot. You all are a bunch of badasses. I met your brother the last time you guys were up. He told me about you living on your own for a while. That took some balls, dude."

"I don't know about that," Cory says as Paige approaches with Parker. He immediately notices a change in Dale's demeanor at the sight of Parker. There is a degree of dislike in his dark eyes.

"There's definitely a place for you here if you change your mind. It'd be great to have another qualified instructor," Dale offers.

"Thanks, but we stay pretty busy on the farm. I don't think they'd like it if I up and left," Cory tells him with a friendly smile. He introduces Paige to Dale, who offers a cordial handshake. Cory notes the wedding ring on his left hand, although he does regard Paige with the typical appreciation that most men have when they look at a woman as beautiful as she.

They talk for a while with Dale, and Cory offers to help him out for the rest of the afternoon. Paige leaves with Parker, which seems to piss her off that she has to and even sends a nasty glare Cory's way. He suspects that she is angry to have to go with him by herself. Cory's pretty confident that the guy will keep himself in check and not do anything stupid where she is concerned. Cory also offers him a look of warning, one that lets him know that he's treading on thin ice with him.

He makes a lot of progress with Dale and a few other instructors and even offers some ideas on how they could improve the training center. Then he goes to the firing range where they have even more people practicing. It seems to be men with a little more experience doing most of the shooting, and they explain that it is to conserve ammo in case they even need it. Some of the people shoot well, but others need a lot more range time. He volunteers to work with one of the women who is struggling with her rifle, which seems ill-suited to her in size and weight.

"Where are the actual soldiers in your group?" Cory asks her.

She is a petite brunette who reminds him a little of Sam, only that her eyes are brown not blue, and she seems older than him.

"They usually go out in the morning and don't return sometimes till late or even the next day," she explains as she reloads her magazine.

"Oh, I see," he answers and helps her by loading another mag for her. It's something with which he has a lot of experience, so he can do it faster than her. "What are they doing?"

"Looking for supplies and more people to join the group. It's the same as it was at the bunker," she offers.

"You came from the bunker? I thought you might've come from a nearby town or something."

"Nope. Came all the way from Colorado," she says.

"Must've been pretty bad out there."

She looks at him and rolls her eyes. "Yes, it sucked. The President isn't such a bad guy most of the time, but we rarely saw him. He had a lot on his plate. Most of his soldiers were nice, too, but some of them…"

She groans and goes back to her work.

"Were they ex-military? Like legitimate soldiers?"

"I think so. I don't know, though. They seemed good at yelling at people," she says.

Cory chuckles. "There's a little more to it than that."

She smiles and says, "Some of the men here were ex-military. That's who they send out on supply runs. They've been bringing back a ton of stuff, too."

"Like Parker, you mean?"

She wrinkles her nose and says, "No, he's just with the general all the time. He never goes off the base. He does make a lot of the decisions, though."

"What kind of decisions?"

"Who can live here and who can't. That sort of thing."

This piques his interest. "What do you mean? I thought anyone who wanted to come here for sanctuary was admitted."

She shakes her head and frowns as if she finds this a silly idea. "No way. He turns a lot of people away. If they can't offer up some sort of service, they aren't allowed in. He said we can't all pull the slack for others who would bring down the group."

This pisses Cory off. This is precisely what they were doing in Colorado that the general was so upset about. Supposedly. He obviously wasn't that upset over it if they're doing the same thing here. They don't do that in Pleasant View. Those who are too old to work are either taken in by younger people or are looked after by the community with support. Some teach at the school, which is invaluable.

"What other decisions does Parker make?"

She sighs and says, "Oh, the usual. Who gets assigned what jobs, how much food gets rationed to each family, where they'll be housed on the base. I guess you could say he keeps things running smoothly."

"Isn't that why you guys left Colorado? To get away from this sort of living arrangement and to gain more freedom?"

She snorts, "Yeah, well, old habits I suppose…"

He nods and frowns but continues to help her and some of the others with their marksmanship skills until the call for dinner is brought by a messenger. When he arrives in the mess hall, he spots Paige and Lucas sitting together. He goes through the line and takes a tray of offered food before joining them. He purposely sits across the table from her because Cory knows she wouldn't like it if he sat next to her, which he'd actually prefer to do.

"Where's your buddy?" he asks her.

She rolls her eyes and says, "I think he was mad I wouldn't join him for a private dinner. I also think he might've figured it out that I was lying about having to help Derek."

"Hey, leave me out of it," Derek says as he joins them. "You gotta let the guy down gently. You're obviously his first crush."

Cory chuckles at his surly response about Parker.

"Ha!" Lucas retorts. "Not the way it was in the bunker."

"What do you mean?" Cory asks.

Luke looks around to make sure nobody is listening in on their conversation and says, "He was quite the lady's man out there."

"For real? Are you just messin' with us?" Cory jokes.

"No, and he wielded his authority to get whatever he wanted from whomever he wanted, especially women. I can't believe my dad put him in charge here, his second in command. I was hoping he wasn't going to invite him here."

Cory is surprised that Luke is telling them so much. He's usually the quiet one between him and his sister. Of course, Gretchen doesn't give him much of an opportunity to speak.

"What do you mean about throwing his authority around?" Derek asks, his interest piqued.

"Well, he didn't force women to be with him or anything like that, but he sort of bribed them with what he could provide for them, either from the food store or supplies. He was a real dick out there. He wasn't anywhere near the rank of second in command, though. He was just a lowly officer, way low, and a lot of people did not like him."

"Great, so now he has more pull," Derek says.

"I don't like a lot of what we saw and heard today, either," Cory tells Derek. "We'll talk about it later in private."

"I thought they were leaving the model of socialism behind in Colorado?" Paige asks Luke.

"Yeah, me, too. My dad's acting like this is all just temporary until everyone's on their feet, but I think when he wants to change things, Parker's gonna be a real problem," Luke answers and removes his ball cap. "I think he likes it like this."

"I agree with that assessment," Cory says with a nod.

A moment later, Parker, Doc, and Robert casually stroll up to them.

"I thought you needed to help Major Harrison?" Parker asks Paige directly.

"She is. As soon as I'm finished, she's going to help me with some physical therapy. She's great at it," Derek lies, a lot more smoothly than Paige had.

"One more pleasant surprise," Parker says with a smile.

"Yep, that's me, full of surprises," she answers with a fake grin.

"I was telling Robert that we should return to the farm in the morning, but first, I'd like to speak with you, Derek. There are some matters here that we need to cover before we leave," Doc says.

"Yes, sir," Derek says with a nod. "Get something to eat, Herb. You need to. I know you were in the lab all day. Gotta get some nourishment in you before we make the trip home tomorrow."

Parker takes it upon himself to sit next to Paige with his tray of food. Cory would like to stab his butter knife into the side of his neck. Doc and his son walk away to get their own food, which looks like it is being brought to them by workers instead of them standing in line.

"Too bad you have to leave tomorrow," Parker starts. "You could always stay, you know. There is plenty of open housing. I could see to it that you get a private room."

"How? By throwing around your weight?" Cory asks bluntly.

This apparently is not something Parker is used to because he shoots Cory an expression of surprise.

He recovers and says, "No, of course not. I just mean that she'd be treated as an honored guest. She'd have whatever amenities that she'd require."

"And how would you go about securing those amenities?" Cory questions.

"By whatever means necessary, of course," he answers.

Cory isn't going to be put off so easily, so he says, "By taking from others because you can, because you're the second in command?"

He clears his voice. His face is turning red, especially since he is slightly pale already. He reminds Cory of an albino sometimes with his light, cold eyes and super pale blonde hair.

"No, I wouldn't do that. What is it exactly that you're insinuating?"

Cory stares him down for a long moment before saying, "Nothing. Just making observations based on what I've seen here."

"Don't make judgments based on living on this base for a mere two days."

"Almost three," Cory mocks, then grins with sarcasm.

"You certainly don't know enough about this place to pass judgment on us."

"I'm not passing judgment on everyone. Just you," he challenges and watches the man's nostrils flare.

"Um, I'm done!" Paige announces and stands. "Cory, could you walk me back to our rooms so that I can get a shower?"

He sits there and stares down Parker for another full minute before nodding to Paige and rising. All the way to the rooms that the McClane family is sharing while on the base, Paige lectures him to keep his cool and stop trying to incite Parker into a fight. In Cory's opinion, it would be a short one. He drops her at her room and makes Paige promise to stay in it for the remainder of the night. Then he goes on an intel mission, but he doesn't leave Robert's base.

Chapter Twenty
Sam

Tomorrow she is returning to Dave's camp and does not know if she'll ever come back to the McClane farm for a visit. It's just too hard being around them, and it makes her miss the family so much more when she's living on Henry's farm away from them.

Dinner is wrapping up, and chores are being completed. The old house feels stuffy and hot, even in shorts and a tank top, so she slips on her flipflops and walks to the goat barn to check on a nanny and her new twins. The little kids have been in here most of the day playing with them and holding the newborn, pygmy goats, which are so adorable.

Sam opens the small, wooden gate and lets herself in with the goats, of which they have fourteen now with the birth of the new twins. The dairy goats are a bit bigger than the pygmies and are kept in a different pen closer to the pigs. Some of the nannies come over to greet her, looking for treats. She feeds them the leftover vegetables from tonight's dinner of pork chops and potatoes. The salad was one of raw vegetables from the garden, of which they had some left since so many of their family members are up at Fort Knox. They never waste anything, though, and all scraps are fed back to the pigs, goats, and chickens. The twins' mother also comes over for her fair share, which Sam places in a separate bin to ensure that she gets enough. Then she is able to sit in the straw and hold the babies. They are so stinking adorable and weigh practically nothing in her arms. In typical fashion of naming all of the goats in their herd after Greek gods, the kids are calling them Hera and Artemis. If the herd keeps expanding, they will inevitably run out of names. The soft little whines and cries of communication that they make cause Sam to smile down at them.

"First Charlotte and now baby goats," Simon says from the gate as he also enters.

"These were easier to deliver, though," Sam comments with a smile as he squats next to her.

"I doubt if that nanny would agree," Simon jokes, causing her to smile again.

He extends a hand and strokes the smaller one, the female. Just because she is smaller than her brother certainly does not mean that she will be pushed around by him. Like most creatures in the animal kingdom, the female goats tend to rule the roost. She'll likely be as bossy as her mother, who doesn't take much from the billies in the herd.

"You forgot to leave something in the shed," she says, pointing to the stethoscope still hanging around his neck.

"Oh, yes, I suppose I did," he answers, touching the cool, metal head. "I was just checking Charlotte again."

"Good grief. Leave that baby alone," Sam scolds with a grin of teasing. "She's only been in this world for three days, and she's already been examined twenty times between you and Reagan."

He chuffs and nods. "I suppose you're right."

Sam goes back to petting Hera on her tiny nose, which she does not seem to appreciate.

"I heard you were going back tomorrow," he says.

Sam looks up at him and nods. "Yes, after the clinic day. As long as Dave's men come and pick me up, that is."

"I'm sure they will," Simon agrees with a frown. "I'm sure everyone over there is missing you, what with this dual residency thing you've got going on."

"Actually," Sam says, stands, and places the babies back on their small nested place in the straw. "I think this is going to be my last visit. I need to stay over there now."

She walks around Simon, who looks shocked by her announcement.

"What? Why?" he asks as he follows her from the pen and secures the gate after them.

Sam just keeps going, hoping he'll drop it. Unfortunately, halfway down the dark aisle, Simon steps in front of her. The only light is from the lantern he carries.

"Because, Simon, I can't keep doing this. I need a clean break. This is just prolonging the inevitable."

"What's that supposed to mean? What part of living over there and visiting here is inevitable?"

"I just feel like my life here is done, has come full circle, and I need to move on. I need to make things work over there and stop visiting so much. It's like I keep putting a bandage on just to rip it off again, and the pain is becoming unbearable."

"I don't understand how that makes sense. Your friends and family are here. This place is your home. That other place is… it's just a temporary housing situation. This is where you should be happiest, with your family. If you do this, the family is going to be devastated."

Sam wishes that he would've phrased that so differently, which is aiming at the heart of the problem, the main reason she needs to stop visiting Grandpa's farm so often.

"Right. The family," she repeats but detests how much she reveals in those few, clipped words.

"Exactly. Everyone will be so disappointed. Your visits mean so much to…them."

"The family," she says again for clarity.

"And me," he finally admits, igniting a glimmer of hope in her heart like he always does right before he rejects her and tramples out the flame again. His teeth clamp together, and his jaw flexes before saying, "I am also thankful for your visits."

"Why?" she asks point blank, yearning for him to reveal something new, something she's never heard before.

"Um…because you're great at the clinic, and the kids love you, and the sisters miss you…"

"Simon," she says, interrupting and surprising him. "Stop. Just stop. I can't do this with you every time I visit the farm. It's exhausting."

"You just need more rest. I always say this. You work too hard and push yourself too much."

Sam chuckles at him, earning a frown of confusion from the perpetually confused Simon. She sighs and pushes his hair back from his forehead. "Oh, Simon."

"What?" he asks, looking more like a naïve, little boy than a man who has seen so much, too much in his young life.

The flame extinguishes, but literally this time as his lantern goes out.

"Oh, shoot," he curses, or as close to cursing as Simon usually gets. "I knew I should've added more oil to this."

"It's fine. I've got a flashlight," she says and reaches into her pocket. "Crap. I must've left it at the goat pen."

"Wait, I might have one," he says, fishing around in his jeans pockets after he places the burned-out lantern on the barn floor.

"It's not that far. I can see light from the moon at the other end of the aisle," Sam says after her eyes begin to adjust to the darkness.

"Just wait. I don't want you to stumble over something and get hurt," he warns with his usual vigor for safety and caution.

This makes Sam smile. Simon will never change. He's resolute in who he is and comfortable in his ideals and character. It's one of the things she likes about him.

"Simon, I'm hardly going to die if I take a tumble," she points out.

"Hold on," he says, digging in his back pockets now. "I'm sure I had one."

Sam groans and tries to brush past him with a show of impatience and independence. Simon's snatches her arm to stop her and steps closer.

"Sam, I'm serious. Just wait."

"I have been, Simon. I've been waiting for a lot of things where you're concerned," she says, looking up at him to gauge his response to this. His hair is rumpled and longer than normal. She can just make out the blue of his eyes set against the dark, summer tan he's carrying with him.

"Uh…" he stammers nervously as Sam readjusts her weight and ends up much closer to him. He still has his hand clamped down on her upper arm, not in a painful manner but firmly.

"I'm leaving in the morning. I'm going to take a break. I may not come to the clinic for a while after tomorrow, either."

"Don't do this," he pleads softly.

"It's what's best, Simon," she admits and pushes his hair back from his forehead again, which is damp from the humidity and heat. His face is covered in a five o'clock shadow, giving him a rugged appearance.

"It's not. It's not what's best at all. It's actually the worst possible case of horrible."

"For who? The family? They seem to have adjusted quite well to my departure."

"No, of course, they haven't. Nobody has," he says, squaring up his body to hers.

"Who then?" she prompts.

"Uh…Huntley. He's been moping around here a lot."

Sam rolls her eyes and says, "Huntley's fine, Simon. He's adjusting fine and has been busy doing more military training so he tells me. Who else?"

"Hannah," he says, this time his voice sounding faint and unconvincing.

"No," she retorts, her frustration with him growing.

"Everyone really."

"Not good enough," Sam says with finality and pulls back only to have him grab her other arm, as well.

"Me, ok? Is that what you want to hear? That I miss you? Of course, I do. I don't know what you're trying to prove. It should be obvious. You're the one who used to go around saying I was your best friend all the time. Now you hardly talk to me at all."

"You know why. It's not like it's some great mystery, Simon."

"Everything about you is a mystery, Samantha," he says and steps tentatively forward, closing the already narrow space between them.

"No, I'm not mysterious. I was rather transparent with you. It was you who was and still is the mystery."

"It's just because I don't want you to see the monster that I really am inside," he says almost brokenly and looks at nothing between them in the darkness.

Sam's brow furrows, and she frowns hard. "What are you talking about, Simon?"

"I can't explain it. I don't want to, either. Not to you. I'd never want you to think of me in that way."

"Simon, seriously. You and I were close once. I'd never judge you," she says.

Sam slips one arm loose. Then she cups his cheek. Simon places his hand over hers and closes his eyes. His face is an expression of a man tormented by something so profound and hidden within him that Sam feels sorry for him. She pulls her other arm loose and lays her hand against his chest where his heart is racing. She knows he once felt desire for her. He showed her that much the night they were in her parents' home. If he feels guilty about that, he shouldn't. It was and still is the best day of her life so far, and she doubts it will ever be topped.

Sam decides in that split second to take a chance and rises on tiptoe to place her lips right next to his, which startles Simon. His eyes pop open as she lowers back down to her heels.

"Don't be sad, Simon," she whispers, the words feeling like some of the most intimate they've ever shared, even though they are standing in the middle of a barn aisle in the dark while the rest of the family is likely all over the property taking care of the animals.

He swallows hard and says, "Impossible where you're concerned, Samantha."

This makes her feel depressed. She'd never want to cause him sadness, and it breaks her heart.

"What can I do to make this better?" she asks, offering herself up to the slaughter should he reject her again.

Simon reaches out and strokes her hair, which is loose and hanging down her back. She'd planned on braiding it later after her shower to keep the heavy cluster from making her even hotter when she goes to bed. His fingertips slide through her hair, causing goosebumps to sprout down her neck.

"Make me stop wanting you?" he suggests in the form of a question.

This rocks her to her core. Simon wants her? He seemed like he did that fateful night when he'd almost made love to her, but ever since has treated her like a distant relative who has overstayed their welcome.

"Simon…" she whimpers brokenly.

244

He pushes his fingers into her hair more deeply until his palm is cradling the back of her neck. Then he pulls her up against him where he can capture her mouth with his. The kiss is searing, not sad and depressing at all. It's as if something has switched within him and turned his melancholy into passion. His mouth moves on hers as if he has memorized every detail of her. Simon steps into her, pushing Sam backward three steps until her back is against the wood wall behind her. His hand cradles her head so that she doesn't bump it. His other arm encircles her waist and tugs her tightly against him all while not breaking contact with her lips.

It's as if he is a starving man, and she his final meal on this planet. Sam slides her hands up his chest, mostly for support because she isn't sure if she can remain standing.

Simon jerks back and whispers against her mouth, "I want you to stop kissing him."

"Wha...what?" she stutters, not understanding his sudden inquisition about kissing.

"Your new boyfriend," Simon clarifies as he moves to her ear, then her neck and collarbone. He presses his palm into the curve of her lower back, causing it to arch. Then he puts his mouth against the base of her neck where her pulse is undoubtedly pounding.

"Boy...what?"

"Henry? Do you like kissing him?"

"What?" Sam asks breathlessly as she clings to his biceps this time. Is he trying to control her? She's not sure she cares right now.

He jerks her to him roughly and says against her mouth, "Do you like kissing him more than me?"

Then it registers as to what he's referring, and she whispers because talking is impossible, "No. No, I don't."

She can feel him smile against her throat as he makes his way back to her mouth where he positively ravishes hers. Sam sinks her hands into Simon's thick, wavy hair and holds tight, marveling at the softness. He smells fantastic, too, like the herbs he's always grinding mixed with cut grass and his own sweat.

He hooks a hand under her leg and pulls it up against his hip. Then his fingers explore the back of her thigh while holding her tightly against him.

"Simon," she begs on a plea of breathless excitement.

He simply groans against her mouth and slides his hand up further until he is cupping her bottom and pressing her against the hardness between them. Sam has her own agenda and slips her hand under his white t-shirt to explore his stomach, which causes his muscles to flex and jump under her fingertips.

"I'm already going to hell, so we should make this worth it," he says against her ear as he kisses her there.

"What?" she asks as his words begin to filter into her brain. That makes no sense. Why would Simon be going to hell? He is a good and perfect man, a paragon of simplistic innocence among men. Why would he think his fate is sealed in eternal darkness? She doesn't care. She'd join him there if it meant that he'd kiss her like this every day of their fiery eternity.

He doesn't answer but kisses her again and grinds his hips against her. Sam moans softly, which seems to ignite Simon's inner fire because his tongue plunges into her mouth.

"Sam, Simon!" Huntley calls from the other end of the barn somewhere.

"Simon, stop!" Sam says, trying to push him away. She turns her head, but he only lavishes more attention on her neck.

"Where are you guys?" Huntley yells again.

"Simon! Let me go. Huntley's coming," she says, pushing against his chest. "Simon."

He releases her a split second before Huntley comes into view at the other end of the aisle.

"Come quick! There's trouble!" Huntley calls to them and waves before running away again.

She looks up at Simon, who is barely sobering from their heated encounter. This is unlike him. He is always in control and can immediately recover his stoic composure from just about any situation in which he finds himself.

"Are you ok?" she asks tentatively.

He frowns and says, "Of course. Come along."

He takes her hand as he walks quickly to the barnyard where the family is gathered. She drops his hand when she sees everyone. Simon looks down at her as if he finds this move surprising. She was just beating him to the punch. Sam is under no false pretenses that after sharing yet another passionate kiss that Simon is ready to yield to his baser urgings and be with her. It will never be that simple between them. It will also probably never happen at all.

"What's going on?" she asks John.

"An attack. We need to go. They just hit a friend's compound southeast of Nashville and Paul and K-Dog think they might be coming for them next. If they do, they're in trouble. Their village is in imminent danger, and K-Dog just called us for backup. We're picking up Chet and a few of the Johnson boys. We're moving in ten."

"What if they don't go there next?" Sue asks.

"They're coming there. K-Dog's friend sent a tracker to follow them, and he said they're making a straight line toward the condo village. If they don't decide to attack somewhere else tonight along the way, then they're coming for the condos."

"Were there any survivors at his friend's place?" Sam asks.

John nods, "Yes, but they took a hard hit from these people. Guess they lost dozens of members of their small town but were able to hold them off for the most part. They ended up breaching their wall, which K-Dog said wasn't all that great, and ransacked many homes. They got flanked. Paul and K-Dog don't have the numbers it'll take to hold off that many."

"How long till they get hit?" Simon asks intuitively.

"An hour, maybe an hour and a half."

"I'll get my rifle," Simon says and jogs away.

John rests a hand on Sam's shoulder with a deep frown and says, "Sam, I need you to watch over Reagan and the kids. I don't have anyone else to ask, little sister."

"Got it. Don't worry about us. I'll guard them, John," she tells him. "How many are there?"

"They think it's the highwaymen. He said maybe forty to fifty, maybe less. They've got roadblocks set up, but it won't take much to circumvent them. They'll be pinned down and need backup from us to get out from under this."

"Who's going?"

"Kelly, me, Simon and the neighbors," he answers.

"Is that going to be enough? Maybe I should go, too."

"No, stay here. If they come this way…" he says, drifting off with worry over his newborn and wife.

"If they do, I know what to do, John. Don't worry. Just concentrate on your job."

He pats her cheek gently and jogs away to join the others.

Huntley comes up to her and says. "I'm volunteering to go, too."

"No, stay, Hunt. If they make their way here, I'll need all the help I can get. The condo village is not far from here. I can't fight off that many people alone. If the men fail…I'll need you."

"Ok, shadi," he says.

"Help them get ready, though, Hunt."

He salutes and takes off at a sprint. She is left alone in the barnyard with Sue and her oldest son, Justin. He looks ready to take on just about anybody who steps onto this farm. Sam feels the same way. Justin, although he is still young, is quite capable with an M4, so she knows he can contribute if it comes to that.

They go to the house to help the family get ready for a possible battle, and the men prepare to leave.

Simon comes into the kitchen and straight to her, "Stay inside. Keep the lights out if possible. Wayne's coming over with Bertie, the kids, and Talia. It'll be better if someone decides to attack either farm while we're short on people to defend them."

"Oh, good," Sue says from the other side of the kitchen. "I'm glad Wayne's coming over."

"We radioed Dave's compound, too. They're sending some men to help us out and a few more over here, as well. Watch for them. They know to call in before approaching."

His fingers purposely brush against hers between them.

"That's good," Sam says to him, looking up into his worried, blue eyes. "Don't worry about us, Simon. Just go take care of whoever's doing this. We're fine."

He nods but still seems on edge. His night-vision gear is already strapped to his head, and he has changed into black cargo pants and a black tee. Gone is the cute, messy hair hanging down on his forehead to be replaced by the warrior with green and black paint on his cheekbones and the sniper rifle suspended from its strap on his shoulder. Gone is his boyish charm and inhibition replaced by a trained killer who knows he is being called up to do it again and has the confidence to get the job done. He has that feral, yet calm look in his eyes which darken when he is facing down their enemies.

248

Sam knows how much he worries all the time about these types of scenarios and leaving the farm without enough security in place to keep it safe. The people who are about to attack the condo village should be more worried when the sniper in the family gets there. Simon is deadly when the time calls for it. Their fates tonight have already been sealed. The hour draws near.

"Just be careful," he warns. "Remember the escape plan if the farm falls."

"It won't come to that," she says. "Just take care of yourself."

He nods and pulls her in to kiss her forehead quickly before turning away. They all meet in the back yard to send the men off right as Wayne pulls in with his family, and Chet switches vehicles to go with the men. Reagan has tears streaming down her cheeks holding her baby as she kisses John goodbye. Hannah isn't doing much better and is being comforted by Sue. Sam stands there with Huntley wishing she could kiss Simon farewell in front of everyone.

They gather in the kitchen before sending the children to bed in the music room where they always have to sleep on the floor together when things like this happen. They don't question or complain because they're used to it. Sue sits with Hannah on the sofa in Grandpa's office with a pistol on the stand beside her, and Reagan reclines while breastfeeding her daughter in a leather chaise. Her own sniper rifle is resting casually on the floor next to her. Huntley is sitting on the back porch with Wayne while Bertie and Talia and their kids have taken up residence in the music room with the children. Sam sits near the window in Grandpa's study where she can see the front driveway, which is never used anymore, and the drive from the neighbor's farm that is their only point of ingress onto the farm. Sam knows that nobody is actually going to sleep. They are merely reserving their energy in case they end up fighting for their lives later tonight. Everyone is very quiet, the mood somber. Mr. Johnson calls over a short time later to let them know that men from Dave's compound are on their way through, having passed his farm and checked in there first.

Shortly before eleven p.m., Henry pulls down the drive with six men. Sam can barely contain her disappointment that he is not Simon. It's going to be a dreadfully long night until she sees the men arriving back home safely.

Chapter Twenty-one
Cory

"Where the hell have you been?" Paige asks as she rounds a corner and runs into him.

"Checking things out. Learned quite a lot, too," he answers. "I thought I told you to stay in your room."

"Come on, Cory," she says and walks away at a brisk pace. Then she starts jogging as if she's in a rush.

"What's going on?"

"There's been an attack. Sue called in a few minutes ago and got ahold of Derek. The guys went to the condo community to help Paul's group. People near them, less than an hour away were attacked, and their scout says he thinks they're headed straight for the condo village."

"Damn it!" he says through gritted teeth and picks up the pace.

Before long, they are in the communications room where the rest of the family has gathered along with Robert, a young soldier manning the radio, and, unfortunately, Parker.

"What happened?" he demands of Derek.

His friend sends him a disapproving look for not being present when he needed him but answers, "We aren't sure yet. K-Dog and Paul are about to be under attack. They think it's the highwaymen."

"How many?" Cory inquires, his mind already racing on how to get down there quickly.

"Maybe fifty," Derek says.

"Shit. I need to go. I can take a few men from here and go. Or hell, go by myself. I don't care, but I'm not leaving John and Simon to hog this one out with my brother. They're gonna get overrun."

"You take off, and you're getting an Alpha Charlie," Derek warns.

"I need in this, sir," Cory pleads with his friend and ranking, commanding officer. He doesn't want the 'Ass Chewing' that he was just warned of, but Cory wants to help his friends and brother.

"It would take too long," Parker says.

"I could be there in two hours, maybe less if I push it," Cory argues.

"Dave's sending some men," Derek relays. "I think he's going in, too."

"What if there's more than fifty? We know this group has much bigger numbers than that," Cory reminds him. "They could and probably will call for reinforcements."

"I know," Derek agrees and rakes a hand through his shaggy hair, having abandoned his high and tight hairstyle ever since his accident. If it gets any longer, it'll be worse than Cory's.

He can tell that his friend is feeling just as impotent and helpless as he is right now. It's frustrating as hell being so far away when the family needs them.

"I could send men," Robert offers. "Cory would be welcome to ride with them."

His eyes dart to Robert's, and for the first time since he met the man, he's actually feeling the tiniest spark of respect for him.

"Yes, I'll go," he is quick to agree.

"Wait, we don't even know if they need our help," Derek says. "And if you leave to join this, we're stranded here until you come back. I don't want to travel with Doc, Luke, and Paige back to the farm without you."

"Right," he agrees. "Let's go now then. We can ask Robert for extra men to make sure you get home safe with the family, and I'll split off from you right before the farm and head to the battle."

Derek is quiet a moment while he contemplates this. Robert nods in agreement with Cory.

"I think that would work," Paige agrees.

He looks at her and nods. They both want away from the general's compound. He really wants her away from it and Parker.

"Fine, gear up," Derek finally says. "Robert, I would appreciate a few men as an escort to the farm if you can spare them."

"Them and more. Parker, get your team ready to move out," Robert orders, earning a look of surprise from Parker.

Cory has to hold in a groan of disappointment.

"We move in ten, people," Derek says, encouraging everyone to grab their gear and pack up quickly.

"Paige, help Herb," Cory requests, gets a nod, and runs from the room.

He jogs along the corridor until he comes to the apartment he's sharing with the family. He's already prepared to leave since he packed earlier today after the tour. He was going to suggest their departure later on this evening to Doc and Derek after his latest series of covert, nighttime discoveries on the base.

Within minutes, they are moving. Robert gives him a set of night-vision binoculars, which are different than the ones they use at the farm but appreciated nonetheless. He also gives him three extra mags for his rifle and another two for his .45 Smith. This may not be enough if a lot more than the suspected fifty men show up. He knows the numbers rank near a thousand or more for this group. Robert's men are following in two vehicles; a car and a pick-up truck painted in camouflage colors. It's pretty corny looking, but the fifty cal mounted in the bed helps improve the status just a little. Paige rides in the backseat with Lucas and Doc while Cory drives and Derek rides shotgun. They are speeding along route 65 going south at a pace that will likely get them all killed should a herd of animals run in front of them.

"I want to go with you," Paige announces from the back seat.

"Negative," he shuts her down.

"I don't think that's a good idea, Paige," Derek adds. "This is a night attack. It's totally different tactically than what you've been in before."

"I'd like to be a part of this, sir," Lucas says next. "I do have the experience, and I snaked a few extra clips for my AK from my dad's arsenal."

"What do you think?" Derek asks Cory. "You've worked with him and G a lot more than I've had the time for."

"As I said, this isn't my first time," Luke says.

Cory wonders what he's referring to because most of the time, Lucas is quiet and reserved, not a big talker.

"In Portland," he explains but just barely.

"I don't know, man," Cory says.

"And while we lived in the woods out there and then again at the bunker and on the way to the farm multiple times. I can handle it. I won't need a babysitter when the shit starts," Luke says, surprising Cory even more. Also, this is probably the most he's ever revealed about himself.

"Fine by me then," Cory says.

He glances in the mirror to see Paige giving a pouty look.

"I need you and Doc at the farm to help Derek. If we're all gone, that ain't good, Red."

"All right," she says in agreement but still looks pissed.

"Yes, I am quite sure the girls are very nervous right now," Doc acknowledges about his family. "We must get home to the farm. I guess I was wrong that it was going to be a good time to leave. We shouldn't have left the farm or stayed so long at Robert's base."

"Don't beat yourself up over it, Herb," Derek says. "I agreed with you that it'd be ok. This stuff happens. It happened all the time in the Army. You plan, prep, and crap happens at the last minute that screws it all up."

"Right," Cory says, not wanting Herb to blame himself for the actions of a few renegade assholes. "Nobody can predict when idiots are going to start acting like idiots."

"I suppose you're right. It was just bad timing on my part," Herb tells them.

"I'm glad we're all riding together, though," Cory says, changing the subject to alleviate Herb's guilt. "I wanted to talk to you guys tonight anyway."

"About what?" Derek asks.

"I did a little more exploring tonight on the base- that's where I was when you couldn't find me."

"I figured you were out chasing women," Derek harasses.

He shoots him a look that lets him know he doesn't appreciate that. Derek immediately looks to the back seat at Paige and says, "Sorry. I was just messin'."

"You don't have to apologize to me. What'd you find out, Cory?" she quickly asks, obviously not wanting to get into their relationship in front of everyone.

"They had a building way off the main stretch where they had stashes of stuff."

"What kind of stuff?" Derek asks.

"Food and weapons, meds, clean water," Cory answers.

"Who? The people? You mean they're stealing?" Paige asks him.

Cory chuckles and says, "No, I wouldn't guess that it's the people doing it. It's all under lock and key."

"How'd you get in?" Paige questions.

"Really?" he scoffs.

"Oh."

"Why would anyone have these things hidden away?" Herb asks.

"It's the same as it was in the bunker," Lucas says quietly.

"What do you mean?" Herb asks his grandson.

Luke sighs as Cory carefully maneuvers the vehicle around a wrecked oil tanker on the freeway.

"My father and the government out there- well, the government officials, not so much my father- kept enough food, rations, and supplies to keep the government running should the system fail, in case of a drought or some sort of natural disaster."

"They were hoarding food and meds for themselves?" Paige asks with an incredulous note in her voice. "To keep themselves alive if they ran out of food for the people?"

"It never happened, of course, but it was there just in case," Luke answers. "The new government felt it was a necessary precaution in case of a collapse. They thought if they all died, too, from either starvation or disease, then the whole city would collapse."

"Gee, how noble of them," Paige criticizes.

"I agree," Luke says. "I believe Parker had a lot to do with putting that policy in place. My father was not so keen on the idea, but others were."

"There were also three working vehicles hidden behind that building," Cory offers.

254

"Escape vehicles in case the system fails and the people turn on the government," Luke tells them. "We had the same thing at the bunker."

"Wow," Paige comments, not bothering to hide her shock. "I feel like I just woke up in the middle of the Bolshevik Revolution."

"Has traces of imperialism, I know," Lucas agrees.

"But this is why you left Colorado in the first place," Derek says. "I don't get it."

"Is this just history repeating itself in a new location?" Cory asks Luke.

"I hope not," Luke says. "It's just that…I don't know."

"What?" Derek pushes.

"I was hoping he would leave some of his men behind. They aren't all so well-intentioned as my father."

"People are flawed," Herb says. "It's just a fact of nature. Perhaps my son felt that they could make a change once they arrived here and had the opportunity. For now, it probably makes him feel more comfortable being surrounded by people he knows and trusts. Their flaws are something that he might feel he can work around."

"*If* they are willing to change," Derek says. "So far, it seems like there are so many of the bunker's same policies that have followed them."

"The model that they used out there may work here for a while, like Herb is saying," Cory says. "They will have to make changes to it all soon or else the people will become just as disappointed with the way things are being run as they were at the other place. Then they're going to have a real shit storm on their hands."

"They are doing great things in their medical research facility," Herb tells them. "That's one positive piece of news to report, I suppose. I worked with some of their doctors who are trying to manufacture vaccines. We discussed the diseases they've seen so far and the ones with which we've come into contact, as well."

"That is good news, I guess," Paige observes quietly.

Cory knows she is likely still thinking about Parker. The guy is an obnoxious asshole who has the hots for her, and Cory would like to lay him out flat on his back. Or put Simon on him. He's good for that, too. Instead, he tries to join in the conversation about the scientists on Robert's staff and their medical advancements. Doc seems a little jealous of their facility. It's funny because Cory has always just thought of him as a farmer first and the town's doctor second. To hear him speak about their research, of which he is quite fluent, just seems out of the box for him. He realizes how smart Herb really is. Then he brings up Reagan and her love of research, too, and Cory is also reminded of what a super brain Little Doc is, as well.

"Cory, there is a matter I'd like to discuss with you in the next few days, one which I'll need your help with," Doc says.

"So don't get your keister shot off tonight," Derek jokes.

"Yes, sir," Cory replies. "And, yes, I'll make myself available whenever you need me, Doc."

"Thank you, son," Herb replies.

Cory really hopes he isn't about to get lectured by Doc for messing around with Paige without being married to her. Kelly already warned him that he'll likely get his ass chewed for it, but it has yet to happen. He admires Herb a lot and doesn't want to displease him.

The time on the dash reads 12:30, and Cory pushes the vehicle even faster as their surroundings become more familiar. As soon as they are within five miles from the condo village, Cory calls a halt to their trip, leaves the family to make it home to the farm without him and Luke, and hitches a ride with the remainder of Robert's men. He watches with a heavy heart as the truck carrying Derek, Paige, and Doc speeds away, led by the other men from Robert's base. Paige's eyes were filled with dread and worry as she slid in behind the wheel. Two of Robert's men jumped into the bed of the truck to guard it while their buddies kept to their own vehicle to lead the way. Together they made a team of eight, and Cory hopes that will be enough men to keep her safe if they are attacked before they get home.

He radios John and his brother as they speed toward the condo village. Cory taps the roof of the cab to let them know to stop. They pull off the road as John comes over the radio.

"Gotcha', brother," John says.

"We're coming in to help. What's the sit rep?"

"Vacation over so soon? Miss me too much?"

"Affirmative. How's the weather at the community pool?"

"Taking on heavy fire from the south," he returns, sounding slightly winded.

Cory can just barely hear the shots in the distance as he and the others disembark. He moves the team forward with a hand signal. Luke follows close behind him as he leads the way.

"Come in from the north," John orders. "You should run into Kelly before you get there. I'll let him know."

"I'm here," Kelly responds. "I'm about to move in, so hurry your lazy asses up."

"Got it," Cory answers. "Be there in five."

He orders the men to speed up and sprints ahead. His brother and John are in a dangerous situation. He's not sure how long it's gone on, this battle, but he's eager to get involved.

It doesn't take long to find Kelly, who has Chet Reynolds with him. He quickly explains that John has the Johnson boys with him. They squat as his brother sketches his plan of attack in the dirt at their feet. Cory pushes his night-vision gear up and waits for orders. He swigs from his water bottle and stashes it back in his pack.

"We need to flank, gain entrance. K-Dog's gonna meet us at the back gate and let us in. These asshats don't know there's a gate back there. John's group is taking fire here," he says, indicating the mark in the dirt with a stick. "Once we're in, we'll come at them from the inside. John's taking on heavy fire. We need to get him some relief. Cory, you take your squad and push in from the east. There's a line of trees here," he says, pointing with the stick. "Use caution. They hit the wall with an RPG about twenty minutes ago. They just haven't been able to get in yet because K-Dog's men and John's group are holding them off."

"Got it," Cory says.

"We could also come at them from this position," Parker says, at once getting a glance from Kelly. "This seems to be the better point of entry."

Kelly looks at Cory as if to say, "who's this idiot?" He even rolls his eyes for good measure.

"You remember Parker from Robert's camp?" Cory reminds him. In the distance, he can hear the single tap-taps from John and his men's rifles. They are conserving ammo but also keeping their enemy under control.

"Uh-huh," Kelly answers.

His brother will not tolerate someone stepping into a battle and within two seconds ascertaining that he knows better. None of them even know if Parker has experience with this.

"I want eyes on that technical, too," Kelly says, ignoring Parker completely. "They've got one parked out front. Simon already took out the shooter, but like most rats, they'll send another one from the nest soon. We need to disable it."

"Where's the Professor?"

"Where you're headed. Work together and push forward from his position. Leave us three men and take the other three with you. Push them hard. We need to end this. We just didn't have enough men to get in there to help K-Dog and Paul yet. Wait for my signal," Kelly tells him. "Good luck, brother."

He bumps his fist against Kelly's and leaves through the cover of the small forest behind the condo units. Luke jogs right along with him, pace for pace. He seems calm and quite at home in this situation. That's good. Cory can't afford for anyone to wig out right now. He calls Simon on the radio and gets an affirmative that he won't shoot them, even though Cory thinks his friend would like to, at least shoot him. Knowing Simon, he already saw them coming through his scope.

"We're moving in from here," Cory tells Simon the plan once he's found him in the woods.

Parker steps forward and says, "I'm the ranking commander here, and I say we push in from the west side. There's more cover of trees and less obstruction to get in our way."

"You are not the ranking anything here, dude," Cory corrects him. "Just follow us."

He stands behind a tree and waits until he sees the green, laser from Kelly's rifle pointing into the night sky. Even if their enemies see it through night-vision goggles, they won't understand what it means to them. He does, though. It's Kelly, and he's inside the condo village's perimeter and in place. He's ready for them to push into the crowd of assholes.

They move forward, but Parker and one of his men take off in another direction.

"Damn it!" Simon hisses, mimicking Cory's thoughts.

"Fucking prick," Cory remarks.

"Let's go," Simon orders and begins jogging again.

Cory continues on with Simon, ignoring the change in plans issued by the new ranking commander. If Parker's men take on friendly fire, it's on them. Cory won't lose sleep over it. If there's one thing they never do, it's change plans in the middle of a mission unless it is absolutely necessary or they are under attack and need to get out of the area fast.

Cory glances one last time their way before tightening up the space between himself and Simon. Parker's men who stayed with Cory seem to know what they're doing. They don't bunch up but move one at a time until their partners can run ahead to keep the area clear and to cover one another. It's the same way he and Simon were taught by John, Derek, and Kelly. He notices that Lucas moves with the same precision. He also notices that Luke stuck with them and ditched Parker the second he decided to split from the group. The only one on their team who doesn't move with tactical practice is Parker. He is screwing up their formation.

As they draw nearer to the scene, Cory can see at least six vehicles and men hiding behind them. This is a different modus operandi than the highwaymen have used before. They've never ambushed people at night that he knows of, and they usually attack people on the road, travelers. With the exception of Dave's compound and possibly that night with Paige at their cabin near Clarksville, neither of which was able to be confirmed as their work, they usually attack in broad daylight. This night attack will work to Cory's advantage. A daytime assault is much different than one in the dark. Confusion and panic can set in quickly if their plan falls apart, which he has every intention of making happen. If they are not equipped with night-vision gear or have experience doing this at night, then they will easily defeat them.

There are at least fifty men, maybe sixty or seventy, a few additional dead ones on the pavement. Cory takes cover behind a house across the street from the gated community. He knows that his brother and John came here years ago and ended up freeing the women and children who lived in these condos from their captors. Now they must help their closest allies again. Simon runs past him and takes cover behind a dirty car parked in the side yard of the home. Cory is sure it was abandoned there and not actually from before the fall. It has that apocalyptic look about it. Missing side door, faded and chipped paint, weeds growing up and out of the windows and hood, half of it burned to a crisp. He's pretty sure this wasn't a soccer mom's carpooling vehicle. It's good cover, though, and he joins his friend, pressing his back against it. Luke runs to the house next door and squats low at the corner near the front porch. He's got good cover, which makes Cory glad. He doesn't particularly want to return Doc's new grandson to him with a bunch of holes in him. Also, he's a lot more afraid of G and what her reaction would be if Cory got her brother killed on his first mission with them. She's a feisty little shit.

"Crap, someone's gonna get on that fifty again," Simon says as he peers through his long scope.

"We're in position," Cory says into his radio, hating that he doesn't have his throat mic with him.

Before he gets an answer from his brother, Parker's group begins firing.

Chapter Twenty-two
Paige

She swerves around a dead deer in the road, forcing the truck onto the berm for a second. Her nerves are rattled, fried, at the prospect of what Cory is going into and what her brother is probably already in. Paige is tired of warring and battles and violence. She'd had enough of that when she was on the road with her friends. Most of the time they tried to steer clear of it, but sometimes they had no choice, especially if people were trying to steal what meager provisions they had on hand, usually food.

"You're doing just fine, Paige," Herb praises from the back seat.

Beside her, Derek has his rifle propped out the window just in case. She hopes he doesn't have a need to use it. Just in case scenarios can quickly become likelihoods with far too much frequency for her taste.

"Thank you, Herb," she says. "I'm sorry if I'm swerving around too hard. I'm just a ball of nerves."

"They'll be fine," Derek says and pats her arm. "Don't worry about your brother. Cory's gonna meet up with them. He won't let anything happen to Simon."

Paige nods as they pull up to the gate in Pleasant View, which Doc ordered her to do. Derek greets the guards, and they are permitted entrance along with the truck of Robert's men behind them.

Paige parks in front of the town hall, and they get out. The sheriff comes out of the building, where he lives full-time, and shakes Doc's hand, then nods to her and Derek.

Herb explains the situation that is taking place at the condo community since it is so close to the town.

"Yes, we know about it, and we've heard the shooting," their sheriff explains. "We've had extra men on guard all night. We haven't seen anything, though."

"No stragglers on the roads near here or people buzzing by?" Derek asks.

"No, nothing. It's been a quiet night, other than the occasional shooting in the distance," he answers.

"Have you talked to anyone else who has had problems with anyone tonight, the highwaymen?"

"No, not yet."

"Keep a keen eye, my friend," Derek says and shakes his hand. "Call it in if you see anything."

They leave a moment later after Doc checks on the clinic, always his first priority. She helped him pack six boxes of medical supplies into the back of the truck before they left Robert's compound. He doesn't leave them at the clinic, though. She suspects he is nervous the town will be attacked tonight. Paige has no idea what the family will do if it is. Will they abandon the farm to come to town to save the people? She questions if they should; she also questions her own values because she's not sure if she was in charge that she'd make the right call. There are many women and small children who live in this town who won't be able to put up much of a fight.

They arrive safely at the farm where the rest of the family awaits. Robert's men set up a perimeter to keep watch while the rest of them go inside. Derek and Herb rush to his office so that they can be ready to communicate with the men or their town.

"What's going on, have you guys heard anything?" Paige prompts as she places her backpack on the first step to the second floor.

Reagan answers, "Nothing. I'm going nuts here!"

She's holding a swaddled newborn, which Paige cranes her neck to see. Reagan obliges by tipping her daughter toward her.

"Oh, my, Reagan," she says. "She's so beautiful."

"And quiet for this second," she complains half-heartedly. "I'd like for her to grow up with a father."

"Don't worry, dearest," Hannah says and comes over to rub her sister's back.

Sam walks into the room and hugs Paige for a long time.

"I'm glad you're still here," Paige tells her.

"Me, too," Sam says. "I hope they're ok. I don't know what to do. I wish I was there helping."

"Don't worry," Paige says, mimicking Hannah.

"Sure, that'll happen," Reagan replies as Sue also enters the kitchen.

"I'll take her, Reagan," Sue offers. "Grandpa wants to see her."

"Thanks," Reagan says and relinquishes her hold on her baby. "My arms could use a break."

"That's because you haven't put her down since she was born," Sue scolds with a smile.

Reagan frowns and says, "She said she doesn't want me to."

Hannah laughs and kisses Reagan's cheek. "You'll spoil her. If Grams were still here, she'd be yelling at you for that. You're going to create a habit that you come to regret."

"Having a free arm is overrated anyway," Reagan says and touches her sister's cheek. "God gave me an extra."

Paige is glad to be home. She misses the family more and more every time she leaves, and that actually scares her. To become completely attached to the McClanes would be to surrender some of her heart to the possibility of what could be here on the farm. Unlike Cory, she's not ready to forget what can happen in the blink of an eye, that moment when you lose everything you care about; your possessions, your shelter, your food, and your friends. She's been through this too many times and isn't ready to revisit it again.

"How are you feeling?" she asks Reagan.

"Not too bad. I'm feeling like my body is mine again- or, at least until I can finally stop breastfeeding."

"That's good. We were all worried," Paige confesses.

Hannah says, "No worries. Simon and Sam had it all under control."

Paige laughs, "That's what we were worried about."

"Not me. Simon had it under control, but I was a nervous wreck," Sam admits.

"You did great," Hannah praises. "Simon told us how wonderful you were."

Hannah wraps a slim arm around Sam's waist and pulls her hip to hip. Sam lays her head on Hannah's shoulder affectionately.

"I'm sure Simon was a wreck, too," Paige says.

"No, he did great. He was very cool, very professional," Reagan tells her. "I was really proud of him. Grandpa would've been, too."

"Oh, good," Paige says, also feeling proud of her little brother. He's so serious all the time. She's sure he was a frazzled mess on the inside the other night when Reagan went into labor, and he had no one else to rely on but himself. "And they said the baby's healthy and all right?"

"Yes, of course," Reagan boasts. "She's a perfect little angel in every way. Of course, not when she wants to nurse at three a.m. Then she's annoying and bothersome like her father."

"Uh-huh, sure," Paige teases, getting a smile from the new mother. "Oh, hey, your grandpa brought a lot of stuff back from the Army base for the clinic. He was pretty impressed with the research they're doing up there. I guess the doctors from the CDC and some other types of doctors were doing vaccine and disease research."

"Cool," Reagan says without her usual zeal for medicine.

Normally she'd head straight for the shed to check out new medicine and equipment for their clinic. Tonight, she only has time for her baby and, apparently by the looks of the fatigue under her eyes, worrying about her husband. Paige knows just how she feels.

Sue rushes into the kitchen and fires up the coffee machine. "Grandpa said this is bound to be a long night. Anyone, want some?"

"No, thanks," Reagan says. "I'm breastfeeding. I'm supposed to be responsible now or something. I don't know. It's just what I've heard."

Paige chuckles and shakes her head at Sue.

"Right," Hannah says with an ornery tone, "You'll have to eat something more than candy and junk."

"Wrong," Reagan argues. "We never have the good stuff anymore."

"Hey, we made honey candy the other day," Hannah reminds her sister.

"Yeah, and I didn't feel good, so I didn't get any. Those little monsters ate all of it."

"Oh, I'm sure you have a stash of candy somewhere in this house," Sue teases.

Reagan doesn't say anything but winks at Paige, who smiles in return.

After Sue has Doc's coffee made up the way he likes it, they join him and Derek in the office.

"Anything?" Reagan asks.

"Not yet," Grandpa answers and embraces Reagan in a long hug while holding her baby in his other arm. "How's my new mother?"

"Fine," she answers. "No thanks to you!"

He chuckles and says, "I know, honey. I'm sorry I wasn't here, but I knew you could do it."

"That makes one of us," she says with sarcasm.

He pats her back and kisses her forehead. "She sure is a little cutie, Reagan. Is she latching on and suckling?"

"Yes, sort of. Breastfeeding sucks. I've had to pester Sue and Hannie constantly about it. It's harder than it looks."

"Yes, I'm sure it is. She seems healthy. Her color's good. I listened to her heart and lungs."

"I have no doubt," she comments.

"In the morning, I'll give you both a thorough examination," he says. Reagan just offers a smile of appeasement, her light eyes joyful at the sight of her grandfather.

Paige steps closer and looks down at the dark-haired baby. "She is adorable, Reagan. She has dark hair."

"Probably our moms," Reagan tells her. "Wanna' hold her?"

"Oh, um, I don't know. I'm not that great with babies."

"What do you mean?" Reagan asks. "You took care of Maddie for almost three years."

"She was a lot bigger than that when we took custody of her," Paige tells them as Reagan places her baby into her arms anyway. Lucky for her, Charlotte is fast asleep and barely stirs when transferred to her. Paige takes a seat on one of the leather sofas. Reagan's daughter is so tiny, feels like she doesn't weigh much more than a sack of sugar.

A cool evening breeze passes through the large window near her. It almost seems as if it will rain. She hopes it doesn't because it would make the mission her brother is on more difficult. There was fog settling in during the last few miles to the farm.

"Is anyone hungry?" Sue asks.

"I could use some fuel," Derek tells her. "Doc and I didn't eat much at dinner. We were busy with your father."

"Oh, great," Sue says. "I'll grab some food from the kitchen."

"I'll help," Sam offers and rushes from the room, probably eager to have any task to do to keep her mind off the night's events.

Sue leaves, but her husband does not. Derek is busy at Doc's desk with maps and pens.

"If they move this way, if the men push them and some escape, this is a possible route they'll take. Or this one here. This is the one we don't want them to take. It could bring them here."

"Or our town," Doc says.

Paige is too much in awe of the small bundle in her arms to look at the maps. Charlotte's tiny eyelids flutter from time to time, but for the most part, she is content to be cuddled.

"They've been warned," Reagan says. "They have enough people to defend it."

"If they go that way, I'm sure John will follow," Derek says about his brother.

Paige can tell by his body language that Derek is a tense ball of anxiety. He keeps clenching his fists and nervously tapping his pen on the desktop. He's also leaning heavily on his cane as if he is exhausted and sore.

"There is the possibility that none of them will be able to escape. I know John's not going to want any of them getting away," Reagan adds before taking a seat next to her.

Derek says, "No, but with numbers that high and it being dark out, there could be some stragglers that escape."

"What do you want to do?" Herb asks. "It's your call, Derek."

"I'm going to send a few of Robert's men and a few from Dave's to these two roads. They'll act as roadblocks to prevent them from escaping. No prisoners. No escape. We have to eliminate them, make a show of force. If they escape, you can bet they'll be leading more men back immediately."

266

"If that's how you want to handle it, I'll support your decision."

Derek nods and limps from the room. Paige assumes he is going outside to speak with the men who are guarding them. Minutes later, they are pulling out, and Derek returns to his position at the desk.

Huntley comes in a moment later and hovers near Derek. She saw him earlier standing guard in the music room where all of the kids are sacked out on the floor. Gretchen was sitting at the window seat reading a book. She also comes into Herb's office.

"What the hell? How long's it gonna take before we hear something? This friggin' sucks! Luke shouldn't have gone."

"No swearing," Hannah corrects her new sister.

"Awesome," Reagan states. "Swear more, G. It gives Hannie someone else to yell at besides me."

"No," Hannah says firmly and takes a seat. "I just need to keep a bar of soap in my pocket for you two."

"He'll be fine, G," Reagan says, referring to her new brother and ignoring Hannah.

"I'm sure he will," Gretchen says, chewing on her darkly painted fingernails, exposing her anxiety.

"Does he have the experience to handle himself in this sort of situation?" Reagan asks.

"What?" she asks distractedly. "Yeah, of course. He went through military school before college. Plus, Dad always spent summers teaching him and forcing him to read military books and crap."

"I didn't know he attended military school instead of regular high school," Hannah comments.

Paige notices that she keeps wringing her hands and twisting her fingers in her long dress. Hannah is also stressed out.

"Yes, four years," she answers. "He went to private school like me until the general forced Luke into military academy."

"That probably wasn't a fun place," Reagan says.

G grunts and says, "Yeah, no crap. But he did learn a lot."

Sue walks in carrying a tray with a pot of hot tea, cups, saucers, hard-boiled eggs, and biscuits with a little jar of berry jam. Paige passes. She's too nervous to eat.

"Where's Sam?" Paige asks her.

"I think she's outside with Henry," Sue answers.

"Hm, interesting," Hannah says as demurely as ever, even though Paige knows what a little schemer she is.

Reagan asks her new sister, "You said before that Luke had to deal with people when you guys lived in the forest or something up in Portland?"

"Right," she says. "He got good at taking care of us. Plus, well, there was the trip to the cabin. That got pretty hairy."

"What do you mean, dear?" Herb asks her.

"Oh, the usual. Idiots trying to rob us and shit…"

Hannah jumps in on this one, "Miss Gretchen!"

"Sorry," she apologizes and swipes a hand through her short, dark hair. "Tried to rob us and *stuff*. Luke took care of it."

"Where was Robert?" Sue asks of her father.

"He wasn't there yet, remember?" G says. "He was trying to get to us from the other side of the country. Luke came for me and Mom and got us out of there. We didn't really need the general. We just waited for Luke."

"Where was your brother?" Paige asks.

"Seattle. It took him a while to get to us, too. That was scary. We had to wait a few days for him to arrive, and it was just Mom and me."

"Did you two have any problems?" Reagan inquires.

G shakes her head and says, "Not really. We tried to stay inside, not go out."

Paige believes that she is hiding more than she is revealing. Whatever her family went through in the northwest must've been harrowing because she definitely doesn't want to talk about it.

"And you had trouble in the city trying to get out once Luke got to you?" Reagan asks.

"Of course," G answers and plops down into a leather chair near Paige.

Everyone pauses and looks at her. She doesn't continue but sits cross-legged style and opens her book again.

"And?" Sue presses. "What happened?"

Gretchen's head snaps up, and she says, "Oh. I don't know. The usual. My mom did a lot of the driving while Luke laid down

268

suppressive fire. One group of ass...sorry, jerkwads tried to steal our car when Mom got stuck in traffic."

"What'd you do?" Paige asks quietly so as not to awaken the baby.

"Luke took care of them," she answers. "I helped, but it was mostly my brother. He punched one guy out the window and shot two. I don't know what happened to them, if they died or lived. Who cares, right? They were trying to jack our car."

"So the city fell when you guys were still in it?" Reagan asks.

"Yeah, but we got out safe. It was only dangerous in certain areas. Once we got outside the city, it wasn't so bad. Well, the one time it was, but we still made it to the cabin. Then it sucked 'cuz we had a long hike to get to it."

The baby begins to stir, wanting to be fed, so Paige passes her carefully to Reagan, who drapes herself in a soft, cotton blanket to breastfeed. She is tired from the trip and being away from home where she didn't sleep well on that Army base, but she is way too keyed up and worried about her brother to go to bed.

"How long were you in this cabin out in the woods by yourselves before your dad got to you?" Paige asks.

"Um, a while. I think a few months. I don't know. You lose track of the days when you're so isolated."

"Don't I know it," Paige concurs as her concern for the men grows. She stands and decides to pace the room instead. She wishes that she could've been involved in this fight, too, but understands why she couldn't. If the men are defeated along with their allies, the highwaymen could hit the farm next. She's not going to fool herself into believing that if the men can't defeat them that she could. She's not that delusional.

"Damn it!" Derek swears softly at Doc's desk.

"They'll radio soon, son. Don't worry," Herb says, trying to console their leader.

"I should be with them," he growls angrily.

Doc lays a hand on Derek's shoulder briefly before saying, "If you were, then we'd be in trouble if those men come this way. We need you here just as much if not more than your brother does."

He groans quietly and hobbles from the room on his cane. Everyone is quiet for a moment. Then Sue goes after her husband with an expression of pain on her face. His disability is affecting his whole family. Paige has observed him falling deeper into despair with each passing day. She suspects that Herb requested his presence along for the trip to Fort Knox just to get him out of the house.

Hannah finally breaks the silence by saying, "I feel so terrible for him. This has been so hard on Derek."

"I know," Reagan says softly.

"I wish we knew what to do," Hannah says.

Reagan looks at her and replies, "We're working on it, Hannie. Give us some time. We might figure something out for Derek, and if not, he'll just have to reconcile himself with the fact that this is his life now."

"But so many veterans…so many vets who were injured and disabled…" Hannah says, drifting off with sadness.

Paige knows she's speaking to the suicide rate of veterans. It was always something she was familiar with because her father worked hard in the Senate to make the lives of injured vets easier. She'd even started a charity at her college to raise money to go to veterans' causes. It hadn't gone over well with the hippy progressive kids, but Paige hadn't cared about their reproach. As the kid of a senator, she was used to it. Respecting the men and women fighting for her freedoms was something instilled in her at a young age.

"It won't come to that, Hannah," Reagan says. Then she adds in an almost scolding tone, "Don't even say that."

"He's so down, though," Hannah counters.

Doc comes over and takes her hand in his, "He'll work this out, honey. Don't you worry about Derek. He'll get better, even if his body does not. The Good Lord doesn't give us more than we can handle. Don't let your faith falter. He knows what Derek can take, and for some reason, this is the path that was chosen for him."

"Right, Hannie," Reagan says in a more cheerful tone. "Childbirth alone is something that I didn't think I could handle, that it was more than anyone could ever go through, and we made it. I didn't think I would about halfway through, but I did. I'm sure as hell not ever doing it again, but I did it once."

"Reagan," Hannah reprimands for the swear.

"Yes, you did," Doc says and walks over to touch the top of her head. "And we sure are glad you did, too."

"Do you want her? She's done. She seems to like to feed for about five minutes and then sleep for an hour. Hope this trend ends soon."

"Who needs sleep? It's highly overrated," Herb asks rhetorically and with a broad smile as he takes his great-granddaughter into his arms. "Boy, your grandmother would've loved seeing this little one. She looks a little like your mother, Reagan."

"Really? You think so?"

"Oh, yes," he says and kisses the baby's downy head.

"Cool."

"Let's just hope she doesn't inherit her mother's vocabulary," Hannah teases.

They take turns passing around Charlotte Rose while Herb and Derek listen for the radio and check and re-check the maps. Derek also goes out to speak with the remainder of Robert's men and Dave's backup. She doesn't know how much experience Robert's people have with this sort of thing, but she knows firsthand how well-trained Dave's men are. His men have all been through the same as Derek's. They are ready for anything that happens tonight. Henry and Sam join them a short time later, and he takes a position near the desk with Derek.

"They're getting desperate," Henry notes.

"I know. A nighttime attack, maybe not the first, and hitting villages that clearly have security," Derek observes.

"It shows that they're willing to take more chances to get what they need."

"Our signs on the roads are interfering with their business," Derek says.

"After tonight, this is it. We have to stop them."

"It's time for our ambush. I've been putting some thought into that, too."

"I have, as well, and so has Sergeant Winters," Henry agrees with a nod. "We're ready when you are, Major Harrison."

Paige isn't sure why he still uses everyone's ranks, but it must be a military thing. Either that or he is trying to hold together the last remnants of order and structure. In her opinion, that ship sailed four years ago with the first nuke overseas.

"Let's just get our men home safely before we plan the next mission," Doc tells them, calmly sipping his second cup of coffee.

"Agreed, sir," Henry says and looks over at Sam, who is holding Charlotte.

From what Paige can see in his eyes, he'd like for her to be holding his baby, their baby. His regard for her is undeniable. Paige just wishes that her brother felt so comfortable offering the same, open admiration to her little friend.

Tonight, though, she isn't worried about her brother's love life. She just wants him to come back in one piece.

Chapter Twenty-three
Simon

"Fuckin' moron," Cory swears again.

His friend is upset about Parker, who has taken it upon himself to call the shots for his team which happen to be different plans than John is ordering. They are firing pell-mell at the men who are also firing at the wall of the compound. Basically, they're all wasting an exorbitant amount of ammo. K-Dog and Paul's men are doing a good job keeping the invaders at bay, though. Simon takes a second to review the scene before him. There are at least fifty men, maybe as many as seventy-five scurrying around, taking cover behind cars, trucks and anything they can. Others are shooting at Paul's men inside the compound and don't seem too concerned about wasting ammo. Luke is taking cover behind the car next to them.

"Hold your positions!" John yells into the radio. "Wait for my order!"

"It's not us, brother," Cory tells him. "It's that fucking moron from Robert's compound."

"Idiot. Some help," John says. "Derek's sending men to block the roads out of here. Don't shoot them if you run too far out of perimeter."

"Yes, sir."

"Give Kelly cover if he needs it but wait for my command to move forward."

"He's in position, sir," Cory whispers.

"Got it," John says. "Hold your positions."

"This guy is an imbecile," Simon agrees with John's assessment of Parker, who is going to get himself killed.

They wait a moment while Parker offers up to their enemy some firepower. The enemy gives it right back from the cover of their vehicles. Cory taps off a few rounds from his AR10 with the .308 rounds. It is loud and speaks with authority.

John says into Simon's earpiece, "Move in, Professor. Come hard."

"Yes, sir," Simon replies. Then he turns to Cory and signals, "Let's move."

Cory just gives a nod and rises from his crouched position. Within seconds they are in the battle and pressing forward. He just hopes he doesn't get shot by one of Parker's men.

Simon can hear men shouting and see their silhouettes in the dark, outlined by a fire that has been lit near the wall of the condo community. It is blazing thirty feet into the air and illuminating the darkness, the orange flames licking the inky sky like a dragon's forked tongue.

"Hey there, asshole," Cory whispers and pops off a shot, killing a man twenty feet to their left who was trying to sneak around furtively.

Simon sweeps right with his short barrel rifle, having slung his sniper weapon behind his shoulder, just in time to see two men with an RPG aiming right at the wall. Unfortunately, it is also pointing toward them.

Simon takes aim and fires, hitting the trigger man. The rat has fired it off too quickly, though, and the RPG is flying at them. He shoves Cory to the ground and covers him with his body after yelling, "Incoming!"

Others take cover and dive for safety, as well, as the RPG hits the wall right in front of him. The blast wave shoves the car they are hiding behind. They both scramble to their feet again, and Cory fires a few rounds on fully auto to keep the enemy at bay.

"Thanks, bro'," Cory yells and pats his shoulder.

Simon nods and takes aim again, shooting over the hood of the car. He shoots a man who is stalking toward them. The scene has become chaos. If there's one thing he's learned from fights like this it's to take control and not let the situation manipulate you. Simon squats and aims again. He is able to hit a man in the calf before he is

274

dragged behind a car by his comrade. Luke is farther ahead than them, moving at a faster pace.

"Overlapping coverage. The Hulk's in. Move, people!" John shouts into Simon's earpiece.

He and Cory push forward, making it to another vehicle in the road where they catch up to Luke.

"What the fuck is that...." Cory asks rhetorically.

Simon mimics his surprise as he looks up, "What..."

"Fucking drone," Cory says and shoots it down.

The small, metal drone lands with a clank and skids ten feet down the road until it comes to a stop. Then someone shoots at them from behind. Luke covers and fires back.

"Goddammit," Cory swears and swings, firing from his rifle.

Simon does the same, and together they take out three men who have flanked or who were hidden at the next house over that they didn't notice. Luke kills another with a headshot. The enemy's ability to flank makes the hair come up on the back of his neck. If three were able to circle them, others could, too.

They pause and stay low. Cory shoots around the front of the car at people. Luke does the same from the other end of the vehicle.

"Be careful," Simon relays to the others who have throat mics and earpieces. "They've got drones."

"Roger," John says. "Take out that truck of men in front of you, Professor."

"Got it," Simon answers.

Beside him, Cory is shooting at men far in the distance away from them. He shouts to him.

"Shoot at the truck. There are men on the other side of it."

"Ten-four, brother," Cory says. "Cover me."

His friend low jogs to the next abandoned car over and squats again.

Simon and Luke cover by firing a few rounds down range to suppress bad behavior. These men don't seem to have a lot of fear, leaving Simon to think that perhaps they have not come up against much resistance before. Maybe they are just that stupid, too. Either way, their enemy seems fearless. They shoot back, forcing him to squat. Cory waves at him that he's ready. He remembers the many dead people and the two raped women on the sides of the road. It fuels his hatred and acts as a shot in the arm of bravery. Simon takes a risk and pops up to shoot again.

Cory does the same, pushing the enemy into squatted positions. Cory rises and tosses a grenade, surprising Simon. They don't have much like that at the farm. This must have come from Robert's compound. Cory offers a big, boyish grin at Simon before turning back to look.

It hits directly in front of the men hiding behind their truck. A second later, it explodes, and men scream in pain. Others do not, leaving him to believe they are dead. Cory rushes, so Simon follows to offer assistance. Luke is right behind him. They both round opposite ends of the truck and fire upon the enemy, killing three more men. They squat in the wreckage and take a breath before pursuing planning their next move.

"Damn it," Kelly says into his mic. "Someone, take out that fifty. Son-of-a-bitch."

"Professor, can you get eyes on it?" John asks.

"Yes, sir," he says. "I'll have to leave Cory."

"He's a big boy," Kelly jokes.

John says, "Take it out, Professor."

"I'm going high," he says to his friend, tapping Cory on the shoulder and pointing up. "I gotta leave you."

"I got this," he returns and fires a few rounds toward another cluster of men, which sends them diving for cover. Cory has hit one, and the man is wailing in pain. Cory gives a thumbs-up and says, "See you soon. Stay safe, brother."

Simon nods and jogs away as their enemy begins to realize they are not getting out of this without a fight to the death. Parker has effectively blown their cover, but he is keeping them from scurrying down the road in retreat. At least Luke is with Cory.

John says into Simon's earpiece, "Professor, when you get into position, take out that fifty."

"Yes, sir," Simon returns, knowing the dire need of this situation. Someone has taken command of the fifty and is rapid firing it right at the front gate of the community and his teammates. Kelly is fighting behind those walls now. He has to get rid of the fifty shooter.

Simon sprints back to the house where he and Cory were squatted and hiding initially. He kicks in the front, locked door of the home and does a quick scan of the room, which is actually a combined living room, dining room, and kitchen area. It was abandoned years ago because dust, cobwebs, and dirt cover every square inch. He sprints to the stairs and runs up to the second floor. Simon does a quick search to make sure he's still alone. Then he rushes to the master bedroom that faces the road. The rest of the team is blasting away.

After quietly prying open the window, Simon rests his rifle against the sill. He takes a deep breath and scans the area below him, sighting in on the truck with the mounted .50 cal. He pulls the trigger, watching the follow through until the man drops. Another runs over, and Simon takes him out, too.

"We're gonna need a medical evac," John states.

This concerns Simon, but he tries to remain professional and shoots three more men before they realize he is hiding in a house sniping at them. Then an entire cluster opens fire. He grabs his short rifle, slings the sniper rifle, and dashes. The home is not brick. Those rounds will come through the exterior walls. Bullets thud against the house and shatter windows. Tiny fragments of glass rain against his back as he retreats. When he reaches the hallway, a sound from the first floor immediately alerts him that he is not alone anymore. Men's voices clarify the theory. Simon backs silently into another bedroom not facing the barrage of gunfire being pounded at the front of the house. Then he squats and directs his rifle at the stairwell. It takes them a few seconds, but they eventually run up the stairs. Simon is able to shoot one, but the other realizes what he's gotten himself into and flees, tripping over his dead friend as he goes. Simon knows this is a no prisoners situation, but they do want to keep a few for questioning. He hits him in the right butt cheek with a round and puts him down. The man falls end over end down the stairs with a howl, but Simon pauses a moment to make sure there aren't others who are going to rush him the moment he comes down the stairs.

"Throw out your gun!" he barks as he keeps his weapon trained on the man on the floor. He doesn't answer, so Simon threatens him, "Throw it to the side, or I'll shoot again."

"I don't have it!" the man cries out.

Simon scans the area and spots it. He approaches cautiously, kneels and hogties the guy's hands behind his back with zip ties.

Then he rolls him over and pats him down for another gun, which he doesn't find. What he does discover, though, is a teenager, not a man. The kid can't be more than sixteen.

"I'm dying!" he cries out with fear.

"You aren't dying. Stay quiet. Stay down. I'll be back for you. Don't get back up, kid. You'll likely get shot again."

"Please, please don't kill me. I won't tell them where you are…"

"Shut up," Simon says, silencing his pleas. "Stay here. If I come back and you aren't here, I'll hunt you down and kill you. Understand me?"

"Ye-yes. Yes, sir," the kid stutters nervously.

Simon rises as his earpiece goes off again.

"Professor, get over here," John says. "Go around back to Kelly. He's got injured. Cory will meet you and provide cover to get you in."

He exits the house the same way and finds Cory and Luke right at the edge of the porch squatted low.

"Got a kid tied up in there," he tells his friend.

"Kid?"

"Teenager," Simon clarifies.

"Gotta get you inside the compound. My brother needs help," he says.

As he is about to answer, another grenade explodes. This time it takes out the technical. The truck explodes a moment later, taking the fifty cal with it.

"Robert's men," his friend explains.

He follows his friend in the dark through the woods and whispers, "You guys got some good toys from the general."

"Yeah, but we got Parker, too. Kind of a shitty deal, you ask me," Cory jokes.

Simon grins and jogs behind his friend. Strangely enough, the highwaymen don't have people set up in the woods to take out anyone making an escape.

"Plus, the dude's got the hots for your sister, so I really just wanna' shoot him in the fucking face," Cory tells him.

"Yeah, lot of that going around lately," he says and punches Cory in the shoulder, very hard.

He just gets a laugh from his former friend. Luke is not joining in, though. He is serious, intense, not like a scientific student of DNA research right at this moment.

"Admit it, you still love me, bro'," Cory jokes. "If you didn't, you wouldn't have saved my ass back there from getting an RPG up it."

"Reflex," Simon replies as they come to the back gate unscathed. "Thanks for the envoy. Now get lost."

Cory laughs obnoxiously and leaves as Kelly lets him in the gate.

"They still don't know we have a rear gate," Kelly tells him as they jog through the compound.

"That's good," Simon says with hope. "I've got a teenager tied up in one of the houses across the street."

Kelly nods and says, "Assholes shot up a few of K-Dog's men. We need medical help, brother."

"Yes, sir," he answers, starting to feel the weight of his value, which he does not hold very high. "I'll do what I can."

"They'll need evac'd to our town for medical care, surgery, whatever the fuck," Kelly says with stress. "We gotta get 'em outta here. This is a shit storm."

"How're we doing?"

"Better since you got that asshole on the fifty off our tails," Kelly answers as they come to a temporary medical site in one of the condos.

K-Dog's wife, Anita, is there working on the wounded with her husband. She is doing whatever she can but is not a nurse or doctor. Simon slings both rifles to Kelly's care and gets to work. He takes off his pack and kneels beside one of the men, who is holding a white rag to his bloody side.

"Let me take a look, sir," Simon implores and rests his hand on top of the man's for just a second to reassure him.

He has clearly been gut shot, but upon further inspection, it seems as if the bullet has passed through, clean through his back. In the distance, the shooting continues.

Kelly rests his hand on Simon's shoulder for a moment before looking at K-Dog and then back to Simon and saying, "We gotta get back out there, little brother. I'll try to get you an evac for these people. Till then, do what you can."

"I'll help," Anita offers. "Tell me what you need. We'll get it."

"Yes, ma'am," he answers. "Go, Kelly. Get out of here."

Kelly nods and takes off with K-Dog.

"I need sterile towels and hot water," he orders.

Then Simon gets to work as a triage nurse, trying to assess whose injuries are more life-threatening and the most urgent. He finds a woman shot in the upper right quadrant of her chest. Her breathing is labored. The bullet passed through, coming out through the fatty tissue and muscle near her scapula. He decides to treat her first.

"Press here," he orders Anita, who does as he says. "Keep pressure on the wound. Lots of pressure, Anita."

Then he steps away to talk to the men over his mic, "We need to get these injured people out of here. We have critically wounded who aren't going to make it if we don't move them now."

He waits a second to get a response and walks back to stabilize the woman.

"Easy, talk to me," he tells her. "Try to calm down. Are you having trouble breathing?"

"Yes, I'm scared. Don't let me die, Doctor," she begs with fright clearly showing in her eyes.

"I won't. Stay calm," he orders patiently as he tries to listen to her chest. It's clear. There isn't wheezing. He's not sure if she can't breathe because her lung has been punctured or because she is in shock. "Give me a deep breath. You can do it. Good."

She's clear. She's just in shock and panicking.

He turns to find a teenager there to assist him. He believes he may be the son of Anita, "Keep her calm. Press down here."

Simon rushes to another person who has been shot in the back and takes a listen to his lungs and his heart. This man is not so lucky because the bullet is still inside and has not passed through. He is bleeding, but the blood is coming out in a slow leak, which should mean that a main artery has not been hit.

"I can't feel my legs, Dr. Murphy," the man says, obviously remembering him from the clinic in town. "I got no feeling from the waist down. Am I paralyzed?"

280

"Just take a deep breath, sir," Simon orders. "Easy now. Stay calm. Don't panic. I'm here to help, and we're going to get you all out of here."

Simon presses bandaging against the man's wound. He doesn't know if he will be paralyzed or not, but he is confident they can get that bullet out. He's going to need Doc's help.

He moves on to a man who has been shot just below the knee. Simon whips out a tourniquet and ties it off tightly.

"Damn it!" Kelly shouts as he runs toward him, the front door having been left open. "Professor, I need you in that tower to the south."

"But what about my patients?"

"They'll have to wait. They're hitting the wall with RPG's and a battering ram. These assholes just don't quit."

"Yes, sir," Simon answers and looks at Anita's son. "Just keep the pressure to these people's wounds until we can get them moved. I'll be back as soon as I can."

He grabs his rifles and rushes out the front door behind Kelly. Passing a frightened woman on the way, he shouts at her, "Go help the medics. They need help back there!"

She nods shakily and turns to go. At least the kid will have some help. It's better than nothing.

He jogs to the south tower, somewhat familiar with the layout of Paul's condo community and their guard towers.

John is there now and yells above the melee, "We'll cover you. Climb!"

Simon hurries up the ladder to the top of the second-story platform while John and his group provide cover fire to keep him from being shot and killed. When he gets there, he can easily see why they need him. Their other sniper from Parker's group lies dead in the erected, wooden tower. He wonders if he'll be next.

"Behind you," Cory says as he joins him.

Simon hefts himself onto the platform, kneels behind the wall, which is double layered with metal to prevent the guard from being shot, and waits for Cory to do the same.

"What's the situation?" Simon asks.

Cory points to their south and says, "RPG's coming in hot and fast, continuous. We gotta figure out who's doing it and take them out. You get them. I'll take care of the battering ram assholes."

Just then, a loud explosion rocks the tower and the ground below them. Men's bodies go flying into the air. Something other than a simple RPG has been fired at them. This is a new threat.

"Fucking mortar fire?" Cory shouts. "You gotta be fuckin' kidding me. Take out those assholes, too, Prof."

Simon nods and prepares to scan the area through his starlight scope. He avoids wasting time looking in the near vicinity because these rounds, mortar and RPG, are coming from further away. Beside him, Cory tap-tap-taps out a rhythm of suppressive fire. Simon has no doubts that not all of it is only to suppress but to kill. He's not a big waster of ammo.

Within a few minutes, another mortar round is fired into the complex and lands on a condo unit, the noise deafening, the earth shaking. He takes a steadying breath to calm his rattled nerves and ringing ears and tries to zero in on whoever is doing that. He doesn't see a mortar, but Simon does spot two men firing RPG's farther down the road. He takes very careful aim because he doesn't want to just frighten them off. These rats will return to another area and begin firing anew. He breathes deep. He squeezes, letting the shot startle him. One target disabled. The man will not get up from that one. Simon has hit him center mass in the chest. The other one using the RPG gets spooked and turns to run. Simon leads the shot and squeezes again. Smack, the deadening thud hits the man square in the middle of his back. He will either bleed out, be crippled for life, or will die instantly.

"Good job, Professor. Good shots," Cory praises. "Now find that asshole with the mortar I'm heading down to take out the morons at the front gate."

"Yep," Simon answers calmly.

He scans slowly but doesn't come up with the shooters. He knows they could be very far away. Mortar rounds can travel from miles away. Simon adjusts his scope and scrutinizes the area farther out. Then he hears it. Another mortar round is coming.

Simon shouts down to the group, some of whom are family, "Take cover! Incoming!"

He gets right back on his scope scanning carefully. He finds them. The man firing the mortar is smoking a cigarette. Simon spots him through his scope, picking up on the light from the tip of his cigarette. There are also men running around with flashlights that give away their position. He is nearly a mile away, maybe further. He can just barely see them through his scope, which is not equipped for this range in the dark. It'll be a difficult shot, likely impossible. Simon is doubting his ability, but he knows he must take that man out of the equation. And from what he can tell, the man has many friends scurrying around the area with him, probably helping load the shells. They have brought a full artillery assault and have no plans of losing this. Simon feels the same way. They cannot allow these thugs and animals to take over this community. Simon knows these people do not take prisoners. Their friends, even the women and children will be murdered, some may also be raped first.

He presses his hand to his throat mic and says, "I gotta come down. I can't hit him from this range. I know where the mortaring is coming from. There's a pack out nearly two clicks."

John immediately says, "Cory and Luke will ride shotgun."

"Got it."

He climbs quickly down again and runs to the back gate, immediately met by Luke.

"Where's Cory?" he asks over the noise of gunfire.

"Pinned down working with another group now. It's just me and you."

"Let's go," he says, slightly nervous about the fact that he hasn't ever really fought with Luke.

They double-time it and run through the woods. Simon sprints up a steep incline, intending on flanking them. Luke grabs his arm to halt him. Then he signals to the bottom of another short hill. They have circumvented two men, who are clearly supposed to be watching the woods on this side of the battle for stragglers. He and Luke have gotten lucky by not being seen. One of the men is urinating behind a tree, his partner ten yards from him smoking a cigarette, or perhaps a joint by the way he is smoking it and holding the inhale for a long time. They are not taking their job too seriously.

"I'll take the one..." Simon starts.

"No, I've got this. We can't alert the men on the mortar launcher that we're closing in. Wait here and cover."

Luke slinks away before Simon can argue. He hopes his new friend knows what he's doing. Simon squats, rests his weight on one knee and brings his rifle up to watch the area so that Luke isn't shot in the back. He can see him moving through the woods, but Simon doesn't hear him. He is as silent as a doe sneaking around. Simon swings left and then right, keeping a keen eye open. Then he swipes back to watch the men in case they spot Luke. They don't. One man is already on the ground. Simon observes as Luke takes the other man by surprise, the pot smoker, and slices his neck. He allows the man to slide down to the ground as silently as he just crept up on them. Then he is sprinting back to Simon. He nods as if nothing has happened, and they continue on, Simon in shock at what he's just witnessed. He had no clue that Luke was so lethal.

They close in on the men surrounding the launcher, and Simon signals for Luke to flank to the other ridge. Simon likes his position where he is for sniping but doesn't want anyone to escape their wrath. Luke waves his laser in a circle toward Simon, which only they can see unless there are others in the woods with night-vision. He hopes they are high enough that the men below them cannot spot their laser pointers.

He takes a deep breath and zeroes in on the man who is getting ready to launch another mortar. Simon squeezes, disabling the man with a headshot. He deserves this. Firing mortar rounds on innocent people is a sickening thing to do. Luke wastes no time and fires, as well. He takes out another man. Simon hits one who is in the middle of diving for cover behind a tree. Luke does the same. Two other men run. Simon leads one and pegs him in the leg. He goes down, and Simon shoots again but misses because the man rolls down a hill. He scans the area as Luke continues to pop off rounds. He sees another person trying to escape, so he takes a shot, wings him in the shoulder. Another squeeze and he has killed him. Luke is holding his own as he takes down another person. Simon hopes none of these people are teenagers.

He moves in closer and meets Luke at the bottom of the hill. They have taken out everyone in this cluster. There are no survivors.

He calls it in to John, "Targets disabled. We're coming back."

"Roger, Professor," John answers. "Get back to the wounded and send Luke to Kelly."

"Affirmative," Simon says and adds, "Be advised, there were men hiding in the woods as lookouts."

"We know. Cory found a few."

It is all that is needed said. If Cory found them, then they are dead.

"Let's take this with us," Luke suggests, indicating the mortar tube.

"We can hide it and come back for it," Simon adds.

"Good. Where the hell'd they get an M224 anyway?"

Simon shakes his head and says, "Same place all these creeps get everything. They steal."

"Right," Luke agrees.

He's not sure how Luke knows what caliber and model it is, but he seems rather proficient in military weaponry. He is also quite capable with the AK47 he's carrying, even though, in Simon's opinion, they have too loud of a bark. He prefers the smooth action of his sniper rifle to the more rustic and heavy design of the foreign rifles.

They pick it up, both carrying one side. It is heavy but manageable with both of them lifting it. They walk quickly back up the hill. They have quite a distance to go, and both keep an eye out for more jerks in the woods to come upon them and kill them. They stash the launcher away behind the condo compound in some thick weeds when they get there. The fighting is still going on, but now they will be able to gain the upper hand.

He is admitted entrance again through the compound's back gate and heads straight for the medical facility. There is a pick-up truck out front that is now holding three of the wounded in the bed. Simon checks on the ones still in the house. There are many more now.

"The mortar fire," Anita's son explains. "People were hurt by the debris that went flying. One landed on the house down the street. Kids were in there hiding. We thought it was safe."

Simon rushes to a particularly bloody child, not more than ten years old, and kneels beside him. He slings his pack to the ground digs in it for gauze bandaging. The child has a head wound that is bleeding down her forehead. She is crying loudly.

"Easy, little one," Simon assures her as he examines her scalp. He looks at Anita's son, who has come to assist him again. "She's going to need stitches."

"There's another little boy who keeps saying his arm hurts," the young man says. "I think it's broke. I don't know."

"Here, hold this pressed against her laceration. I'll be right back."

Simon rises and runs to the other room where three more children are sitting either on furniture or the floor and are being treated by the citizens of the community.

"Doctor!" one of the women yells. "Help over here!"

He speeds past the others and looks at the teenage girl lying on the kitchen table. There is a deep laceration on her head and another on her right shoulder. She is also unconscious and unresponsive.

"We think she was hit by debris," the woman says. "Our house was bombed, the roof caved in. Allie was upstairs hiding with her little sister. We had no idea she was in danger up there. Oh, this is all our fault."

Simon suspects the woman is her mother but doesn't have time for small talk. He listens to her breathing, which is even but shallow. Then he checks her pulse, which is a little slow. He bandages her head tightly. The real worry is the cause of her loss of consciousness and if she has any serious head trauma or eventual brain damage.

"Don't let that truck leave yet," Simon says into his throat mic.

"You got it, Professor," someone answers over his earpiece, although he isn't sure which person it was since it wasn't John or Kelly. He thinks it might've been Dave the Mechanic, but Simon thought he hadn't come to this fight. Some of his men were dispatched, but Dave was detained at the compound for other problems.

"You two!" Simon calls to several young men standing in the doorway. "I need to move her stat."

They hurry over, dread on their young faces, and Simon shows them how to transport her to the truck.

286

He checks on three other patients who have minor cuts, abrasions and some lacerations that will require stitches. Most are in shock or in a state of paralyzed fear. He's thankful that the shooting victims have only added another two in numbers, and both he can handle himself because they are mere grazes instead of fully impacted bullet wounds.

Simon goes outside again and finds Dave and Sam's uncle by the truck. They must've just arrived. "We gotta get them to Doc at the clinic in town."

Sam's uncle rounds the other side of the vehicle, and Simon nods to him.

"I'm going, too," he tells Simon.

"Good. Some of them are in really bad shape."

Simon proceeds to tell him which ones are more critical than others. Within moments Dr. Scott is speeding away with three of Dave's best soldiers toward Pleasant View.

"Has Dr. McClane been advised?" he asks Dave.

"It was either call him or have us dumb jocks sew these people back together," Dave says with his usual humor and chill attitude as rounds are being fired not fifty yards from them in an all-out battle for their lives and the lives of their friends. "Got him comin' to town in the middle of the night on an ER call. Poor old dude. This shit's gotta be hard on him."

"He doesn't mind," Simon reassures him. "He wants to help."

"Twilight of his retirement," Dave jokes.

"Sir, should I get back in this or treat the injured?" he asks.

Dave shakes his head and says, "Nah, I brought another dozen men with me. It's all but over now. They're full-on fucked. Got a call from the men Derek sent to blockade the roads. They've already caught at least twenty or more fucking cockroaches. Some were set up there to prevent us from escaping, and some were in the middle of trying to escape themselves. Dumbasses."

"I don't think they were prepared to meet with this much resistance," Simon comments.

"This ain't fuckin' Disney World. Those dudes are fuckin' well-fucked. Later, Professor."

Simon watches as the world's most prolific cusser jogs away as if he's just out for a Sunday run before church. His Garand is out front at the ready, a cigarette hanging out of his mouth, and his knife hand is issuing commands to his men as he goes. Simon frowns, shakes his head, and runs back to the condo-turned-medical clinic and meets Lucas there.

"John sent me to help," Luke says.

He has worked with him a few times at the family's clinic in town. Although Luke's preferred science was research and DNA studies, he has been very valuable at their clinic and has helped immeasurably when Sam isn't present.

They manage to sew up four patients who needed stitches, bandage others who do not, and treat the less critical injuries like broken bones and contusions. As soon as he can, he'll try to hitch a ride to Pleasant View to help Herb. He doesn't want to leave him with so many people to attend to with just one other doctor and Sam. There are bound to be more injured or shot civilians and soldiers. If he knows Dave's men as well as he does John and Kelly, they will likely keep on fighting even with a few bullet holes in them.

As he works with Luke, he tries not to let his mind wander to Sam. Cory shot down a drone tonight, which they have confiscated along with the wrecked fifty cal from the technical, the mortar, rifles, and ammo. If these people have been using technology like drones since they started their nefarious endeavors of being mass murderers, then they will likely soon find Pleasant View and the McClane farm. They probably used one to find Dave's compound, too, but hadn't thought they'd need to send very many men to overrun it. Her safety is in jeopardy. If she stays at the McClane farm, then the likelihood of her coming into harm's way by these people is very high, too high. If she goes back to Dave's, the same will happen. Taking out less than a hundred of these men tonight is just chunking away a tiny chip from the massive rock of their numbers. They'll come again. The next time they come, she could be in their path.

Chapter Twenty-four
Reagan

She went against Derek's final word and her grandfather's lecture and decided with firm finality to join Grandpa at the clinic to treat the injured people of the condo community. It doesn't matter that she gave birth a few days ago. She feels fine, and this is more important than sitting at the farm where she is of no use to anyone. Derek was worried with her leaving, too, that there wouldn't be enough security at the farm, but Henry assured him that he and his men could help him should danger arise. So, she went to town, and it is nearly dawn.

She, Grandpa, and Sam and her Uncle Scott have treated twelve people so far. The sun is just cresting on the horizon, but just barely because a light drizzle started a few hours ago. A bead of sweat runs down her brow as they await the next wave of patients that her husband called in a while ago to tell her were on their way.

"Sweetheart, here, drink," Grandpa says, handing her a cold mason jar of water from the farm. "Sit, Reagan. Take a breather."

She takes his advice and sits in the receptionist's former chair in the lobby of her grandfather's practice.

"Rest a while, honey," he orders and takes a seat near her, reviewing patient charts.

"I can't believe we lost two people tonight," she admits with shame.

Her feet are tired, her body is fatigued, and she'd been forced to pump milk for her daughter before she left the house. Thank God baby Daniel is finally on goat's milk, or she'd be pumping enough for both of them.

"Focus on the patients still coming who need our care, Reagan," he says. "You know better than that. There's time later for second guesses and misgivings."

"I know," she says sadly.

"Take a break," he says again. "The ones who needed it have been moved across the street. Our townspeople are taking care of them and watching the critically injured."

"I know, but I feel like I should be over there until the next group arrives."

"Reagan, you just gave birth three days ago. You shouldn't even be here."

"I read once that some women in third world countries give birth and go back to the rice fields the same day. Compared to them, I'm a real chump."

"My granddaughter is not a slacker, and I'll not have you talking about her that way," he teases with a grin and pushes his readers higher on his nose.

Reagan smiles and observes him for a moment writing notes and scanning patient charts. It reminds her of when she was little, and a pang of fear that he'll die soon, too soon for her daughter to get to know him, hits Reagan right in the chest. The air in the stuffy clinic suddenly feels too thin.

Her grandfather doesn't notice and keeps on talking, "Simon did well this evening, too."

"Yeah, so I heard," Reagan agrees, remembering John's report. Simon and Luke took care of many of the superficial injuries. "That took a lot off our plate."

"Yes, he's becoming quite the young doctor," Grandpa praises as Sam comes out of the back with soiled sheets and passes through the door to the outside. The linens will be boiled out back to contain and kill any contaminants.

"I'm glad he was there," she says.

"I'm just thankful that all of our family is going to come home safely and uninjured," he adds.

"I'll believe it when I see it. John always gets hurt."

"Have a little faith," he teases her.

Reagan sips the water and swipes the back of her hand across her sweaty forehead. She'll be glad when summer is over. Normally, it's her favorite time of year, but this year with being pregnant and now the massive hormonal flux, she'll be relieved when fall arrives.

"What did John say about the highwaymen? I didn't get to hear the whole transmission."

"No survivors that they know of," Grandpa says.

"Some could've gotten away," she acknowledges and gets a solemn nod from him. "They could still come back, come at us again."

"I know, honey."

Reagan sighs and waits for him to finish jotting down notes. Tonight has been stressful and harrowing for them and the men in the family who went out to confront this danger head-on. She admires their bravery, but she's not sure she feels the same about a lot of this now. Once her daughter was born, Charlotte changed her views on things. She no longer wants to leave the farm to join a fight, and she's not so sure she wants John to do it anymore, either. But these were not just allies who were being attacked; these were their friends, too. They couldn't stand by and watch them be slaughtered like so many were on the road. As worried as she was about her husband and family members in this fight, she was equally concerned about Derek.

"Grandpa, did you notice how upset Derek was tonight?" she asks and pulls a bag of homemade crackers from her pocket.

"Good girl. Keep your calorie intake high, Reagan," Grandpa praises. "You need to keep your milk going. Plus, the baby will rob you of key nutrients if you don't. Your body will produce, and the baby will take what she needs. Then you'll start having problems with your teeth and bones."

"I know."

"And, yes, I did notice," he says reluctantly.

"He's so depressed lately. I wish I'd studied post-traumatic stress syndrome more thoroughly. I don't know what to do about him."

"I know, dear," he says and drags his chair closer to hers. Then he pats her leg and continues. "I've been working with the CDC doctors up north. We did some pretty advanced research work together while I was there, and I feel confident for the first time in a

291

long time that we're going to conquer all of this and flourish someday again."

"What's that got to do with Derek?"

"I was also working with one of the other young doctors there who specialized in orthopedics. Bright young lady. We reviewed Derek's case quite thoroughly, and I think I may have a solution. I'm going to need Cory's help, but we worked on a design for a brace that she was using with similar patients before the fall. I think with Cory's knack for mechanical engineering and this new idea for a brace that we can build it."

"That would be great, Grandpa," Reagan says.

"I'll show the drawings to you when we get back. I've just been so busy…"

"You mean in the eight hours since you rushed back from the fort so that the men could get involved in this war?"

He chuckles and scratches at his whiskers. "I suppose so."

"Time flies in the apocalypse," she jokes.

There is shouting outside as another truckload of injured people is brought to their clinic.

"You can go to my office and sleep if you need to," he offers as he stands. Then he lays his hand on the top her head.

"No, I'm good. Those crackers-and-water Soviet prison food were just the thing to get me going again."

"What would I do without you?" he says with great affection, smiling down into her face before caressing her scarred cheek and leaving.

Dr. Scott comes in from the front porch to tell them what they already know. From what Reagan has learned of him, he is a good man, and Sam is lucky to have him back in her life.

This wave of patients is not so critical, for which Reagan is thankful. The exam rooms are a wreck when they finish again. The sun has risen and is trying to push through the heavy cloud cover. Sam and her uncle volunteer to clean the rooms along with three women from town. She is more than thankful for the help. They insist she sit on the sofa in the lobby and rest. Reagan doesn't argue this time. She finally breathes a sigh of relief when the next vehicle brings the men to the clinic. She rushes out to hug her husband, heedless of what people think.

"We're ok, babe," John says, crushing her to him with one, strong arm while holding his rifle with the other. He kisses the side of her head through her curls. "We're fine."

"I know. I know," she whispers.

They separate, and Reagan steps back. She presses her hand to John's cheek but notices blood on the side of his head.

"What…"

"Not mine, babe. I'm one piece."

"Let me get you cleaned up," she insists and tugs his arm.

"Luke's way worse than me."

"My brother?" she asks, the words tasting strange coming out of her mouth. She has not referred to him as this yet, not out loud. It was a chapter of her life that she wanted to be a bad dream, her father disgracing himself by having a whole other family secreted away from them.

"Yeah, apparently your new brother is quite the proficient when it comes to hand-to-hand combat."

"Oh, gross," she remarks honestly.

"Gross it may be, my love, but handy it was in the battle."

"How's everyone else? How's Simon?"

John looks over his shoulder and points. "He's coming. He was invaluable tonight with his long-range shots and taking care of patients for us."

"I know. I'm so glad he's safe. That's all that matters."

"Everyone's fine. Paul's people took the biggest hit. A few of Dave's men, but you probably already know all this. We have so much to go over later at the farm when we get time."

"Ok, good. We were all worried and left out of the loop. Your brother's about to lose his mind."

"I radioed to let him know the mission was a success."

Reagan frowns and says. "That's not what I mean, John. Derek's in bad shape. He didn't handle it well that he was left out of the fight. He needs more to do than run the damn radio at home."

"He did. He sent men to stop the runners on the road. It helped us a lot."

"I know, but you don't get it. Your brother…we'll talk later," she says and presses a quick kiss to his mouth.

She spends some time collecting clean, scalded rags from behind the clinic and passing them out for the men to wipe down. Some are covered in black soot, others blood, and some have grease and gunpowder on their faces. Lucas is, indeed, the worst one of the bunch. His demeanor is calm and cool, however. It leads her to believe that this is not his first skirmish as G had conveyed to them about their new brother. He simply washes up, dumps a bucket of water over his head and walks away with his rifle slung again.

Sam and her uncle volunteer to remain in town for a few days to look after their patients for them while Reagan and her grandfather will return to the farm for some much-needed rest. Simon also volunteers to stick around in town to keep watch over Sam and her uncle, who absolutely do not need him to do so with the extra guards in place, the sheriff and his men, and the few men from Dave's who are already planning on staying until their friends are healed up and ready to go home. He is going to stay anyway. Reagan doesn't think it's such a bad idea, though, since there are so many patients that require their help.

"Call us if you hear anything else, brother," Dave is saying to Kelly as she and John join them in the street.

"You got it," Kelly tells him. "You do the same."

"K-Dog's got a patrol unit out right now looking for strays, so if I hear anything, I'll let you know. There were bound to be a few that got away."

Kelly nods and says, "Not such a bad thing. They'll make it back to their people and let them know what happened. Hopefully, they'll leave the condo community alone now."

Her husband says, "They're gonna be wondering where their people are who don't make it to them, if any do at all. I'm sure we fluffed their nest tonight. But, at least they know who they're messin' with now."

"Hooah," Dave says and bumps Kelly's fist, then John's.

"Safe travels, brother," John tells their friend.

Dave nods and shouts expletives to his men to mount up.

"What about Paul's group?" Reagan asks her husband. "How will they protect the community now?"

"They'll be fine. The sheriff here is sending some men that way to help."

"Will the town be ok without them?"

John nods and says, "Yeah, babe, they'll be fine. They're gonna have Simon here for a few days and some of Dave's men. We're only a few miles away if something happens to the town."

Reagan and the other doctors take the time to check their patients again before leaving with Cory, Kelly, and John for the farm. Derek dismisses Henry and his remaining men, who agree to go to Pleasant View and help keep an eye on their town and also their laid-up comrades at the medical house across from the clinic. The men agree to discuss the night after a few hours' worth of shut-eye. After showering, John hits the sack like a comatose person. Cory and Kelly do the same. Luke says he is too keyed up to sleep, so he's going with G on a perimeter check. Reagan is exhausted but feeds Charlotte. She hopes her grandfather is also going to get some rest, but knowing him, he'll stay up and review those patient notes he brought home, having left the actual files for Simon and Dr. Scott.

Their bedroom is dark and cozy from the cloudy, melancholy day and the rain, and John has opened the doors to the balcony allowing a crosswind to flow through. He is sleeping so soundlessly she'd like to check his pulse but refrains. She slips in beside him and is immediately pulled into his embrace, although he does not even open his eyes. John always does this, holds her tight when he sleeps. She isn't sure if it is an insecurity issue, that he is afraid he'll lose her, or if he just finds it comforting. Usually, it's option C. He just wants sex. This morning, however, he is dead asleep and doing it out of habit. Either way, she's fine with being tucked up against him and held firmly there by his strong arms. She was worried sick last night about John. She can never lose him. He and their two children are her whole life. Charlotte just changed everything again. She has to hold her little family together.

Her dreams are plagued with macabre images of a battle that she has not witnessed and does not believe occurred last night. It is more premonitory in scope. She sees Kelly dead, a bullet wound in his chest, bled out on the ground near their barn. Cory is also dead, having been hit by something intense like a grenade. As she stands in the barnyard watching the scene before her, Reagan witnesses family members either in a state of dying or already having left this earth. Her children are also there, not much older than they are now. The house is ablaze, barely anything left of it. The barns are also torched and standing with just the antique beams glowing a brilliant red-orange in the middle of the day. Smoke burns her lungs and causes her to cough. Her son, although he is only maybe six years old, is cradling Charlotte close to his chest, and they are both crying.

She awakens with a start to the cry of her daughter in her bassinet near them. Already trained to snap to instant alertness, she slips from the bed without awakening John and retrieves her hungry baby. Reagan takes a seat in a rocker that John brought up to their room and feeds her daughter again. Her palms are sweaty, even though their room is not overly hot since the rain has brought with it cooler air and a heavy breeze. The time on the bedside clock reads a little after noon, surprising her that she slept so long. She's also surprised Charlotte slept long, too. She usually wants fed every few hours.

Stroking her daughter's downy head which is covered in dark, silky hair, Reagan reflects on the nightmare. She hopes it is not a foretelling of their future. She hates mystical bullshit and premonitions or anything of hokum, but it felt so real. She tries, instead, to focus on what she needs to accomplish today and works hard on blocking the images of that dream from entering her mind again. It doesn't work all that great, and she knows it will be the first thing she thinks of when she turns in for the night later this evening.

Around three in the afternoon, everyone is awake, alert and more rested, even Grandpa, who probably fell asleep in his office. They eat a late lunch made by Hannah and Sue of baked beans, sweet corn, pulled pork sandwiches and fresh watermelon. It feels more like a Fourth of July party than the day after an intense battle for survival. Perhaps this is how their forefathers felt, too, when they won independence from England. Either way, she's thrilled with the meal until her sisters force her to eat seconds. Then she feels gross and bloated. They don't miss a beat and lecture her about her calorie intake. Grandpa joins in, too, until she gives him a sneer. He just smiles.

Later, the men do chores and clean weapons until they all meet for a light dinner in the evening. They gather in Grandpa's office after to discuss last night's events while the kids take care of cleaning up after dinner. Gretchen volunteers to hold Charlotte while Reagan talks with the adults.

"Come on, kid," G says to her baby. "I've got some things to teach you. I mean, since you are my niece and all."

"Like what? How to light a cigarette?" Reagan razzes and gets an impudent shrug from her little sister before she walks onto the front porch with the baby.

Reagan sits in the only chair left while John stands behind her. He takes a second to bend over and kiss her cheek and stroke her hair. This sort of thing would've embarrassed her just a short time ago, but now it is simply comforting. Just knowing he's still alive is also somewhat of a comfort after a night like last night.

"The enemy had mortar rounds," Cory starts in with.

"What are those?" Paige asks.

"A weapon that takes a crew to handle," Kelly answers, taking Hannah's hand in his and looking at his wife, who is distressed by all of this talk of violence. "It's bad. They can do a lot of damage without getting too close to the scene of the battle. They did last night. There was some heavy damage to a few of the condos and buildings in their community."

"There were RPG's, too," John explains. "Those aren't what we'd consider heavy artillery so much as just dangerous. But they can also do some serious damage."

"Rocket Propelled Grenade," Kelly jumps in to help explain since not everyone is on the same page. "The insurgents used a lot of them against our forces in the Middle East. Sometimes they even blew themselves up first. That was always funny."

He snorts with an ornery grin and gets a disapproving look from his wife, for which he immediately apologizes. Then he looks at Reagan and winks and nods and mouths, 'it was funny.' Reagan smiles. Hannah elbows him, and Kelly looks very well put in his place.

Cory says to Paige, who is sitting across the room from him, "I'll show you and everyone else what heavy artillery looks like later. I have a book."

"I have no doubt," Paige jokes, getting a grin from Cory.

"Anyway," Derek states impatiently, "We didn't know they had that kind of firepower. The ones who attacked Dave's compound weren't using anything that heavy duty. This is new. It's good to know now. Let's us know who we're up against. I just wonder where they got that kind of weaponry."

"Probably an old base," John guesses. "They might've found 'em at Knox, maybe Campbell. I talked to their leader, Melora. She said there wasn't anything left when they got there. She and Hardy searched the base extensively for anything like that but came up short of any weapons at all."

"Yeah," Kelly agrees, "We never found anything left like that on a base, either. Heck, our own base was overrun and raided as we were leaving it. It was either shoot a bunch of civilians or leave."

"We made the right call," John says.

Cory jumps in again to add, "Some of them also had night-vision gear like the ones who attacked the cabin when Paige and I were staying there waiting for Sam and the Professor."

"Yeah, I saw that, too," Kelly says. "Some were wearing Kevlar again, too, just like before. Made taking them out a little harder."

"But we managed," Cory brags and bumps his brother's fist from his standing position behind the sofa. This also earns a scowl from Hannah, which makes the brothers instantly stop their shenanigans. "Sorry, Hannie. It had to be done. There were so dang many of them that they could've overtaken the town or here if they made it that far."

"Do you have a final tally?" Grandpa asks.

"Seventy-two," John answers.

"Whoa," Reagan says with a gasp of shock. "I thought it was like forty or fifty."

"No, and we're sure that a few got away. There's never a way to prevent it. We tried our best. Derek setting up men on the road with the blockades was perfect. We think when it first started at the beginning of the night they realized pretty quickly that they were in trouble and sent a runner for more men."

"Still, it's staggering," Reagan says, reeling.

Derek nods and says, "I think, all things considered, that it could've gone a lot worse."

"I agree with that assessment," John says and nods to his brother.

"We have to do more. This can't go on like this. They'll continue to attack our allies and neighbors and friends until they

298

eventually establish a foot in the door and take over one of the communities, possibly even here," Derek says and perches his weight on the corner of Grandpa's desk.

"We spoke with Robert," Grandpa starts and comes around from behind his desk, too. "He agrees to lend us troops and whatever firepower we need to defeat this group."

"But we'd owe him," Reagan immediately says, knowing her father so well.

"I didn't get the impression that he would want the favor returned. I think he just wants to keep us and all of our allies as his own allies, as well," Derek explains. "I got a feeling that he was being genuine about it, too."

Reagan rolls her eyes in disbelief.

Sue looks at her and admonishes with a simple, "Reagan."

Derek says, "I'll be honest here, guys. I don't know if we could do this without him. I think we are going to need his help. We can discuss it further, but I really think we're going to need more men and maybe even our own heavy artillery on this."

"We should implement our ambush plans, too," John says. "We tried questioning some of the men we captured, but none of them has agreed to talk yet."

"Where are they now?" Grandpa asks.

"We have them detained in the jail in town. The sheriff's keeping an eye on them for us," Kelly answers. "We'll go again tomorrow and interview them. There's three. We'll see how it goes."

"I'm sure at least one of them will talk," John says.

"We need to go back to town tonight to treat our patients," Reagan says.

"No way, boss," her husband says. "You need to rest. Do you remember that you had a baby a few days ago? You're staying home tonight."

"Besides," Paige breaks in to says, "Simon called home a while ago to let us know that the patients are doing well and that he and Sam and her uncle have it under control."

"Bet that's going to be a fun night," Sue says.

"What do you mean?" Reagan asks.

"Henry went to town, too," her sister explains.

"Oh, boy," John says.

Kelly jokes, "Glad I'm here. You should be too, bro'."

Cory looks at his brother with confusion.

"The Professor already whipped your ass once for you," Kelly says and gets a solid thump to his head from his wife. "Sorry, baby. But it's true. The Professor doesn't seem to have a lot of patience lately, and with Henry in town, it could get real interesting."

Everyone jokes for a while and even razz Cory a little more, but Reagan excuses herself to check on the baby. She's fast asleep in G's arms in the music room now, and the other children have gone to bed.

When she retires to her own bedroom with John, their small son is already there.

"We're gonna need a bigger bed," he whispers with a bright smile.

"You could always sleep in the closet," Reagan suggests.

"Or I could drag the twin bed back up here and sleep in the corner like a dog like you used to make me," he exaggerates as he climbs in on his side.

"You managed to work your way into my bed easily enough, Harrison," she teases with a smile, getting a bigger one in return from her studly husband.

Reagan lies Charlotte in the bassinette Kelly and Cory built her. John leans over Jacob and kisses her. They hold hands across Jacob's middle, and she watches her husband fall asleep. It doesn't come so easy for her, so Reagan rises a while later and works on medical research at her desk. She studies bullet wound surgery and deep tissue lacerations. The nightmare from earlier has resurfaced into her brain. She doesn't want to lose anyone else in her life. She just hopes it is only a bad dream fueled by lack of sleep and exhaustion and not some foreboding warning from the beyond.

Chapter Twenty-five
Sam

She awakens confused by her surroundings. Sam sits up and rubs her eyes. She's in a strange bedroom, one that looks like it used to be inhabited by a teenage boy. She swings her legs over and remembers. She and her uncle are staying in one of the empty homes a few doors down from Grandpa's practice. Simon chose to sleep at the clinic in Grandpa's office to keep a closer watch on the three men who are resting there.

Having not slept for over twenty-four hours, she still feels tired after finally crashing last night. There are people who need to be checked on and cared for, so there's no time for a pity party over missing some sleep. She hauls herself from the bed and pulls on fresh clothing, jeans, and a black, v-neck tee. The clock on the nightstand is stuck at 2:20, the batteries having long ago ceasing to work. She consults her watch instead. It's still early, just past dawn.

She sneaks from the room and quietly down the stairs so as not to awaken her uncle just across from her in the master suite. People in the community brought them food and water yesterday, and she has a piece of bread, some dried berries and nuts, and a glass of water before getting ready to leave. Everyone in town always takes care of them when they are away from their own homes like this in order to watch over patients who can't be moved.

Henry and one of his friends also stayed the night in the house with them, but she doesn't see them on the sofas in the living room where they'd decided to sleep. She plucks a ball cap from the hook near the door and slaps it against her thigh to remove some of the dust. She doesn't know who this used to belong to in this home, but Sam needs it because it is drizzly and rainy today. It's a good thing. They have been worried about a drought because it has been too dry all summer. At both farms, they are watering gardens daily just to keep the dirt from resembling the Mohave Desert. She decides to leave her gear upstairs and exits through the front door.

The town is starting to awaken, some people out and about at their chores, a few working in the distance on the wall from what it sounds like.

"Hey, Sam," Henry says, startling her as he comes up behind her.

"Hi," she replies. "Get any sleep?"

"Sure, enough. You?"

"Yeah, I think I went into a coma."

"That's good. You needed some rest," he says with concern.

"So do you," she reminds him. "Are you guys leaving today?"

"Nah, don't think so unless you release the men from our group."

"I don't know. It'll be up to Simon and Uncle Scott, not me. But two of them still seem like they shouldn't be moved."

He nods with a frown. It isn't because he wants to rush home to his farm but because he is worried about his friends. Both required blood transfusions and are very weak. One man, a personal friend of Henry's, suffered severe head trauma and required over thirty stitches. He was lucky, though. Others have died; two on Grandpa and Reagan's watch and one yesterday afternoon while in her uncle's care. Simon believed the woman had internal bleeding from being shot in the stomach. She'd taken it upon herself to join the fight at the condo community and didn't have the experience to do so. She also didn't have the permission of Paul or K-Dog. They were both devastated when they found out that she'd succumbed to her wounds.

"Hi, Samantha!" Melora greets as she comes upon them.

"Oh, hey, Melora, what's going on? Enjoying the weather?" Sam jokes as their new ally from Fort Campbell joins them on their walk.

"Is your uncle up yet?" she asks.

"No, sorry. Is it a medical emergency?" Sam asks. "Simon's at the clinic."

302

"Oh, it's a pediatrics thing. I just wanted to talk to him about a few things with our kids. I'm surely not a doctor, so a lot of what we've been doing with the kids is guesswork."

"He should be up soon. He's not usually a late sleeper."

"With what you guys have been through the last few days, I don't blame him for sleeping in."

Sam offers a grin. She seems nice to Sam. Just the fact that she and Hardy were willing to take in a bunch of orphans, victims of the apocalypse, and look after them, feed them and clothe them speaks a lot to her character.

"Uncle Scott's your man then. He was a former pediatrician."

"I know. I heard. I mean, I wasn't asking around about him or anything. I just…I'll catch him later."

Melora's cheeks redden, and she quickly walks away. For a woman who is so sure of herself most of the time, she got embarrassed awfully quick.

"Sounds like someone's got a crush on your uncle," Henry says as they reach the clinic.

Sam chuckles and says, "Yeah, maybe. That was weird."

"It's in your blood, Sam."

"What? What is?"

"People are just drawn to you, and obviously your uncle, too. Although, my interests in your family are just in you. Just to set the record straight."

Sam laughs and says, "I would hope so!"

"No batting for the other side, rest assured," he clarifies and grasps her hand as she steps up onto the first step of the front porch. "Will I see you later?"

"I don't know where else I'd go," she says, trying to seem nonchalant. He does not let go of her but presses a kiss to the back of her hand. Suddenly his eyes darken and dart past her. Sam turns around to see Simon standing inside the open door of the clinic, casually observing them while leaning against the door jamb and drinking something steaming from a mug. He's dressed in khakis, a white tee, and a white doctor's jacket. His stethoscope is hanging around his neck, and there are patient files tucked under his arm.

"I'll have my radio with me. If you need me, don't hesitate to call," Henry says, gaining her attention again.

"Ok, thanks, Henry," she says, trying to slip her hand free inconspicuously.

"She won't," Simon says bluntly, and a little too loudly.

Henry looks as if he'd like to say something but doesn't. He reluctantly releases her hand and walks away.

"That was rude," she says to Simon and squeezes past him to the reception area. He doesn't follow her but continues to stare at Henry's back. It makes her so mad that he doesn't follow her or acknowledge her at all, so Sam stomps back over to him and says in a much more authoritative tone, "You don't speak for me, Simon."

Simon simply turns his head to look down at her. He stares at her for a long time. His eyes trail down her face, then her body and back up. They rest for a long time on her mouth, so long that she thinks she must have a crumb or something there. Sam swipes her fingertips over them to make sure she doesn't look like a fool but doesn't discover anything. Then he slowly takes a sip of his tea and turns his attention back out the open door as if she hadn't just said anything. Sam grits her teeth, shakes her head and frowns. She throws her hands in the air with frustration, snatches the files from him, and leaves.

Sam heads straight for Grandpa's office and sits behind his desk, opens a file and begins reviewing the case. The cot in the corner is made up neatly, which she is quite sure is how Simon left it. He's about as meticulous as one man can get. The room still smells like him, as if he has branded it with his scent from sleeping in it just one night. He strolls in a few minutes later, walks behind the desk and rests one palm flat on it beside her. He is apparently going to read over her shoulder.

"Do you mind?" she asks in a snippy tone.

"No, do you?" he asks as if he hadn't thought the notion of him reading over her shoulder would be offensive at all.

She harrumphs and says, "No, I guess not."

"Mr. Markel across the street at the medical house has a fever," he says, pointing to where he notated it on the man's chart. "I'm watching him closely. It could be a sign of infection."

"Right," Sam says, not liking how his warm breath is tickling the side of her face. "That would be bad."

"If that's the case, we'll need antibiotics from the farm," he says. "I'm waiting for Herb to call in for his morning report, and then I'll tell him what's going on, see what his opinion is."

They discuss two more cases and their patients' care before Sam asks, "Did you get any sleep last night? It sounds like you were up again all night."

"No, I went to bed around two."

"Oh, well then, no wonder you're so full of vigor this morning!" she jokes and looks up at him. Simon smiles at her, but there is something in his eyes this morning that is different. His guard is down for some reason.

"Maybe it's just the tea."

"Ew, yeah right. That wouldn't make anyone chipper."

He smiles wider, and again his eyes focus on her mouth until Sam looks back down at another file on the desk.

"I didn't ask you how it went... you know, during the...thing," she questions, not wanting to say war or battle or even skirmish. It all sounds so horrible.

"Uh..fine. It went just fine."

This drives him away and he takes a seat off to her left a few feet. He naturally doesn't wish to discuss it, but Sam does. She wasn't there and wants to know.

"What happened?"

"The usual," he says in a clipped tone and sets his tea on the desk in front of him.

"Talk to me. I wasn't allowed to go. I want to know what happened."

He squirms, leans back in his chair, and interlinks his fingers behind his head. She wheels her chair closer.

"You don't need to know, Sam. It was the usual violence and mayhem."

"How many were there? Were women fighting, too?"

"No, no women, not that I saw."

"How many?"

"Over seventy."

Sam is floored. This is crazy news. "Wow, how did you guys take out that many?"

"It wasn't too hard," he lies and looks at his knees instead of making eye contact.

"Yeah, sure. That's believable." She removes her wet ball cap and places it on the desk.

"Enfilading fire. John was set up in front of the enemy, Kelly, too, eventually. Then we came in from the sides and behind the enemy and took them out. Basically. Nutshell version."

He shrugs and crosses one foot over his knee, trying to appear casual. She knows how much he hates killing and hurting people. It had to be so hard on him.

"Did you snipe?"

"Of course, Sam. Why do you want to know all of this?"

She frowns and says, "I just want to know what happened. I was worried about…all of you guys. It was stressful. It's always stressful when you have family in trouble and can't be there with them to help out."

"Everything turned out all right," he says. "Except for the few that we lost."

"All things considered, I'd say it went better than we could've expected," she says sadly.

"Right."

"John said something about you saving Cory's life," she says with curiosity.

"Not really. I'm sure he would've been fine even without my help."

She bumps her knee against his. "Don't be so humble. What happened?"

"RPG. They had a lot of heavy weaponry. I just didn't want him to take shrapnel from the wall or have stuff hit him. He's pretty valuable in a fight."

"And in the family," she points out. "And as your friend."

He snorts and wrinkles his nose in a sarcastic way.

"He is, Simon. Cory's your best friend. Don't be that way."

He looks at her and says, "You always say that you're my best friend."

"Not anymore," she says without missing a beat.

He allows his leg to lean into hers and says, "We could be again. If you want to."

Sam quickly looks away and then at her feet.

"I already told you how I feel. After we get through this, I'm going home to Henry's farm and staying there. Maybe I'll come to town for a visit in the fall or something."

"If you just come to town, you won't be able to see everyone back on the farm who doesn't come to town."

"Then I won't."

"Won't come to town or won't come to the farm?"

Sam sighs and says, "Maybe I won't come to either. I'll just go home to Henry's farm and not come back. It's probably what's best anyway."

"I hate that you're starting to consider his farm as your home."

His expression is pained but also holds a lot of anger and contempt.

"It's where I belong. My uncle lives there. I've made new friends. It's my new home."

He rises swiftly, grabs the arms of her chair, yanks her to him using the wheels, and tips her back. Her feet no longer touch the floor. Then he leans down over her, hovering there, coming eye to eye, nearly nose to nose. Sam can feel his breath mingling with hers. He's not wearing his eyeglasses, so she can see the gold specks in his blue eyes being this close.

"You belong at the farm. *His* farm is *not* your home," Simon growls.

She opens her mouth to argue but instead inhales sharply, holding it. Apparently, it draws his attention there because Simon's eyes shift from her eyes to her mouth.

"What are you doing?" she finally whispers after a long moment.

"I hardly know anymore," Simon admits as if he is a defeated man.

He leans in, his eyes hooded as if under the influence of some sort of euphoric drug. Then he presses his lips lightly to hers.

"Simon, no," Sam says weakly and turns her head to the side.

He doesn't snap back as she expected he would but presses his nose against her neck below her ear. His hands tighten on the arms of the chair, making the leather squeak and groan from the pressure. He inhales deeply and presses his lips against her skin, sending a chill down her spine.

"Simon, don't," she whispers pathetically.

He doesn't but continues to kiss a trail down her neck to its base where it meets her clavicle. Part of her wishes that she would've chosen a more concealing t-shirt than one with a deep vee. He tugs the chair closer until her neck is forced to arch. Then he kisses another trail up her neck and to her chin.

"Say it," he says, hovering over her mouth with his own. "Say you don't belong there."

Sam's brow furrows and her eyelids feel heavy.

"You belong on the farm," he repeats.

Sam tries to shake her head, but Simon captures her mouth with his to silence her. It is a control tactic, but she can't seem to find the courage to push him away or argue. His mouth moves greedily on hers, and the second she yields, Simon swiftly encircles her waist and pulls her off of the chair, off her feet and up against him as he stands in one fluid motion. It has a dizzying effect on her senses. His lips never leave hers, and Sam is forced to hold onto his shoulders for support.

She wants to stop him but can't manage to find the words. His kiss is intense and unforgiving, and she has longed for him. He is not giving her the opportunity to argue with him as his tongue touches lightly against her lips, seeking entrance. He doesn't ask permission. He is simply taking as he plunges his tongue into her mouth and groans. Sam is left breathless and panting against him.

Simon steps forward and places her bottom on the corner of the desk. Sam leans back, breaking contact with him for an instant. His hands slide down to her hips and tug her close. Then he insinuates himself between her legs roughly without asking again. He shoves both hands into her hair. Simon still smells like rainwater mixed with medicinal herbs but tastes like mint tea. He pulls her face upward into his again and proceeds to kiss her in a more leisurely manner as if he has nowhere else to be. His stethoscope swings between them, bumping into her chest. Sam clings to his shoulder with one hand and slides her other up his chest until they find purchase in the top of his t-shirt where she grips it tightly. Her fingers brush back and forth against the base of his neck. Simon moans into her mouth and allows his hands to flow down her back to rest on her hips. His fingers dig into her skin through her jeans, igniting an all-new fire within her. She pulls his stethoscope from his neck and lets it fall, somewhere.

One hand slides up her back to grasp a handful of her hair. Then Simon tugs, pulling her head back so that he can kiss her neck, causing her to shiver under his touch.

"Hello?" someone in the lobby calls. "Dr. Murphy?"

They both look that way, but Simon doesn't release her. She sobers and tries to scoot back from him, which he will not allow. His eyes keenly watch the open doorway to see if someone is going to come in. His fingers on her hips stay her from moving away. Then he looks back at her and grins with something akin to a malicious glint in his eyes. Instead of stepping away, Simon wraps one arm around her and lifts her from the desk until she is standing in front of him looking up into his face. He slowly bends in front of her to retrieve his stethoscope. He rises even slower until he is standing straight again, staring at her body the whole way with the same lopsided grin.

"Don't threaten me not to come to the farm anymore," he warns quietly.

Sam is too stunned to retort a response, and he is gone in the next instant anyway. She takes a second to right her clothing and tries to appear composed, although she feels anything but. Sam joins Simon in the lobby where he is speaking to Melora. She seems upset as Sam approaches, pulling a rubber band into her hair to keep it back in a bun.

"Hi again, Sam," Melora says with a worried smile.

"What's going on?" she asks, avoiding looking at Simon, although she can tell he is not doing the same.

"Two of the kids woke up just now with fevers and chills. I don't know what it is. We had a problem like this a few weeks ago, but this seems worse. I don't know what to do. I felt bad for even coming here for help because I know how busy you were last night and probably today, too."

"It's no problem," Simon tells her and rests a hand on her shoulder like Grandpa does with patients' families. "Sam, I'll go take a look at the kids. Would you like to start on morning rounds and check on the patients across the street?"

"Um, sure," she replies, not sure why he doesn't want her to go with him and also not sure how he is so calm and collected while she is a ball of nerves inside from their kissing episode. She can still feel the impression of his lips on hers.

Melora is more than thankful and tells them so many times as she waits on the front porch for Simon to gather what he needs. He returns to the reception room a moment later with his bag.

"The radio's in the office. Call *me* if you need something," he orders. Sam doesn't answer but stares at him. He prompts her impatiently, "Sam?"

"Fine, I'll call you."

"Will you be alright while I'm gone?" he asks, standing directly in front of her.

"I'll probably be better," she smarts off with a frown.

Simon chuckles. "Probably. Probably safer, too."

Sam squints at him, trying to appear cold and angry. It must not come off that way because Simon chucks her under the chin and leaves. Her emotions are a mess. She isn't sure if she wants to throw something and hit him in the back or beg him to return soon and kiss her again.

She sighs long and hard and retrieves the patient files to begin checks. One of the men across the street is still running a fever, so she makes a special note on his chart. He doesn't complain or ask for pain reliever, but the fever is a concern because it could be an infection. Two of their patients now have their wives with them, leading her to speculate that Henry sent for them using his men. She is quite sure that just having their spouses with them will aid in the healing process.

She finishes at the Victorian house across the street and checks the men in the clinic, one of whom is complaining that he wants to leave already. Sam smiles patiently and pats his arm. His blood pressure is still low, so she'd like for him to rest until Grandpa comes to town later.

Jotting down notes at the front counter, she's surprised that over an hour has passed since Melora led Simon away. She is grateful for the work because it keeps her mind occupied. Unfortunately, she's all caught up with her work, so she strolls outside to get some fresh air. She works on a sketch she's been doing. Her feelings are so conflicted about Simon. Why does he kiss her if he doesn't have

310

feelings for her? What does he care if she stays at Dave's compound instead of the McClane farm if he wants her to move on?

"Everything ok, Sam?" Henry asks, startling her as she rocks in one of the white rocking chairs on the front porch. She swiftly stows the drawing away.

"Yes, fine. Thanks. What are you doing?"

"The sheriff's wife invited some of us down to the town hall. Guess she made everyone lunch, her and some of the other people here in town."

"That was awfully nice of them," she says, consulting her watch.

"Would you like to go with me to lunch?" he asks kindly.

"Um, I kind of feel like I should wait here until Grandpa gets here or Simon comes back."

"I talked to Joe's wife, one of our men who's staying over there," he says, pointing to the house across the street. "She said she'd keep an eye on the patients so you can get a bite to eat."

"Oh, that was…thoughtful," Sam says, appreciative of the gesture.

She nods and stands, following Henry down the front stairs of the practice right as Simon strolls up with Melora.

"Where are you going?" he asks with unconcealed anger and a deep crease between his brows to match.

"I'm taking Samantha to lunch," Henry says, capturing her hand gently in his.

"You aren't taking her anywhere," Simon growls angrily, drawing a surprised look from Melora, who probably just witnessed his tender and caring side as he took care of the ill children in her group.

Henry's posture immediately stiffens up, and he says, "Excuse me?"

"Simon," Sam warns and narrows her eyes at him.

"Hey, guys!" John says as he jogs over to them.

"John!" Sam says and waves with a false smile. "When'd you guys get here?"

"Just did," he says. "Brought Doc with me. He's detained talking to people, of course. Watcha' up to, kiddo?"

"Going to lunch," she says, her hand still enclosed in Henry's, which feels strange.

Simon steps forward, but John literally steps in front of him and presses a hand to his chest.

"Professor, I need to talk to you about something if you don't mind and got a sec," he says.

Simon's eyes dart to John's and then around him at Henry. Sam needs no further encouragement and tugs Henry's hand. By the look in Simon's dark eyes, there is about to be a fight. She's seen this before in him, usually when he gets ready to kill someone. He looked like this when he'd clobbered Cory to a bloody pulp in the dirt. It's definitely time to get out of here. She's sure of what Simon can do, but she does not know of Henry's abilities.

"Ready?" she says, trying to appear cheerful and anxious instead of frantic and nauseous.

"Yes, ma'am," he says in a lower than normal tone, also staring down Simon.

They are not going to be friends, Sam can tell by this one, simple moment. John looks over his shoulder and raises his chin to her, letting Sam know to get the heck out of the area. She wastes no time and actually walks faster than Henry, who is considerably taller than her.

Henry glances over his shoulder twice to look at Simon, who is standing there now arguing with John and sending his own seething looks their way. He finally throws his hands in the air and stalks off to the medical house, leaving John with Melora.

She and Henry walk to the town hall where they run into Kelly, who she greets, and also who doesn't miss the fact that she's holding hands with Henry. He raises his eyebrows once and offers an ornery grin. She isn't sure why, but his reaction tells her that he is in on something of which she is not privy. How had John instantly known that something was about to go down between Henry and Simon, too? Maybe they are just more intuitive than most men.

Sam dines with Henry, observing him around his friends, one of whom swears in front of her, which earns him a look from Henry- a simple raised eyebrow. The young man, likely her age, immediately apologizes to Sam and looks put in his place. The sheriff's wife, Doreen, has made a feast of slow-roasted turkey, roasted vegetables, and fresh berry lemonade. The McClane family also has lemons that get donated, but Grandpa reserves them for medicinal use instead of consumption. One of the other women in town brings baskets of fresh-baked rolls. It all tastes great, but Sam is too conflicted to eat much.

Her heart is torn and confused. Henry smiles and talks a lot during lunch, more than usual. She even laughs a few times at the things he says and the way he jokes with his buddies. But the feel of Simon's lips on hers is still fresh in her memory, and it is those memories on which she keeps focusing. From time to time, she even loses track of the conversation around her because she is thinking about him touching her, pulling her close, demanding that she respond.

"I should head back," Sam says to Henry the moment she is finished with her meal. She really does need to return. There are patients who need their help, and she'd still like to know what is going on with the Campbell Kids because she hadn't had the opportunity to speak with Simon about them because he was a boiling kettle.

"So soon? You do need to take breaks, ya' know," Henry teases.

"I do. I take breaks, but with so many wounded, they'll need all the help they can get."

Sam swings a leg over and exits the picnic table. Then, being completely ungraceful trips on the curb when she steps down. Henry grabs her arm and pulls her back up, and against him.

One of his men says, "Are you alright, ma'am?"

"Oh, yes," she says, totally embarrassed for being such a dork.

"Careful, Miss Sam," another says. "Don't want the farmer to have a heart attack."

"The farmer?" she asks.

"Nothing, are you ready?" Henry says and leads her away.

"What'd they mean?"

"It's nothing. Just a nickname," he answers as they walk.

Sam smiles. "They call you The Farmer?"

She just gets an awkward shrug and a shake of his head.

Sam laughs and says, "Yes, I suppose it fits."

Henry attempts to hold her hand again, but Sam pulls back. At his hurt expression, she apologizes, "Sorry. That...that's just...sorry."

She doesn't know how to correctly express what she's feeling. She can hardly tell him that she'd been kissing Simon this morning, not when she's not even sure why it happened, either. It's confusing for her, so it will be even more so for Henry.

"That's fine. I'm a patient guy, Sam," he tells her with a kind smile.

Everything about Henry is kind. He's sweet and giving, open and honest, so many things that Simon is not, especially about being transparent with her regarding his feelings.

"Yeah, I know," she acknowledges.

They walk side by side to the clinic where she finds Kelly and John standing near the front porch. Their backs are turned to them, and they appear to be in a deep conversation. It sounds like they are discussing the looted weaponry that they confiscated from the enemy. She overhears something about a mortar launcher and RPG. They both turn and send friendly waves in their direction, and Henry returns theirs with one of his own.

"I'd better get back to work," she says with a nod. "Thanks for lunch."

"Thank *you*, ma'am," he says.

Sam turns to go, but Henry grabs her hand and swiftly pulls her to him where his arm slips around her back. He kisses her fast and briefly, just a speedy peck against her mouth, but it catches her off-guard, nonetheless. It is also much more intimate than what he's done in the past. And a whole lot more public. He releases her as quickly as he'd captured her. It was definitely a sneak attack.

As she is stepping back from him, the screen door to the clinic slams and Simon comes onto the front porch.

"Bye!" she blurts and fast walks away from Henry, not bothering to wait for a response.

By the looks on John and Kelly's faces, they've seen the kiss. What she's not sure of is if Simon has. She hopes not. He was already in a bad, confrontational mood before she left.

"Well, well, well," Kelly says and whistles for good measure, causing her cheeks to redden. "No wonder you haven't been coming around for visits as much."

314

Sam would like to slap some duct tape over his mouth, but she loves Kelly too much to be angry with him. He's also clueless about things like this unless Hannah is telling him what to think about it. Maybe Reagan is right, and all these big warriors are deaf, dumb, and shell-shocked. Sam usually admonishes her friend for such comments, but maybe Reagan hit this one on the head. She only wishes Hannah was here to stop Kelly from meddling and making things worse. She'd probably club him in the back of the head with something or give him one of her words-are-not-even-necessary looks she gives that puts him right in his place. Man, she misses Hannie.

"What? No, I still love coming to visit," she lies through her teeth.

She avoids eye contact with Simon until she reaches the porch. Then she allows her eyes to drift slowly up to his as John asks her a question she barely hears. Simon is furious. The cold hatred she saw earlier for Henry has turned into a black flame of murderous intent. She is truly afraid for Henry's life. Simon must've seen him kiss her. However, it wasn't like she'd asked him to. Henry had obviously felt his own motivation to do it. She hadn't encouraged it. None of these facts make Sam feel any better about the way Simon is staring her down.

"So? What are you thinking?" John repeats.

"'Bout what?" she croaks.

He chuckles and says, "We'll talk later, kiddo. Anyway, the Hulk and I gotta go question another prisoner. Stay with the Professor today, ok? After the other night, we're not sure what to expect if they decide to regroup and retaliate. I'll see you later."

She wants to beg John not to leave her alone with Simon but doesn't. Sam bids him the same cordial farewell and turns to climb the stairs to the clinic. Two people ride by on horses and wave to them, recognizing them both from the clinic. Sam sends a wave back. She feels like these townspeople that she barely knows are easier to understand than Simon and his strange behavior.

"Too bad he didn't say for you to stay close to your boyfriend that I see you're still interested in," Simon states angrily.

"Simon, don't," she says and tries to brush past him. He allows her onto the deck with him but stands in front of her. "I don't need you judging me right now. I have enough on my mind with taking care of our patients right now. And you. You're stressing me out, too. What the heck was that earlier in Grandpa's office? What's wrong with you?"

He sighs as his eyes drift off to the side to stare at something only he can see, something that must be unpleasant because he frowns.

"That, *that*, my dear Samantha is what I've tried to warn you about, what I never want to show you," he confesses softly.

Sam shakes her head and says, "I don't understand. What do you mean?"

"You wouldn't understand. You're too innocent," he says angrily, his mood shifting.

"*I'm* too innocent? Um, I don't think so, Simon."

"You're so young and innocent," he argues. "And…and I don't want you to hate me."

"Simon, I could never hate you," she admits. "I get mad at you and frustrated, and then I want to choke you, but I could never hate you." She reaches for and takes his hand. "We've been through too much together."

Simon strokes the top of her hand gently with his thumb. Then he pulls away as if he has been burned.

"That's the problem, isn't it?" he asks as if she understands his meaning.

"What is? What we've been through? That only makes us stronger and closer, Simon," she says softly.

Simon looks over her head, scanning the area. His jaw flexes as if he is clenching it tightly together to keep from speaking. His eyes harden when he looks at her next.

"Let's get to work," he states coolly, his controlled demeanor having returned.

"I'll work with Grandpa," she says in an equally cruel tone.

"You'll work by my side and not leave it," he growls. "Do I make myself clear, Samantha? And you won't be hanging out playing kissy face with your boyfriend anymore today, either."

Sam glares at him but knows that John already told her to stay with Simon. She's not even sure where Grandpa is at the moment. Simon makes her so mad she'd like to slap him in the face. Again.

316

"Well, Simon," she starts in a huff, "I sure as hell won't be playing kissy face with you, either!"

She stomps past him into the clinic. He meets her at the counter, and, at once, she can see a switch come over him. He is being a professional doctor again.

Sam stares at him, frowns, and says, "What's going on with the Campbell Kids?"

"They're very ill. They now have six children who are sick over there. Doc is having them moved to a quarantined house where we can care for them without infecting others."

This makes Sam forget all about their petty argument on the front porch, and she asks, "What is it?"

"He thinks Scarlet Fever," he says in a serious tone that shows his concerns.

"Oh, my," she says, feeling the same level of worry.

"We're safe. Doc already confirmed that he and I would've been vaccinated for it," he tells her in a gentler voice. "We need high potency antibiotics for treatment, but we're going to be forced to use the homemade tonics we've concocted. This illness could lead to other problems like rheumatic fever."

"Oh, dear," Sam says, knowing that such an illness can also lead to heart and nervous system deterioration. "Where do they think it came from?"

"He's not sure. It spreads very easily, though, which is why he ordered the quarantine," Simon answers. "We're taking preventative measures by suiting up with gloves and masks when we take care of the kids, too. Melora said she and Hardy were up to date on all their vaccinations before the fall, so she's going to take shifts there, too."

"And Grandpa and you? Are you staying in town longer to take care of them? And me, too?"

"Yes, we are, but we weren't sure about your vaccines. Do you know?"

"My uncle made sure we had everything, remember?" she answers, to which he nods.

"Doc said you were probably vaccinated for it," Simon tells her. "I'm sure you were. We just don't want to take any chances. I know for sure that I was."

"Of course, you do, Simon. You're Simon! I'm sure you were annoyingly in control of everything around you even when you were a little kid."

Simon regards her with irritation boldly plastered to his handsome face. A stray lock of auburn hair falls over his forehead, and Sam pushes it back.

"I'll help with our patients," she says and walks away. She says over her shoulder, "Then I can help with the sick kids, too."

Simon follows her to the storage area where they take bandaging and tape, antiseptic solution and scissors.

"We'll get started across the street first," Simon tells her. "I checked them all this morning but didn't change any of their bandaging."

"That'll be just fine. Where's Grandpa?"

"Working with your uncle," Simon answers.

She frowns, "Oh, I didn't know he was here. What are they working on?"

"Baby Daniel has a hernia. Your uncle may have to perform surgery," Simon explains. "He came to the farm to check on him, and I think they're bringing the baby to town later today to do the procedure."

"Why didn't you tell me?"

"He came down to the clinic when you were gone on your *date*."

Sam furrows her brow at him as he hands her another sterile towel.

"We could go on a date, too, you know. If you asked me."

Simon looks shocked at this. Sam is more shocked that she said it.

"Maybe we could go to my old house again. That might be interesting."

Simon looks down at her, but this time there isn't surprise in his eyes but something different.

"It was the last time," Sam reminds him. By the look in his eyes, he remembers just fine that night.

"What part? Getting shot at or me getting stabbed or hiding in the snow together?" he asks with unhidden irritability.

"Kissing upstairs in our game room. And when you touched me," she whispers hoarsely.

318

Simon swallows hard and looks as if he'd like to do those things with her again. The corner of his mouth twitches.

Sam has to find some sort of fortitude when it comes to Simon, so she says, "Come on, Mr. Kissy Face. Let's go."

She squeezes past him, ducking under his arm where he has rested his hand on the shelf above her head. It takes all her strength to resist him, but Sam can't keep letting him kiss her with no accountability. If he's just looking for someone to sew his wild oats with, then he'll have to find someone else to practice on. Melora had looked at him with interest. Maybe she'll suggest that to him later. For now, she has to get away and catch her breath. No matter what Henry does or says, she cannot deny that Simon makes her feel different than Henry. There is something deep and raw within her that wants to be set free, and Simon seems to be the only one who can do it.

Part of the reason she wants to go to her old house with Simon again is that Sam needs him to explain the strange and bizarre things he says to her sometimes, and it is usually hard to find time alone with him. He starts to talk to her about their relationship, but then he'll throw something weird into the conversation that she just doesn't understand. Later today, she's hoping for some clarity.

Chapter Twenty-six
Cory

Three days have gone by since their battle with the highwaymen, and Cory is itching to get back out there. They've inherited a mortar launcher, a grenade launcher, and a trashed drone, which he has been working with Derek on repairing since they found its remote by one of the dead highwaymen. He has to admit, he was a little jealous of their toys. They've had meetings throughout each day and have questioned the prisoners multiple times.

They haven't given anything up, and John and Derek are having a meeting tonight about what to do. Cory is pacing the street in front of the courthouse waiting for them. They finally sent Simon back to the farm yesterday to get some rest and to clean up at home. Sam and her uncle also returned to Dave's for rest and showers, but she is coming back later tonight or first thing in the morning. Simon will also return soon but for different reasons. None of the doctors, with the exception of Simon, know yet, but they may have more bodies to sew up by morning. He and the others are heading out soon to set up their first ambush on these assholes. Robert's men are still with them, Dave is coming and sending another four men, and K-Dog insisted on being a part of their next move.

While Simon had been in town taking care of the patients, Cory had made an attempt to speak privately with Paige, but she'd avoided him. This morning he'd tried again to talk to her before he left the farm, but Simon was having none of it. He'd caught them in Gram's rose garden. She'd been doing some weeding, and Cory had approached her. It lasted a nanosecond before the Professor had come upon them and started making accusations and forced Cory to leave. Paige hadn't argued with her brother, either. The look on her face let Cory know that she agreed with Simon and that she wouldn't put up a fight. For some reason, she acts like she is carrying a burden of guilt over their relationship. Cory isn't sure why, but he doesn't like it. She shouldn't feel that way.

Last night at the clinic, Sam's uncle and Doc performed the first, invasive surgery there. Between their supplies, items they brought back from Robert's compound, and Dave's contributions, the two doctors performed a hernia surgery on baby Daniel and put him all the way out for it. They also performed his circumcision while he was out. Cory felt bad for the little dude. He's bound to wake up pissed. He sure as hell would be if someone messed with his junk while he was out. Unless it was Paige, of course. There's always an exception to everything.

John and Kelly come out of the building with the sheriff on their heels. They shake his hand and leave him.

"What's going on?" Cory asks.

"We're rollin' at seventeen-hundred hours," his brother answers. "I'm callin' the farm now."

Kelly walks away to use the radio while John stays with Cory.

"Get anything from them?" he asks his friend.

"Nada," John answers. "They aren't budging. I think they're mostly scared."

There are three men, two of which are teenagers, who they are keeping in the newly built jail inside the town hall.

"I don't think we need them," Cory says. "If they're still operating on the east to west and back again thing, then we're bound to be able to run into them with an ambush tonight."

"The only thing I got outta' the one kid is that they usually do their work during the day and head home after the sun sets or close to it. Lately, though, they've had to change it up, which is what we'd already guessed."

"They haven't retaliated yet. I don't think it's gonna happen. I don't think they know who we are or where we're from."

"Maybe," John says. "If they find out, we're gonna have trouble on our hands."

"Did they give you any indication of who their leader is?" Cory asks.

"Nothing yet," John tells him. "We aren't done with them, though."

"Want me to take a crack at it?"

"Maybe later," he says. "Right now, we need to get ready to mount up, brother."

Cory walks down to the clinic to let Doc know what's going on before they leave. He is with Reagan reviewing notes of some sort in a file when he gets there.

"You're leaving soon?" Reagan asks, concern in her green eyes.

"Yeah, we're just waiting on the Professor and Dave's men to get here. Then we're out."

"Be careful, son," Doc says with a firm nod. "Tomorrow we'll start on that project."

"Yes, sir," he answers Doc, knowing what he means.

He and Herb have drafted and sketched out a design for a metal brace that he will fabricate for Derek's leg. It is something that Doc discussed with the orthopedic doctor up north at Robert's compound. She told him some techniques she'd had success with while at her practice in Boulder, Colorado, using similar braces for disabled vets, a cause she kept close to her heart. They have the rough sketch ready, and he will work with Doc doing the metal fabricating. He's anxious to get it started. They both are because they know how frustrated and depressed Derek has been.

Doc says, "Besides, you need something to occupy your time while a certain redhead we all know and love comes to her senses, right?"

Cory's eyes dart to Herb's quickly before he chuckles nervously and says, "Yes, sir."

"Yeah, right," Reagan says with a snort. "I think she's worse than me. She's never getting married."

"We'll see about that," Herb says with a playful wink. "Until then, we need to keep you busy. Idle hands and all."

Cory grins sheepishly, feeling put in his place with just this one simple turn of phrase. They have been so busy dealing with the family problems, highwaymen, travel and everything else that the lecture he full anticipated never came.

"I can think of some chores that need to be done back at the farm," Reagan chimes in.

Cory shoots her an unappreciative glance, getting a cocky grin in return.

"Now, where's my idiot husband? I need to say goodbye in case he gets himself shot later."

"He'll be fine, my little honey," Herb says and pats her shoulder.

Reagan snorts and leaves the clinic. They follow and meet in front of the town hall building again to go over plans. Minutes later, Henry arrives with Samantha and a truckload of men, including Dave the Mechanic. Simon pulls in at the same time, having caught a ride with Chet Reynolds, who will also be helping them.

"Hey, Professor!" Dave calls out to Simon.

Simon walks over and shakes their friend's hand, "Hello, sir. How are you?"

Cory shakes his head and chuckles at Simon's formality. He was definitely born in the wrong era.

"I brought a little present for you," he says to Simon with a grin that reveals he is up to some sort of mischief.

"A present?" Simon asks.

"Got a few of the women to work on something for you and my other sniper," Dave tells them and yanks something from the bed of their truck. It's a full-length ghillie suit.

"Oh, wow. That's awesome," Simon says with appreciation as he takes it from Dave's grip. "This is perfect. Thank you, sir."

"No problem, brother. We gotta keep our snipers hidden," Dave says. "Don't want our snipers to get fuckin' sniped, right? I heard General McClane's sniper was killed the other night. Can't have that happening to these dudes."

He says this to Cory, who bumps his fist to Dave's, who in turn smiles widely and nods. Cory notices that Dave's sniper is also with them and talking to Kelly about something. He walks over to join them.

"Yeah, they're hot as shit but definitely do the job," his sniper, Lucky, says. "Looks pretty much the same as the one I used fighting the rag-heads."

"Really?" Cory says. "Cool."

"We're movin' in ten!" John shouts from the front of the building where he is talking to Reagan and the sheriff.

"Get ready, you rangy, mean, sons-a-bitchin' bastards!" Dave calls to his men and walks away.

"Hey, kiddo," Cory says to Sam and gives her a hug.

She smiles when they break apart, "Hi, Cory. How's everyone on the farm?"

"Doing fine," he says and ruffles the top of her head. "Could be better if you were there, but we're managing."

"How's Paige?"

He chuffs and says, "I wouldn't know. The Professor doesn't like me spending time with her if you know what I mean."

She smiles patiently and says, "I understand. Just give him time, Cory. He'll come around. He loves you. He just loves his sister so much that it will take him some time to get over it. I know he wants her to be happy, and you make her happy, so it will work out eventually. Be patient with him."

"I don't have much of a choice," Cory tells her. "The Professor isn't letting us alone for more than a few minutes at a time, and he won't talk to me about it. I don't force the issue. She's acting like I'm a leper right now, but I'm hoping she'll change her mind. We'll see."

"Right, just give it some time. I know Paige loves you. She just doesn't want to hurt her brother, Cory. Plus, let's face it," Sam says with a sad, little smile, "she's going to fight this kicking and screaming because she's scared to death of it."

Simon walks up and says, "Hello, Samantha."

"Um…hi," she says, stammering nervously.

"Are you staying here with Doc?" he asks.

"Yes, just until you guys get back. Then I'm probably going back home."

"To the farm. Good," Simon says with a nod.

Cory stands back and watches it unfold, knowing this isn't going to go well.

"No, home. Back to Henry's farm," she says firmly, her tone and demeanor turning impatient with Simon.

"His farm is not your home, Samantha. We've already covered this," Simon argues, beginning to lose his own temper.

"It's where I live now, where I eat and sleep," she counters. "I'd say that's my home now."

"Samantha, I'm losing my patience for this," Simon retorts angrily. "We've already gone over it. Don't make me do something that's going to upset you. I will. You know I will."

"You'll do nothing, Simon. Do you understand? I'll live where I want. I'll go on lunch dates with whomever I want. And I'll sleep where and with whomever I want."

Simon's eyes about pop out of his head and he steps forward as if he is going to physically drag her back to the farm on the spot.

"Save it for when the fighting starts, Professor," Cory says, jumping in and standing between them. "Doc's in the clinic, Sam. You should head over there."

"Oh, going to the clinic, Miss Sam?" Henry says, stepping in on their conversation. "I'll walk ya'."

"Son-of-a..." Simon starts.

"Let's roll, brother," Cory says, yanking Simon's arm and giving him a light shove to the shoulder. Then he slaps the back of his shoulder and keeps his hand there as he leads him away. Cory says in a quiet voice, "Let it go, man. You can deal with him later. Now's not the time."

His friend looks over his shoulder at Sam being led away from them by Henry.

"I don't like that asshole," Simon admits.

Cory nods and tries not to laugh because his statement is so obvious, "I know, Professor. I know. But now isn't the time to get into this with him. You want Sam? Fine. Go for it. We ain't gonna stop ya'. But don't do anything right now. Get your head in the game. We need you today. We need you in this, brother. Forget the women. Forget the farm and fighting over Sam. Just concentrate on our plans and defeating these fuckers."

Simon frowns, shrugs off his hand, and says irritably, "Fine. For now. That's it. For now. Later, I'm dealing with this. I'm tired of that guy, Cory."

"I know, brother," Cory says, although he believes Henry is a pretty good guy. He's never heard a single bad thing about him, and he has been generously allowing people to live within the safe confines of the walls of his farm. "Just say your goodbyes and get your head in the game."

Simon nods, his eyes coming into focus, and walks away from him. His pep talk worked for now, but Cory wonders if the Henry situation is about to become a fuse waiting for the right spark to ignite it. Simon hasn't been himself since Sam left, and Cory would like her to return to the farm. However, he's hardly in a position to give his best friend advice on his love life when he was sleeping with his sister in secret. Instead, he slings his rifle, double checks his pistol and joins the group of men getting ready to embark on their first offensive mission against these assholes.

"Payback time, boys," John says as he joins them and climbs into the driver's seat of the truck.

Reagan is standing with a small crowd of people and walks away with a pissed off expression on her face. This is normal for her, though. She's always full of anxiety when John leaves for something like this.

They mount up, all of them, including him and Kelly in an RV they've borrowed from a family in K-Dog's town. They'll be the bait, but these assholes won't know what's in store for them. They drive about ten miles out and park in the middle of the road. John, Simon and the others leave in their trucks, waving as they go.

"We've got 'em choked down into this road or the next, so we've got a fifty-fifty chance of them coming down here," his brother says as he lifts the hood of the RV to make it seem like they are having mechanical problems.

"Well, then let's hope it's this road," Cory says with a wink and a smile.

"You fucking know it, brother," Kelly says and bumps his fist against Cory's. "I've had about enough of their shit."

"Me, too. Assholes."

"They're preying on the weak and helpless, and that shit's over," Kelly declares. "After today, they're gonna know exactly who they're fuckin' with."

"Hooah," Cory says and grins.

This was the nature of their meetings for the last few days with Dave, the Reynolds and Johnson brothers, K-Dog, Paul, and, unfortunately, Parker, who nobody listened to anyway. They've had enough of these people terrorizing, robbing, and killing innocent travelers. Now that the family has cut off some of their sources of potential victims by placing the signs on the other roads, they are starting to hit towns and communities. Enough is enough. The McClanes are not going to stand by and allow this to happen. Not one more time.

"Hell, I'm even glad that asshole, Robert, is contributing to the fight," Kelly tells him.

"No doubt. Doc talked to him last night on the radio, and he's agreed to send more men and weapons as soon as we let him know when to," Cory says as he lights a cigarette and offers one to his brother.

He shakes his head and says, "Nah, Hannie will smell it on me."

"Pussy," Cory teases.

"You will be, too, soon enough, tied to that redhead," his brother says.

Cory chuckles and shakes his head, "I don't know about that. My woman isn't exactly racing me to the altar."

"She'll come around," Kelly says. "If not, Doc will force it sooner or later. Ain't no booty calls allowed on the farm, bro."

Cory laughs and nods.

"He's gonna be throwin' Scripture at your ass," Kelly says.

"Is that what happened to you?"

Kelly chuffs and raises his chin a notch as if to confirm this. Then he says, "Fuck it. Gimme a smoke."

"Oh, so you do have a set in your pants still."

"The gunpowder will cover the smell."

"Jesus, you're a real badass."

Kelly smirks and smokes his cigarette. His brother's hands do not shake with trepidation of the impending battle. He is not nervous, and neither is Cory. They are ready for this, prepared and enthusiastic even. This has been a long time coming, and these people are about to get what they deserve.

"You guys ever have trouble with drones like that before?" he asks Kelly.

"Yeah, sometimes. We had nerd support from people like Derek, though, who flew our own drones. At the end there, it was pretty high-tech. We even had drones capable of shooting down the enemy's drones. Made it kinda' convenient."

"Yeah, I read about those."

Kelly says, "Yeah, I should've figured you already knew about them."

Kelly looks at him for a long time and finally shakes his head with a smile.

"What?" Cory asks.

Kelly shakes his head again and says in a tone that almost seems remorseful, "All I ever wanted to do was keep you, Em, and Dad and Janet safe by doing what I was doing overseas. I never wanted this life for you. I never wanted you to join, even though I knew that's what you wanted- even if your mom didn't. And look at you now. You're so deep in it anyways."

"I was joining, Kel," Cory says and adds about his mother and Kelly's step-mother, "And Mom woulda' figured it out soon enough. She was a lot like Hannah. Hard to hide shit from."

"Yeah, I just wanted you to go to college and stay outta' this shit, man. Fightin' and war, it ain't no picnic."

"The way I see it is maybe some men were just born for it, maybe we both were. Shit, man, John for sure as shit was. That dude's DNA was formulated with nothing else in mind."

"Yeah, but neither of us ever wanted this for the people we cared about."

"I know, but we don't have much of a choice anymore. Look at Simon. He wasn't cut out for this. That nerd woulda' done some shit with his life, ya' know? Been a politician like his old man or some big famous scientist or some shit."

"Yeah, sucks."

"He's still doing shit. It's just different. He's smart as hell."

"And good with that rifle."

Cory bumps his fist against Kelly's and nods, "No doubt. Some people are just naturally good at sniping. I'm not as skilled in that."

"No, you're like me, Cor," his brother says. "We were meant to be in the trenches of it. John, too. Derek was the one meant to play on the sidelines drawing up the plans, doing the tech stuff behind the scenes. I mean, don't get me wrong, there's no better soldier, but Derek was always good at leading men and keeping up with the technology shit."

"Yeah, and he's frustrated as hell now 'cuz he's forced onto the sidelines and out of the fight completely."

328

"To tell you the truth, Cor, I'm glad he's out. He's got a lot to take care of on the farm. I'm disposable. Derek's not."

"I don't think Doc feels that way or he wouldn't have left the farm in your care when he dies someday."

Kelly shrugs as if he doesn't agree and stamps out his cigarette.

"And I don't feel that way, and neither does your wife or daughter."

"If anything happens to me, today or anytime, promise you'll take care of them for me."

"You know I would. You don't even have to ask."

Kelly looks at him and nods solemnly.

"It won't ever come to that," Cory states emphatically, suddenly nervous that he could lose his brother. "You've never even got a scratch during anything we've been in."

"Never know when your ticket's gonna get punched, little brother. Don't ever live your life like there's gonna be a tomorrow."

Cory pauses a long time before asking, "Do you like her, Kel? I mean, do you approve? It matters to me."

"Yeah, I like Paige just fine. She's been through some shit. You weren't there when she came to the farm. She was...I don't know how to describe it. She was like a caged animal. She didn't trust any of us and looked most of the time like she wanted to bolt. She's come a long way."

"Now she just wants to bolt from me."

"You want Paige? Take her. Take her for yours. Don't let her push you away. She cares about you. I've seen it when she thinks nobody's lookin'. Tomorrow's never promised to any of us, especially us, especially now."

Cory looks at his big brother, the man he's always admired and revered, and nods. They stand there another moment until Cory puts out his cigarette.

"Now quit being a total pussy and get ready," Kelly orders, to which Cory laughs raucously.

"Yes, sir."

He conceals his throat mic and earpiece by pulling his scarf up around his neck. Using the butt of his rifle, he breaks out both back windows of the abandoned sedan nearest him, shattering them to oblivion. Cory pops the hood on the vehicle and hides his rifle under it. He lowers the hood without locking it. Kelly's is behind the driver's seat in the RV, easily within reach. He uses a small mirror and signals that they are ready and gets a return signal from John and the others hidden in the woods. Simon also sends one from higher up the hill. He is completely camouflaged in his new ghillie suit gear. Dave's sniper signals in the same way from the other hill across the street.

"We're in position," Dave comes across his earpiece.

They are farther down the road and will act as a blocking force and will push inward as the fighting starts to prevent stragglers. Chet reports the same. His group is doing the same at the opposite end of the road. Cory knows they will be well-hidden in the forest around the road until it starts, their vehicles hidden, too.

Kelly lights a fire, causing a cloud of smoke to rise in the late day sky, hoping to draw in sharks. He slides the stack of debris which contains mostly old newspapers mixed with some chunks of cut up tire scraps under the RV to make it appear as if it is having radiator or engine problems.

They wait and then wait some more. Over an hour passes, and still, there is no sign of them. Kelly makes sure the fire stays lit enough to continue puffing out long, tenuous plumes of black and gray smoke high into the sky. A low rumble of thunder in the distance echoes down through the trees. It makes no difference to Cory or his brethren. They'll fight this out in a monsoon if need be. It is time to send these people a clear message. Their days of tyranny have come to an end.

"We've got a visual," Chet says through his mic.

"What've ya' got, Four-wheeler?" John asks, using Chet's new call sign since he's always the one repairing everyone's ATV's.

"Three trucks…" he says but pauses. Static ensues. "No, wait, four trucks, one's a deuce. They've got a fifty cal mounted on one again."

"Hold the fuckin' door, Batman," Dave says next in his own mic. "We've got us a little maneuver going. I've got two trucks full of what appears to be gen-u-ine assholes approaching from this direction, too. Fuckin-A, Bubba."

"They're boxing in the road," Kelly says.

"How'd they even know we're here? Drone? The smoke?"

Kelly shrugs, "Could be." Then he presses his throat mic and says, "Watch for drones, people."

"Let them come," John says, his tone deep and menacing. "Wait for the signal."

The signal that John is referring to is Cory. He is to ascertain that these are the highwaymen and send a signal to Simon with the mirror. Unless, of course, these dickheads kick it off sooner. He feels bad in a way because they sent Parker to the farm to manage the command center from there with Derek. The part he feels bad about is that Derek is stuck with him. They got rid of him because the dullard can't follow orders and thinks he is in charge of every operation. Mostly, he's a pain in the ass. He's going to be dead soon if Cory finds out that he spent his time on the farm hitting on Paige again. He and his men have been staying in Derek and Sue's empty cabin in the woods since he and his family are living in the big house again because of his injuries. He'll be glad when Parker leaves. Robert's men are pretty cool, some of them very well-trained, others not as much, but their intentions are honorable. Parker, he's not so sure of.

"Hey, show time," Kelly calls to him and snaps his fingers twice as the convoy that just passed Chet comes into view on the horizon. Cory heads over to the abandoned car to be in position to grab his rifle and also signal Simon.

The lead truck with the fifty cal pulls up within thirty feet of them and stops. The others follow his lead but pull off to its sides, effectively blocking escape. Cory looks the other way but doesn't see the ones that Dave spotted coming toward them. They must hang back and wait to see if their buddies need help. This is how it was before, too, when he and John had trouble on the road, and the cavalry came in for backup.

A man hops down from the bed, followed by the driver and front seat passenger of the lead truck.

"Car trouble?" the driver shouts to Kelly.

"Yeah, piece of shit radiator took a dump," Kelly yells back.

Cory's grip on the hood of the car tightens. This is them. He can feel it.

"We can help," the man says in a quieter tone as he approaches. "Got anything to trade?"

"Yeah, sure. That'd be great. What do you need?"

"Food, weapons, medicine," the man says.

Cory gets a closer look at him. He is clean cut like the others they've killed from this group. His clothing is not filthy, which lets them know that they have certain amenities worked out. He doesn't look skinny or starving. The other men in his group appear well-fed and clothed, as well.

"Sure. We've got all that," Kelly lies.

The only thing they've got that they're willing to trade is lead.

"How many are with you?" the apparent leader asks.

"Just my son there and my family inside the RV."

"How many?" the man repeats with less patience.

Kelly's eyes narrow and he says, "My wife and two daughters are inside."

Cory watches as a flicker of interest jumps between the men at the mention of women. He knows how this would go if it were all true. They'd either rape and kill them or take them if they are going to be useful. Children are killed, not taken or spared.

Others have come forward in a flanking maneuver. All together there are at least twenty that Cory has counted. Good, their flanking maneuver is what they'd been hoping they'd do.

"She's a good cook," Kelly expands on his lie. "She could make us up some dinner if you all could help us get this hunk of junk running again."

"Dinner?" the man asks, his tone becoming more threatening. "Why don't you just step away from that RV and let us have a look inside?"

"I don't think that's a good idea," he says.

"I don't remember asking," the man insists and signals to his men to search it.

"Hey, we're willing to trade," Kelly says. "It doesn't have to be like this."

"It's all like this," the man says. "Now get your women and girls outta there and let us have a look at them. Then we'll make a new deal."

"What do you mean?" Kelly asks, playing stupid.

"I could always use another wife," the man taunts. "And how old are your daughters?"

"Wait, this isn't an acceptable form of trade. I don't think we need your help after all."

The man shouts laughter to the sky and says, "You actually thought we were gonna help you? That's classic."

His men are heading around the other side of the RV to climb inside.

"So you're the ones?" Kelly asks, looking for clarification. "You're the ones that people put up signs to warn everyone about?"

The man bows and says, "At your service. And the assholes who put up the signs? Yeah, we're about to take them all out."

"How's that?"

"My boss is workin' on a plan," he answers unknowingly.

Kelly looks at Cory, and he instantly knows that they need this man alive for questioning. Cory gives an imperceptible nod.

"Aren't you the boss?" Kelly asks.

"Me? Nah, I'm just one of the drones."

"Drone?"

"Worker bees. We gather the nectar, and the boss spreads the honey."

"Seems like an unfair deal," Kelly comments, trying to get more information out of the man. "You seem smart. Why are you letting someone else call the shots?"

"'Cuz he brought us all together. He did the hard work to get us to where we are now. Ain't nobody starvin' anymore."

"How many of you are there?"

"What's it matter to you?"

"Just curious," Kelly says. "Maybe I wanna' join your group."

The man laughs, "You ain't got the stomach for what we do. I can tell. You're soft, weak. Like a little teddy bear."

Cory can hear John in his earpiece, "Pick your partner, dos-i-do. I've got the guy on the farthest right."

Dave says, "I've got Mr. Bright Red shirt down here on our end."

They all sound off in Cory's ear who they will pick off when the shooting starts.

"Yeah?"

"That's why I'm gonna kill your son, take your woman if she interests me, and take everything you own, teddy bear."

Cory's eyes shift quickly to Kelly's. Then he sees the corner of his brother's mouth twitch as if he is trying to suppress a smile.

"Hey, boss!" one of the men calls from the other side of the RV. "There ain't no women in here!"

Cory flashes the signal to Simon, and all hell breaks loose. Shooting ensues, long range from Simon and Lucky as they take out the men on the .50 cal quickly, within a second of the other's shot. Kelly shoots the leader in the knee, and the man goes down in a scream of surprise and extreme pain. Cory draws his pistol at lightning speed and pulls the trigger, taking out a man directly beside the leader. He can hear shots being fired from both sections of forest on either side of the road. John is leading men in taking out the RV explorers because Cory can hear bodies bouncing off of the outside wall of the vehicle as bullets slam into them. He squats and pulls his AR from under the hood.

"Kevlar," John says into his mic.

Cory knows he needs leg shots or headshots. By the way the men are falling, he also knows that Simon and the other sniper already figured it out as their body count rises. One of Robert's men tosses a grenade, hitting the crowd around the .50 cal as they were approaching it to take over. They dive for cover, even the man who was about to open up on the weapon. Someone shoots him when he pops up to go to work because the man slumps forward onto the machine gun. Kelly has taken cover in front of the RV and is popping off rounds into the group of men from the rifle he snatched from behind the driver's seat. Each shot takes down one man. His brother is not a teddy bear. His brother is a grizzly.

Cory uses the open windows of the sedan to fire shots through and strikes another man in the back. He is not wearing protective gear because blood splatter hits the white truck behind him like a Rorschach drawing, and he goes down and doesn't rise again. Cory shoots another as a barrage of heavy gunfire continues from the woods. Then he hears more shooting in the distance. Dave must be engaging with the assholes who were hanging back waiting to supply backup. The man he shoots returns fire, so Cory aims in and finishes him off with a headshot.

Someone shouts, "Grenade!"

The RV is rocked. Cory offers suppressive fire toward the enemy with a quick tap-tap-tap and sprints to the front of the RV

334

where Kelly was using it for cover. He finds John there with his brother, dragging him away. His heart stops. Then Kelly gets his feet under him and runs alongside John and scurries down into the ditch beside the road. Cory joins them as his heart resumes pumping.

"Man, you scared me, bro."

Kelly shakes his head and says, "I was just funnin'."

"Yeah, fucking hilarious," he adds with sarcasm.

Cory knows his brother wasn't joking. He must've been knocked off his feet or else John wouldn't have been pulling him clear.

"Professor, take out that dude going for the fifty," John says into his throat mic.

A second later, a loud report is heard and nothing else. Simon wasn't even in a good mood when they left today. He's taking no bullshit from these assholes. More shots are fired from the woods where Robert's men are still hiding. They are definitely holding their own.

"There's a truck heading your way, Four-wheeler," John says to Chet.

"Got it," Chet answers over his own throat mic.

Cory worries that their ally will have trouble, but he has seven men with him. Another long-range shot rings out, and one of the men in the back of the truck making its escape falls out. Then another as a second shot is fired, this time from the other hill. Apparently, the Professor and Lucky are having their own competition.

"Cory, take the hill. Flank 'em," John issues. "I'll lay down some cover fire."

"Yes, sir," Cory says and crawls out of the ditch as the highwaymen continue to fight it out. He sprints into the woods and quickly up a hill that isn't as well concealed with trees. John keeps them off of him by shooting a pop-popping spray of designed fire.

He pushes hard and runs parallel to the road. A splinter of wood hits a tree near his head, and Cory ducks. The shot did not come from the road. It came from ahead of him. He doesn't see anyone.

"They're scattering to the woods. Watch out," Cory says into his mic, getting a response to the affirmative.

Below him, the borrowed RV is on fire now. He doesn't think the man that lent it will be taking his family on any camping trips anytime soon, so it hardly matters. He wanted to fight actually, but he is seventy-three. They'd assured him that his place was at the condo community helping to keep it safe.

Another shot rings out in the woods. There is more than one man ahead of him. He has to eliminate them because they could find Simon or shoot at his brother or John from the cover of the forest.

A light drizzle begins as Cory rises and stalks carefully, quietly forward. God is smiling on him, offering the splattering of raindrops to cover his footfalls. He can hear them but doesn't see them yet. He decides to move up the hill a little further to see if he can look down on them. It does the trick because he finally spots them moving around, whispering to one another, and taking cheap shots at Cory's comrades in the road fighting back at their own friends. Cory heads down the hill and stops halfway. Then he kneels and aims.

"Don't take that shot, asshole," someone says behind him.

Cory feels the barrel of a gun pushing into his back. A moment of indecision hits him. Then Cory lifts his right hand in the air in submission and lowers his rifle to the ground, unsheathing his dagger from his boot at the same time.

"Get up!" the man says but not loudly.

Cory begins to rise very slowly. Then he stabs the man in the calf and spins to finish the job. The man crumbles, though. A headshot has disabled him. A second later, Simon sprints up to him.

"Sorry, Cor," he apologizes. "I saw him but couldn't get a shot off. Too many trees."

"Thanks, brother," Cory says.

"Hm, looks like you were gonna deal with him anyway," Simon says, covered in green camo from head to toe.

"Thanks anyway," he says again.

"What are you doing up here?"

"John sent me to flank, but there are assholes down there in the woods hiding."

"Want some help?"

"Hell, yeah," he says with a nod.

They move out together and find the men quickly. There aren't two. There are seven that Cory finally counts. They squat and observe for a moment.

336

"Where the hell'd they come from?" Cory whispers. "I don't think these dudes rode with them."

"No, I agree," Simon concurs.

"I'll head that way. You push forward from here," he says, getting a nod. Then he adds with a wink, "They won't see you coming."

"Not funny. This thing's hot as hell."

"Quit your bitchin'."

Simon nods, pulls his face mask back down and leaves. Cory walks quickly and as quietly as possible and ends up behind the men, who have not spotted him. They are too intent on shooting his teammates near the road, mostly Robert's men who have come out of hiding to join the fight more head-on. Cory sights in and pulls the trigger, taking one down. Simon does the same from his position. Only he takes out two more in quick succession. Cory can't be outdone, so he shoots another man. This one is in mid-dive for cover, so he only wings him in the leg. Two more to go, but they run away. Simon shoots one in the butt cheek, and Cory offers the other a faster mercy. Then the sniper takes deliberate aim and hits another man at over a hundred yards.

"Nice shot, brother," Cory says as he joins back up with Simon and punches his fist against Simon's.

"Cover me. I gotta get outta this monkey suit."

"You got it," Cory says and swings around to keep watch. No one else approaches, but he scans the area carefully.

They rush down into the fight again, and within minutes, they have the job finished. The shooting at the end of the road stops shortly after, too. Dave comes out of the woods and meets up with the rest of the group.

"Good job, men," John says, patting shoulders and bumping fists.

"My men are taking care of survivors," Dave says. "That piece of shit," he points to the leader of the group, "we'll take back to town."

"You know it," John says with a nod.

Suddenly, an explosion rocks the ground under them, and Cory's ears are ringing. Round two has begun.

Chapter Twenty-seven
Simon

A mortar round has struck in the middle of their fighting position. Their backup has arrived. One of them or many of them must've called for help from their people once the fighting commenced. He's not sure if his teammates are injured or not, but he dives for cover with Cory, his brother, and John.

"Take cover!" John and Dave both shout to the remaining men.

Everyone scrambles as they try to figure out where the attack is coming from. The sound of heavy equipment moving on the road vibrates under his feet.

"Talk to me, Chet," John says into his mic.

"It's not coming from my area. The road's clear," he says.

They look at Dave. The rest of their group jumps into the ditch with them and await orders.

"Not from ours. We took care of them, too. There wasn't anyone left, and we took the keys to their trucks."

"New group," Cory guesses.

"They've sent for new reinforcements," Kelly says.

"Head for the woods. We need to split up, flank that mortar launcher, take it out," Dave says.

"They're coming in something big or heavy, could be a tank or similar," John says.

"We'll head east," Simon says of himself and Cory.

Another round hits the already burning RV. They make plans to encircle the road and take out whoever is coming down it. He and

338

Cory are to track the ones using the mortar launcher like he did with Luke the night of the condo attack. He runs beside his friend through the forest.

"I don't think that was mortar fire this time," Cory says as they blast up a hill, heedless of noise. "That looked like a round from a bazooka or an AT-4."

"Whatever it was, we need to take it out," Simon says.

"Agreed," his friend confirms.

It doesn't take long to find the next wave of men coming through the woods. They are less fearful of them and making a commotion as they move together toward them.

Cory says, "Uh…we have a group of maybe fifty men up here toward the ridge."

"We're coming," John says.

"Spread out," Simon orders, although he doesn't think Cory needs his advice.

They run to the farthest points on the ridge, about sixty yards apart and take up positions of an offensive nature. Simon kneels and readies his rifle for multiple shots. He locks in on the man using some sort of grenade launcher or mechanism of that type. Without waiting for the others, he squeezes the trigger. The man goes down. Then the enemy all start shooting, but he and Cory lay down rounds of more lethal intent. Pieces of bark and chunks of wood splinter off of the trees near him, but Simon knows they are just mindlessly shooting. It doesn't mean he won't be hit, either, so he stays low, belly crawls to his right just a few yards and sets up a good spot for sniping. He remains prone and starts picking them off. Cory is moving around shooting, too. He knows this because his friend's rounds are hitting men from different angles.

Dave and John join him in the resistance a few minutes later. The others hook up with Cory at the opposite end, and they all spread out, effectively barricading in the men below them. Dave sends a hand signal to three of his men to start flanking. Simon knows they are about to surround the men below them, which will block them in and prevent them from escaping or retreating. This is a no-surrender, no-retreat battle. Sympathy will not be given. An armistice will not be offered. They will fight these men and kill them or be killed in the process.

Most of John's men are kneeling behind trees or lying prone like Simon. A few have their backs turned to the approaching enemy to scan behind them lest anyone decide to circle them, as well. Simon continues to shoot men as they enter into open areas. Something about this feels like a scene from a documentary about the Civil War that he'd watched one time with his father. Men of the same country, fighting it out in the heartland, in the forest like monsters full of hate and anger instead of fellow countrymen who should be working toward the same goals and who share the same values. These men are nothing like them, though. They are pure evil.

Somewhere down the line, one of Robert's men throws a grenade into the crowd coming at them. It does a lot of damage because the men were bunched together, and it throws clumps of dirt and debris into the air, causing the scene down there to become frantic and chaotic. Many of the opposition is taken out in the next two minutes because they are panicking, some trying to retreat, others trying to hide, and the worst situation possible trying to rush them, which is resulting in numerous and swift casualties on their side. Simon fires into the men in the cluster. The others do, too, and soon they have this group taken care of like the ones down on the road. They were coming to help their already fallen comrades but were met with the same expedient punishment.

One of Chet's friends from town has been shot through the top of his shoulder, so Simon quickly treats him, preparing him to be transported to the clinic. He binds the wound and ties a sling for stabilization.

"Think that was it?" Kelly is asking rhetorically.

John shakes his head and wipes the sweat from his forehead. He frowns and says, "Not sure. Maybe."

Dave offers, "I'll send runners."

They head back down the hill after investigating the area and confiscating weapons. Cory had been right about the AT-4, or so his brother had confirmed. There is one survivor with a bullet hole in his side and the mouthy leader that John shot in the knee. Simon is thankful that none of them look young like the two teenage boys in the jail in town. As with the others they've fought, they are well fed and clothed and very well armed. They take the survivors with them. If they live, they'll be questioned along with the others. Although these fights will help to suppress the highwaymen, there are still hundreds of them that can hurt people.

They listen to a few of the radios they found on the men, but nobody makes contact. The highwaymen have gone radio silent. They head back to their town after eleven p.m., having waited a while for another barrage that hadn't come. Chet's friend is shown to Doc's clinic where Herb and Dr. Scott treat him.

Sam rushes over to him and says agitatedly, "What happened? Is everyone all right, Simon?"

"Yes, fine. Everyone's fine."

"Did you run into them? Did they take the bait?

Simon washes his hands under the spigot behind the clinic and splashes cold water on his face. "Yes," he says in between dousings. His hands come away with just as much dirt and grime after he's run them over his face. "We took care of them. Many of them."

"And nobody in the family was hurt?"

"No. Not at all," he answers. He stands straight again and takes her shoulders in his hands. "We're all fine. It's over."

She nods nervously. Her hands are trembling and twisting between them. Simon takes them into his. Hers feel so small and cool to the touch within his. He nods reassuringly.

Cory rounds the corner of the building, skidding to a stop, "Come quick, Simon. There was an attack on another road. This time there were about a dozen survivors, but some are in pretty bad shape."

"Are we going back out?" he asks, jogging beside his friend, Sam on their heels.

"No, the people said the men took off quick," he explains.

He frowns, wanting to go after them, "Who found the survivors?"

"Dave's runners who went scouting for more of the highwaymen who might've escaped us," Cory says. "Guess they weren't more than a few miles from us. We didn't hear the shooting because we were doing so much of our own."

"Man, that sucks. We could've helped them," Simon says, angry and frustrated, the high of the win squelched by this new defeat.

"I know, but at least some of them got away. They said that only three of their group was killed. They said the highwaymen took off in the middle of robbing and killing them and left survivors. We're guessing that they heard over their radios about us fighting their friends."

"It could be if they were that close that they heard our shots. The idiots on their team were shooting friggin' bombs at us, so it's hard not to hear that, too. Maybe those men we fought last in that ravine were the ones who fled from the people who survived. Maybe they came to join the fight," Simon speculates.

"I'm not sure," Cory says. "The survivors said they went northwest, so they got back in their vehicles and fled east. That's how they ran into Dave's men. We never did find whatever was making the ground shake. Dave still thinks it was a tank."

Simon joins Sam and her uncle as the truck carrying the survivors pulls up to the clinic. The family has also taken the highwaymen's vehicles. Two men jump out of the back and immediately call out for assistance as they carefully lower an older lady on a stretcher. He and Sam help care for the injured people in the clinic while Doc and Sam's uncle do the same. It's going to be another long night.

The townspeople volunteer to get people moved and shuffled around across the street in the medical house to make room for additional patients. Others open their own homes to some of the survivors until they can decide what they want to do, whether it means leaving in a few days or staying on in Pleasant View. They would still have to be vetted first if they want to stay.

He and Sam finish with their patients around four a.m. and wash up, sanitizing their hands and any exposed skin thoroughly. Some of the town volunteers working in their clinic clean the two rooms where they treated patients. Her uncle and Doc are still in the surgical suite. Simon thinks they may be performing surgery on a man who was very badly wounded by gunfire.

Simon collects the patient files and directs some of the men where to transport their patients for rest and healing.

Dr. Scott walks up to him and Sam and says, "We lost him. His internal bleeding was too extensive by the time he arrived here and we started working on him."

"Sorry, Uncle Scott," Sam says, touching his shoulder.

Her uncle's face is one of bereavement and frustration. Simon knows the feeling all too well. He diligently studies the pre-apocalypse surgical techniques and medical procedures but will probably never be privy to using any of them. This rustic, barbaric form of medicine they practice now is second rate at best.

"Herb is speaking with the family. I'm gonna go clean up. Simon, can you have his body moved for burial?"

"Yes, sir. Right away," Simon answers and immediately goes to find help.

It is almost dawn by the time things settle down. He helps Cory load the fifty cal confiscated from their enemy's truck, along with the AT-4 and about thirty rifles and pistols into the back of the McClane family truck. The rest is divvied up among the townspeople, Dave's group and K-Dog. They are now the proud owners of three additional trucks, too. One will go to the farm, the other to Dave's and one will be given to Chet's family.

Cory walks past him and slaps his shoulder, "Done! Fuckin' finally. I'm getting hungry as hell."

"You've been hanging out with Dave too much," he says and frowns at his friend's language.

"Doesn't mean I'm not hungry as hell. Killing assholes is hard work."

Simon scowls and says, "Probably the exertion and adrenaline."

Cory chuckles at him and says, "Dork."

"Imbecile," Simon counters with and grins.

"You stickin' around?"

Simon's eyes inadvertently drift toward Sam, who is sitting on the top step of the clinic's front porch taking a well-deserved break. His adversary, Henry, is standing a few steps below her conversing, his booted foot resting right next to hers, his arm bent at the elbow and propped on his knee. He needs to stand back about three feet, or thirty, or just go back to his own damn farm.

"If you're staying, you better keep that pistol harnessed, brother. Don't wanna' piss off the Mechanic by shooting his friend."

He fires off a sneer at Cory and says, "Dave has poor taste in friends."

Cory laughs and says, "Nah, Henry's all right. You're just jealous that he's hanging out with your girl."

"She isn't my girl, idiot. I'm just tired of him acting like Sam belongs to him. It's absurd. And, yes, I'm staying. Herb can go home, and I'll watch the patients."

"Good, I'll let them know. You know, Simon, maybe it's time you staked your own claim," Cory suggests, this time without humor or his usual charming wit that others find so engaging and Simon finds so irritating.

"Why would I do that?" he asks as he wipes down his rifle with an oily rag from his pack.

"Because you love her. For some reason, I think she feels the same, although I can't see why because you're such a dick."

Simon scowls at his friend's humor.

"Because if you don't, she's going to end up marrying someone else. Hell, probably that guy."

Simon looks sharply at Cory and says, "Do you know something I don't?"

"No, not really, but I've seen the way Henry looks at her. And I've seen the way other men do, too."

"I'll kill them," Simon growls.

Cory chuckles again, "You can't kill everyone, buddy. She's a pretty girl. She's also smart and funny and sweet. She's a real catch. Hell, you won't let me marry your sister, so maybe I'll have to make an offer for Samantha."

Simon explodes. He's had enough. Testosterone and adrenaline have been coursing through his veins for last twelve hours at full speed. He slams down his rifle on the tailgate of the truck and shoves Cory hard in the chest with both hands.

"Hey, hey, hey!" John says from his spot a few feet away where he'd been talking to Kelly and Dave. He steps between them.

"Save it for the enemy, boys," Dave comments with a laugh. "Jesus Christ, it's like watching a pack of D-boys going at it after a battle."

Kelly laughs and says, "Or before. Remember the briefings beforehand?"

"Fuck yeah, I do," Dave says. "Those were always testy times, lots of tension and stored up adrenaline."

"Remember when Mitchell and Dr. Death went full-on MMA in the dirt over the plans?" Kelly asks, referring to John and someone named Mitchell, who must've been on their team.

"Fuck yeah, I do. Dr. Death was always a little off, if you catch my meaning," Dave jokes about John.

"Gee, thanks, brother," John jokes. "In my defense, his plan sucked."

They all laugh, but Simon grabs up his rifle, slings it, and starts walking away.

John stops him and says, "Are you staying today and tonight? If so, we're packing it in, and I'm taking Doc home. He looks beat."

"Yes, sir," Simon answers.

"Ok, good. Thanks, Simon. I can *always* count on you to do the right thing," his friend says, although Simon suspects there is a lot more than just friendly praise behind his words.

"Sure," Simon returns but keeps his eyes leveled on Cory's behind John. "I'm...I'm going to hit the hay for a while before I get back on medical duty."

"That'll be just fine. I'll let the others know. They can hold down the fort for a few hours," John says and pats his shoulder as if he is unsure of Simon's mood. "See ya', Professor. And, hey, steer clear of Henry for me till he's gone."

"Sir," Simon says and gives a curt nod before turning to go.

Cory shouts at his back, "Hey, let me know when I should start ring shopping!"

"Dangit, Cor," John is saying as Simon keeps walking. "Stop with the Paige thing. He's under..."

"Not his sister. I was talking about Sam."

"Oh, Jesus. That's below the belt, little brother," Kelly says, their voices growing quieter as he puts some distance between them. "Give a guy a break, man."

Simon picks up the pace and jogs. He needs some time alone, so he heads to the house where he stayed the other night with Sam and her uncle. There's running water, so he can grab a shower. He's seen many times in movies where people take cold showers to let off steam. Or maybe it was sexual tension. Either way, it sounds good right now.

He lets himself in and goes upstairs to the master suite where her uncle had stayed. The house is not locked; most of the homes in town are not since everyone trusts everyone else in town. He's not sure if Scott will stay in town today, but if he does, he can have the master bedroom again. The shower down the hall doesn't work, but the one in the master does. Simon just needs the use of the shower for a while, maybe a long while so that he can cool down, calm down, and clear his head. It's been a long night.

He drops his gear on the made bed, laying his rifle and pistol out and tossing his pack near it. The stress of the day has been too much. The endless war, the killing, the people who are always shot full of holes and need put back together. Turning on the water in the long, walk-in shower, he steps right into the stinging cold spray and allows it to ease his tired muscles. The home is an older one but has had extensive remodeling done, probably right before the fall. The patterned, gray tile walls of the shower and the floor of the shower are cool to the touch. Despite wanting to linger, Simon washes up quickly using the homemade soap from the farm and gets out, not wanting to use too much water, and not wanting to freeze to death. The water never really gets all that warm. He looks in the mirror, observing the fact that he needs a shave and a haircut but won't get either until he returns to the farm. It still feels better being clean. Simon wraps a towel around himself and grabs his gear before heading out into the hall. He'll go back for the guns in a second, but first, he needs some clothing. He brought some of his and Doc's clothing with him the last time he stayed here in case they'd need it when they're in town. With the battles and attacks that keep happening, Simon has a feeling they'll be using this house a lot in order to pull long hours at the clinic.

His mind drifts to Sam like it does most of the day when he isn't completely preoccupied with the business of staying preoccupied to avoid thinking about her. His feelings have intensified, those feelings of lust and desire, the same ones that make him sick to his stomach. He recalls the moments they shared in Doc's office just a few days ago when he'd been fully prepared to make love to her right then and there on the desk or the floor or wherever. The softness of her in his hands, his mouth on hers.

"Simon!" Sam states in the hallway as if she is startled, nearly running him down.

346

She smacks right into his bag, causing Simon to lose his towel. It falls between them on the carpet, and they both freeze.

"Oh, my goodness!" she screams.

Her wide blue eyes dash down the front of him, so Simon covers himself quickly with his backpack. Her eyes dart away as if she has scorched them by looking there.

Sam spins around and says, "Sorry! I didn't know you...what the heck? Why are you naked?"

"I wasn't!" Simon retorts, grabbing his towel from the floor and re-wrapping it around his waist.

"Uhh...you look very naked to me," she states, keeping her back to him.

"I just got my shower in case you or your uncle wanted one," he explains, leaving out the part about needing a cold-water splash to cool his temper. "I didn't know you were going to come home right now."

"I just brought you some food. I thought you might be hungry."

"Er, thank you," he says. "That was thoughtful. Just let me get dressed."

Her shoulders shimmy. Then she bursts out laughing.

"Stop laughing this instant, Samantha. It's not funny," he reprimands, still thinking about how she felt under his hands. He'd like to drop his towel and drag her into his room.

She continues to laugh, "Yes, it was. It was very funny."

Sam turns back around to face him. Simon scowls down at her.

"You of all people. That had to happen to you!" she teases and starts laughing again.

He just groans with frustration, some of it not from losing his towel. She sobers a moment, and her eyes drop to his bare chest.

"You've changed so much," Sam says, stepping closer.

"What? What do you mean?"

She lifts her hand and places it on his chest, the muscles there jumping in response to her warm touch. His skin feels vampirically cold from his shower.

"You aren't a skinny boy anymore," she observes as her fingertips trace the ridges of his pectorals.

Simon's mouth opens, but he quickly closes it for fear of what he might do or say. He has found lately that he cannot control himself very well around her, not like he used to.

"Don't put on any of my clothes by accident," she says, her demeanor changing, and turns to go.

Simon frowns, "What the heck's that supposed to mean?"

She says over her shoulder, "I moved my clothing into your room because someone in town needed a dresser the other day and I told them they could have the one in my room."

Sam turns the corner, and Simon can hear her skipping down the steps, whistling as she goes. He tries to regain his composure and takes a deep breath. It's a good thing she didn't look down again. The settling effects of the cold shower wore off the second she placed her hand on him. Simon lets out a sigh of relief at her departure and goes to his room. This time he closes and locks the door.

He rummages the top drawer in the dresser where he stashed clothing the last time and pulls out a very small pair of pink and white lace panties. His imagination races because he knows exactly whose body these belong on. He stuffs them back in only to pull out another pair, this time satiny black with a tiny ivory bow on the waistband. And yet another find is one of her bras, also pink, all lace, no padding, which makes him swallow hard.

"You've got to be kidding me," Simon mutters to himself and pulls out a big handful instead. The torture is too much. There in his fist is a collection of her intimates. Lace, silk, satin, delicate, colorful, everything that encapsulates who Sam is. He shoves them back in and slams the drawer closed, opening the next one down. She has moved his socks and underwear to this drawer. It was rather presumptuous of her, but Sam hardly asks for permission in such matters, or pretty much in any matters.

A few minutes later, he has combed his hair and dressed in clean clothing, although his jeans have seen better days with the rips and snags and even a few, unpatched holes in them. At least his button-down, blue plaid shirt looks slightly more professional. Herb never shows up to the clinic to wait on patients dressed like a bum, so he won't, either. He goes downstairs to find Samantha in the kitchen.

"I set your plate over there," she says, pointing to the island.

He nods and takes a seat at one of the barstools. "Aren't you eating?"

"No, I'm going...I'll eat later," she says evasively.

"Where are you going?"

"Simon, I don't want to get into this with you right now. Just drop it."

"Are you about to tell me you're going somewhere with Henry? Is it another date?"

She groans with irritation and great exaggeration. "You aren't my father."

"I'll tie you up and lock you in this house."

"Don't threaten me," she says, turning with a butcher knife in her hand. Then she realizes that she's holding it in an offensive manner and lowers it down to continue cutting the watermelon on the counter.

Simon doesn't argue but eats in silence his donated meal of biscuits and sausage gravy, or venison gravy- he's not sure which. Whatever it is, it hits the spot but is not as good as Hannie's. He won't tell the woman who cooked it, though. He's not too smart about women, but one thing he does know is that they don't like to have their cooking criticized. One small woman wielding a knife at him in a single day is plenty.

"I forgot to tell you, Tessa spoke today," she announces.

"Really? That's great. Finally," he says of the little orphaned waif who follows Cory around like a lost puppy.

"Yeah, she said 'Cory', and then she said, 'Daddy.'"

Simon smirks, "Uh-oh. Sounds like he's in trouble."

"I don't know. Grandpa was there when it happened, and he said he wonders if perhaps she didn't have a father who looked like Cory. She touched his scruffy whiskers on his face and then his hair in the ponytail."

"Maybe she had a father with longish hair and a beard," Simon comments. She nods and hands him a chunk of the watermelon, to which he nods and says, "Thank you."

"Yeah, that's what Grandpa said, too. About the beard and his hair."

"Wish we had a child psychologist in town," he says.

"Uncle Scott said he'll try to work with her some while he's here."

"Good idea. He probably took a lot more child psych classes since he majored in pediatrics."

She nods and packages all of the cut watermelon chunks into a plastic container she finds under the island. How she knows her way around this strange kitchen, he'll never understand. Women just seem better at finding things. It's okay with him because Simon knows men are better at other things like killing people. He doesn't wish for a role reversal anytime soon. Women are naturally smaller and built differently, not for war and dragging men out of a firefight, but for giving birth and nurturing a baby. To him, their jobs seem a heck of a lot harder with a much grander amount of responsibility. He would have no idea how to raise a child. It would grow up more screwed up than him. People have always called women the weaker sex, but they must not have ever met any women like the McClanes.

"All done!" she announces. "Gotta go. I'll be back tonight."

"Wait," Simon says to her and stands. "Where are you going?"

"The town's having a party to celebrate the victory, and I'm going. Duh! It's more of a necessity actually since so many people are here right now and away from their homes who need to be fed. Weren't you wondering why I just cut up two watermelons?"

He looks around her in the sink and sees an excess of peelings. She must've cut the first one while he was rifling her panty drawer like some sort of perv.

"I'll get those scraps later. Loretta's chickens and ducks love them."

He has no idea who Sam means, so it's probably a woman in town she's befriended. Sam befriends everyone. People just naturally love her. He can't blame them, but he would like certain people to stop loving her quite so much. And stop inviting her to lunches and parties. If he sniped Henry from the roof of this house, would anyone know it was him? He smiles ruefully as she rambles.

"...then some of the townspeople are going to be playing their instruments. It's going to be a relief, especially for the people in the medical house who will be able to hear the music. Music's good for..."

"Are you going to be gone after dark? I need to sleep a few hours before I head to the clinic."

"I'll be fine, Simon. Everyone will be there, even the soldiers who are still here."

"*That* hardly makes me feel better," he retorts, his temper rising. He knows she is saying that Henry will be there. He's sure there is no such luck that Henry left town, especially not while Sam is still in it.

"Well, bye!" she says with a huge, defiant smile on her face.

"I can carry that for you," he offers, trying to stall her for any reason, reluctant for Sam to leave.

She laughs gaily and says, "Simon, I hardly need help taking these to the party. Goodness."

All he can see is Henry kissing her in front of the clinic. It makes him so angry and disgusted. He doesn't want her going to this party but can't stop her, either.

"Right. I'm sure you can take that with you," he says, his mind racing. Inspiration strikes and Simon leans in and tells her, "Take this, too."

Then he slides his hand behind her neck and tips her mouth toward him for a quick kiss. It isn't like the one that Henry gave her. It lasts much longer and is more intimate. She leans into him, the giant bowl of watermelon between them. Simon pulls back and stares down at her, at the flushed color of her cheeks, the dark hue of her soft lips.

"Have fun," he whispers. "I'll see you later tonight."

She stutters and even stumbles forward, "Um…ok, thanks."

Simon grins as he watches her walk awkwardly toward the front door, glance over her shoulder at him, to which he waves, and leave the house. Good. He doesn't want her hanging out all day with Henry having fun and not thinking about him while he's asleep so that he can stay up all night watching their patients. He doesn't even want her going but knows he can't stop her. Until she finds someone that he approves of, Simon will keep interfering in her interest in Henry. It may be the only tactic he can use to keep them apart. If this fails, then the sniping from the rooftop option is still on the table.

Chapter Twenty-eight
Reagan

"Reagan!" someone whispers in the stairwell to her and John's bedroom.

He is dead asleep to the world, Charlotte is in her bassinette also asleep, and Jacob is in the basement being one of the big kids tonight, but she is studying at her desk with the small lamp still on. She looks at the time. Two-thirty a.m. Reagan rises and goes to the opening to the second floor and sees Paige.

After going carefully down the dark stairwell, she asks, "What is it?"

"I think I need your help. I didn't want to wake your grandpa. He was so tired when they got home today."

"Yeah, he was," she agrees, worried about her grandfather, who keeps pushing himself too hard as if he is still twenty-five and can work the long, grueling hours of an E.R. physician. "What's wrong?"

"I don't know. I've never had this problem before. I'm kinda' freaking out," she says, holding her stomach.

She realizes Paige has come to her with a medical problem. The way she's holding her stomach makes Reagan worry that something has gone terribly wrong from her shooting incident, although that seems illogical since it was a while ago and she hasn't presented any signs of long-term side-effects since then.

"Tell me your symptoms," Reagan says and touches Paige's shoulder briefly.

"I'm bleeding. Like really bad," Paige answers.

"From where? Vaginally?"

She nods, her face a picture of fear and dread.

"Come on," Reagan says, leading her downstairs. "Let's go out to the shed."

"No!" Paige whispers frantically. "I need to use the bathroom again."

"Ok, I'll wait," she says. Then a thought hits her, and she grabs her arm and adds, "Paige, don't flush, 'kay?"

Paige shoots her a funny look as if she finds the idea unpleasant but nods anyway. She uses the first-floor half bath off the kitchen and comes out quite a few minutes later, so long that Reagan asks her twice if she's doing okay.

"You didn't flush, did you?"

"No," she whispers, her color pale.

"Meet me in the shed," Reagan says.

Paige shakes her head, "There's no bathroom out there that works."

"It's fine," Reagan reassures her. "We'll use buckets to flush the toilet out there. Don't worry. You can still use that bathroom."

She's referring to the toilet closet in the back of the building, which they rarely use. Paige nods reluctantly and leaves. Reagan hurries in to inspect the contents of the commode and has a terrible hunch. She flushes, washes her hands, and leaves out the back door where she runs into Kelly on the porch.

"Everything ok? I just saw Paige go into the med shed. What are you two doing up?"

"Um, yeah, everything's cool, Kel," she tells him and furrows her brow. "Don't tell Cory we're in there, ok?"

He frowns but nods and says, "Sure. What's going on?"

"Just don't tell anyone we went in there and don't let Cory come in."

Her brother-in-law frowns harder but says, "Got it. I'll make sure."

"Thanks," she says.

Reagan rushes to the shed where Paige is sitting on the exam table already.

"Did you flush the toilet? I don't want anyone to see that. What a mess. It's so embarrassing."

"Yes, I flushed it. Don't worry. When did this start?"

"'Bout an hour ago. I thought I was just having a rough period."

"Has it been heavy like this before?"

"No, never."

Reagan sighs, "And the other times you went to the bathroom tonight, were they just as heavy and filled with clumps and clots and…tissues?"

Paige nods. "Am I dying or something?"

Reagan shakes her head and says, "Pass anything particularly large?"

Again, she gets a nod in return, "Yeah, the second time I went to pee when I noticed bleeding. It felt like a ping-pong ball size. That's when I really started freaking out. I didn't wanna' wake you."

"No, you did the right thing. Wake us. Always wake us."

Paige nods with frightened eyes and bites her lower lip nervously. Reagan takes her pulse and temperature. Her heart is racing, but she's pretty sure it is from fright.

"When was your last normal period?"

Reagan doesn't even start a chart on this. There's no need.

"Um…let me see," Paige says, clearly counting the weeks in her head. "I missed last month. Well, I didn't miss. I just spotted lightly. And the month before about the same. I thought maybe I was just losing weight again like I did when I was on the road. I never had a period then."

"Right, because your body weight dropped too low. Happens to anorexic and bulimic girls all the time, or apocalypse survivors," she says, attempting light humor to relax Paige.

She smiles and nods. "Then, of course, as everyone knows, I thought I might be pregnant and took that stupid test and everyone found out!"

Reagan offers a sympathetic frown and says, "You were."

"What?" she asks with confusion.

"You *were* pregnant. You're miscarrying."

"What?" she repeats much more loudly and in obvious shock, touching her fingertips to her lips.

Reagan frowns, tries to offer a comforting touch to Paige's bare knee and says, "I'm sorry."

"I took that test. It was negative. This has to be something else."

354

Reagan shakes her head and says, "I should've insisted on a blood test. The pregnancy tests at the clinic are four years old. They might not be so reliable anymore. Or you tested too soon, and the hormones weren't setting off the trigger. I'm sorry I didn't more thoroughly test you."

"It's not your fault. If I'm not miscarrying, then what else could it be?"

"You are. I'm positive," Reagan declares with confidence.

Paige looks at her hands in her lap and frowns. Her slim hands are shaking. "I can't believe this."

"It's gonna be all right," Reagan states.

Paige grimaces.

"Need to go again?"

She gets a nod before Paige scoots off the exam table and walks quickly to the bathroom.

"Damn," Reagan whispers to the empty room.

Then she goes outside and pumps a bucket of water. When Paige has finished, Reagan pours it down the toilet to force it to flush. She returns to find Paige at the sink washing her hands. Over the next few hours, they repeat the process quite a few times. Reagan doesn't mind the sleep she's missing, but she only wishes it wasn't happening for this reason. Paige is a dear friend now. She's Simon's sister and Cory's love interest. She's a part of their family, and Reagan hates to see her going through something so traumatic, especially alone. Of course, if Simon were here, this would be a lot worse. They'd all be dragging him back off of Cory.

"I know you aren't going to want this, but I'd like to check you just to make sure everything is doing all right. If you don't pass this entirely, you could get a very serious infection."

"Sure," Paige says weakly.

Her color is pale, which is also making dark circles stand out under her silvery gray eyes. She looks exhausted and spent.

Reagan checks her, careful to be as gentle as possible because she knows how raw everything is feeling right now. When she is finished, she presses sterile, thick cloths against her and helps Paige slide her panties up to hold them in place.

"I don't think there's much left to pass," Reagan says, helping her sit upright again. "You'll probably have something similar to a heavy period for the next few days. I want you to take it easy."

"'Kay," Paige says, her head hanging, her eyes avoiding meeting Reagan's.

"Why don't you lie down on the cot in the back of the building. I'll stay in the one next to you. There's no sense in going back to the house. I need to keep an eye on you for the next few days, tonight very closely."

"Why?" Paige asks in a flat tone, following her like a zombie.

"Just in case you'd start hemorrhaging or having a fever. We don't want either of those things to happen. Plus, I'll help when you need to use the bathroom."

"I don't want you to have to sleep out here," she argues weakly as she sits on the low cot.

"I'm fine. Used to it actually. I'll just run up to the house and let Sue know to feed Charlotte when she wakes up."

"Wait!" Paige blurts quickly and grabs Reagan's hand with desperation on her face.

"What is it?"

She looks around before saying, "Please don't tell anyone, Reagan."

"I won't. Not Cory, either."

"I mean it. Your family probably already thinks I'm the biggest whore there is for coming here and sleeping with Cory. And then, come to find out, I really did get myself knocked up like a loser."

Tears slip down Paige's upturned face. Reagan squats to be at eye level with her. She is shaking, so Reagan slips off her own sweater and wraps Paige in it.

"Hey, don't say that. Nobody, *nobody* thinks that."

Paige shrugs as if she doesn't believe her. Then her shoulders slump.

"I mean it, Paige. Nobody in this family believes that. And trust me, dear, there also isn't anyone in this family without sin."

"Your family is so old-fashioned and reserved, though. Plus, now they all know about me and Cory."

"So? I slept with John before we got hitched," she confesses softly, earning a surprised look from Paige. "Yep, it's true. We had

356

sex. Quite a few times, actually. He wanted to get married- kinda' like Cory. I didn't, so he left."

"He did?"

"Yes, that asshole," she admonishes jokingly. Paige smiles gently. "Went to live over on the Johnson's farm because they were still driving around the country looking for their relatives. He took Jacob, too. That really pissed me off."

"I'm sure," Paige agrees.

"It all worked out. We got married. I even wore a damn dress if you can believe that," Reagan jokes, getting another smile.

"But someone like Hannah...I don't know...I really like her. I feel like such a skank when I'm around her now, now that she knows about me and Cory."

Reagan chuckles. "Yeah? Hannie? Pure as the driven snow? I almost had to kill your boyfriend's brother."

"Cory's not my boyfriend."

"Yeah, whatever you say."

Paige frowns, "Why'd you almost kill Kelly?"

"He was sleeping with my little sister. I found out 'cuz she got a UTI," she says. At Paige's frown, she explains, "Urinary tract infection. Bladder infection. Same thing basically. You get it from not urinating after sex. Men are gross. They can give us cooties."

Paige chuckles.

"No, I'm just kidding. But they were gettin' it on under all our noses. Grandpa wasn't too happy about that one, either. I'm sure it was all Hannie, though."

"What do you mean?"

"It's Hannah!" Reagan says with a smile. "Once she set her sights on Kelly, he didn't stand a chance."

"I can see why he would've been so drawn to her."

Reagan nods. She has no doubt that Hannie's innocence is what drew Kelly to her. That and her big boobs, probably.

"But your grandfather..."

"Would never judge you. He doesn't hate you. As a matter of fact, he likes you. He's said it many times. He's just strict about stuff, but don't worry. It doesn't make him dislike you. Grandpa's got a past, too. Everyone has sinned. It's what we do. We're humans, sent here to do God's works, but He knew we would never be without sin."

"Some more than others."

"Yep! You are flawed. You're supposed to be," Reagan says, brushes Paige's red hair behind her ear, and stands again. "And I'm as fucked up as the next asshole. We all are. Now, lie down and rest. I'll be back."

She leaves to the sound of Paige laughing. It's a good thing. The not-good thing is that she finds Cory and Kelly standing near the shed outside.

"What's going on? Is Paige in there? I just went up to check on her, make sure she was all right…"

Reagan frowns at Cory, "Why were you checking on her?"

He shakes his head. "She didn't eat anything at dinner and looked sick or in pain. Is that who's in there? Is she sick or something?"

"She's fine."

"What's wrong with her?"

Reagan looks at Kelly, then at his little brother, who is very distraught at the thought of his lover being ill. Unfortunately, as much as she'd like to tell him the truth, she made a promise to Paige.

"She'll be fine tomorrow."

"But what is it, Reagan?" Kelly asks this time.

She weighs her decision quickly and says, "Girl problems. You lugs gonna help with that?"

They both cringe, step back physically, and shake their heads.

"Oh, ok. Sure. No prob," Cory says. "Just let us know if you need anything."

"Buckets of water. Just leave them outside the door," she says, knowing they won't question.

Reagan laughs and walks around them. She calls over her shoulder to them not to enter the shed. She probably doesn't really have to say this, though. With the looks on their faces, she doubts either of them would've done so.

She returns a short time later after she has pumped and taken Charlotte to Sue for her feeding. She brings Paige some hot tea laced with painkillers. She is lying down under a blanket, resting her head on a pillow.

"Were you talking to Cory?" she immediately asks.

358

"Yes, don't worry. I didn't tell him anything."

She breathes a sigh of relief, "Thanks. Sorry I put you in that position. Can you not tell your family, either?"

"No, I won't tell anyone," Reagan says as she sits on the other cot near her. "Did you go again?"

"Yeah," she answers. "It was a lot less this time."

"It will be. It'll let up. Here, drink this. There's medicine in it to help with the pain."

Reagan lies down and raises up on her elbow, resting her head on her hand.

She asks after sipping the hot beverage, "Are you going to tell Cory?"

Paige shakes her head. "I don't think so. I don't think that's a good idea."

"Drink some more," she orders. "Why not? Why would you not tell him?"

"I don't want this to influence him."

"You don't want him to feel obligated to marry you? Too late. He already wants to."

Paige nods and starts crying. Reagan stands and pulls her cot closer so that she can rub Paige's back.

"I don't even know why I'm crying!" she exclaims. "It's not like I wanted to be pregnant. I was glad when the test was negative."

"I know," Reagan says with understanding. "It's the hormone dump. Your body is changing again from being pregnant one minute and literally the next being not so. It's dumping all the hormones you just built up being pregnant. This is normal. Don't worry about it."

"I didn't even know I was pregnant. This just sucks."

"Are you sad because you miscarried, Paige?"

She shrugs.

"It's ok. I won't tell anyone."

"I didn't want to be pregnant. I was so stressed out when I thought I might be. I was freaking out trying to figure out how to tell Cory. Then I was freaking out more thinking of a way to break it to my brother. But I didn't want to have it."

"Sometimes we don't even know we want something until it's gone. Maybe it's time to stop worrying about what's gonna happen and just try to find some happiness for *now*."

She shrugs and frowns. Her gray eyes are tortured.

"I would never want to bring a child into this world."

Reagan nods. "I know. I felt the same way. But then Jacob came along, and I was okay with that. He changed me a lot, changed my mind about children. Mind you, I still wasn't wanting to have any. I was afraid I'd die or the baby would die or both of us. I was afraid that this world is just too ruined for children to exist in it. Then Charlotte. She really changed my perspective about a lot of things. When I look at her, really look in her eyes, I feel like I can see hope for the future, and that's not something I've felt in a really long time."

"She is precious."

"I always felt like it was unfair to bring a baby into a world like this. Look at Daniel. I wasn't even sure he'd live, but he did. And you know what? This world isn't so bad, not always. Sometimes I think it might actually be better."

Paige snorts in disbelief.

"I had my whole life planned out. I'm sure you did, too. And I'm sure when you thought of your future and kids and all that, you never thought it would look like this. I never even wanted kids. Or a husband! Life's complicated. It was even before this all happened, but we have to learn to adapt. There's no reason you can't be happy. If you love Cory, just love him, hold onto him and don't let go. And I was never the kind of person before who would've given someone relationship advice like this, but now that I have John and my little family, I understand what it means to be truly, truly happy and content. I just want the same for you because I care about you."

"Thanks," she says softly. "I care about you, too. And the whole family. Crap!"

The tears start again. Reagan smiles sympathetically and rubs her back some more. Paige uses the bathroom two more times. She eventually drinks all of the tea. Then she finally falls asleep right before five a.m. after they talk longer and discuss her regrettable situation.

Reagan takes her temperature and monitors her heartbeat. She is concerned that with Paige's blood loss only months ago from the shooting she'll become anemic again from this. She will have to closely keep an eye on her for hemorrhaging.

She rises from her cot and stretches her back, having forgotten how uncomfortable it can be not sleeping in her own bed. The sun will rise soon, one of her favorite times on the farm, so she goes out onto the cement stoop in front of the shed and sits with her blanket wrapped around her shoulders.

"Hey, sexy mama," John says as he approaches, taking her breath away like he always does.

"I told you to stop calling me that," she reproaches. "Plus, these," she says, indicating her breasts, "aren't gonna last forever, ya' know. As soon as I stop breastfeeding, they'll be just as small as before."

"You weren't that small. I mean, you are small, but your breasts were just fine. They're perfect," he says and pulls her to her feet for a long, searing kiss. "Kelly said Paige is in the shed for girl problems? What's really going on?"

She figured that lie wouldn't work on John. He's not afraid to tackle women's issues, either, so he would go in to check on her even if she was just having cramps. Nothing seems to embarrass him.

"Don't tell anyone," she says, getting a nod. "She miscarried last night."

"I thought…"

"Yeah, well, we all did," Reagan says. "I should've checked her myself instead of relying on a test from the clinic."

"Oh, man," John says, hanging his head and sighing. "Man, that's too bad. Is she ok?"

"Health wise? Yes. I think she's pretty sad right now, though. She didn't know, either. She believed the test."

"Cory?"

"No, he doesn't know, and she doesn't want him to."

He nods. "Got it. Can I help? Does she need anything?"

Reagan shakes her head.

"Do you need anything?"

This is one of the things she loves most about her husband. He's always thinking of her, putting her first, sacrificing anything he must to ensure her happiness and comfort. Reagan shakes her head again.

"I don't know how I'm gonna keep this from Grandpa," she explains. "I mean, he's not going to believe this whole farce of her needing to be in the shed for a difficult period."

"Let her rest," John says, touching the side of her face, the side with the fading scar. "Then talk to her about it. Not everyone needs to know, but explain to her that your grandpa should be kept in the loop in case there's a medical emergency with her."

"Well, yeah! I would like him to be in on this," Reagan admits.

"Right," he says, agreeing with her. "She's just traumatized right now by it all. And probably scared."

"Yeah, she is," Reagan says with a nod. "I feel bad for Cory, too. He doesn't even know."

"She'll probably tell him. Just let her do it on her own. It's too soon, and she's probably too upset."

"She was," Reagan says, always surprised by her husband's intuition.

They sit on the cement stoop together and watch the sunrise between kissing and holding hands.

"I'm glad you're home again," she says, leaning against his arm.

"For now. We're not done yet. We're going on another ambush tonight," he reveals.

Reagan nods against him but doesn't say anything. She wants him to stop putting himself in danger but knows that what he's doing is saving many people's lives, including children.

"The Professor was great the last few trips," John tells her. "He's such an expert."

"Good," Reagan says. "Too bad he's not as good with relationships."

"I think him and Cory will eventually work out their differences. I mean, they both want the same thing, right? Paige to be happy."

"No, I meant Sam."

"Oh, right," John says with a sigh. "He better dig his head outta' his rear-end before Henry snatches her up for his own. And we aren't gonna stop him, either. He's a good guy."

"Why do you think he's doing this, this pushing her away thing that he does?"

362

John shrugs. Reagan shoves into him.

"Come on," she urges. "You're the expert at this crap."

Her husband chuckles, a deep-pitched and comforting sound, "My best guess is that he sees her as a kid still. I don't know, babe. This one's a mystery even to me. Obviously, he has feelings for her, right? Obviously, he doesn't want her to be with Henry because the dude about blew a gasket the other day in town. That almost got bad. I think we all saw what Simon's capable of. That wouldn't have been good."

"No, I would hate to see our relationship with Dave and his men go sour, too."

"Nah, Dave wouldn't allow stuff like that to come between us. He'll always be our ally."

"Good," Reagan says and pauses a moment before continuing. "You know, Sue and Hannie wanted me to talk to Simon about this issue."

"About Sam?"

She nods and says, "Yes, me. I mean, are they serious?"

John kisses the top of her head and says, "You're probably the closest with him. It makes sense. He looks up to you and your grandfather more than anyone else on the farm. He can't talk to Cory about it. Heck, I don't think he would even if he wasn't having problems with Cory right now. Simon's a very private, quiet, introverted person. He's always in his own world. Hm, reminds me of someone I know."

"Shush," she scolds.

"If you think for one second that he does love her, you'd better intervene soon, or she'll be lost to us for good."

"I don't want that," Reagan frets.

"None of us do, but there isn't going to be anything we can do to stop it," he says casually. "Plus, I do want her to be happy. If she can be happy with Henry, then that's what I'll support."

Reagan swallows hard. She'd been hoping that Sam would return to the farm soon to live. She'd genuinely believed that she was just over there to help her uncle establish the clinic and that she'd come back when it was done. Now, she seems to be coming for visits less and less, too. This leaves Reagan feeling a moment of panic. She wants her little friend, their little Sam to come back. The family hasn't been the same without her.

She sits with her husband a while longer until he decides to run a patrol route through the woods. He also wants to check in with the three men from her father's compound who are staying in Derek and Sue's house.

Sometimes her life feels like a pressure cooker ready to burst. There is always some source of stress and anxiety in her life. Paige just miscarried last night. Simon doesn't know yet, but she's pretty sure he will eventually and they'll all have to worry about what he'll do in retaliation to Cory. Sam is gone and may never return to the farm. The highwaymen are a considerable threat in their lives. Her father is a pain in their ass, or maybe just hers.

She sighs, stands and stretches out her back. She can't wait to start running again. Not exercising is contributing to her lack of stress relief. In today's environment, she'll die before her thirtieth birthday from a stress-induced heart attack.

Reagan tries to think of how Grams would handle all of this. It helps. She yawns, arches her back, and heads into the shed to get a little sleep. Grams always used to say that everything would look better in the morning after a good night's sleep. She crawls into her cot and closes her eyes. She hopes her grandmother was right because life couldn't possibly be more difficult or fraught with stress.

Chapter Twenty-nine
Paige

Two days after her miscarriage, Paige is still feeling like crap and staying close to the house. She'd been such a fool. She was still having the same, strange symptoms like intermittent nausea and tenderness in her breasts. She shouldn't have ignored it. Reagan has assured her that it was nothing she did to cause the miscarriage, that they happen all the time and are in no way indicative of future pregnancy results. She can't help but blame herself, though. For not wanting to be pregnant in the first place, her level of guilt over the loss of the baby is eating at her.

The men left again yesterday to perform another ambush against the highwaymen. This time according to John and Kelly when they'd returned, they hadn't been as lucky. One of Robert's men was killed. They also didn't manage to take out quite as many of the highwaymen, either, only twelve. To make matters worse, the prisoners in town won't talk. The only ones left are the two teenagers, and Paige is left to speculate about what happened to the others. She can only imagine.

Years ago, she might've felt differently about using torture tactics with prisoners of war, but not anymore. She's seen what these animals do, what they did to women and children whose most nefarious deed was to be traveling on the same road as them. These people get what they deserve.

"Feeling better?" Cory asks as he sneaks up behind her in the music room where she is sketching out an architectural drawing.

"Yeah, thanks," Paige says. It's not a total lie. She does feel a little better, sore and achy but better.

Cory kneels down in front of her since she is perched on the bay window seat. It has the best light in the house.

"Cory, don't," she says, looking over his head toward the open doorway. "Simon's back. You shouldn't even be in here with me alone."

"I know. I'm just worried about you."

"Don't be. I'm fine."

He scowls and touches the back of her hand gently. "You're so pale, and you look really tired."

She frowns and says, "You really know how to flatter a girl."

Cory reaches out and lets the backs of his knuckles skim down over her cheek. It causes a shiver to run through her, though she tries to hide her reaction from him.

"You know what I mean. Something's going on, isn't it? Are you hiding something from me? Are you sick, Paige?"

The use of her actual name makes her insides do a little flip. Paige tries to steel herself against his charm, even though she really doesn't think he's trying to be charming.

"No, I'm not sick. I'd tell you." Talking in the kitchen draws their attention. "That's Simon!" she hisses. "Go. Go away now before he comes in here. I don't want to upset him."

"Not until you tell me what's going on," he bribes.

"No way."

There's really no way to get into that conversation in less than five seconds anyway.

"Then I'll wait for your brother to come in, and then we'll discuss it- all three of us together."

"Cory," she pleads with frustration. "Damn it. Fine. Later, though. Not right now."

"When?" he says, standing up again.

"Another day…"

"Today," he dictates.

"Fine, today. But now right now."

"When?" he demands.

She can hear Simon's voice growing louder as he comes closer to the music room.

"Um, after dinner, ok? I'll meet you behind the horse barn in the woods."

He nods, leans down and grabs the back of her head, pulling her toward him. Cory presses a kiss to the top of her head and then leaves. Her brother walks in a moment later.

"I'm going out to collect herbs. Need anything?" he asks, obviously not having seen Cory making his sly escape.

"Can I come with you?"

He frowns and says, "Sure."

Paige has been cooped up, not wanting to wander too far from the nearest bathroom for a few days. It'll feel good to stretch her legs.

They walk together toward the woods behind the barns, and luckily her brother isn't in a hurry. He seems slightly more relaxed than usual.

"When are you guys going back out?" she asks, looking up at him, observing his auburn hair in the sunlight, his pale blue polo shirt, and khaki pants. He looks like he's headed to a high school debate competition, not out for an afternoon stroll collecting medicinal herbs in the post-apocalyptic countryside.

"Don't know. Maybe tonight. We're waiting on Dave's call over the radio."

"Right," she says with a shaky nod. "I wish you didn't have to go. I get so scared when you guys are gone, like you won't come back, Simon."

He offers a pained grin and says, "I'm in a lot less danger than the others. They usually have me somewhere high taking care of business while they're down in the thick of it."

She nods, completely and fully comprehending what he means. She doesn't like this, either. It means the other men, Cory included, are in the most danger.

"Plus, with the new ghillie suit, it makes my job even easier."

She frowns and says, "Yeah, I suppose so."

"It does! The other night, I had a person walk right past me. I mean, right past, as in within inches and he could've stepped on me. That thing's great."

She nods, her eyes widening at the thought of one of those creeps being so close to her brother. It makes her sick to her stomach.

"If only you could all where ghillie suit thingys."

"Nah, wouldn't work. The others need to be able to move more quickly than me. My whole tactical motive is to move around in a sneaky, slow motion. Not like the others. They're zipping around quickly trying to find the best advantage."

"True."

They arrive in a glen, and Simon squats to do some picking of weeds that have white flowers coming out of the tops of them. Paige takes a seat on a fallen log.

"Cory fell down last night, got some road rash on his back," he tells her. "Guess he lost his rifle in the dark on some hill."

"Oh, good Lord."

"Yes, I'm sure he was saying some prayers of his own," he teases with a smirk.

"What'd he do?"

"In typical Cory fashion, of course, when he fell down, two men saw it happen and attacked him."

"What?" she asks, a bit hysterical, earning an admonishing glance from her brother.

"He's fine. He did what he does best, if you know what I mean."

"How? If he lost his rifle?"

"Cory doesn't need a rifle to kill people. You of all people should know that."

She does. She saw a lot of violence in him when they went on short runs together. It was a totally different side than she was used to. She didn't judge him for it, though. It's what kept them alive.

"Guns are just an accessory for Cory. He certainly doesn't require one to be effective in combat."

"Right," she says, furrowing her brow and nodding.

She leans her head back, soaking in some vitamin D as the sun's rays shimmy their way down through the branches of the massive trees around her. A light breeze causes the loose hairs of her ponytail to tickle her cheek and nose. It just feels good to be outside again.

"What's going on with you lately?" he asks out of the blue.

Paige is startled out of her daydream and blurts, "What? Me? Nothing."

"You seem...I don't know. Is something wrong?"

368

Guilt eats at her gut as she shakes her head. She can't tell Simon about the miscarriage. He already hates and blames Cory for everything.

"Is this about Cory? Because I don't want you to be with him?"

Paige shrugs and feebly shakes her head.

"Sam thinks I'm a big jerk for keeping you apart, you know."

This causes her to smile. "Well, I guess that depends on how highly you value her opinion as to whether or not to believe her."

"Do you? Do you think I'm being a jerk?"

Paige sighs and says, "No. You're just doing what you think is right because you're my brother. It's fine. I told you, I don't want to marry him. I was just…I don't know. I was just lonely, I guess."

Simon looks at her with speculation and finally joins her on the log.

"I just don't want you with him because out of everyone on the farm, I know Cory best. But I want you to be happy, and lately, especially the last couple of days since I've been home, you seem completely miserable."

She offers a shrug again because words are too difficult. She's never been a good liar. The worst one she tells with frequency is about her feelings toward Cory. Now, she's carrying a big, fat whopper of one around, and it feels like a malignant tumor on her shoulders.

"I'm fine," she finally manages to say, holding back tears that are threatening to spill over.

"You're really pale, sis," he observes, making her look away quickly. Simon uses his thumb and index finger and turns her chin toward him again. "Hey, you're really pale. What's going on? Are you sick?"

"Sick? No, I'm fine."

"Has Herb or Reagan tested your blood lately?"

She shakes her head, "No, remember? I'm doing fine. My blood's back to normal." Minus the miscarriage blood loss, she's normal. She doesn't say this part.

"You don't look right. You're pale and…" he picks up her hand, "cool to the touch. Did you get hurt while I was gone and you're not telling me?"

"No!" she says, nervous he'll start questioning people. "You've just been gone so much lately that you're misremembering my coloring."

"That's silly. Your coloring is the same as mine, and I can clearly see that you're very pale."

"Just tired," she lies.

Simon regards her another moment and finally nods. He doesn't look like he believes her, though.

"You weren't around any of the Campbell Kids, were you? You know there's a breakout of Scarlet Fever going around town, right?"

She nods. "Yes, I know. I wasn't around them. I swear. I'm just tired or something."

"You need more rest," he says in a bossy tone.

"Me? You've been running on empty for weeks. Working at the clinic, going on missions, working at the clinic some more, never coming home."

"I'm fine because I'm used to it."

She changes angles and says, "I'm going to get Sam to gang up on you and force you to slow down and get some rest."

"You mean if she ever gets out of bed today?"

She laughs. Sam and a few of Dave's men returned with Simon to the farm to rest for one night and return to the clinic with more supplies. She slept in Paige's room last night.

"Simon, is the situation between her and Henry getting serious? Everyone's kind of been talking about it around here."

His eyes dart to hers and turn cold with hatred, "They have?"

"Yeah, well, some people have been."

"Has she said anything to you?"

Paige shakes her head, "No, we haven't talked about it. Do you want me to ask her?"

"No, I'll deal with Henry if it comes to that," he says with confidence.

"Why would you do that? If she likes him, there's no reason they shouldn't be together. He seems nice…"

"What someone seems like and what they're really like are sometimes two different things, Paige. Don't be so naïve."

She scowls at his back as he turns to stoop and pick more weeds.

370

"He seems nice to me. He has good manners. And he definitely likes Sam. I've seen that much."

He grunts and doesn't comment.

"Don't you love her, Simon?"

Her brother stops all movement and is frozen in time, as still as a statue.

"It seems like you do," Paige adds.

Without turning all the way toward her, Simon says over his shoulder, "Sam is like a sister to me. I just want to protect her. I feel a lot of responsibility toward her."

"Because of what you went through together?"

"Because she's a part of the family, and I feel the same about all of the women in the family."

"That doesn't sound right," she argues. "It seems to me like you have stronger feelings than brotherly ones about Sam. I mean, I know she drives you crazy, too. I've seen your temper when it comes to Sam. You want to go and beat up Henry, who as far as I can tell, is a pretty good guy. If you wanted her to move on, move away and be happy, then it seems like his farm was the perfect opportunity."

"I never told her to move away!" he says, his voice getting louder. "She did that on her own. As a matter of fact, I forbade her from doing so, and she did it anyway."

"Forbade? Oh, little brother, you've got a lot to learn about women."

"I think I've got a lot of it figured out actually. You're emotional, irrational human beings, who care very little for your own safety and well-being for the sake of being defiant."

Paige just laughs at him. She rises and walks over to him, resting her hand on his shoulder. Then she bends and kisses his cheek.

"I sure do love you, Simon," she confesses and notices his grouchy scowl and turn of disposition. "I'm heading back."

"I'll walk you," he says, rising instantly.

"Nah, I'm good. Keep picking your weeds and stuff."

"They aren't weeds," he says irritably.

Paige leans in and gives her brother a hug, even if he isn't so little anymore. She just wishes she could take away his pain, of which she's sure he is in.

She leaves him to his picking and walks back toward the barns where she runs into Luke and G. He's been going on the missions, too, when the men decide it's safe for him to leave the farm to do so. Either he or Kelly stays to add protection while the others are gone.

"Don't be such a dumbass, Luke!" G is saying as Paige enters the horse barn.

"Language, young lady," he scolds.

"Whatevs, bro."

"What's going on, guys?" Paige asks as she approaches them where they are saddling two horses.

"Going on a patrol ride," G tells her. "Wanna' go, oh great horse whisperer?"

Paige chuckles and smiles, "Yeah, right. No, thanks."

Gretchen giggles with ornery intent.

"What were you arguing about? Is everything ok?"

"Nothing!" Luke blurts quickly.

G laughs again and says, "My brother has a crush on someone in town."

"Gretchen!" he states angrily. "Do you mind?"

"Oh, really?" Paige says slyly.

"Yep, and he's being a chicken-shit and won't ask her out," G reveals, earning a contemptuous glare from her brother.

"Who?" Paige asks, genuinely curious.

"Nobody."

"Melora," G says loudly over her brother's response.

"Melora, huh? She's really cool. I only got to meet her a few times, but she's really nice."

"And super pretty," G adds.

"I don't have a crush on her. I just happened to tell bigmouth here that she was attractive. It was only because Gretchen was pushing me to answer a bunch of childish questions."

"Like what?" Paige asks.

"I knew he'd been acting weird lately, so I entrapped him into playing a game of answering questions about stuff like who was the smartest person and who was the prettiest out of all the people we know. And who was the nerdiest. Your brother won that award. Unanimously."

"Obviously and well-deserved, too," she jokes.

"I just happened to say that Melora was attractive and now her overactive imagination is running away with it."

"And who did you say was handsome, G?" Paige inquires.

"Cory."

"Oh?" Paige asks with a grin.

"Yeah, but he's too damn old for me and obviously into you."

Paige laughs heartily. She's never known someone so young to offer up their opinion so easily. Maybe Sam.

"Huntley's a little closer to your age," she points out.

"Huntley?" she asks with a scowl as if she has tasted something bad. "He's so annoying and too damn bossy!"

"Huntley? He's so sweet."

G scoffs in a most unladylike manner and gives a snort, too. "Not to me. He's an annoying jackass. He thinks he's my boss, especially when my brother leaves."

Paige spies the tiniest grin spread across his face. He must've told Huntley to keep tabs on G while he's gone. She overheard John and Cory discussing how great Luke's been as an addition to their team. She would never guess it to look at him. He's tall like his dad, built wide, but is always quiet. When the men get together to plan and scheme their next battle, Luke usually just sits in the corner. She's seen him taking notes, too. She just can't see him as a trained killer. Of course, she never would've thought that of her innocent, gentle little brother, either.

"Maybe he just feels like he needs to keep an eye on you when Lucas is gone," Paige suggests.

"Whatever. He's a real jerk."

Paige smiles. Huntley is anything but. He's a good kid, kind, sweet, caring and very protective of the family. He and G do seem to clash, though. Paige figures it's probably just their age bracket that sets them at odds.

"Nice, G," her brother says with sarcasm. "Maybe it's your bubbly personality that puts him off."

She snorts at her brother, making Paige smile.

"So?" G prompts her brother.

"So what?"

"Are you gonna ask her out?" she presses.

"Not right now. I'm gonna take you for a patrol ride," he deflects, getting a snippy look from his little sister.

"Not funny," she says angrily.

"I'll leave you two at it," Paige says, excusing herself.

She walks to the house and heads straight to the bathroom. The bleeding has already let up some, which is a relief. Reagan has checked her numerous times for fevers and questioned her many other times about her stats.

She volunteers to help with dinner, but Reagan comes in and sends her away to rest. It draws confused looks from Hannah and Sue, but Reagan distracts them with medical mumbo-jumbo. Instead of helping in the kitchen, she goes to the music room to finish her drawing.

Sue walks in with an armload of towels that have been drying on the outside clothesline.

"Have you seen my sketchpad?" she asks.

"Um, no. I thought it was over there by the window," Sue tells her and sits on the sofa to fold her bounty.

"Let me help," she offers and sits next to her.

"You sure? Reagan was acting like you're not in good shape right now."

"Oh, I'm fine. Whatever it was…" she lies, the words bitter on her tongue. "I'm over it."

"Good," Sue says. "Thanks for the help. G was supposed to be helping me, but she took off somewhere. I'm learning with her that it's normal behavior. She's not into housework."

Paige chuckles and says, "Yes, I don't think she's a big fan of housework or anything that has to do with being in the house at all."

"No, she's a real tomboy. She made me chop off her hair again. It was just starting to grow! I don't think she knows she's a girl yet."

"I think you're right about that," Paige agrees. "She is cute, though. She makes me laugh."

"Yes, she's ornery as heck."

"And her brother's so quiet," Paige adds.

"Ying and yang," Sue concurs. "I'm really glad they're here, though. I'm glad my father finally brought his family here."

"I'm happy for you guys that you have more family now. It's great. They've been such a good addition to the family."

"I still can't believe he never told us, but I'm glad we finally got to meet them. It also clears up a lot of stuff in my mind, missing gaps in timeframes when I'd talk to Dad on the phone, his evasiveness."

She pauses, then starts folding again. Paige hands her one to put back into the basket.

"Why'd he do that, do you think?" Paige asks.

Sue shrugs. "Why do any of us do the things we do? Maybe he was ashamed. You see how Reagan reacted, how she still feels about him. It's not like we were going to roll out the red carpet and welcome him home, and that was before we knew about the other family. Grams would've been very disappointed."

"I'm sorry you had such a bad relationship with him," Paige sympathizes. She can't relate. She loved her father greatly, still does, and always will, even if he is gone to her forever.

"It's ok. I forgive him," she confesses softly.

"Really?"

"Yes. He's my father. He's the only one I have. I want us to all heal our relationships with him. Grandpa said he was not looking well again when he went up there. I don't want something to happen to him while he thinks we all hate him. Reagan will probably never come around, but I just want to move past everything."

"That's really mature."

Sue shakes her head and offers a sad smile, "Not really. We all do stupid things for love. If my dad loves Lucy, then I'm glad that he found love in his life. I don't think he ever loved my mother, not like I love Derek or like Grandpa loved Grams. I'm not saying he was relieved that she died, but I am happy for him that he was able to move on and find love."

"True. And that's a selfless way of seeing it."

"No, I just understand why he did what he did. I'm sure you do, too. We all do foolish things for love."

Paige swallows hard as a new ripple of guilt washes over her.

"Thanks for the help!" Sue announces cheerily as if she didn't just drop a bomb on her. She places the last, folded towel in the basket.

Paige excuses herself and heads upstairs to her room. She still doesn't find her notebook with her latest sketch. Perhaps Sam has seen it and mistook it for one of her drawing sketchpads. She searches Sam's desk, shuffling drawings around but carefully putting them back in order. The drawing on top catches her eye. It is of Simon. She has seen Sam's pictures of Simon before, but this one is different. It is a bisection of his face; one half depicted with lightness and joy, the other dark and something akin to sadness mixed with anguish. It is disturbing but also fascinating at the same time. Paige places the lightweight tissue paper over it again. Instead of drawing, she writes in her journal.

Later, the girls call for dinner, so she figures her search for her sketchpad will have to wait. She helps carry trays of food to the dining room and makes plates for the children. Cory walks through the back door in mid-conversation with his brother. They are loud and raucous and oblivious to everyone else in the space, as usual.

Their meal goes well, and the girls have gone out of their way. They made homemade pasta noodles and created ravioli with sausage, a multitude of colored peppers, garlic and red sauce from last year's store. They are getting ready for canning season, so she helped circulate the old jars to the next shelf over in the basement last week to make room for what is coming. For dessert, the girls have made peach cobbler, which Paige usually loves but doesn't partake. Her system is still in a funk and not back to normal.

"You all right?" Simon asks beside her.

"Yes," she answers, her eyes drifting across the table to Cory, who is watching them intently. She was so relieved when Parker finally left for the base. She'd applied a lot of avoidance tactics, except when he'd wanted to sit next to her during dinner. Gross.

"You didn't eat much. Perhaps I should do a blood sample," her brother suggests.

"She's fine," Reagan corrects him and shakes her head for good measure.

"But she could..."

"I said no," Reagan lays down the law. "She's fine. We don't need a blood sample. This is something that you can't understand, so just drop it."

Simon looks at Reagan and then her before finally saying, "Yes, ma'am."

A moment later, Paige looks back at Reagan again and gets a subtle nod from her. Then she glances at Cory, who is regarding her with even more curiosity. Luckily, he drops it, and Paige doesn't have to come up with a terrible lie. They finish dinner soon after, the kids clean up, and Hannah and Sue head to the kitchen to lay out articles for the start of their canning season. Paige helps the kids put away the washed and dried dishes. It makes the work go faster.

"I'm heading out for a walk," she tells Simon after the rooms have cleared, and the family has dispersed to their own activities.

"I'll take you," he offers.

"I actually just want to be alone for a while, hon'," she says, trying to ensure that her brother will not follow.

"Sure," he says with understanding. "I'll be in Herb's office for the next few hours studying if you need me. He wants me to look over the patient files from town. Also, he wants to go over the treatment of the Scarlet Fever cases that seem to be spreading."

"Happy studying," she quips, getting a smile.

"Have you seen Samantha? She should be in on this, too," he says, looking around.

"No, I think she might've gone for a ride with Huntley," she tells him. "I thought I heard them talking about doing that after dinner."

His brow wrinkles as if he is concerned for Sam's well-being.

"Don't worry, Simon. They'll be back soon, I'm sure."

He nods and says, "Don't go too far."

She smiles and kisses his cheek in compliance. Then she pulls on her sandals, a new addition to her footwear thanks to Cory. She also grabs a pale blue cardigan from the laundry room to ward off the evening air's chill. Then she heads straight for the wooded area behind the horse barn where she promised to meet Cory. He isn't there when she arrives, so Paige sits on a stump and waits for him. It gives her some time to think about what she wants to say.

Within a few minutes, he strides toward her through the darkening forest. "Sorry I'm late. Got detained by helping Doc."

"With what?" she asks but doesn't rise to greet him.

"We finished the brace appliance we made for Derek. We showed it to him. At first, he seemed a little pissed."

"Really?"

"Yeah, well, it's to be expected," Cory says, plucking a leaf from a low-hanging branch. "Guy like Derek, he doesn't want people fussing over him. But we talked him into trying it out. I think it's gonna work great. He was able to walk without his cane. Well, somewhat. It's gonna take some getting used to."

"That's so amazing, Cory," she says with genuine inflection. She's truly happy that Derek is going to be slightly more mobile now. He's been so depressed and angry lately. She was so worried about him.

He walks over and sits next to her. "Yeah, it is," he agrees and takes her hand in his.

Paige pulls away and says softly, "Don't do that."

He nods reluctantly and pulls something from behind his back, "I heard you were looking for this."

"Oh, great! Thanks," she says, taking her architectural drawing pad.

"I found it," he tells her with a smile.

"Wait, the one I was working on is gone. What the heck?" she asks, looking through it for the missing sketch she's been working on for the last month. It was of a small white cottage by the sea, a fantasy dream cottage. She'd always seen herself having a family someday and spending her summers on the beach in a tiny town where all the homes were small and quaint and cozy like the one she'd drawn.

"Hm," Cory says with a frown. "Must've got torn off by someone. I'll look for it later for you. Could be one of the little kids found it and took it to draw on."

"Probably," she says, thinking about the many little ones running around on the McClane farm. "It doesn't really matter. It wasn't that important." And it isn't. That silly little cottage on the beach fantasy is long since dead and gone, no hope for resuscitation.

Cory tucks her loose hair behind her ear.

"What's going on with you? What are you hiding?"

She doesn't know how he can tell that something is wrong, but apparently, Cory is more sensitive than she thought.

"I didn't want to tell you, but I feel like crap about not telling you."

His mouth turns down, and lines form at the corners of his deep brown eyes.

"Tell me what?"

"The other night in the shed?" she asks, getting a nod. "I had a miscarriage. I wasn't having girl problems. I made Reagan promise not to tell anyone."

"What?" he asks with a sharp hiss of shock. "But I thought…"

"Yeah, me, too," she agrees with wide eyes. "Reagan said the test must've been a false negative or something like that. I was pregnant this whole time."

"Jesus," Cory swears under his breath and looks at his feet. "Damn it, Paige. This shouldn't have happened."

"No kidding! You think I'm happy about it?"

"No, I mean we should've been married. That's not right."

She scoffs and offers a single laugh that comes off as sardonic and without humor. "We shouldn't have been screwing around in the first place. That was the problem."

"You're right," he agrees, nodding. "I should've forced you to marry me…"

"What? Cory, get real. This isn't two hundred years ago. I don't want to get married, and you know that."

"Doesn't matter what you want. What we did had consequences. It was wrong. People were hurt. The family, your brother, us. And now you've miscarried our baby."

"I know! I'm so stupid."

She looks away, and he says, "No, you're not. We just made a mistake, a lot of them, but none of it was your fault. If anything, it was mine. I'm the man of the situation. I shouldn't have had sex with you outside of marriage. It wasn't right, and I knew it but did it anyway because I wanted you so damn much. But this isn't your fault, and I don't want you blaming yourself. Women have miscarriages all the time. You've been under a lot of stress lately, too. That couldn't have been good for a pregnancy. Listen, I don't want you blaming yourself, you hear?"

He wraps an arm around her that Paige tries to shirk. However, Cory persists and pulls her close. She can feel the waterworks turning on again. She sniffs hard to prevent herself from crying and leans back. Cory gets down on one knee in front of her and pulls her forcefully into a full embrace. Then she's done for. The tears start again. He rubs her back soothingly and strokes her hair.

"Damn, I'm sorry I couldn't even be there for you. You shouldn't have had to go through that alone."

"I had Reagan," she says as she regains her composure and he pulls back again to look at her.

"That's not the same. You were pregnant because of what I did. That means I should've been there with you. It was my responsibility. You're my responsibility."

She vigorously shakes her head, "This doesn't change anything, Cory."

Paige scoots agilely around him and stands. She walks toward the edge of the woods where she can see the barns of the McClane farm. He comes up behind her and rests his hands on her shoulders, which makes her feel small and fragile in Cory's large grasp.

"Is everything ok now? You aren't having any complications or anything like that?"

"No, Reagan has been staying on top of the situation. I'm fine now."

"Were you in a lot of pain?"

"Not too much. It was mostly just scary," she admits as he massages her shoulders gently.

"I wish I could've been there for you, sweetheart."

She dislikes his use of endearments. It's better when he calls her a beanpole or Red. Things like sweetheart are just too intimate.

"I'm fine," she says, stealing herself and stepping out of his grasp. "Like I said. This doesn't change things. I still don't want to get married, and I am definitely never having kids."

"Have you told Simon?" he asks, ignoring her comments.

"No!" she whispers, frantic that someone could hear them. "And don't tell him, either. I don't ever want him to find out. Or anyone else. Reagan's the only one who knows, and I swore her to secrecy. I can only imagine what the family thinks of me already. I don't need this to add to it."

"They love you," he counters softly. "And I won't tell Simon. It would only further solidify his hatred of me right now. Plus, I don't want him to have to dwell on what we've done. He's been through a lot lately."

She'd like to know more about what he means, but she can hear the kids near the barns coming their way.

"We'd better leave and split up," she says, getting a deep scowl in return.

Cory pulls her gently to him, kisses the top of her head, then her closed mouth, and releases her.

"You go back first," he says, to which she nods. "And come and get me if you have any more problems, alright? If you have complications or anything, you come and get me no matter what."

"Fine," she agrees, knowing full-well that it's a lie.

Cory strokes her cheek, runs his thumb over her eyebrow, then kisses her there before releasing her again.

"Be careful," he says as she turns to go. "And get some rest."

She nods and walks quickly toward the barns, getting away just in time because Ari and Huntley are running toward her, probably in the middle of some game or another. It would be so nice to be young and carefree right now. Instead, her life has become a whirlwind of traumatic events, bleakness, and the heavy burden of lies. All she wants is some peace and quiet and a little cottage by the sea to rest her head at night and listen to the waves lapping at the shoreline.

Chapter Thirty
Sam

They returned to town again yesterday, nearly a week having gone by since their last battle. They've been treating patients non-stop. The men went on another ambush but were met with a lot more resistance this time, and many of their enemy escaped. They weren't too happy about that. The highwaymen are becoming more cautious and not revealing themselves.

Another attack occurred, this time on a small community they weren't even aware of closer to Nashville. They'd heard about the family's clinic by word of mouth, so the survivors came to them for help. Most of their patients from the last battle had already been cleared for release by her uncle and Grandpa, which made the addition of even more patients a little easier. Now the medical house across the street is full again, and the people in town had to open the smaller, double story home next to it, as well, to accommodate so many.

The men went last night again to hunt the highwaymen but did not find any running their usual routes on the usual roads. The family had a meeting about it, and most came to the conclusion that the highwaymen may be heading in another direction to avoid the confrontations with them. It is becoming a sore subject, although Sam is secretly glad they didn't skirmish with this enemy again. They frighten her more than any others they've come up against so far. Plus, the men are confiscating their weapons and vehicles when they defeat and kill them. They will want those back and the revenge that goes with it. Sam doesn't want to see anyone in her family get killed fighting these men. She fears she is about to lose people she cares deeply about.

382

She and her uncle are working today with some of the ill children from the Campbell Kids group. There are nine of them and two children from town who are also sick with Scarlet Fever.

"She's doing a lot better today," her uncle says, jotting down a notation on the little girl's chart.

Melora, who has been helping, says, "Yes, she is. I took her temperature last night after you guys left, and it was finally down."

"Good," he states. "Samantha, let's see if we can't get her on some solid foods for dinner today."

"Got it," she says, her face mask causing her to sweat underneath it. They are taking a lot of extensive precautions with these children and their sickness so that they don't spread it further around the town.

"I want the last two on broth," he states decidedly. "They aren't keeping much down, but if we can at least get some broth into them, it's better than nothing. This one and the three in the dining room can have solids. Some bread, a little meat, some soft, cooked vegetables. Whatever you can manage but no dairy or fruit."

"Yes, sir," she answers Uncle Scott. "I'll get right on it."

"Wash when you leave. Don't forget," he reminds her.

"Dr. Scott," Melora is saying as Sam leaves. "When do you think they'll be able to return to our house?"

Sam knows the answer is going to be a timeframe at least a week from now. She'd already discussed it with him before Melora arrived. She's been great, though. Helpful, kind, so tender and caring with the children. And they love her, too. Sam also believes that she may have a crush on her uncle. Sometimes Sam sees her looking at him as if she is interested. Her uncle does not seem to return the sentiment, however. Sam knows that his girlfriend was killed in the beginning. Perhaps it is not something he is able to get over just yet. Perhaps he never will.

She walks to the community building where they are preparing late day meals for the volunteers and the sick who are staying in town. The sheriff's wife is cooking with the help of many town volunteers. Sam orders the appropriate amount of plates for the sick children, and the volunteers begin loading them onto trays. They don't allow her to carry anything, though, and insist on doing it for her. She does, however, ensure that the volunteers know which children should receive which meals. Then she charts their food intake and leaves the files for her uncle, who is still working in another room with Melora. He's been staying in this housekeeping constant watch over the children. Sam is pretty sure Melora has never left once, either. She cares so much for all of the orphans that she and Hardy have taken under their wings. They both have huge hearts.

Sam leaves the medical house and heads to the clinic where the family who came to town with her is supposed to be meeting for their own dinner. Simon and Reagan are there along with John and a few of Robert's men, who are still living at the farm in Derek's house.

"Need any help?" she asks Reagan when she arrives. Her idol is cleaning her hands behind the building. Sam joins in to do the same.

"No, we're all done. I'm going to the town hall with John now, but everyone's been seen, and the patients have been cleared out. All you and Simon need to do is lock up."

"But I thought we were having dinner together," Sam complains.

"Sorry, kiddo," she says. "John and I will eat later. We've got some stuff to go over. Dave's in town with some of his men, and we're making plans."

"I didn't know they were coming to town tonight," she says. "Who all came?"

"Your new boyfriend," Reagan teases.

"He's not my boyfriend," Sam whispers uncomfortably. "I don't know why everyone's always saying that."

"Seems that more than one person has seen you kissing him. If you don't want people to come to their own conclusions, then maybe you ought to stop kissing him." Reagan smiles and bumps her shoulder against Sam's. Then she continues on to say, "Unless you like kissing him, of course."

Sam doesn't know what to say to this. She's never sure of herself around Reagan, who always speaks so bluntly.

"Do you?" she prompts.

Sam offers an impish shrug in answer. It's the best she can give because she doesn't know how to feel about Henry. Other than the McClane family, Sam has never fully trusted any other men. But now she feels like that about Henry. He watches out for her when they're on his farm. He is protective and kind and considerate of her.

384

She hardly wants for anything when she's living there, and he goes out of his way to ensure her comfort. And now he says that he's in love with her. Sam really doesn't know what to think of it all.

"Do you love him, Sam?" Reagan asks, uncharacteristic of her.

She swallows hard and frowns. "I don't know. No, I don't think so. Maybe. This is all so confusing."

"Sounds like you'd better figure it out soon. You don't want to string poor Henry along if you aren't interested in him, if your heart still lies elsewhere."

Sam's eyes nervously dart to Reagan's. She hopes that her feelings and intentions are not so easy to read because she's been working so hard at being just the opposite.

In the next moment, Simon jogs over to them. His lab coat is still on, but he's carrying his sniper rifle. It comes off as strange looking.

"We've got a problem," he says preemptively.

Reagan turns to see him, "What's going on?"

He is slightly panting. "I just came back from the tower at the main gate. A guard there needed help with an infected cut on his arm."

"And he couldn't come to the clinic?" Sam asks.

He shakes his head with frustration and says, "That's not the problem. Look, we're leaving. Someone in town, someone working the patrol on the fence, spotted a drone. He shot at it but missed. John and some of Dave's men and I are going out. We have to find out who's behind the drone. If we spot it, it could lead us to them."

"Oh, dear," Sam frets with genuine fear.

Reagan goes for a much angrier response, "Wait a damn minute. That's only a few of you. What if you run into a big group of them like last week?"

"We're not going to attack if we do," he explains as he turns to go. She and Reagan follow after him. "This is strictly recon. We'll come back for reinforcements."

He shrugs out of his doctor's smock and hands it to Reagan, who scowls. Sam understands how she feels. This could be disastrous. By the time they reach the men, John is already on a four-wheeler, and Simon hops onto the back of another. One of Dave's men rides behind him. Henry is going with them and will follow in his truck with two more men. He walks over to her before joining his men. Sam can feel Simon's eyes on them.

"Be careful while I'm gone," Henry warns and touches her arm.

"Yep. Sure will," she says, trying to appear casual and blasé about the situation. Behind Henry, Simon revs the engine on his four-wheeler. Henry tosses a look of contempt his way and turns to leave.

"You guys be careful, too!" she calls after him, to which he tips an invisible hat.

She glances toward Simon, noting the sneer on his handsome face. This can't go on. She has to put an end to it. Reagan is right. Henry doesn't deserve her aloofness, and Simon doesn't really deserve anything at all from her. He has no interest in her romantically and is only showing her attention and kissing her lately to force her to lose any budding interest in Henry. He's trying to manipulate her since she stood up to him. She's not as stupid as he obviously thinks she is.

"Let's eat," Reagan states angrily and stomps off as her husband drives away, fully expecting Sam to follow, which she does.

To ease the burden of feeding so many extra mouths right now with the new citizens, care of the highwaymen, the sick children and the wounded victims, Hannah and Sue have prepared meals for them to take to town for today and tomorrow until they return home. Depending on how it goes this evening on this recon mission, the men may not be returning for a while. They may need to go back out soon for more than just some reconnaissance.

"What are we having?" Sam asks, unpacking the cooler that John probably placed on the front porch of the practice.

"Who cares? I wouldn't even be eating if I wasn't breastfeeding," Reagan complains and takes a seat on one of the rockers.

"Yum, chicken salad sandwiches," Sam comments. "I love these. Sue always adds walnuts and apple pieces from the apple trees on the farm."

Reagan just nods distractedly.

"Here," Sam instructs, handing her a sandwich wrapped in paper. "Eat. Charlie needs your milk. You need your strength. And…"

"Charlie? What's that supposed to mean?"

"Charlie, you know, short for Charlotte?" Sam says with a bright smile toward her big sister.

"Where'd you get that?"

"John. He and Huntley keep calling her that. Well, I think they mostly call her that when you're not around."

Reagan scoffs and says, "They better stop calling her that. She's gonna grow up to be a tomboy."

"Like you? What's so wrong with that?"

"Everything," she jokes and begins eating.

They enjoy their meal in silence, savoring the flavors and aromas of home. Sue has packed them herb-infused water in canning jars that hits the spot. Her greenhouse has been completely rebuilt and is back up and running since the tornado demolished most of it. They also built a new chicken coop, which is even bigger. Paige drew up the plans for both buildings. Sue now has solar panels on her greenhouse, which will help in the winter with supplying a small amount of heat to it.

"Are those butterscotch bars?" Reagan asks, always the dessert junky.

Sam just nods and hands her one. "Did you eat all of your meal or are you skipping to dessert? Charlie's never gonna grow if you supply her with breastmilk filled with sweets and sugar."

"Shut it," Reagan warns with a grin. "I'm the doctor, remember?"

Sam smiles in return and also helps herself to dessert.

"Have you given any more thought to studying more like your uncle wants you to and becoming a doctor?" Reagan asks.

"Nah, I don't think it's for me. Don't get me wrong. I like helping our patients, but I just don't want to do this forever."

Reagan nods and says, "I understand. Hell, this isn't exactly what I signed up for, either. I thought my field of study was going to be modern medicine…with modern technology and science. Not this survivalist medicine bullshit."

"But you're good at it," Sam points out. Reagan snorts. "I think studying further would take up too much time from the other things I like better. I'll continue to help my uncle, but I don't know if I want to become a doctor, too."

"That's fine. You weren't meant to be a doctor…or probably not even a nurse. You're good at it, but it would eventually squash your artistic side. Do what makes you happy, kiddo. Life's too short."

"You can say that again," Sam concurs with a wink. "I think Melora is really interested in studying medicine, though."

"Really? She's never said anything about it. Of course, she never talks all that much when I'm around."

"It's not you," Sam tells her. "She's just really shy. I think she's been through a lot, something really bad."

"And you haven't?"

Sam swallows the lump of emotion in her throat, suppressing the nightmares of her past, and says, "I had you guys, though. It helped."

"I don't know about that. I think it was Simon that helped more than us."

This isn't something Sam wants to hear, so she looks away.

"Are you finished?" she asks in a friendly manner. "I'll clean up if you want to go in the back and rest, get off your feet for a while," Sam offers smoothly, hoping Reagan will drop the topic.

"I think I'm going to walk back down to the town hall and talk with the sheriff. Derek wanted me to go over a few things with him."

"He seems to be doing a little better since Cory and Grandpa finished that brace."

"He may never fully recover back to where he was before, but he can at least be mobile without a walker or a cane."

"That's better than being in a wheelchair, too," Sam adds with hope alive in her heart for her adopted older brother.

Reagan just nods and looks away. "You sure you got this? I can help."

"No, I'm fine. Come back later to the house and sleep if you want," Sam suggests.

"No, I think John and me are going to sleep in the medical house upstairs tonight before we head home tomorrow morning. I have a few patients over there I want to keep a close watch on.

Besides, your uncle and Simon are sleeping in the other house with you. It isn't that big."

"True," Sam admits. "If this all keeps up, we're going to need to build a doctors' dorm."

Reagan chuckles and nods before leaving. Sam cleans up after their mess, making sure to pack away food for Simon and John for later, hopefully not very much later. She wants them to come home safely and soon.

"Samantha," her uncle says behind her as she finishes washing their dinner plates.

"Hey, Uncle Scott," she greets him with a smile. "Finished for the night?"

He shakes his head and chuffs, "Not even close. I just came to see if there was food for us or if I should go to the town hall for a meal again."

"No, no!" she interjects. "Sue made sure to pack a ton. There's plenty for you."

"And Melora? She's staying the night over there with me, too."

"Oh, really?" she asks with a sly grin and a lot of implication.

He chuckles this time. "Samantha, I am working. She's a good assistant when you aren't with me. But neither of us can work with no gas in the tank."

She smiles and says, "Uh-huh, whatever you say. Here, let me get you a bag to carry stuff back to the house to share."

Sam leaves him in the waiting room and rushes to find a bag. She doesn't come up with one but does find a basket in the storage room. Then she packs him sandwiches, two thermoses of vegetable soup for later if they get hungry on the midnight shift, apples, and cheese slices. She also places inside the basket two small containers of Sue's homemade trail mix that contains walnuts, dried berries, and salted sunflower seeds.

"This is great, honey. Thanks," he says and kisses her forehead.

"So you aren't coming back to the house tonight to sleep?"

He shakes his head, sending a strand of dark hair over his forehead. "I don't think that's a good idea. Some of the children need constant care. I'd hate to leave them in someone else's care in case they get even worse. Two of them are spiking fevers. Oh, hey, by the way, thanks for getting them all fed. That was helpful. We need to keep the food and liquid to them."

"No problem," she says.

He grins, touches the side of her cheek gently, and says, "I'm so proud of you, Samantha."

Sam's eyes well with tears. "I love you, Uncle Scott."

"Ditto, honey."

He hugs her close, balancing the basket in his other arm. Then he pulls back and kisses her forehead.

"Are you going back to the house now? I'd like to know that you are so that I don't have to worry about you while I'm at work."

She nods. "Yes, I'm tired tonight. I think I'm going to turn in soon."

"Shower first. Too many pathogens that we're dealing with lately."

"Right," she agrees.

"And go straight there now, so I know where you are," he orders more firmly.

Sam rolls her eyes and chuckles, "Uncle Scott, I've been living without you for four years. I think I got this."

He narrows his eyes and says, "That may well be, young lady, but I'm in charge of your care now."

"All right. I'll go home now. Like I said, I'm tired. Plus, I don't want to crash your date with Melora."

He gives a slightly less patient look but eventually grins. Sam laughs, though.

"Not a date. Just taking care of patients," he corrects.

"Too bad you don't have a nice bottle of wine and some candles."

"Ha, well, we better hope the solar panels hold up better tonight. We were working by candlelight last night."

"Ooh, romantic!"

He shakes his head and smiles, "I'm leaving on that note."

Sam laughs again and watches him go. She's so lucky to have him back in her life. She wishes that every person who has lost everything and everyone they love could reunite with even just one family member again. Having him in her life again has been a blessing. Even if he is driving her nuts lately with his hovering. The only time that he doesn't hover is when he knows she is on the McClane farm. Unfortunately, that doesn't agree with her anymore.

Sam closes the clinic, locking the door behind her since there isn't a single patient staying in it tonight for a change. Every patient is being kept across the street in the medical house and the one next to it. She walks down the street to their temporary house, wiping her brow twice from the humidity and heat. Once she arrives and lets herself in with the key Simon left her, Sam checks it just to be sure that nobody is already there or up to no good. Since the highwaymen, Simon's been locking it. Then she heads upstairs to her bedroom and strips out of her clothing. Tomorrow, she'll scald them in boiling water behind the clinic. But for tonight, Sam just wants her own shower, minus the high temps. When she's finished, she dresses in a pale pink tank top and sweatpants that have seen better days. She goes back downstairs to the living room and works on a sketch she's been doing of baby Charlotte. They have to preserve their memories without the aid of modern electronics like cameras for now, so this is the only way she knows how to do so. Last week, she drew one of her uncle, and the week before one of her friend Courtney and her new husband. They keep her busy over at Dave's compound.

Without the aid of lighting in the house and just the use of a single oil lamp, Sam's eyes grow weary, and the next thing she knows, Simon is kneeling beside her on the floor shaking her shoulder. It startles her awake.

"Simon?" she asks in a rush of disorientation.

"Yes, it's me."

"Is everything…is everyone…" she asks groggily.

He nods and says, "Everyone's fine. We're back."

Sam clears her throat and sits upright, "What happened?"

"We saw the drone. Took us a while to track it down, but we found it," he tells her. "We had to split up. Then it got even harder once the sun had set, but we managed to find it."

"And?"

"It didn't lead us back to their place, but it was heading toward the farm. John ordered it shot down. It's a dead-end lead, but at least they won't find the farm."

"Do you think they know about the farm already and have been spying on it?"

Sam rubs her nose and stretches, which draws Simon's attention to her chest. Her watch shows the time of two a.m.

"No, I doubt it," Simon answers.

Sam shivers, so he pulls his black hoodie off in a flash and wraps it around her.

"Thanks," she says, trying not to read anything into his kind gesture, which for Simon, that's all it is and all it will ever be. "Is anyone going back out?"

"John has some men patrolling the area to make sure nothing happens, but as far as I know, we're done for the night."

"Good," she admits. There is a long pause as they stare at one another, Sam trying to wake fully and Simon doing whatever it is he does when he looks at her like he is. "Did you eat? I brought food here for you."

"Thanks, but I think I'll pass," he says. "I'm just heading up to…bed." Simon's voice cracks slightly, and his gaze falls to her mouth. "I'll let you get back to sleep, too. Sorry to wake you."

"No, I'm glad you did," Sam tells him, swinging her legs over, causing him to stand and step back from her. "I'm going to bed, too." She scoops up her art supplies and slides around Simon. "G'night."

Sam glances over her shoulder to see him standing there looking down at his upturned hands, which seem to be shaking.

"Simon?"

His head jerks her way, "What? Oh, yeah. Good night. Sleep well."

"I will now that you guys are all back safely."

He chuffs, offers a lopsided grin, and a nod. "Get some rest."

"You, too."

She leaves him, going to her own room and tucking in for the rest of the night. In the room across the hall, Sam can hear him moving around. Then the house falls silent. Sam tosses and turns for a while. Sleep will not come to her again, so she rises and lights her lantern. Staring at her sketch pad doesn't help, either. Sam can't take this anymore. She goes downstairs and finds a notebook in the home office, left there by whatever family used to own this house. She takes it back to her room and flips it open to the first page.

The blue notebook with the white flowers on the front must've belonged to the mother who used to live here. There is a

392

grocery list with the usual items like milk, eggs, a loaf of bread and the like. The next page is a list of errands that includes picking up dry-cleaning, shopping for kneepads for her daughter who must've played volleyball, and buying sweatbands and tennis balls for "Nick," a person that Sam believes must've been her son. The farther Sam goes into the notebook, the more ominous the lists become. The next page reveals a different kind of list that looks more along the lines of someone preparing for a camping trip. After that, it becomes increasingly portentous. Lists of bottled water, making sure their children's vaccinations are up to date, medical supplies like antibiotic cream and bandaging. Then there is a page that bodes even worse. She has made a note of the family members they are going to try and pick up on their way out of town and who they will not be able to fit in their mini-van. She has crossed off some names. The final page that was written on is directions to a campground and the names of their friends who are going there. It is mostly thoughts of the person who wrote it, though, because there are doodles of flowers and squiggly lines on the sides and the space at the top. It makes Sam feel depressed peering into what was probably the last glimpse into a family's life before they abandoned their home to go wherever they went. She wonders what happened to this family. Did they make it to the campground? Are they together now and surviving? Are they even still alive?

Sam quickly flips to a blank page and begins writing. She pours out her heart saying what she needs to express. When she is done, tears have fallen, but she feels slightly better.

Folding the paper in half, Sam sneaks to Simon's bedroom and watches him sleep a moment. He is on his back dead to the world, one arm flung above his head in a carefree manner. She removes his hoodie, folds it and places it on the nightstand beside him. Then she lays the paper on top so that he is sure to see it.

Simon groans softly in his sleep and turns his head toward her, eyes still closed. Sam reaches for and pushes his hair back from his forehead. He stirs slightly and rolls to his side, exposing his back to her.

Sam creeps slowly out of his room and back to her own where she packs her belongings in her bag. Then she goes downstairs and out into the cool night air to find Henry.

Chapter Thirty-one
Cory

"Thanks for breakfast," he says and kisses the top of her head.

"You're welcome, Cory," Evie Johnson says with a gentle smile as she clears away the dishes from the small dining table in their kitchen.

"And thanks for being there when I needed someone to talk to," Cory adds.

"That's what friends are for," she says and gives him a long hug. "Be safe."

"I will. I'm going on a patrol ride from here back to the farm, and then I'm headed to town later to go on another run with John and Simon."

"Want me to send some of the guys over to the farm?" she offers kindly.

"No, Derek and the others will hold down the farm. Luke's there now, too. They'll be fine."

"Be careful later then," she says, swiping a loose cluster of blonde hair from her sweaty forehead. She'd been in the middle of canning in the back yard when he'd rode up this morning on his horse hoping to catch her. Evie frowns up at him and says, "I don't like these people, Cory. They remind me of the kind that killed our family up north. Same type."

He nods with understanding and says, "We will. We're taking extra precautions. Soon, we'll figure out where their main division is coming from, and we'll finish this."

"I heard my brother saying that you all found clusters of people living in homes in the woods around the area. Do you think that was them?"

"Yeah, probably. Very likely actually," Cory explains. "We think these places in the woods that we keep finding- like the other two that some of Robert's men found again last week closer to Nashville- are like their outposts, their sentry posts or something. Then the person in charge can radio them to run routes and attack different places that their scouts find like the condo village and Dave's compound."

"Why's that? How did you come to that conclusion?"

Cory says, "Because when we pinned the different locations on Doc's map, they made a big circle, probably twenty miles in circumference. It encompasses a huge amount of space. They just missed Pleasant View, but it goes out as far as the outskirts of Nashville and Clarksville. Somewhere in that circle has to be the main headquarters. Once we find that, we coordinate with Robert McClane, he sends men, we take them out."

"Sounds awfully simple."

The skepticism in her soft voice makes Cory smile.

"It will be. That is if we ever find the damn place."

She mimics his smile and touches his arm gently. "Just be careful. These people, these men...they're pure evil."

"I know, but we'll be fine," he assures her.

She hugs him again and says, "Good luck."

"Thanks, but I've got my weapon. That's good enough luck for me," he jokes.

"I didn't mean good luck with the highwaymen," she corrects.

"I know," he says with a wink.

He leaves a moment later and runs his horse on a quick patrol skirting a few miles beyond where they usually ride just to be sure that the highwaymen are not encroaching. Then he hurries back to the farm as the family is finishing their own morning meal. Cory washes up in the mudroom and joins Derek and Doc in his office to finalize plans. His brother is also there, bent over the desk already looking at the map.

"Chet's coming with you," Derek informs him.

"Cool," Cory replies. "Is he bringing an ATV?"

"Yeah, you'll both go on ATV still like we planned, but I'm sending you towards Clarksville instead," Derek says. "Someone said there was activity out that way yesterday on the freeway."

"Alright," Cory says with a nod.

"John's going to meet you," Doc puts in.

"Yes, sir," Cory complies.

Derek tells him where to set up camp to wait for John. Then they go over the contingency plans, communications, and what's expected. The meeting concludes, and Derek heads off to find Luke, who will stay on the farm to work with Derek and Kelly in case of a problem here.

"Cory," Doc says behind him as he's making his exit from the office, too. "Stay a moment, son. I'd like to speak with you."

"Yes, sir. Of course," Cory says and rests his rifle in the corner behind the door and closes it, but not before his brother winks at him from the hall and slices his finger across his own neck to signify that Cory is in deep shit.

"Take a seat," Herb offers a chair and sits opposite him on one of the leather sofas.

"What is it, sir?"

"This matter with Paige..."

Cory hangs his head a moment, not sure how he wants to deal with this. The only conclusion he can deduce is that he doesn't want to deal with it at all, not with Herb.

"Yes, sir?"

"She and Simon are my responsibility, in a roundabout way, if you will," Herb explains as he sips his hot beverage.

"I can understand why you'd feel that way."

"Are you making any progress, son? Seems to me that your intentions are honorable, but that she doesn't want to get married? Am I understanding this correctly?"

"Yes, sir. That's about it. Although her brother would say that my intentions are less than honorable."

"That's understandable," Herb states. "She's his sister. He feels a lot of responsibility for her. He wants to make sure she's safe and healthy and taken care of in the best ways he knows how to provide. You've stepped on his toes, so to speak."

396

Cory nods, shame setting in as if he hadn't consumed enough of it already.

"What steps are you taking to improve this situation you've made for yourself?"

He has to hand it to him. Herb can be frank when he wants to be. He is definitely laying the full brunt of the situation at Cory's feet, deservedly so. It is entirely his fault that this all happened. He knew better. He knew what he was doing, what he was getting himself into, and he took the wrong path. He just couldn't resist his own temptations.

"I'm working on my relationship with Simon. Trying to earn his trust. It hasn't been easy."

"No, I'm sure it won't be, either," Doc concurs with a nod. "You have a long row to hoe there, I'm afraid. And Paige?"

"I have a plan. It's taking me a little longer to make this one come to fruition, but I'm working on it. With everything that's been going on around here with these highwaymen idiots, my situation with her has come to a standstill. I'd like to have more free time for my plan, but that would take time away from helping the family."

Herb nods, sighs heavily, and says, "I understand. Courtship is quite a bit different now than it used to be, as well. Fear can drive us to be too cautious sometimes. She is likely worried about this affecting her brother, as well. She lived for quite a long time without anyone but her two friends. Trusting people is going to take an exceptionally huge effort with Paige. She was off-putting and rather withdrawn when she first arrived on my farm. I'm glad that she's come around so well. I can only imagine what horrors she must've witnessed while living on the road all that time. But, I do enjoy her company and believe she is an added benefit to our farm and the community. Her fears and distrusts are something that she will have to overcome on her own. If she truly has feelings for you, she'll eventually stop trying to run away from those feelings and learn to adapt. Tomorrow is not promised to any of us."

"No, sir," Cory agrees and shakes his head with a frown of understanding. "I will make this right, though. I give you my word on that account."

"Good. That's what I want to hear," Herb states. "I believe that you are a good man, Cory. You have honor and value and a place in this family. Your mother and father would be very proud of the man you've become."

Cory swallows the lump of sudden emotion in his throat. Doc is tugging at his heartstrings. Yanking, pulling and rendering would be a more suitable description. He tries not to think of his mom and dad too much. It hurts.

"Thank you, sir," he manages to say.

"You'll do the right thing. I have confidence in you and your decisions as a dutiful, conscientious man."

"Yes, sir," Cory answers.

"You'd better get ready now," Herb says and stands, concluding their meeting.

He walks over to Cory and offers a handshake, to which Cory complies. Then Herb pulls him in and embraces him warmly, surprising Cory that he has so much strength. He pats his back twice and finally releases him. Cory doesn't even hesitate. He collects his gun and gets out of there before more feelings get filleted and old wounds reopened.

Hannah hands him a bag of food for his backpack, then hugs him goodbye as if he is going off to war in a foreign land.

"Don't worry, Hannie," he says. "I'll be back soon, probably by tomorrow morning."

She slides her hand up his arm until she reaches his face where she cups her small palm against his whisker-filled cheek.

"Take care of Kelly for me," Cory says in a light tone.

Hannah smiles and nods as Kelly comes into the kitchen. His brother punches his shoulder.

"Having fun?" Kelly teases, knowing full-well what just occurred in Doc's office.

"Time of my life. Can't you tell?"

Kelly laughs and says, "You ready?"

"Yeah, I just wanna' say goodbye to…some people before I split," he says with zero finesse.

"She's in the rose garden," Kelly answers, knowing who Cory means.

He nods and tips a salute to his brother. Cory finds her easily enough in the rose garden sitting on one of the faded white cast iron benches. The morning sun is hitting her in profile causing her red hair to look like actual flames. She has it down and loose, which is how he prefers it, instead of pulled back. The roses are in their final bloom of the season, according to something he overheard Sue discussing the other day, and the flowers' colors and scents surround her as she reads her book. There are even yellow roses climbing the white wooden trellis behind her.

"Hi," he says as he approaches so as not to startle her. She looks up and actually offers a smile. Paige is wearing a white tank top and pale yellow cardigan paired with blue-jean shorts. Her long legs are tanned from the summer sun and working outside. "Watcha' reading?"

"Good morning," she says. "Where were you?"

Cory takes a deep breath and answers honestly, "Visiting with the Johnsons."

"Oh," she replies and watches her smile fade.

"I needed to return a tool to Mr. Johnson," he says. It is the truth. They borrowed one of his tools that they needed for fence repair until theirs can be fixed. Guilt starts in on him, so he comes clean. "And I also wanted to visit with Evie."

This gets her full attention. She looks like she's clenching her teeth together. Her feathers are ruffled.

"I needed to talk to her about something," he explains.

"What did you need to talk to her about?"

He shrugs and takes a seat next to her, causing Paige to swing her legs over and place them on the ground.

"Nothing important. Girl stuff," he attempts a joke. It doesn't work because she chuffs. "You're not jealous, are you? I mean, it wasn't like that. I…"

"No, of course not. We're not together. We don't have any sort of a commitment to each other. Why should I care who you visit?"

"You may feel that way, but I don't. I'm fully committed to you, whether you want it or not."

She sighs and frowns a second later.

"I just came out to say goodbye. I've gotta go."

Her gray eyes flit nervously to his, "Where?"

"I'll be back. Don't worry. Meeting John and your brother to check on some things in Clarksville."

"Another raid on the highwaymen?"

He shrugs and offers up a lie to spare her from the concern he sees growing on her face, "Nah, just patrol type stuff. How are you feeling?"

"Oh, fine. I'm fine. Well, be careful."

He stands, and Paige follows.

"We will. Stay close to the house while I'm gone, ok?"

She shakes her head and argues, "I'm fine."

"I mean it, Paige. They're using drones. We've shot down two of them. They could very easily find the farm using those. If they do, you'd better believe they're gonna hit us, the Reynolds and the Johnson family. These farms would look like paradise from a sky view. Especially to people like these assholes. They'd rob and kill all of you. Stay close to the house," he reiterates. "Luke's staying and so is Derek and Kel. Don't stray. And definitely don't go into the woods."

She nods, her fair eyebrows pinched together with worry. Cory pulls her carefully into his arms to offer an embrace. He is very concerned that those men will find this place while he's gone.

"Listen to Kelly. We have contingency plans in place if the farm is ever overtaken. Listen to my brother when I'm not here. Stick to the plans he issues. It's the only way I'll be able to find you if all hell breaks loose."

"It won't," she says against his chest.

Cory leans her away from him and presses a soft kiss to her closed mouth. She doesn't return it, but she also doesn't pull away or protest. He'll take anything he can get. It's progress.

He kisses her forehead and turns to go.

"Be careful," Paige calls softly.

Cory turns and gives her a wink before leaving to go pick up Chet next door. They take their four-wheelers to Clarksville and await John in the abandoned Home Depot, a place they've deemed safe many times over during their travels to the city. It's also a place they've nearly wiped out of supplies which they store at the farm in the top of the horse barn and on the racks and shelves in the back of the equipment shed.

"I'm gonna take a look around. I need some door knobs and hinges," Cory tells Chet, who agrees to stay on lookout.

He does a quick sweep of the store and finds a few of the things he needs. Most people are scavenging for dehydrated food products or packets of seeds. Shopping for granite countertops and a sub-z fridge have been put on the back burner for most people for now.

John and Simon show up a few minutes after he exits the store and has stashed his loot in the pockets of the leather saddlebags on the ATV.

"What's the plan, sir?" Cory asks John.

His friend runs a hand through his blonde hair and says, "We heard about a raid on some people holed up just outside of town here. K-Dog sent two men over last night to talk with the survivors."

"Were they living in a community?" Chet asks.

John nods and explains, "Yeah, I guess they had about a dozen homes surrounded by fencing like the condo community. They just didn't have the firepower to keep them off for very long. Only two families made it out. Now K-Dog and Paul are taking them in."

"What'd they find out from the survivors?" Cory asks.

"The usual. It was the highwaymen again. Apparently, they weren't deterred from this behavior by our resistance at the condo community or our planned attacks on them. They've moved on to terrorize other people. This time, though," John states with a smile, "we might just have a better idea of where they're from."

"How's that?" Cory prods.

"One of the victims who survived said he recognized two of the men."

"Seriously?" Chet asks with the same surprise Cory feels.

John nods and answers, "Yep. Said he recognized him from t.v. Well, from before this all happened. Guy was some big car dealer, owned a bunch of huge dealerships around Tennessee."

"A fuckin' car dealer?" Cory asks, incredulous.

"Marchiano, Saviano, or something like that, something Italian was his last name," John tells them. "They couldn't remember."

Cory notices that Simon is silent during this interaction. He has a very distracted and rather pissed off look on his face. He just wonders if he's done something to make Simon mad again or if maybe he is just anxious to get this thing with the highwaymen over and done with. Cory couldn't agree more.

"This guy saw him and recognized him?" Chet asks.

"Yes, he hid in the tree line and spied through his binoculars on the highwaymen as they raided their small village and took whatever they needed."

"Assholes," Chet comments.

Cory asks, "So the television car salesman is the leader of the highwaymen? No wonder they all drive such nice, new-looking vehicles. The guy had access and keys to all the vehicles on his lots. Whatever wasn't stolen in the beginning, he just drove off the lots. A car dealer, though? Un-fucking-believable."

"And get this, it gets even better," John elucidates. "There was another guy there, another leader type shouting orders."

"An ambulance chaser?" Cory jokes.

John chuckles and says, "Worse. A local politician, some senator douche-nozzle. So, yeah, probably a former ambulance chaser, too, since most politicians were lawyers of some kind or another before they got into politics. Also, probably the reason our government was so screwed up."

"This sounds like the start of a bad joke," Chet says with a look of disbelief. "A used car salesman and a senator walk into a bar…"

Cory chuckles and questions, "No doubt. Wonder if they were there the night they hit Paul and K-Dog's condos?"

"Could be," John says.

"Or maybe they were watching and listening on radios from far out," Cory suggests.

John nods and says, "Possible. Let's head over and check out the scene for ourselves."

They drive in the truck and leave the ATV's hidden to conserve fuel. When they arrive, it is obvious that the scene of destruction and murder has been performed by the same men they've been tracking. Only what they needed was taken; food, clothing, fuel.

"So, we're thinking if these two idiots are in on this together, then they may be running it out of their personal homes," John says as they step over dead bodies to get back to their vehicle.

"We find out where they lived before the fall, then we might have a chance at taking them out," Cory says.

Simon is still quiet, pensive and wearing a deadly expression.

"Right," John says. "We've come up with a theory, Dave and I. They may be running this from two different home bases. Then they have the small base camps around the area to work it, like the cabins in the woods we found. We've had spies on those places since we found them, and not one person has returned to them. That tells me that they're not too worried about shelter because they abandoned them. It was worth more to them not to be discovered and taken out than it was to stay and hold onto their properties."

"It also tells us that they have somewhere else to go when they do get found," Cory adds, getting nods of agreement from Chet and John. He's not sure Simon is even listening.

"They run a very tight ship, smooth operations, and are tactically smart. Somewhat. They don't necessarily have the best-trained soldiers, but they have a heck of a lot of firepower to make a mess when they need to," John says.

"We need to question the prisoner again," Cory says.

"That kid's too scared to talk," John says, shaking his head. "None of the others would. He's all we've got left, but I'm not putting down a teenager. Especially one whose only sin so far as we can tell, is being lumped in with a bunch of morons and thieves."

"He could be a murderer," Cory reminds him.

John sighs hard, "I know. But he might not be, too. He could've been a scout, an aide to the men on the line. We just don't know enough to make a final call about his fate. Plus, Herb's not too keen on killing a kid."

Cory nods with understanding.

John continues as they board the truck again, "This thing is looking more and more like a two-headed snake, run from two different command centers. It explains how they have so many people going on so many different routes in the area. We find one head and chop it off, it might make it easier to find the other."

"And we can encourage the first prick to talk if we find him," Cory adds. "What if there are more than two leaders?"

John shakes his head and says, "I'm surprised there are two, to begin with. We may be wrong on that. Perhaps one or the other is simply the second-hand man. Most people don't like sharing power."

"If it works to their benefit, they might," Chet says.

"True, but more than two seems like too many chiefs in the mix," John counters.

"Maybe the senator's in charge, and the car dealer prick is the one supplying the men, weapons, and vehicles to do the dirty work," Cory offers up.

John nods, "Maybe. That's a good theory. But why would they need the senator then? Why keep him in on it?"

"Maybe he's the gun runner instead of the car dealer," Chet says.

They all nod. There is a lot of theorizing about the highwaymen, but at least they now know that two men are likely running the group and who they are.

"Let's head back to town and ask around about these two men," John says as he drops them back at their ATV's. "Someone's bound to know something."

They follow the pick-up truck back to town, and Cory is left puzzling out a lot in his mind during the silent trip. He wonders about Simon's quiet disposition today, the highwaymen and their bizarre leaders, and mostly about Paige and his plan to win her over. If it fails, he's not sure what else he could do to convince her to marry him.

Immediately, they begin questioning people from town, the newly taken in survivors of other attacks, and the injured men and women in the two medical houses. None of them are as familiar with the leaders as the man that K-Dog has already questioned. Cory heads to the library to talk to Mrs. Browning, who seems to know everything about everyone. As usual, Cory finds her behind the counter in her freshly pressed, navy blue cotton dress, pantyhose, low, conservative heels and pearls. She is ever the consummate professional.

"And what can I do for you today, Mr. Alexander?" she asks in a courteous tone.

"I need to find articles in local newspapers or magazines about a few men, men who we think might have something to do with the recent attacks."

"Oh, dear. Those are quite tragic, aren't they?" she asks, her hand pressed to her heart. She nods, smooths her hair as if a wisp of it is out of place, which, of course, it is not, and smiles agreeably.

"Since you brought me a load of new books last week, I'd be happy to help. Who are these men?"

"A former senator from Tennessee and a local car dealer, something Italian, maybe starts with an 'S'."

"Let me get to work on it. It's going to take a while, so you don't have to wait. I don't have computer access any longer, but I'll do what I can. Many of our periodicals were destroyed in the fire, but I managed to save quite a bit."

"Thanks, Mrs. B."

She sends him an intolerant look, to which Cory smirks and offers a thumbs-up. She shakes her head and leaves.

Cory also leaves but runs into the blonde who teaches school and came with a group of the survivors. He can never remember her damn name, though.

"Hi, Cory," she greets.

He sends a cordial wave instead.

"Off to school?" he asks, hoping she has her hands full with the twelve or so kids on her heels.

"Yes, would you like to join us?"

"Ha! No, thanks. I didn't like school even when I had to go."

She smiles and laughs as Tessa breaks free of the group and holds her small hands up to him. He picks her up, of course.

"Hey, kid," he says as she hugs him tightly around the neck.

"Cory," she returns.

He shoots the blonde teacher an inquisitive glance.

"Yes, she's talking more and more. Aren't you, Tessa? You're doing so great, sweetie."

Tessa buries her face in his neck and refuses to speak further.

"Come with me now, Tessa. Come with Rachel," the blonde says, sparking his memory. Rachel is her name. "Professor Rex is going to tell you guys a story today, a really great story about our country. You'll love it!"

Cory can appreciate what the teachers in their town are trying to do with the children, especially the younger ones who will never know what America was like before this all happened to it. They need to understand that it wasn't always like this, that it was once a beautiful and great thing that weak men allowed to be destroyed. He hopes they never make the same mistakes when they become adults and inherit it.

"Mr. Alexander!" Mrs. Browning says, rushing toward him from the library's main door. "Wait up, sir. I have something!"

Cory and Rachel turn toward her as she catches up to them. She hands Cory a newspaper, the page turned and folded back to reveal a story at the top.

"I believe this might be one of the men of whom you were speaking," she says, pointing to the article.

A man is featured in a picture with a caption below it. He is standing next to a blonde woman, presumably his wife by the tagline. They are dressed impeccably. The smiles on their faces couldn't possibly be any more forced or fake.

"Senator Warren Armstrong and wife Kitty," Cory reads aloud. He flicks his wrist to adjust the paper as it attempts to bend over. Tessa whines. "Sorry, kid. Hold still."

She whines again and quickly looks away, hiding in his neck.

"What's the matter with her?" Mrs. Browning asks and rubs Tessa's back. "What's the matter, little one?"

"Bad man," she whispers against Cory's ear.

"What?" he asks, unsure of her meaning.

"Bad man. Bad man. Bad man," she repeats as if her vocabulary skills have been reduced to that of a skipping record.

She points with her tiny, thin index finger at the black and white photograph of the senator.

"Him? He's a bad man?" Cory asks.

"Bad man," she repeats and nods vigorously. "Kill Papa. Kill Mama. Kill Sissy."

"He killed your papa?" he asks her, hating the terror he sees in her young eyes.

She nods with even more vigor this time.

"He did that? He killed them?" Cory prompts.

This time she shakes her head, "Bad people kill Papa."

What a piece of shit. This man ordered her family to be murdered, and whatever Tessa has been through, she heard the kill command come straight from the mouth of the "charitable senator" as the article describes him at this fancy gala to raise money for the ASPCA organization. This man who supposedly cared so much about animals has absolutely no problem ordering the murders of

406

hundreds of people to keep himself and his group alive another day. He had her mother, father and whoever 'Sissy' might have been murdered. Cory can only imagine that it was an older sister, probably still under the age of ten years old.

"Ok, kid," Cory says. "I'll take care of him. Don't you worry about that."

She nods and rests her soft little cheek against Cory's chest.

"I'll bring her back later, Rachel," he tells the blonde, who is always looking at him like a fresh piece of meat. She nods, clearly shaken by this turn of events. "Thanks, Mrs. B."

"I will go back and find more. I'll search all day if I have to, Mr. Alexander."

"Thanks. I'll be down at the clinic most of the day. Send someone to get me if you find anything."

"I will," she says and leaves.

Rachel also leaves with the children. Cory carries Tessa with him back to the clinic where he shares the information he's learned with the rest of the group. John goes off to radio it in to Dave to see if he can find out anything from the people he has also taken in who survived the highwaymen's attacks. Simon is doing his rounds with the injured in the medical house, and Reagan leaves to give him the update.

Everyone disperses, high on this new information and eager to dig up more. He is left with only Tessa and his thoughts as she sleeps on his chest and he studies the article some more. The sound of her soft breathing his only comfort as he memorizes every line of the senator's evil face. The ridiculous article is nothing short of a bullshit piece of ass-kissing journalism full of high praise about the senator and his cold-eyed wife.

It also names a few of the donors who made rather large donations to the Senator's wife's cause. Right there in black and white is the next name in their puzzle. Tony Romano of Romano Motors out of Nashville. Cory wonders how legit any of the contributions to the wife's cause were and if they actually made it there. He may have been a simple kid from the Midwest, but he understood a lot about shady politicians from listening to his dad. Romano and the senator may have met at this charity gala, but they might've actually have known each other before. It still gives him something to work with. He'll head over to the library when Tessa wakes to share this information with their librarian. She's bound to turn up more dirt on these two jackoffs.

Cory holds the small girl close, stroking her back and her hair occasionally and thinking about what the child of him and Paige would've been like. Would it have been a girl or a boy? Would he or she have favored Paige? Would she have had red hair and freckles? What the hell kind of father would he have been? That thought terrifies him, so he focuses his attention back on the article again.

He hadn't even known she was pregnant. It scares the shit out of him that she could've died during that miscarriage and he wouldn't even have known what she was going through. Reagan was obviously in on the lie, but he doesn't blame her, especially if Paige swore her to secrecy. He just feels terrible that she went through it without him. It was his fault that she got pregnant in the first place. They weren't careful enough. She was probably pregnant when they went on that run and she passed out in front of John and Dave the night of the tornado. So many things could've gone even worse in this situation. He's just thankful she's still alive. He doesn't care if she can never have children. That doesn't matter to him. All he wants is Paige.

He wasn't lying to Herb. Cory really does have a plan, one that he's been working on for quite a while, months. It's just taking a lot longer to implement because of everything that's been happening. Soon, it will be completed, and hopefully, it will help him to win her over. There's only one clear outcome to Cory, and that's making Paige marry him one way or another. Getting this all approved by Simon is another thing. He's also working on that project. A few more sleepless nights are nothing in the long run if it means that he can be with her.

He glances down at the article again. This piece of shit government employee's days are numbered. He is a murderer, a thief, and basically a typical politician. Unfortunately for him, the rules of the game no longer apply. He will not be protected by the laws that once governed their great nation. He will not live in the comfort of whatever mansion he used to dwell with security alarms, armed guards, a brownstone in D.C. where he stashed his mistresses, and private jets. He has a reckoning coming his way, one that Cory intends to personally deliver if for no other reason than the fact that he made this little girl an orphan.

Tessa stirs but doesn't awaken because he begins gently rocking in the rocking chair on the front porch of the clinic again. Tonight might be a good night for another ambush.

Chapter Thirty-two
Simon

It is near dusk, and they have been set up for nearly two hours on a dirt and gravel, rutted, rough road that has been encroached by the surrounding forest. It runs parallel to the main road where they have flagged it down with warning signs. They are hoping to squeeze the highwaymen into this enclosed, narrow back road. Fog is setting in, as well, which isn't going to help them. He doesn't think they're going to show tonight. They may be holding back because they've met resistance in a few of their plans to rob and kill people. Dave had called in again to report a similar attack southwest of Nashville that he'd heard about from newcomers when he went to his own town this afternoon. If this report is right, the highwaymen should pass by them if they need to head northeast to get back to their base camp or camps.

He is working in tandem with Cory tonight, hiding in the forest, thankfully having removed the hot ghillie suit a few minutes ago after the sun started its slow descent.

"Here's your food, bro'," Cory says, handing him a paper sack.

"Thanks," Simon replies taking it and sitting in the dirt behind a tall oak. There are large boulders and shale rock sticking out of the side of the hill in front of them that will provide cover if needed. Even without the monkey suit, he's still dressed to blend in wearing all black from head to toe. This is where they will dine this evening. It's normal. They're used to it. He pulls out a flatbread sandwich with sliced roast beef nestled inside with arugula and some sort of sauce that Sue makes. The girls have also sent along mason jars full of baby redskin potatoes quartered and baked with bits of bacon and parsley and green beans. The carbohydrates will give them a slowly released energy to pull a long nightshift if they need to. There are peach scones for dessert and peach-infused iced tea to drink. Simon is particularly fond of peach season at the farm. Some mornings he'll walk out into the orchard, pick a few peaches and sit under a tree eating them. It's a good breakfast eating those sweet fruits while watching the sun rise over the trees.

"A meal fit for the gods," Cory remarks as he plunks down on a fallen tree's thick trunk.

"So now you're polytheistic?" Simon asks with a smirk.

"Are you kidding me? That kind of talk would get you an extra hour in Doc's office on Sundays," Cory jokes.

Simon chuffs and nods. They eat for a while in silence, and Simon would like to believe that the rest of their night will go so peacefully.

"Hey, where was Sam?" Cory asks around a mouthful of food. "I didn't see her when I got to town today. I thought she was working with you at the clinic. Did she go back to the farm with Reagan?"

"No, she left," he states, trying to hide his anger.

"Oh," Cory says quietly. "I see. That makes sense now."

"What does?"

Cory hits him with a surprised look and says, "What? Oh, nothing."

"What makes sense?"

"Nothing. You just seemed in a pissed off mood earlier. Sam going home to Dave's compound would probably explain it."

"She doesn't belong over there."

Cory shrugs and says, "If it's what she wants, bro', I don't know how you can stop her."

"She's too young to know what she wants. Or better yet, what she needs. She'd be safer at the farm."

"I don't know about that. They've got a hell of a lot more manpower over there to keep her safe."

He glares into the distance, still remembering her ridiculous letter he awoke to find on his bedside table. Cory has no idea how truly angry he is right now, and how frustrated that he can't take a truck and go get her.

Cory adds, "But if you want her to come back to the farm, just tell her."

"I have. Many times. She's being bull-headed and headstrong. She's like talking to a brick wall."

His friend chuckles, "Yeah, most women are. You just don't have a lot of experience with them yet. They're all like that."

"Probably," Simon agrees.

"She's not that young, though. Samantha is very intelligent, too. And from what I've seen and heard, I think perhaps she has more than just her uncle that is pulling her toward Dave's compound."

"Don't remind me. That son-of-a-bitch is the one that drove her back there in the middle of the night!"

Cory winces at Simon's use of crude language, not used to it. Simon isn't, either, but it feels good to lash out. He hates Henry. It's official.

"How do you know that?"

"She wrote me a note. She said she wasn't coming to the farm anymore or town to the clinic."

"What? Why?" Cory asks with obvious concern. "You guys have a big fight or something?"

Simon sighs. Telling him the truth is not an option, but he doesn't want to boldly lie, either. He's not good at deception, and it always makes him feel horrible to do so. He does it all the time with Sam, but he tells himself it's for her own good.

"She's…mad at me or something. I don't know. She's being irrational…as usual."

"So apologize," Cory merely states.

"What do you mean? You don't even know what she's mad about."

"Doesn't matter. Women like us to apologize. When they know we feel like shit because of whatever it is or isn't that we've done, it makes them feel better. They like apologies. It's how their brains work. Even if you didn't do something to piss her off, just apologize."

"It's not that simple."

"No relationships are simple, Simon," Cory says as if he is the guru of love. "But when we're wrong, and in the eyes of all women

412

we're always the one who's wrong, then it's up to us to eat a little crow."

"Look alive, people," Kelly says into their earpieces.

He returned to town to go with them after John dropped his wife off at home. Dave sent extra men to the farm, and they also left two of Robert's men there, as well. Kelly has more experience than any of Robert's men anyway, so Simon is thankful for him being on their team in case things go south, and Wayne Reynolds came to help, too.

They both toss their food items into their bags and set them aside. Simon jumps to his feet and spies through his rifle scope.

"We've got a car inbound. High speed," Simon says to Cory as he watches a blue sedan speeding toward their roadblock, throwing gravel and mud everywhere.

It careens down the road and slides to a jarring stop a few yards from the back end of the McClane family's pick-up truck. The hood is up to make them appear as if they are having car troubles again. Simon and Cory are helpless on the top ridge of the hill as they watch Kelly and John interact with someone in the driver's seat behind the wheel of the sedan. A few moments later, they are quickly waving the people past them and around another parked car and some debris in the road. Then the car is speeding away as if the devil himself is on their rear wheels.

"They're coming," Kelly tells them. "Those people in the car are running from them. Everyone get ready!"

Simon kneels and takes precision aim toward the road, knowing the importance of his role.

Cory lays a hand on his shoulder and says, "Good luck, brother."

Then he jogs away. His order is to flank them from behind where Simon will join him after he has made the first, disabling shots from the safety of his current cover. The other men on their team are doing similar maneuvers and will be working the scene on their specific orders laid out by Kelly and John in town before they left.

A few seconds later, two, very expensive looking pick-up trucks come flying onto the scene. Men are standing in the bed, while others drive and ride in the extended cab back seats.

"We'll draw them in," John says into Simon's ear. "Be ready, Professor. This one's gonna go down a lot faster."

The trucks slam to a halt about twenty yards from John and Kelly, and men immediately jump out. Another car rolls up behind in a slower fashion and parks behind the trucks.

"We've got two cars coming in from the east," K-Dog states. "They're hanging back. We'll take care of them from here."

"Roger," John says quietly as the men approach him.

Simon is the only trained sniper on this task force this time, so his shots must count, every single one of them. There are men stationed on the other side of the road from him, but they are not in a sniper's point up high on a ridge like him. They will push in once it starts and take cover behind trees.

John's mic is left open, and Simon is able to listen in on the conversation. It does proceed more quickly this time. The men are angrier, bolder, and the one speaking seems high on some sort of drugs because his words slur and he barely makes sense. Apparently, he never got the typical lecture in school about the dangers of driving while under the influence. Perhaps that explains the erratic display of bad driving. It doesn't, however, explain the fact that they were just chasing those people in the sedan with the intention of robbing and killing them.

"Professor," John says softly.

It's all the signal he needs. The drunken man asks, "Professor? Do I look like a fuckin'...."

Simon takes him out first. A clean headshot fired from a simple angle with very low wind resistance. It's a good night for this style of shooting. The sun is still setting, low glare issues. The wind is barely even moving, another good factor. No rain. No snow. Just a warm, August evening in Tennessee perfect for executing cruel men who deserve it. The man's blood sprays his friends and the side of the McClane family's white truck. It startles his buddies because they stand there a moment as their friend collapses on the pavement as if someone has disabled his ability to stand erect. The report comes a second later. Then they panic and start freaking out. The fighting ensues, and shots ring out from all directions.

He shoots again, hitting a man straight through the neck. He'll die within seconds from such a wound. John and Kelly are shooting, as well, but from behind the cover of the nearby cars where they'd parked strategically for just this purpose.

The fight only lasts about five minutes total. Simon doesn't even get time to join Cory and change positions. K-Dog calls in to report that they have taken out the men on the other road who were coming toward them. It's a good victory, one they needed. The people who were attacked near Nashville and also Clarksville- probably by these very men- have been vindicated, but Simon wishes that it hadn't had to happen this way.

All total, they have killed another twenty-eight men. Not one survives for questioning, but they are making progress without interrogations anyway.

Mrs. Browning found an article about the Italian man who was a car dealer being suspected of money laundering and drug dealing. It was dated two weeks before the fall of their country. He was never prosecuted for his crimes. He walked away without ever having to face those charges and decided to go into a murder and thievery ring of another kind with his friend, the senator. These men are survivors, kings of a wasteland that once used to be the greatest nation on earth. Simon has news for them. Evil despots always end their lives with their necks on a guillotine. The McClane family is about to drop the blade.

The article listed his crimes and his current residence as being Brentwood, a very exclusive and wealthy area south of Nashville, according to Mrs. Browning. In addition, she found out for them that the senator was also living in Brentwood at the time and was a part of the same financial schemes. The two men knew each other before the fall. They were friends, business partners, and criminals even before the country crumbled and bred maniacs out of formerly normal men. These men were never normal, anything but. They were already hardened criminals and pure evil. Simon just wonders if his father ever dealt with this Senator Armstrong since he was one, too. Highly likely. And Simon's father would've smelled the snake oil salesman quality of the man. He was good at sniffing out the scoundrels in D.C., which is why he tried to stay away from the city as much as possible and preferred to conduct his state's affairs from Arizona instead.

Dave dispatched a group of men to the town of Brentwood to see what they could covertly dig up on the leaders of the highwaymen. Simon's not sure if they will find their lairs or if the men moved out of their homes like so many had after the country fell. They could be anywhere. John and Dave think it's a good chance they are still living in their homes there, though, since they would not want to leave the comforts of them. Only time will tell, but Dave had explained how important it was for everyone to be careful since these men probably have scouts everywhere looking for them. They aren't used to meeting with such resistance, and now Simon understands them very well. They are spoiled by what they've managed to accomplish as a team of scavengers. And that was before the apocalypse struck. Now they are living like there's no tomorrow. Simon couldn't possibly disagree more. The end of their tomorrows is about to come a lot sooner than they ever would've guessed for what they've done to innocent people.

Chapter Thirty-three
Reagan

Reagan awakens the next morning to the soft cries of her daughter, who she immediately pulls into bed with her for Charlotte's morning feeding. Although she is anxious to get to work in the med shed, her mornings are always the quietest time alone with her daughter. The rest of the day, the family monopolizes Charlotte and Daniel's time. They are both bound to be spoiled brats.

John comes into their room a few minutes into her breastfeeding session and leans down to kiss her forehead, "Hey, beautiful."

"You're home," she says.

"Yeah, we just got in. We convinced Simon to come home with us. He wanted to stay, but we stopped him. Kid was runnin' on fumes."

"I know. He's in a bad place right now," she comments as John strips and slides into the bed beside her. Reagan openly gawks at his flat, muscular stomach and hairy chest. Then she clears her throat. John is oblivious to the effect he has on her.

"Yeah, she left. Cory said something about Sam leaving him a note or some such about not coming around anymore."

"Shit," Reagan blurts.

"Hey, you aren't supposed to swear in front of our little angel," John reprimands.

"You mean Charlie?"

He chuckles and nuzzles into the back of her neck. His arm slipping around her waist.

"She likes it," he says, his smile pressing against her skin.

"She likes it, huh? The biggest excitement in her day is the appearance of my boob."

"I gotta say, boss, that's the highlight of my day, too."

Reagan chuckles, groans at him, and says, "Gross. And she doesn't have the capacity to like or dislike her newly assigned nickname."

"I don't know what the gross part of my comment was, but our daughter smiles when I say her nickname," John says.

"Probably a gas bubble," she tells him with a smirk, although she doesn't believe that. She used to. Reagan used to believe everything she studied on the subject of babies. Now that she has one of her own, she knows that a gas bubble would not produce a smile or a soft giggle from a baby. They are genuinely happy and have the capacity to express emotions.

"My little angel doesn't get gas."

Reagan snorts. "How'd it go with the mission?"

"Good. Got rid of a small group of them, so that's good. We also dug up more on the leaders."

"Derek told us some of it," she says of her brother-in-law's communications with John throughout the day. He seemed less frustrated about not being with them, but maybe that is just wishful hoping on her part.

"I'll tell you about it in the morning."

Reagan chuckles, "It is morning."

"I meant in *my* morning," he says and is softly snoring against her shoulder within minutes.

His morning will be in about six hours when he rises in the afternoon. She worries about John, and the rest of them, too. They are exhausted, sleep deprived and tense. There is so much at stake now. Everything they know and have, including their family could be taken away from them if they fail and they all know it.

Reagan rises after Charlotte has finished and fallen back to sleep against her. She has too much to do today to linger in bed, although she'd like nothing better than to rest in the comfort of her husband's arms with their baby tucked in next to her. The children with the Scarlet Fever are not responding well to the antibiotics now. It is as if the sickness is mutating. The situation could become very dangerous if they don't get this figured out. Sam's uncle was also going back to his camp to study and try to find a solution. Grandpa is making a radio call, as well to her father's camp to talk with the team of doctors up there to see if they've run into this before.

After stroking her fingers once through John's thick blonde hair, she pulls the sheet up over him and leaves to get dressed. She places Charlotte on the carpeted floor of her closet, wrapped in a blanket like a little burrito, and then changes into clean clothing for the day. She takes her daughter quietly down the stairs to the second floor where the old antique grandfather clock chimes the three-quarter hour showing that it is nearly seven a.m. It is still dark outside since it is pouring down rain and overcast as she passes Paige's room where the door is still closed. She needs her rest. Reagan is glad to see that she is not up yet. She's been through so much the last six months that Reagan worries about her.

She goes downstairs where she is greeted by Sue in the kitchen.

"Up early," Sue comments. "Want some tea?"

"No, thanks," she says. "I'm going out to get to work. Grandpa and I need to figure this out."

Sue is aware of the situation in town with the Scarlet Fever kids and is equally concerned.

"Let me take her, Reagan," her sister offers and cuddles the burrito bundle closely and even kisses her smooth forehead. "So precious."

"Don't spoil her. You'll make her obnoxious."

"Oh, you mean don't make her like you? Too late. She's got your DNA," Sue remarks with good humor. "We're fine. Aren't we, Miss Charlie? Grandpa's still in bed. Want me to send him out?"

"No, let him sleep. I know he was up later than me last night working on this, and I was up past two."

Sue nods, furrows her dark brow, and leans in to kiss Reagan's cheek. "I'll bring you some breakfast later."

"Thanks," Reagan states and dons a raincoat and black rubber barn boots.

The dash to the shed is a sloppy one, leaving her with mud-splashed jeans. Simon is already there at the counter.

"Damn!" Reagan curses. "I think we should start building an ark!"

"For another apocalypse? We've managed that on our own. No, I think God's turned his back on us for now."

"That's a depressing thought. Thanks! Just what I needed to hear first thing in the morning."

Simon hangs his head and goes back to his notes. "Sorry."

"Why aren't you in bed? You need to get some sleep," Reagan reminds him. John is right. There are dark, angry circles under his blue eyes, and a gauntness about him lately.

"Not tired. I just want to get a jump start on this. Those kids are getting sicker and sicker," he says.

Simon uncharacteristically makes a fist and pounds it on the table.

"Whoa," Reagan comments softly as she hangs her wet rain slicker.

"Sorry, I'm just very frustrated with this," he says.

"Exactly why you need rest. You're fried, little brother," Reagan says as she draws closer to him.

"No, I'm fine. I want to help."

She smiles and says, "Simon, you always help. But you're no good to us if you're sleep deprived and baked extra crispy."

"I don't need to sleep. I'll catch some later today," he reiterates.

"Suit yourself," Reagan reluctantly complies, joins him at the counter and flips open a book.

They work for over an hour, comparing notes and discussing therapeutic dosages and possible changes when Sue sends Huntley out with a tray of food for them. Scrambled eggs, freshly baked biscuits, and grits with bacon crumbles. It hits the spot and is a good source of fuel for brain food.

Simon's mood darkens with every minute. He's so angry and frustrated, but nothing Reagan says or suggests about their studies makes him feel any better. She's not good with people and their emotions.

"I'm going to the restroom," he states and shoves away from the table. "I'll be back."

He leaves through the main door to the outside. Most of the men on the farm urinate outside when they are not in the house. Reagan figures it must be like male dogs marking their territory because she has never once felt the urge to go anywhere but in a closed-door proper facility.

She looks down and notices a slip of paper that is folded in half and half again that he must've dropped. It piques her interest. He must have been working on this in town and took even more notes when she wasn't with him. When she unfolds it, though, she realizes it is not medical study notations but the letter that Samantha wrote him.

She skims it quickly, knowing he will be back soon, and feels terrible for doing it even as she does so. It is explicitly addressed to Simon, but Reagan is worried about him. Perhaps the key to whatever is bothering him lately is hidden in this message. However, as she reads, Reagan realizes this is not the kind of letter that would make his situation any better. Basically, Samantha is telling him off, telling him goodbye, and it sounds very permanent. She goes on about her feelings for him and that they have not changed but have also not ever been reciprocated. Sam writes that she needs to stay at Dave's and not return to town, not return to the farm, and not be around Simon anymore because he is cruel and heartless to do what he has been doing and she is angry with him. Reagan wonders what this part means. Then she says at the end that she is going to give her relationship with Henry a real chance because he is a good man who loves her.

Simon barks angrily, "What are you doing? Where'd you get that?"

Reagan actually yelps in surprise. Then she stands as Simon yanks it from her and smashes it into the back pocket of his chinos.

"I saw it on the ground. Sorry. I thought it was more medical notes."

He glares at her as if he doesn't believe what she is saying.

"Simon, is this recent? Is Sam not coming to the farm again, ever?"

"No!" he states with fervor. "She'll come back, or I'll drag her back myself. She's just being obstinate right now."

"About what? She mentioned that you aren't being fair to her or something? What's that mean?"

"Nothing, this is none of your concern, Reagan," he says, swiping a hand through his auburn hair and readjusting his eyeglasses.

"Sam is my concern," she informs him, her own anger growing at his evasive answers. "She's all of our concern. She's a part of this family."

He chuffs. "Yeah? Try telling that to her!"

"I would, but it would seem that you've chased her off," she accuses.

"Stay out of it," he warns icily.

"And this Henry? He loves her? Did you know that?"

He steps back, his arms hanging at his sides. His fists clenched. Then he paces a few feet in the shed like a wild animal at a zoo longing to be free.

"She sounds really angry with you," Reagan prods. "Did you two have a fight or something?"

"No. Not exactly," he says.

Reagan rises and walks closer to him. "Simon, what's going on between you two? Please, talk to me. I know you won't talk to anyone else, but can you just trust me and tell me what's going on?"

He shakes his head, and his blue eyes dart to the door. Reagan rushes to it, blocking his exit.

"Reagan, don't," he states.

He is a tiger, caged in and ready to maul someone. She's guessing that someone would be Henry if he were here.

"Just tell me. Talk to me. What the hell's going on between you two?" she asks again. He doesn't answer, so Reagan prods, "I know you have feelings for her. I've seen it…"

"No, you don't know what you're talking about. And that would be wrong, so no."

"Having feelings for Samantha would be wrong? Why would it be wrong? What the hell's that supposed to mean?" Reagan asks. Why can't Hannah be here instead of her? She'd know what he means.

"Just drop it."

"No, I'm not going to, and you aren't leaving until you talk to me."

Simon stalks toward her, but Reagan stands her ground. He is feral. She can see it in his eyes. He wants to hurt something or someone.

"Please, move. I don't want to talk."

"Nope," Reagan states with fortitude. "I'm not moving until you tell me. Don't you have feelings for Sam?" she says, deciding on a different tactic to get him to talk. "Is Sam in love with you? It sounds like it in that letter. She seems like she is. I've seen it. I've seen it in you, too. Don't you love her, too?"

"Sam is like a sister to me," he says, his eyes darting around, probably seeking another form of exit.

"Ha!" Reagan counters loudly. "Get real. She isn't your sister. I caught you two making out! Remember? In the supply room at the clinic in town? Your sister's upstairs asleep. Sam is more to you than that. I've seen the way you look at her." This gets a reaction. He looks directly at her as if startled to hear this. "Oh, yeah, I've seen it. You love her. I know you do. Hell, Simon, I think everyone knows you do. What I don't understand is why you just don't tell her."

He runs a hand through his already-standing-on-end hair and then rubs his face with both hands.

"Stop it, Reagan," he says more firmly.

"No, talk. Then you can go. Tell me."

Simon glares at her again, staring her down. "Get out of my way, damn it. I don't want to hurt you by moving you."

His temper is about to blow.

"Do what you have to do, but I'm not moving."

He stalks toward her, realizes he can't touch her, and growls with frustration, making two fists at his sides again.

"Don't do this. Stop. I mean it, Reagan. Move."

His words are delivered through gritted teeth.

"Why do you push her away? Why don't you just let yourself love her? She's going to end up with Henry or some other Henry if you don't do something pretty soon."

"I'll kill him," Simon says with deadly cold menace.

"You can't kill them all, honey," she informs him patiently. "And, trust me, dear, there will be more. I mean, sure, maybe you'd get away with killing one or two, but more will come."

"You aren't being funny right now."

"She's going to marry someone else. Is that what you want?"

He looks directly at her and says, "Yes, I want her to be happy. That's all I want for Samantha."

"I don't believe you," Reagan states emphatically.

He gives her a whole new sneer, this one malevolent.

"Then why not marry her yourself?"

The expression that comes over Simon's innocent face is one of revulsion and, if Reagan is guessing correctly, self-loathing.

"Marry her, Simon. You two are perfect for each other. It's obvious that Sam loves you."

"She's just a child."

Reagan actually laughs, "No, she's not at all actually. She's an adult woman. And as an adult woman, I think I can speak for her. I was a late bloomer in every sense of the word, but Sam's not. She's very mature for her age."

"Don't be ridiculous," he says.

She sighs and continues, "She'll marry someone else, and you'll be miserable."

"Good," he says as if this makes sense. "It's no less than what I'd deserve."

Reagan frowns. "What? What do you mean?"

"Nothing. Can you move, please?" he requests more loudly.

"No, I'm not going anywhere, and neither are you. Not until we talk this out because I am sick to death of not understanding you and Sam's situation."

"There is nothing to report. Stop being so snoopy. You sound like one of your damn sisters."

"Good! If that was supposed to be an insult, it wasn't. Why do you think you don't deserve to be happy, to be with her? She's clearly what you want."

Simon starts pacing again. He even holds a hand to his stomach as if he is nauseous.

"Simon, talk to me. Why? Why can't you be with her?"

"Stop it," he states in a quiet, frustrated tone.

"No, I want to know. Damn it, this affects us all. We're all a family, and I for one am tired of watching the two of you be miserable."

"Just drop this. Please, Reagan," he pleads in a softer tone.

424

Reagan notices that his hands are shaking. She is hitting on something that is important.

"You deserve to be with her. You don't deserve to be unhappy. If Sam would make you happy, then you should be with her."

He groans as if the thought of this is something distasteful. There is a bead of sweat running down his forehead.

"You kids have been through so much together. She trusts you, Simon, and sometimes that's more important than a lot of other bullshit romantic ideas that people put out there."

He offers a sardonic laugh.

"Why are you laughing?"

When he looks at her, Reagan is actually afraid, "You have no idea the irony of what you just said. She trusts me. That's rich."

"Why?"

He shakes his head and says, "Move."

"No."

"Get out of my way," he repeats, his eyes becoming menacing and deadly.

Reagan doesn't back down. She isn't afraid of Simon, but for him. This much rage can't stay bottled up inside a person for so long.

"You think it's ironic that you have Sam's trust?"

He doesn't answer but balls his shaking fist again.

"You want to hit me? You want to hit something?"

Simon flinches as if he doesn't even understand his own emotions right now. He shakes his head, but Reagan isn't sure he realizes he's doing it.

"You're so angry," she says more quietly. It hits her. "You blame yourself."

"Reagan," he warns, looking down at his feet.

"You blame yourself and find it ironic that Sam trusts you because you feel like it's your fault for what happened to her. That's it, isn't it?" It's as if the last four years, his behavior, the sly looks he slides toward Sam during dinner when she still lived on the farm and didn't know he was watching her, the longing she's seen in his eyes, the desire, all of it finally makes sense. Reagan is cracking his code of secrecy. And he's scared to death for it to be known.

"Stop," he says and backs away.

Reagan pursues him.

"Get away from me," he warns.

Reagan keeps following him until Simon has a building support pole at his back. He turns around instead of facing her, but she potentially has him cornered.

"Are you seriously blaming yourself for what happened to Samantha when you two were held prisoner by those people?"

"Go away," he says.

"You've got to be fucking kidding me, Simon. That wasn't your fault."

With a roar, he explodes and punches the steel pole. Reagan wraps him in a bear hug from behind, trapping his arms down at his sides.

"Simon, oh, Simon," she coos. "Don't do that. Darling, it wasn't your fault."

He jerks from her grasp and steps a few feet away.

"You have no idea what happened, so don't you assume you understand, Reagan," he shouts, pointing at her, blood dripping from his damaged knuckles onto the concrete floor. There are unshed tears in his eyes, so he turns away.

"Explain it then," she presses. He doesn't say anything but continues to stand there shaking, this time his whole body and not just his hands. "Explain it to me so that I can understand."

Simon turns to face her, and Reagan can see the pure and utter self-loathing, the hatred, the anger, and the anguish in his troubled eyes. His poor heart is so downtrodden with this burden.

"You want to hear it?" he asks, an almost taunting grin on his face. "Prepare yourself. I guarantee you aren't going to want to hear this. I tried, you see. I tried to hide her so they wouldn't find her in her parents' house because I knew what they'd do. But they found her. Of course, they did. They were the worst sort of human beings you could ever imagine. *He* found her. Bobby. You want to hear how I had to lie awake and listen to my bastard of a cousin rape her? How I was too weak to help her, too outnumbered to do anything, too tied up? How he raped her a total of nine times? How the first night he had her, he raped her twice? How's that for an introduction into our group? How's that for an introduction to sex? She was a virgin and was raped twice by my cousin. She could barely walk the next day. Or do you wanna' hear how I tried to claim her for myself to spare her

426

from what I knew they'd do, but how my cousin had the other men tie me up so that I couldn't help her? They knew me. They knew I was just trying to spare her, that I'd never hurt her like they wanted to. I couldn't claim her. Bobby wanted her for himself the second he laid eyes on her hiding in that closet. Is this what you want to hear?"

Reagan cannot help the tears that slide down her cheeks. She's not the kind of person who cries easily, but this is maybe the most horrific thing she's ever heard. She knew Sam had been raped, mostly assumed it from her behavior, but could not imagine the horrors that they both faced with those wretched people. She's glad they're all dead.

"Do you want to know that the other men also wanted her, but I convinced my cousin not to let them? I heard their disgusting plans for Sam. Huntley's father, Frank. Rick. Buzz. Willy. They all wanted her. I heard their plans. They would each take a turn. I couldn't stop them. I had to do something," Simon says, almost trance-like. "The guy who was already abusing her, my own cousin, I had to talk him into keeping her for himself so that she wouldn't be raped by every other man in the group. Do you know what that felt like? Do you? Could you? I was condemning her to being raped by Bobby, but sparing her from gang rape from the others."

"Simon," she starts and sniffs hard but is cut off again, this time by the anger that has returned to his soft voice.

"Or do you want to hear how I had to help her down to a lake one day after a particularly fun night with my cousin to wash away the blood from her small face and busted lip where he'd beaten on her for lying to him about having her period. The lie that I came up with!" he says, shaking again uncontrollably. "Her thin thighs and tiny wrists were so bruised from him hurting her. Her neck had bruises, too, so I think now that I'm older and know more that he might've choked her. She was so small."

"Simon, for God's sake! You had broken ribs when you first arrived on the farm. You're leaving a lot out here. Huntley and his brother and mother showed signs of abuse. You suffered at their hands, too. We all saw it."

"But she suffered far, far worse than the rest of us. At least Huntley's mother and brother died. They got out a lot easier than Samantha."

"Simon, stop," Reagan pleads, trying to get him to see reason.

"Oh, no. You started this. Do you want to hear how she could sometimes barely walk because he'd been so violent with her the night before? Or how her little doll face and arms and legs would always have bruises on them. How her wrists were bruised from being tied up. But those weren't just from my cousin. Oh, no! Everyone in that group would abuse her, even the women. They'd hit her if she moved too slow getting them things. My aunt would abuse her because she was jealous that the other men looked at her with desire. Or would you like to hear how I found a pair of earplugs in the RV and used them at night so I didn't have to hear Bobby raping her, so I wouldn't have to listen to it happening. Or how I devised a plan of escape, but we were caught. She was beaten for that as badly as I was. Then Bobby chained her to a bar inside the RV. Or how we came up with another plan to escape but Huntley's brother, Garrett, got sick and we couldn't leave them. I told her, begged her to go, to get out without us, that I'd stay with Huntley and his brother and mother so that she could make her escape. She wouldn't. She didn't want to leave without us. 'We'll wait till Garrett gets better,' she'd argued with me. Can you believe that? I had the perfect escape planned for her, but she wouldn't leave Garrett, a kid she barely knew. And why? Because that's Sam. She loves kids, loves people, just loves too much, too easily. She should've gotten away. I should've forced her to leave. I didn't, though. Truth be told, I didn't want her to go. I was afraid of what else could be out there and that I'd never see her again. Does this all sound like a reason for Sam to trust me? I failed her when she needed someone the most not to. Don't you get it? Do you understand now?"

Reagan nods jerkily and wipes at her tears. She looks down and sees drops of blood coming off of his trembling hands and grabs a towel from the counter. She squats in front of him to clean it. Simon follows her and rests his weight on one knee. Then he takes the towel from her and begins wiping at the concrete floor. Reagan instead rests a hand gently on his shoulder.

"Don't," he says. "Don't touch me."

Simon tries shirking her hand, but Reagan rests it more firmly there.

"Reagan, don't," he implores more weakly this time. "Don't do this. Not you."

"Oh, Simon," she says with so much wrung out, raw emotion from listening to the terror that he and Sam suffered. She rests her hand on the back of his neck where the skin is bare and warm. "My darling brother. You and Sam...my God."

Reagan doesn't care if she's crying freely or that someone could walk in on them. She cups his cheek and strokes her thumb gently there. She coos, "Poor Simon."

His shoulder begins to shake like his hands. It's different this time. His emotions have been strung out so tightly that he's cracking. He sniffs hard, and she realizes that he's crying. Reagan rubs his back.

"Simon, I'm so sorry you two went through what you did. No kids should ever have to endure such pain and agony, both emotional and physical."

"She wouldn't have if I'd protected her. But I didn't. I couldn't protect her because I was too weak."

"But, Simon, you were just a kid," she says and pulls him into a close hug. This time he doesn't push her away. She rises and takes him with her to a cot a few feet away where she sits next to him. "You were barely fifteen years old when this happened, darling. Those men were all in their thirties and on up. And higher than kites on every drug known to man, so who knows what the hell they were taking. But they were probably stronger because they were hopped up on drugs and shit."

"They were high all the time. And drunk. But that doesn't excuse me from not protecting her."

"Did any of the other men rape her, or just your cousin?"

"Just him. But I should've stopped it. I should've done so many things differently. She could never forgive me for failing her."

"Don't be crazy. Sam loves you. She knows you tried to save her. What the two of you went through together is like nothing anyone has ever experienced. It was horrible, but it also bonded her to you forever. She understands..."

"Understands. Forgives. Loves. These aren't words that I'll ever reconcile myself to, Reagan, where Samantha is concerned. I could never be with her. It's wrong. It's sick. It's like this disgusting thing inside of me that I can't suppress when she's around. It makes me as evil as him."

"Who? Bobby?" she asks and gets a nod. She grasps his hand tightly in hers. "That's ridiculous. Don't say that. Don't you ever say that. You have nothing to be ashamed of, Simon. Your love for Samantha is pure and good and comes from a place of innocence. It's not the sick desire of a man who would hurt someone weaker than them just because they can. Your love is free of pain and humiliation. You love her so strongly, so purely. She knows you'd never hurt her. She knows you are nothing like them. You're the one who has to let it all go, my darling. Sam has. She moved on. She wants to live a happy life now free from the past."

He scoffs. "As if we could ever be free from that."

"But you are. You tried to kill Bobby, remember?"

He nods angrily, "Of course I remember. If I wasn't so concerned about getting you away from him and out of the danger zone, I would've finished the job."

He's referring to stabbing his cousin in the back when he had Reagan on the ground and was going to rape her just like he did to Sam.

"I know. Sam knows this, too. And she loves you, Simon. She doesn't care about the past anymore."

"Really? She still draws...horrible things when she gets sad."

"Well, maybe that's just her way of dealing with it. And maybe what happened to her isn't the only thing that makes Samantha sad. She's a very sensitive girl. It's just the way she is, innocent and fragile and artistic and beautiful inside. She sees such goodness and lightness in everything. But then we're confronted with such darkness like these highwaymen assholes. I think Sam's sensitive to this sort of evil. She's not self-harming. She's a very well-adjusted young woman for what she's been through. And you're her anchor, Simon. She leans on you so hard for help and support. She has never to this day told any of us about what happened to her, not in detail, not even as much as you just told me. If she told Grams, I don't know of it."

"I could never be with her. I'd never allow myself to do it."

Reagan frowns. "But why?"

"You say that what we went through bonded us and made us close, but it also condemned us never to be together. We can't, not after that," he says and shakes his head. "I couldn't save her. I was just a failure, and I will never forget it."

"You don't have to forget it, but at some point in your life, Simon, you're going to have to forgive yourself."

"No," he says with finality. "What we went through ruined us ever being together."

"Because you see her as soiled goods?"

"What? Hell, no!" he snarls. "Sam is nothing of the sort. Why the hell would you say something like that to me?"

"She mentioned something about it a while back, but I didn't understand why she'd say it. I got the impression she thought that you think of her that way."

"God," he says with frustration and runs a hand through his hair. His fists clench again with anger.

"I also think you should consider her feelings in this, too. She's not getting what she wants out of it. She wants you. I can tell Samantha loves you, but you aren't making her happy because you can't forgive yourself for something that was out of your control to stop from happening in the first place. So by forbidding yourself from being with her, you're also condemning her to unhappiness."

"I hadn't considered it from her angle," he says softly. "It doesn't matter, though. She'll be better off without me lusting after her like some sort of perverted freak."

Reagan scowls, "Why would your attraction to her make you a freak or a pervert? You're not the one who raped her, and you would never do that…"

"Of course, I wouldn't. That's disgusting."

"Yes, but your feelings aren't lustful. They're just normal. It's a natural reaction to feel like that about her because you're in love with her."

He shrugs and swallows.

"Trust me. I don't know shit about relationships. But I do know that my feelings for John are real. I love him, and I never thought I'd feel like that about someone. I lust him, too. It's not wrong. And that's okay because he loves me back."

"Your situation with John is different."

"I wasn't raped," she confesses. "But I almost was, by two men who broke into my professor's lab." Simon looks directly at her with surprise. She'd assumed he knew this. "I ended up having to kill them to escape my own rape and death. They did rape and kill my roommate and killed my professor. I'm no picnic, Simon. I've got a lot of fucked up problems of my own, but John accepts me for what I am. I accept him, too. And Sam seems like she accepts you for who you are. The problem is that you can't seem to accept yourself."

"I never will. It would be wrong to."

She shakes her head and touches his arm tentatively. "No, Simon, what you're doing now is wrong. You're pushing her away, punishing her for what happened, and making her miserable because of it. That letter was written by a woman who is heartbroken because she can't be with the man she wants."

Simon vigorously shakes his head. "She's just being defiant."

"You have to find some way to forgive yourself, Simon. I don't know how to help you with that. None of it was your fault, sweetie. None of it. Not one moment of it. You did what you could. Even if you'd been a grown man like you are now, you couldn't have done anything differently. You were outnumbered by so many. You're just lucky they didn't kill you for what you did do and tried to do to protect her."

He looks at Reagan with tortured blue eyes.

"You have to get her back. She *has* to come home to the farm where she belongs. We all thought she would by now. We didn't realize it was because of all this. You're right about one thing. She belongs here. This isn't something that can't be undone. Sam loves you. She'll come back if you somehow learn to forgive yourself and accept that none of it was your fault."

Simon takes a deep breath and exhales it shakily.

"I think you'd be hard-pressed to find someone now who hasn't been through some messed up shit of their own, but it's how we get past it that makes us who we are. You're in limbo. You're stuck between the past and your future, which you could have with Sam if you just learn to let go of the past. She has. She's willing to move on with her life. You have to learn to do the same so that you can finally be with her, which is what I know you want."

"She's never coming back. I've ruined it with her. I've ruined everything! I'm so stupid. I pushed her away. I drove her away. She hates me."

"She doesn't hate you. Pissed? Probably. But Sam doesn't have the capacity to hate. And she sure as hell wouldn't hate you."

He shrugs as if unsure of Reagan's assessment.

"You need to work this out on your own. Take some time. Think about how you need to handle it. You'll come up with a solution because you're smart and wise and kind, which are all reasons that Samantha loves you."

Simon looks at her again. His tears have dried, his eyes have softened again to the calm blue she knows so well, and he offers a lopsided grin of embarrassment.

"Sorry," he apologizes impishly.

"That pole will forgive you," she teases. "Now, let me bandage your hands so you can go get some rest."

"I'm fine. I should stay up and study."

"No way. Grams used to say that things always looked better with a good night's sleep."

"It's morning," he reminds her.

"Don't be a smartass," she warns and leads him to the counter where she sanitizes and bandages his knuckles.

When she's done, Simon just stands there in front of her.

"Go!" Reagan orders. "Go and get some sleep. You're looking like a damn zombie."

He steps hesitantly close and wraps his arms around her. Reagan doesn't shy away. This is what he needs, and she wants to be there for him. Contact isn't as hard for her as it used to be, not with family. Simon is like her little brother, and Reagan only wants the best for him. Seeing him so miserable for so long has been hard on her, hard on all of the family.

"Thanks, Reagan," he whispers and kisses the top of her head.

She just nods as he breaks away and leaves the shed in a rush of too long pent-up emotions. Reagan goes back to her work after she more thoroughly cleans the floor.

Reagan sighs and says to herself, "I should've studied more fucking psych."

"Everything all right in here?" Grandpa asks from the door, startling her.

"I thought you were sleeping," she says accusatorily.

"I'll sleep when I'm dead," he jokes.

Reagan scowls hard, "Not funny, Grandpa."

"I came out earlier but heard you in here with Simon. It sounded rather…intense. Is everything okay between the two of you?"

"Yeah, better than ever actually," Reagan answers honestly. "Who woulda' thought I'd be giving people relationship advice?"

"Me," he answers.

Reagan snorts and then laughs bawdily. "That makes one of us."

"No, my granddaughter is a brilliant young therapist when she needs to be. I always knew you would be."

"Get real, Grandpa. This shit is your job."

"No, no. I mean it. And I'm glad for it, too. Someday, you may need to help others like you just did for our Simon."

"Again, that's your job."

He smiles gently and touches her scarred cheek. There is something in his eyes, something akin to sadness that tugs at Reagan's heart. She doesn't want to face it but knows what it is. She sees him looking down his own lifeline and finding an end in sight. Reagan is in denial that it'll ever happen. It's a nice place to visit, denial, and she has no intention of leaving.

"So, what's our plan of attack on this Scarlet Fever?" he asks with a chipper smile.

Reagan returns it, kisses his unshaven cheek and joins him at the counter for some research and study. Just listening to his brilliant plans and ideas makes her feel like a little girl again. She misses those days, being a child so carefree and innocent of the future and what it would turn out to be. However, some parts of the present aren't so bad. She has John and their two children. She has her family. She has safety and security and a roof over her head. Simple things are more important to her now.

She looks at her grandfather making notes and talking beside her and can't help the broad smile that stretches across her features. She'll take the little moments like this and be thankful and hopeful for more to come. Their future is not written yet, and the McClane family seems to be pretty damn good at making sure it is one filled with family and safety.

Epilogue
Herb

During the last week since his breakdown in the shed with Reagan, Herb has seen a slow change come over Simon. He is a man coming into his own, not a boy anymore who is unsure of himself and insecure. Kelly told him the other day how selfless he is during a battle and also how completely indispensable. He seems rather resolute about something, determined and single-minded. Reagan told him about their talk, and Herb is confident it is not too late for Simon to convince Samantha to return to the farm. Beating Henry to a proposal may prove the greater challenge.

It is just past dusk, the sun has gone to bed for the day, and he is enjoying a steaming cup of hot tea on the front porch. The men have gone on another night raid. Kelly is the only one still on the farm with him. Herb spoke with his son at Fort Knox earlier this afternoon about their highwaymen issue. Robert has promised more men and is also willing to host them for a spell to work on the Scarlet Fever cure. Herb may be making another road trip soon. The children in town need his help. He's not as young as he used to be, but he doesn't have a choice in this. He has to get those children better. They won't have a future in this country if they can't keep the children alive. He owes them this much. He owes his maker an enormous debt, as well, and doesn't have a lot of years left to repent and make things right. He'd humbly appreciate it if his eternity is to be spent with Mary and is willing to do whatever it takes to see her again. Whether or not his body is aging and failing him more and more every day does not matter. He has to make another trip north to the fort.

Tonight, he is reading a particularly old book with yellowing pages and tabs bent over to mark favorite selections from a collection of poetry. This book means a lot to him because it used to belong to his Mary. He remembered this poem by Alfred Noyes when the men started calling these bandit marauders 'the highwaymen.' However, he also knows the story all too well and will not share it with his family. It does not end well for the people on the road in the story, and he does not want a shred of doubt that they can defeat these men entering their minds, as it has his. They must conquer and destroy them. He peruses one stanza in particular with a critical eye.

Back, he spurred like a madman, shrieking a curse to the sky,
With the white road smoking behind him and his rapier brandished high.
Blood red were his spurs in the golden noon; wine-red was his velvet coat;
When they shot him down on the highway,
   Down like a dog on the highway,
And he lay in his blood on the highway, with a bunch of lace at his throat.

And still of a winter's night, they say, when the wind is in the trees,
When the moon is a ghostly galleon tossed upon cloudy seas,
When the road is a ribbon of moonlight over the purple moor,
A highwayman comes riding—
   Riding—riding—
A highwayman comes riding, up to the old inn-door.

"'When they shot him down on the highway. Down like a dog on the highway'," Herb rereads aloud, contemplating the full impact of these words by the great poet. Although the story is more about star-crossed lovers, the words still feel premonitory and haunting.

Herb quickly rests the book beside him as Hannah comes onto the back porch holding Charlotte, or Charlie as so many are now calling her, much to Reagan's disapproval.

"Come and sit with me, Miss Hannah," he beseeches his granddaughter.

She is dressed just like his Maryanne used to. A long dress, floral print apron over top of it, bare feet and thick, pale blonde braids on either side of her lovely face.

"I wondered where you went off to," Hannah says as she gracefully sits next to him on the porch swing, an item that his own father built many years ago.

"Just catching some fresh air," he tells her.

"Are you worried about the men?" she asks, her sightless eyes searching his face.

Herb reaches out and cups her soft cheek. Hannah, being the way she is, leans into his touch.

"No, they'll be fine," he says with confidence. "They're just scouting tonight. Nothing to worry about."

"Good, I'm glad. I don't want them fighting these men anymore," she says, a little scowl line marring her smooth forehead.

Herb smiles gently and pats her cheek. "They have to, sweetheart. We cannot lose the farm to men like them."

She nods, closes her eyes, pulls back and faces forward, leaning back against the swing.

"Now, let us talk of something more uplifting, shall we?" he suggests, getting a warm grin from Hannah. "What do you think this little bundle of cuteness is going to be like when she gets older?"

The porch door slams, and Hannah's daughter Mary comes out looking for Hannah. She does not like being separated from her mother for very long.

"Come here, Miss Mary," Herb entreats, the name of his deceased wife difficult to say without thinking of Maryanne.

She crawls onto his lap, and Herb sets his unlit pipe on the railing to smoke later.

"Well," Hannah says, "let me think. If Charlie is anything like Reagan, then we're all doomed. If she's like John, she'll keep us laughing."

Herb smiles and strokes Mary's dark curls. She plays with the stethoscope hanging from his neck, her big wide eyes curious, as usual. Herb takes it from around his neck and places the listening pieces in her tiny ears. Then he presses the device to his own chest. Mary's eyes light up with enthusiasm.

"Might be looking at a future doctor with this one, Hannah," he says and explains. "She's using my stethoscope." Hannah smiles gently. Mary reaches for Hannah and presses the stethoscope to her mother's chest, too. Her eyes jump to Herb's with excitement, and he kisses her soft, chubby cheek. The wonderment of little minds is something he'll never get enough of, especially not from his own great-grandchildren.

He takes Hannah's free hand in his. "When are you going to tell Kelly?"

"Soon," she answers without surprise that he knows. She hadn't consulted him about it, but Herb had a sneaking suspicion. Then he'd noticed she wasn't eating much lately. She probably hasn't been feeling well just like last time. When he saw her chewing mint leaves the other day on the back porch, he knew. "It's just been so…"

Hannah sighs sadly and shakes her head.

"Honey, a baby is a blessing no matter the situation. He'll be happy."

"I don't know, Grandpa. With everything that's been going on with these bad people, I didn't want him to get distracted, lose his focus out there when he's… doing that stuff," she says, not wanting to say hunting and killing and battling men for their survival. His Hannah is too delicate for this world. "He doesn't need to worry about what's going on at the farm when he's trying to work."

"He'll be thrilled, Miss Hannah. Tell him soon. Your condition will give you away soon enough anyway. You'd rather it come from you than from him guessing it."

"You're right," she says.

"Oh, I wish your grandmother were here to hear that," he laments jokingly.

Hannah giggles and squeezes his hand. Then she brings it to her face and rubs the back of his hand against her soft cheek.

"No time like the present, dear," he says, indicating Kelly, who is coming their way. Gretchen is tagging along after him with a grumpy expression on her pretty face. Maryanne would've gotten a kick out of Gretchen. She is a spunky little thing. Cussing, smoking, boyish clothing and a pierced nose? Yes, Mary would've loved her free spirit and bold attitude.

"….but that's bullshit!" Gretchen is complaining at Kelly.

438

"Too bad, kid," the big man tells her as he approaches the steps to the porch, probably finding Hannah like a homing beacon in the dark. He is so drawn to her, so protective and in love.

"Whatever!" Gretchen says loudly.

"What seems to be the trouble, dear?" Herb asks her.

Kelly attempts to speak but is cut off by Gretchen, "He won't let me go with them on any of these missions. It's bullshit! If Luke can go, so can I."

"You're a lot younger than your brother," Kelly says patiently. Then he grins down at the feisty girl in front of him, who is not backing down. "Luke's also got experience, and we've all seen him in action. We know what he can do, what he can handle. Paige has more experience than you, and you don't see us taking her, either. This is our job. Your job's here keeping the farm safe while we're gone. We can't have every person who can shoot gone at the same time."

"But…"

Hannah interrupts them and stands, "G, would you please watch Charlie while I talk with my husband? I'll be back in a few minutes. I just need to speak with Kelly."

"Oh…um, sure," Gretchen answers and carefully takes the baby from Hannah.

Once Hannah has the baby safely transferred, she swiftly slaps the back of G's head. "Not in front of the babies, Miss Gretchen!"

She scolds her young sister, who yells, "Ouch!"

"Yes, it was meant to hurt," Hannah remarks calmly. "It'll help you to remember not to curse the next time the mood strikes, young lady. Kelly?"

She reaches out for her husband's arm, who takes her hand while trying to suppress a laugh at G's expense. Herb watches as he leads her down the front steps and out into the yard. It makes him smile observing how tender Kelly is with his granddaughter, who is not as fragile as most people think.

They stand in the front yard out of earshot of anyone who might be listening. Within moments, Kelly is lifting Hannah off the ground and swinging her around with laughter. Herb knew he'd be happy at the prospect of more children.

"What's that all about?" G asks, as clueless as Reagan used to be about matters of the heart.

"Seems you'll soon be an aunt again, Miss Gretchen," he tells her.

"Another baby? Good grief! It's like a damn baby factory around here!" she exclaims.

"Yes, yes, it is," he agrees with a wide smile and takes his granddaughter's small hand in his. She wears a lot of silver rings on her fingers. Perhaps if past lives exist, she was a gypsy in hers. It makes him grin.

Others come out of the house to find out what Kelly is so excited about. They rush out to congratulate them. Sue cries. Paige smiles, but it seems forced. He isn't sure if she is sad because of her miscarriage or if she does not believe in having children anymore because of the way the world is now. He has heard as much from Reagan regarding Paige, but Herb is confident that someday Cory will be able to change her mind.

The children decide that since everyone is outside anyway, they might as well chase lightning bugs and each other. Their laughter fills the farm and his heart.

He wishes he could just live in the joy of this moment. These children will inherit his farm someday, and the men know how important it is that they destroy any and all threats that could stop that from happening. Herb knows what they are capable of, but he does not share their confidence that they can so easily defeat this large group of evil men and their corrupt leaders. Gaining the help his son is offering is going to make it a greater possibility, but it does not stop the doubts from entering his mind as he watches Arianna chase Huntley around the yard, her laughter ringing out in the night like the tinkling of bells. This farm was meant for this, for the laughter of children and the security that the family provides. He looks up to find Derek standing in the open doorway from the front porch to the entry hall. He is leaning on his cane again, apparently sore from using his brace, which is proving the most brilliant contraption he has ever been a part of building. The intensely grave expression on his face, however, mirrors Herb's worries as he, too, watches the children play so carefreely.

Made in the USA
Columbia, SC
26 August 2018